BEWITCHED

Styles grinned satirically. "You will find, Miss Havelock, that I never act out of compulsion, and my gentleman's code of honor is questionable at best."

"Now, you are doing it much too brown, my lord," Theodora insisted, her eyes dancing. "Marriage is clearly out of the question. I do not make it a practice, my lord, to marry my patients."

"But you will agree that ours is a unique case," Styles pointed out.

"It is not unusual," Theodora explained kindly, "for a patient to form a certain emotional attachment for the healer. It is, however, only a temporary condition, which passes in time."

"And if I could give you assurance your fears are unfounded and a reason that has nothing to do with a gentleman's code of honor?" He leaned suddenly near, his hand closing over hers. "What then, Miss Havelock?"

"I should think it would depend, my lord—" She swallowed and lifted her eyes to his, "—on the reason, would it not?"

"Indubitably, Miss Havelock," murmured his lordship, kneeing his stallion closer to Theodora's mare. "It occurs to me that two persons of an inquisitive disposition—" Lightly, he brushed a loose strand of hair from her cheek and curled it behind her ear. "—With a strong proclivity for passion . . . would do no better than to marry."

"Indeed?" Theodora whispered, and closing her eyes, instinctively turned her cheek into the palm of his hand.

THEODORA

Sara Blayne

ZEBRA BOOKS
KENSINGTON PUBLISHING CORP.

ZEBRA BOOKS are published by

Kensington Publishing Corp.
850 Third Avenue
New York, NY 10022

First Printing: September, 1996
10 9 8 7 6 5 4 3 2 1

Printed in the United States of America

To John Scognamiglio, the very best of editors, who has encouraged me, believed in me, and been a good friend to me, with all my thanks.

One

The Devil's Cub had come home—driven to it at last like a whipped dog. No doubt it was an act of Providence that he had done so without having first got himself an heir, reflected the last of the masters of Devil's Keep with cynical appreciation of the jest that had been perpetrated against him. And if there were never to be an heir, what did it really matter? There would be damned few who would mourn the end of the House of Dameron. Least of all himself, he thought. Savagely he threw back his head and downed the last of the port in his glass.

He reached for the decanter and upended it over the glass, then cursed as a single blood red drop cascaded into the bottom of the vessel.

"Bloody hell!" He lurched out of the deep wing-backed chair and staggered, more than a little drunk. But not yet drunk enough. The damnable pain still throbbed. Curse the pain! Curse his tainted blood! He straightened, swaying on his feet, and clutched his head between his hands. The pain raged in his skull with the strength of a score of gnawing demons. His sight blurred, and through the mists, the vision came.

It was not the first time he had seen it. The indistinct form within a white dazzle of light had become a regular intruder on his evening debaucheries, the first indication that he was to be spared nothing in his final degradation. His chief emotion was one of irony. So, he was to experience it all—the pain *and* the encroaching darkness, visited, no less, by the spectres of his cursed existence. Then so be it, but he was damned if he would entertain the bloody ghosts of his past without benefit of his own brand of spirits.

"Renfield!"

Hardly had his voice shattered the brooding quiet of the library and reverberated down the equally silent halls than his summons was answered by Renfield, the butler, bearing a fresh decanter of port balanced on a silver tray.

The servant, of a lofty height and thin almost to the point of emaciation, gave the appearance of one who had been stretched to unseemly lengths on a medieval torture rack. The somber black of his butler's livery afforded him a macabre aspect, an impression that was further abetted by straggling wisps of white hair, which sprouted from beneath an otherwise bald pate, and a cadaverous mien, which seemed peculiarly suited to his gloomy environs. "My lord," he intoned, eyeing his master obliquely out of pale, rheumy eyes.

The Devil's Cub stood rigidly upright in the center of the room. His strong hands were clenched into fists at his sides. His chiseled countenance wore a sardonic expression, his lip curled in a sneer; and his eyes, a hard, glittery black, were fixed on the far corner of the room.

Renfield's glance darted nervously to that same corner and, seeing nothing out of the ordinary, fastened on a point somewhere beyond his master's shoulder. His lips parted, then sealed shut after that surreptitious glance, as if the impulse to say something had been summarily squelched.

"Leave it," commanded the Devil's Cub, indicating the decanter with the gesture of a hand. "And have Erebus brought around."

The old man's lips thinned to an even more somber line, if that were possible. It was past midnight. Hardly the time for a gallop across the moors. But only a fool would try to reason with the Devil's Cub when the black mood was upon him. Glumly shaking his head, Renfield departed to relay the master's orders.

A quarter of an hour later, Caleb Dameron, the twenty-seventh Earl of Styles, thundered through the gates of Devil's

Keep astride a tall rangy stallion as black as his master's heart was reputed to be painted. With his raven hair streaming in the wind and the capes of his greatcoat billowing around him, Styles might indeed have been the Devil's offspring. Certainly he rode as if pursued by the devil's hounds.

Only he knew the demons that drove him and which he sought to banish by taking frequent recourse to the flask he carried with him. With any luck, he would return to Devil's Keep, his senses dulled by drink, his body driven to the point of utter exhaustion, then perhaps to sink at last into oblivion. In the meantime, the night shadows cast by the full moon and the wild flight of the stallion along the edge of the cliffs, plunging sheer to the sea, suited his needs.

He no longer looked for restful repose in the night. It was at night that the darkness within threatened to break through the barriers he had set around it. It was the curse of the devil that the darkness was growing stronger. In the end it must surely break even his iron will. And that was bitter gall to the Devil's Cub.

He neither loved life nor feared death, but he had the devil's own aversion to submitting tamely to a fate not of his own making. And yet how fitting, he told himself, that the long line of Damerons should end in darkness.

They had risen out of the Dark Ages in Normandy eventually to cross the Channel with William the Conqueror as little better than brigands. The succession of the Earls of Styles had been founded on the ferocity with which their favored forebear had shed the blood of the Duke's enemies. They had always been a bold and bloodthirsty lot, counting among their numbers a fair share of pirates, smugglers, murderers, and thieves. The present earl's great grandfather had been notorious for dabbling in the black arts, his grandfather for his avid participation in the Medmenham Abbey Hell-Fire Club, and his father for his gambling, wenching, and duelling.

It was only appropriate that the last of the Devil's Cubs had earned for himself a reputation for depravity that far exceeded anything his illustrious forebears had ever dreamed of achieving. The earl laughed chillingly, coldly amused at the thought that the villagers had taken to using his name to frighten children to obedience.

The moon had long since passed its zenith and the flask was more than half empty when the Devil's Cub at last had a thought for his mount. He pulled the heaving stallion to a walk as the track steepened, descending into a wooded ravine. A chuckle of water served as accompaniment to the croak of frogs and the hoot of an owl, and he caught occasional glimpses of a bourn, shining palely in the shafts of moonlight that slanted through the boughs of beechwood and oak. From somewhere nearby came the sudden crash of underbrush—a deer, startled into flight.

No doubt some deep, inborn instinct had drawn him to the deer park, in which he had used to run wild as a boy. He had vastly preferred the thick wood with its tumbling stream and occasional still pools to the great dreary castle and the uncertain temper of the drunken tutor to whose care he had been given when he was just turned nine. With a distinctly cynical twist of the lips, he tipped the flask in memory of Mr. Josiah Fix, who had been obliging enough to end his life at the bottom of the cliffs hardly before his young charge had reached the ripe age of twelve.

The Devil's Cub had not grieved at the loss. Why should he? Fix had been sadistic and intemperate. He had administered physical and mental punishment with the same relish that he had used to drink to excess. He had had only one redeeming quality—a profound knowledge of a wide spectrum of learned subjects with which he had whetted the boy's natural proclivity for learning. The incident of Fix's death, surrounded as it was by suspicious conjecture, had seen the heir of Dameron bundled hurriedly off to Eton—a circumstance which had not been distasteful to one endowed such as he with an inquiring mind and what was to develop with maturity into a powerful intellect.

With that intellect, he had amassed not only a fortune far

greater than the one his profligate father and grandfather had squandered, but power beyond anything they could ever have imagined. It was whispered that he was the most dangerous man in England, and it was known that his influence was both courted and feared on three continents. How ironic that everything he had achieved should in the end prove so singularly useless and devoid of meaning!

The Devil's Cub threw back his head and drank. Then, swaying slightly in the saddle, he flung the empty flask away.

The track, winding through the trees as it followed the bourn toward the sea, burst suddenly into a moonlit glade. The black flung up its head and snorted a warning as a pale, ghostly form appeared to rise up out of the ground before Styles—or, more precisely, out of a stand of elderberry bushes. The Devil's Cub cursed as the stallion reared, striking out with its forefeet.

Bloody hell! The spectre had found him even here!

Tenderly, Theodora Havelock lifted the sleeping babe from its mother's breast and cradled the tiny body against her own bosom with a sense of immense satisfaction.

"She's a bonny lass, Millie," she said to the woman in the bed. "And she needs you strong and healthy. You're doing neither of you any good constantly fretting about the squire's milch cows. You must think of yourself now. You had a difficult birthing and you need rest. You'll remain in bed until you've had time to heal and win your strength back, or I shall know the reason why."

Millie, watching the other woman lay the infant in its cradle to one side of the bed, smiled tiredly. "I know you mean well, Miss Theodora," she said. "But I've other mouths to feed besides Annie's. It's been two days since the birthin'. If I'm not there on the morrow to do the milkin' and the churnin', the squire'll find some 'un else to do it for 'im, and the good Lord knows where I'll find other work. Now that Tom's been laid off the fishin' boat till the next run of pilchard, what I bring in is all we have to put vittles in the pot."

"And who will put food on the table if you sicken?" demanded Theodora, lighting an incense candle scented with the oils of mint to lift her patient's spirits and cloves to ward off the spectre of disease. "I'll speak to Squire Meeks, I promise. In the meantime, I'll send Ellen's girl, Sadie, to do the cooking and look after the children. And you can tell Tom that Aunt Philippa and I are thinking of expanding the herbal garden. We shall need a man with a strong back to do the digging."

"Miss Theodora, I shouldn't," exclaimed a stricken Millie. Miss Theodora and her aunt were always contemplating expanding the herbal garden or repairing the roof or some such thing as soon as they learned there was a body in need. There was hardly a soul in the village who had not been temporarily employed by the Havelocks in such a manner at one time or another.

"But of course you should," Theodora declared, setting a bottle of elixir on the bedside table before closing her leather pouch of herbs and tonics. Slinging her practical, if wholly unfashionable, white woollen cloak about her shoulders, she smiled down at Millie. "I know you want to spare me a strained back. Tell Tom we shall be expecting him."

Millie smiled mistily. "Yes, Miss Theodora. I will, and thank you. We're beholden to you."

"Then you will repay me by resting, Millie. And promise to take a spoonful of elixir three times a day. Your blood needs rebuilding if you are to nurse little Annie here."

"I'll promise, if you'll give your word you'll go straight home with you, miss. The sun set hours ago. You never should've come all this way tonight after seein' to Mrs. Gladdings. Especially not now that himself is come home to Devil's Keep." Millie shuddered. "It's a sign, Miss Theodora. Someone will die a horrible death, just like poor Mary Wiggins all those years ago, you may be sure of it."

"Nonsense," Theodora retorted with uncharacteristic sharpness, which surprised her as much as it must have done Millie. "The fact that the Earl of Styles has taken up residence in his castle will be a good thing for all of us. You'll see. He is only a man—one who I daresay has been greatly misunderstood. So let there be no more such talk about death and dying," she scolded, bringing her curtain lecture to an end. "As for the lateness of the hour, I had to see how you and little Annie were coming along, now didn't I? And, besides," an imp of laughter danced in her remarkably green eyes, "what should I have to fear in the night? Especially when there's a full moon out? There are those who say the night is my natural element."

Millie frowned disapprovingly. "You ought'n to laugh at such talk, Miss Theodora. You're not what they say you are, and you ought'n to let people think such things of you. Nothing good can come of it."

"But neither shall anything bad come of it," Theodora laughed as she slipped the pouch strap over her shoulder. "I heal people with my herbs and potions. If they choose to believe there is more to it than that, then let them. Very often that is the sort of thing that tips the scales in their favor. Get some sleep now, Millie. I shall be back in a day or two to see how you go on."

Some moments later, having at last taken her leave of a grateful Tom Dickson and the five boisterous younger Dicksons, Theodora secured her precious pouch to the saddle and, mounting Ginger, her dun mare, set off at a trot along the village high road.

The Dickson cottage was nestled in a dale little more than a mile from Weycombe Mere, which, hugging the sea, owed its existence to the small fleet of fishing boats that plied their trade in the Bristol Channel and beyond. The fishing village itself huddled at the mouth of Devil's Gill, so called for the castle perched atop the cliffs overlooking the bay and for the long line of "Devil's Cubs" who had by turns inhabited the keep since the time of William the Conqueror.

How the Earls of Styles had first earned the sobriquet that

had followed them through twenty-seven successions of the title had long been obscured in rumor and legend. Theodora, ever of a practical nature—in spite of her own personal eccentricities—scouted the local belief that it was due to the first earl's having sold his soul to the devil in exchange for what had proved phenomenally good fortune in battle. She considered it far more likely that it had had in great measure to do with the zeal with which he had defended his duke. He was reputed to have been a veritable devil on the battlefield, and certainly he had sent not a few souls to his alleged patron's realm of brimstone and fire. Still, William of Normandy had himself been no less merciless to those who had chosen to take up arms against him. And while the ancient forebear of Dameron would quite naturally have earned the disapprobation of the Anglo-Saxons he had helped the duke to conquer, he had, no doubt, been a vassal worthy of his liege lord. From the duke, he had got himself a rich earldom, after all.

It was not, however, the first Earl of Styles who came to Theodora's mind as she pulled Ginger to a halt at the fork in the road on the outskirts of Weycombe Mere. The cliffs loomed in the moonlight, dark and forbidding, and, though she could not see it, she was tinglingly aware of the castle that had stood guard over the Channel for over seven hundred years. And now the last of the long line of Damerons had returned home to Devil's Keep. Theodora hoped he had made peace with himself and found happiness in the fifteen years since last she had seen him.

What would he be like, now, after that lengthy absence? she wondered, remembering vividly the tall, dark-haired youth who had stood over his mama's grave that memorable day in the church grounds.

There had been no one to mourn the countess's passing, save himself and the clergyman summoned from Porlock Weir to perform the services. The latter had fled after what could merely be considered a decent interval, leaving his lordship to the sole company of gravediggers. *They,* after only a few moments' nervous hesitation, had proceeded to fill in the grave.

Theodora had not meant to intrude, but it had been drizzling, and she had stolen out of the house to hunt frogs in the grave-yard. Suddenly she had seen him, standing all alone in the rain beyond the ironwork fence, which constituted unconse-crated ground.

At ten, Theodora had never beheld a more splendid creature, or one more certain to appeal to her sympathetic nature.

Still, it was not his lofty height or magnificent breadth of shoulders, both accentuated and rendered marvellous in appear-ance by a flowing black cloak which reached to his ankles, that had had such a powerful impact on her child's fertile imagina-tion. No, but then, neither had it been the aesthetic perfection of a countenance made compelling by a high, intelligent brow, long, straight nose, and wide, sensitive mouth. No. It had been the look on that high-cheekboned face with its firm, stubborn jaw.

Even a child could read the baffled anger on the stormy brow and the bitterness about the cynically drawn mouth. But, being Theodora, she had immediately seen much more deeply than that. Indeed, she had glimpsed through the defensive front of arrogance and pride to the terrible anguish behind the re-markable eyes.

The Devil's Cub had been a soul in torment, and instantly her generous heart had gone out to him, followed almost im-mediately by her small, wet and bedraggled person.

Leaving the gravestone behind which she had been hiding, she came to stand beside him.

"Gwendolyn Zenoria Dameron, Countess of Styles," she said, reading aloud the inscription on the carved marble slab. With a child's unaffected frankness, she gazed up into his face. "Was she very beautiful—like her name?"

"Yes. She was very beautiful."

He neither moved nor looked at her, as if it were perfectly natural to be conversing with a complete stranger, and a child at that, over the grave of someone he had only just recently lost.

Theodora, who did not think that at all strange, frowned

thoughtfully, her glance returning to the inscription. "I thought she must be. It is often like that. She wasn't very old either," she observed next, calculating the difference between the two recorded dates. "Not even forty. Just Papa's age. Papa always says only the good die young, in which case I shall probably live to a very ripe old age."

He did look at her then, perfectly gravely, with black eyes of a marvellous piercing intensity. "Are you so very bad, then?"

"Yes." Theodora sighed fatalistically. "Though I start out with the best of intentions, I am forever landing myself in trouble. I shall very likely drive Papa to an early grave."

She waited for his disgust, which was sure to follow, but his expression remained singularly impenetrable. She experienced a strange glow of warmth when he replied, as one equal to another. "Do you really think so? Why? Is he of a fragile constitution?"

"Not at all. He's quite hardy for a doctor who thinks nothing of making house calls at all hours of the night and in every sort of weather. He never thinks at all of himself. Fortunately he has me to remind him to eat sensibly and to wrap up and wear his spatterdashes when he goes out in the damp. He can be terribly absentminded about such things."

"I believe I envy your papa," mused the stranger with the faintest of smiles. "Perhaps you will pardon me if I say I do not believe he is in any immediate danger of being driven to his grave."

"You are very kind, I think, sir," Theodora confided with the unselfconscious candor of extreme youth. "But everyone says so. I'm a witch, you know."

"I shouldn't be at all surprised," he answered, as if she had just declared she was a milkmaid or a fisherman's daughter or something else quite ordinary. "And I am the Devil's Cub. So you may believe me when I tell you that, while you may be different from everyone you know, that does not make you bad. Only unique, and that, in your case, is nothing of which you need ever be afraid or ashamed. I'm sure your papa understands and treasures you all the more for it."

She had frowned at that, instinctively trusting that he would not lie to her and yet unable but to take exception to one thing he had said. She did not believe for a moment that he was a devil's offspring with all that that would seem to imply. "If you are the devil's cub," she ventured, pondering, "then who is your mother?"

It lasted only a fraction of a second, but in that instant it was as if she had snatched a concealing curtain aside and glimpsed into his very soul. "The Lady Gwendolyn was my mother," he said with a chilling lack of emotion. "Pray spare me your look of pity. There was little love lost between us. You might even say it was I who sent her to her grave. And why not? You may be sure others will say it. But no matter. Like a dutiful son, I have seen her to her final resting place, and now I think it is time I saw you home." He held his hand out to her in such a manner as left her little doubt that he meant her to take it, which she did, unhesitatingly, her trust untarnished by anything he had said. She, after all, had seen what he had never meant her to see.

"For a sensible female, you have shown a remarkable lack of sense," he commented as he led her from the church grounds. "You are soaked to the skin. What in hell's name possessed you to come out in the rain?"

"I was hunting frogs," she answered matter-of-factly.

"Naturally. I wonder why I did not think of that. But what the devil for and why in a graveyard?"

"Because," she shrugged, "I had already discovered that toads do not in truth bring warts to the skin. But before I could reasonably discard the theory, I wished to put a frog to the test. I came to the graveyard because I know they abound near the ornamental pond and—well, because Jemmie Wiggins said I would not dare to cross the church grounds in the rain, since I should immediately be changed back from a girl into a frog, which, as everyone knows, is the true form of a witch. It seemed the perfect opportunity to test two theories at once."

For a moment he stared at her as if much struck by the sheer rationality of her methodology.

"Were you not in the least concerned that Jemmy Wiggins' theory might prove sound?" he asked finally.

"Well," she temporized, as she considered her feelings earlier upon approaching the graveyard, "I cannot say I should have liked to become a frog. I should have missed Papa dreadfully and worried about whether he was taking care of himself properly. Still, it would have been a singular opportunity to learn a great deal about frogs and I daresay any number of other things I should never otherwise know."

"I daresay indeed," he agreed, regarding her with an appreciative glint in his eye.

"The worst part would have been being forced to exist on a diet of insects and worms," she continued in a practical vein. "Do you think, once having turned into a frog, one would suddenly find such a regimen entirely palatable?"

Abruptly he stopped and looked at her.

It was then, after only the briefest of silences, that he threw back his head and laughed.

Really, she wished that he had not, for it had been a rich, wonderful, vibrant sound, as potent as Mrs. Tibbitt's elderberry wine. All in an instant, all his bitterness and grief seemed magically to disappear so that she had beheld him as he had been truly meant to be. It was a memory, which, coupled with that other, earlier one of bitter torment, had become indelibly etched in her mind and heart to be forever preserved there— opposing images, one of what he might have been and the other of what the world had made of him.

Not that she had perfectly comprehended all that then, she acknowledged wryly to herself. It was not until later, when she had begun to experience the first budding into womanhood, that she began to realize just how truly devastating had been that singular meeting in the church grounds.

In retrospect, she supposed it was inevitable that, once having caught both her imagination and her considerable powers of sympathy, the Devil's Cub could not but assume the proportions of a beau ideal in her childish imagination—as, indeed, he had.

From the very first, he had appropriated a very special place in her heart. The problem was that no one had ever quite succeeded in dislodging him. Here she was, all of five and twenty, and not once had she been tempted to abandon her spinster state for marriage with a man who did not live up to the ideal she had momentarily glimpsed behind the arrogant facade of the Devil's Cub. Not that she had ever really minded, she reflected with her usual practicality. It would have been deucedly hard to practice her chosen vocation were she burdened with an unsympathetic husband. She much preferred the freedom of her single state and had long since determined that she would always be perfectly happy to remain in it.

Until, that was, Millie Dickson's chance remark had provoked a wholly unexpected reaction from her.

It was not the first time she had heard the superstitious nonsense that death dogged the heels of the Devil's Cub. Nor was she ignorant of the rumors which had seen its birth. She merely considered them wholly unfounded. And if, indeed, it had happened that Caleb Dameron had been born into the world one of identical twin boys, it was hardly his fault that his umbilical cord had somehow managed to become wrapped around his brother's neck, strangling the elder child to death upon the occasion of their birth. From what her papa had said, the attending physician must have been extremely hard put to save the remaining twin. It was all an unfortunate accident, as was the death of the boy's tutor a dozen years later, the drowning of his father in the ornamental pond hardly two years following, and, finally and most devastating of all, the tragic end of his mother. The unexplained circumstances of her death had finally been legally termed a suicide.

She had never for a moment believed the Devil's Cub responsible, either directly by deliberate murder, as many postulated, or indirectly due to the curse of the devil, for the deaths of all those who had been close to him. And certainly she did not hold him responsible for the death of Jemmy Wiggins's sister, Mary, no matter what anyone might say. On the contrary, her heart went out to him at the thought of all that he had been made to suffer.

It was little wonder, she thought, sitting her dun mare at the fork in the road, that he had chosen to absent himself from the scene of so much unhappiness or, indeed, that he had apparently pursued since a wide assortment of exotic pleasures both at home and, most especially, abroad. She could not blame him for seeking that sort of self-indulgence. If she had had as much as he to wish to forget, very likely she would have behaved in a similar manner.

What the Devil's Cub had or had not done, however, was hardly any of her affair, she sternly reminded herself, brought at last to an awareness of the lateness of the hour. Of far more immediate concern was the fact that lately she had found her services to be greatly in demand. So much so, in fact, that she had had neither the time nor the opportunity to replenish her store of certain wild herbs required for any number of her very special potions and poultices. These, unfortunately, were best gathered in the light of a full moon when their curative properties were at their most potent.

Conscious of a longing for her supper, a bath, and her bed, she debated her immediate course of action. The house she had shared until recently with her father and now with her Aunt Philippa lay only a short distance ahead on the village highroad, while to her left beckoned the now little used track into Devil's Gill.

At last, judging that her aunt had long since retired to her bed and, further, that she might not have another opportunity before the waning of the moon to gather the required herbs, she urged Ginger on to the track, which led into the ravine.

* * *

This was not the first time Theodora had ventured into the woods at night in search of her precious health-giving herbs. For as far back as she could remember, she had known what her calling was in life and had pursued it with a single-minded determination which was as much a part of her nature as was her instinctive understanding of pain and those who suffered it. Had she been born a boy, she very probably would have followed in her father's footsteps and become a physician. Instead, she had become a witch, a white witch of the healing arts, and, as such, she had not only studied every aspect of herb lore, potions, and natural cures, but she had made extensive forays throughout the surrounding countryside as well to discover just exactly what herbs grew where and when was the best time to gather them. Her numerous excursions had taught her that not a few of the plants she sought thrived in Devil's Gill.

They had taught her, as well, that she had a natural affinity for the night. It was a whole new world after dark, with creatures about that one never saw in the daytime. Even one's perceptions of otherwise familiar things were different at night. The air was crisper, the sky more intimate somehow and yet vastly more mysterious when lit by an infinitude of winking stars. Sounds in the dark were amplified and made to assume new significance. Every excursion into the night world assumed the proportions of a fresh, new adventure to Theodora, who was of a naturally adventurous nature.

It helped, of course, that she had never been afraid of the dark. In fact, she had never been afraid of anything that she could recall. She was far too analytically minded to allow her imagination to conjure up monsters out of shadows or the wind rustling through branches. She was also too familiar with the various murmurings, scamperings, and night calls and their probable sources to be in the least frightened by them. Having reached her intended destination, she immediately dismounted and set about gathering the celery-like stalks of angelica, which grew along the banks of the bourn.

An hour later, rather tired, but well-pleased to have replenished her supply of St.-John's-wort, plantain, king's cure, and mistletoe, among others, Theodora made her way at last to an elderberry thicket for her final acquisition. Interested in the stems as well as the leaves and flowers, she knelt and felt in the leather pouch for the pruning shears she always carried with her for just such occasions.

She must have been weary indeed, she was to reflect later. The horse and rider were almost upon her before she became aware of them. Startled, she sprang to her feet almost beneath the nose of the equally startled stallion.

Two

Theodora froze, which, in the circumstances, was really all that she could do. The Devil's Cub dragged the stallion aside with an iron arm before the deadly hooves could reach their mark. Beneath him, Erebus snorted and sidled nervously. The drunken haze which had begun to settle over Styles abruptly receded, leaving his head momentarily clear at least. Bloody hell! This was no spectre come to haunt him in his hour of darkness. Not if the horse was aware of it, too.

"Softly, my lad," he crooned, laying a steadying hand on the animal's neck. "I see it."

Shaken, but unhurt, Theodora was startled into a low, vibrant chuckle. "But of course you do," she agreed, both rueful and amused. "In which case it must be obvious that I am not an 'it.' I am sorry I startled your horse. And though I own I might appear to be a wraith, I am not one of those poor tormented souls, I assure you."

"Demented would be more like," observed the earl with a chilling lack of humor. His cold eyes swept over the slender figure, which was unmistakably feminine in spite of the white cloak which obscured it or the deep hood which concealed the face. "I do not question your obvious corporeality. Only your apparent lackwittedness. Who are you, girl? Have you no one to take you in hand? What the deuce are you doing trespassing on my grounds and at this ungodly hour?"

"*Your* grounds!" The hood slid back as the trespasser's head shot up to reveal huge, startled eyes framed in a countenance of uncommon beauty. One might even have said ethereal, reflected the earl, observing the delicate bone structure beneath flawless, translucent skin—had it not been, that was, for the sensual fullness of what were undeniably alluring lips. Whatever she was, Styles noted with a sudden prick of interest, she most certainly was not frightened of him.

"But then," she exclaimed, "you are . . . ? Oh, but of course you are. You are considerably older, of course . . ."

"Almost ancient, as it were," agreed the nobleman dryly.

"But well-preserved," Theodora reminded him.

"Perhaps not so well as I might wish," conceded Styles, with melancholy gravity.

"No, you are a magnificent specimen!" Theodora hastened to assure him. Her glance took in the compelling figure of the earl from his commanding breadth of shoulder to the powerful thighs gripping the horse. A soft thrill started most unexpectedly somewhere deep inside and rippled through her. "Indeed, sir," she said, "you are uncommonly well-constructed."

"I bow to your enthusiasm, ma'am," replied the Devil's Cub, who had not failed to note the unmaidenly leap of her gaze. His smile was distinctly satanic.

Theodora blushed. The devil, she thought.

". . . But other than that," she plunged ahead, "you are just exactly as I have pictured you. And it *was* rumored, after all, that you had taken up residence at Devil's Keep. Had you not taken me by surprise, I'm sure I should have known at once who you were."

"No doubt you are to be congratulated for your powers of deduction, madam," observed the earl acerbically. "None of which is to the point, however. You have yet to answer me satisfactorily. Who are you and what are you doing here?"

Grown men had been known to quail before the Devil's Cub when he employed that particular tone. This slip of a woman had the impertinence to narrow her eyes at him in a manner that he found more than a little disconcerting. He had the curious feeling that he had never before been so thoroughly scrutinized.

"Dear, you are in a rare taking, are you not?" she murmured, touching the tip of an index finger meditatively to her cheek. "I suspect that tea of angelica might improve your disposition. It is very soothing in cases of dyspepsia."

"Is it indeed?" queried the earl with a steel-edged softness. "No doubt I am sorry to disappoint you, but I am not now, nor am I in the least given to, suffering from indigestion."

Theodora grinned, revealing a wholly bewitching dimple at the corner of her mouth. "But I am not in the least disappointed, my lord," she demurred. "On the contrary, I am very glad you are not prone to digestive disturbances."

"No more than am I," granted his lordship in exceedingly dry tones. "The state of my health, however, is not in question here. I am not a fool, my girl. I know when someone is trying to fling dust in my eyes."

"But of course you do," Theodora agreed with perfect equanimity. "In which case, it must be equally obvious to you that I am not a girl. I am a woman of five and twenty and hardly in need of someone to take me in hand."

The sardonic curl of his lip at that moment, she decided, reluctantly discarding dyspepsia as the source of his ill-humor, was hardly meant to be reassuring. Perhaps she should consider the possibility of a choleric condition.

"The fact that I find you roaming the woods alone at night hardly predisposes me to agree with you," Styles was quick to point out. "Obviously you are no man's wife, or you would not be here."

"Very likely not, sir," Theodora assented, moved to irritation at his stubborn insistence that she required a man to govern her existence when he did not know the first thing about her. "You are quite right, however," she declared. "I am not a wife. I am a witch."

The Devil's Cub's fierce bristling eyebrows snapped together at that unexpected announcement. Clearly the woman was a Bedlamite, he reasoned. And yet her words had struck an unexpected chord, rather like an echo of something he had heard before a very long time ago. He frowned, trying to place the event, and was rewarded for his efforts with a wincing stab of pain. Silently he swore.

"No doubt you are to be commended, madam," he uttered between clenched teeth. "That would naturally explain why you find yourself in an unwedded state, but hardly what you are doing trespassing in these woods."

It did not improve his rapidly deteriorating hold on his temper to observe through the mists of pain that the woman was watching him again with her damned, unnervingly pointed gaze.

"I come here often to gather herbs for my healing potions," replied Theodora, who could hardly have failed to note the sudden, swift blurring of his eyes or the way his strong hand clenched the reins. These were obvious symptoms of deepseated pain. Her tone gentled with compassion. "You need not concern yourself, I assure you. I am well known in these parts, and there is not a soul who would wish to lay a hand on me. I daresay I am as safe in these woods as you, my lord. Possibly even more so."

"Which only goes to prove you are either exceedingly naïve or a fool," growled the earl. Slipping his foot out of the stirrup, he dismounted with the supple grace which had caused more than one observer to liken him to a cat in his movements. "I am Styles," he said, dropping the reins and stepping significantly toward her, "and you are a young, unprotected female far from any habitation. These facts alone should give you pause for thought."

He was a very large man, towering well above average height and endowed with the firm, muscular frame of one who would strip to advantage in the ring. Added to these attributes were a fierceness of eye and a deliberately cultivated satyr-like expression which had served to intimidate eastern potentates, at least one crowned prince, and various other heads of state.

Yet this slip of a female appeared singularly undaunted at finding herself face to face with the most dangerous man in England. If anything, she appeared rather amused at the suggestion that she should be in dread of him, he realized with something very nearly approaching irritation. Who the devil was she?

"Indeed, my lord?" she had the temerity to answer, cocking one eye at him, rather as if they were engaged in a wholly stimulating, but purely hypothetical discussion. "And what exactly am I to contemplate?"

The earl moved closer. "That I am who I am should be enough to spark your imagination. You are trespassing on my land, and you are alone. Perhaps I intend to take my pleasure with you and then put a period to your existence. It is, after all, only what would be expected of me. There would be talk, but without witnesses or proof, it would be merely another unsubstantiated rumor to add to all the others. One more tragic death attributed to the curse of the Devil's Cub."

He had painted a vivid enough picture of what she might expect at his hands. By all rights, the wench should have been trembling in her rather disreputably scuffed, but otherwise sturdy, brown half-boots. It was not fear, however, which darkened her eyes, but something very disconcertingly resembling pity.

"For shame, my lord," she scolded. "Trying to frighten me with bogeys. I confess I expected better of you. I shall excuse your lapse purely on the grounds that you very likely were afraid of being a disappointment to me. I assure you, however, that it is not at all necessary to impress me with the absurd things that are said of you. I have never believed there was a grain of truth in any of them."

A single dark and exceedingly arrogant eyebrow swept upwards toward the earl's hairline. "No doubt I should be grateful for your generosity and your trust," he uttered with scathing cynicism, "—were they not so patently misplaced."

Theodora smiled with complete understanding. "Naturally you would say that, my lord. I suspect that, having been made the object of so much idle gossip, you have become accustomed to living up to your reputation. I find that I am prone to do the very same thing myself. It does afford a certain perverse satisfaction to pretend to be as bad as one is made out to be, does it not?"

"It is, in fact, one of my few pleasures in life." He experienced another echo of memory as he heard himself ask with cynical amusement, "Have you the reputation of being bad, then?"

"Not precisely bad, perhaps," Theodora confessed, reflecting upon her peculiar status in the community. "I am much sought after for my knowledge of healing potions. Still, even a good witch must find herself the object of a great deal of absurd speculation. I should warn you, perhaps, that, among my more dubious talents, I am reputedly able to cause a man's hair to fall out with a curse, to turn milk sour and to make a horse sweat at dawn. You will, however, be safe enough from my flights of temper if you wear a sprig of broom in your hat. Or you might try draping your windows and doors with elderberry gathered on the last day of April. Beware, however. A witch finds elderberry, in general, very attractive. It would be wise, therefore, were you to avoid it after dark."

He could not miss in the muted moonlight the gleam of mischief in her bewitching eyes or the fact that she was even then standing in the middle of an elderberry patch. The minx, he thought, aware that he had begun to enjoy himself.

"I shall keep that in mind," he promised, "if ever I feel the inclination to find me a witch." His curiosity now fully aroused, he approached to within less than a foot of her. "Or frighten one away," he added, staring down at her. Witch, hell, he thought. She was a bloody enchantress, intent upon weaving her spell over him.

Next to his imposing frame, she appeared absurdly small and fragile. Her head only just reached to his shoulder, and yet he was well aware her appearance was deceptive. There was a strength in her that had little to do with her size. She did not flinch when he reached up to pull the hood back, letting it drop down between her shoulders, but only stared up at him with a frank curiosity that he found undeniably fascinating.

Her hair, worn unfashionably long, fell in an enchanting disarray from a careless pile on top of her head. It shone in the moonlight—so fair as to be almost silvery. In sunlight, it would be flaxen, he judged, experimentally crushing a handful in his fist. It was thick and soft and exuded a pleasing, delicate aroma. He pressed the springy mass to his nose and inhaled.

"So sweet," he murmured thickly, savoring the scent and his own arousal, which was as heady as it was unexpected. When was the last time he had felt the need of a woman? He reached for the folds of her cloak where they met in front.

"Cloves and rosemary, my lord," drifted meaninglessly to him through the heat mists clouding his brain and his need to see beneath the cloak to the treasures it hid. Vaguely he wished he had not indulged so freely in intoxicating spirits. It would seem to be having a disturbing effect on his powers of reason.

"What—?" His hands went still, as he forced himself to focus on her face. "Rosemary—your name?"

"No, my lord. Oils of rosemary and cloves," she repeated patiently. "Aromatic herbs. I scent my soaps with them."

She gazed at him askance, clearly thinking him either drunk or demented. Perhaps he was both, he thought, a warning sounding somewhere in his brain. Plainly this was no country wench, used to the ways of men. Country wenches did not smell of cloves and rosemary. Still, she had need of being taught a lesson. A young, desirable female should know better than to traipse through the woods at night, alone and unprotected.

She made no move to stop him as he thrust aside the folds of her cloak.

Her gown was of a soft grey wool and so severely plain with its chaste, high neck and prim round collar, that, save for the lack of a wimple, it might have belonged to a novice in a nunnery. Hardly the sort of gown one might expect a self-proclaimed witch to wear, he mused, intrigued by the seeming contradiction. Even so, it did little to camouflage her feminine charms or the fact that she wore very little beneath it. She was undeniably lovely.

Hellsfire! To say she was lovely did not begin to describe what she was. Her rounded breasts, peaked beneath the fabric of her bodice, appeared specifically molded to fit his palms. Her waist was not greater than the span of his hands around it, he judged, strangely pleased at the thought. She was all small and slender and delicately made, and yet womanly, he realized, noting the well-rounded curve of her hips. The devil, he thought. She had not lied when she claimed she was a witch. His groin was taut against his close-fitting breeches.

Theodora stood quite still beneath his scrutiny, prey to a bewildering assortment of reactions to this unexpected turn of events. Not the least of these was a delicious tingling sensation along her spine and the incipiency of an odd sort of ache in the region of her belly. These peculiarities she found most particularly thought-provoking, never having experienced anything remotely like them. It occurred to her that, in stubbornly adhering to her single state, she had overlooked a broad spectrum of physiological science which offered intriguing possibilities for study. She had had no idea that the mere proximity of a man like Styles, coupled with what could only be described as a look of probing passion, could induce so pleasurable a bodily chemical reaction. It was really quite intoxicating. With a keen sense of wonder, she studied the nobleman's face in an effort to determine if he were experiencing a similar physiological response.

The earl's harsh features did indeed demonstrate a marked alteration. The (she was certain) deliberate satyrlike expression he had worn from the very first of their encounter had now assumed the rigid contours of a determinedly impenetrable ironlike mask of control. Obviously, he was intent upon concealing his thoughts and feelings from her. Naturally he could not know that *she* was a highly skilled sensitive or that she had been gifted almost from birth with the faculty for apprehending and identifying with the sensibilities of those with whom she came in contact. She was, in short, possessed of what her father had been wont to call "acute empathic powers of perception," which had proved invaluable in aiding her to detect and assess the physical and emotional conditions of those she treated. She looked at Styles now with a discerning eye.

The earlier blur of pain she had detected in the fierce, black eyes had vanished, she noted at once, to be replaced by a smoldering heat of discomfort.

"My lord?" she queried, moved to immediate alarm. He flinched and then froze, his burning eyes fixed on her face as, instinctively, she laid her palm against his forehead before sliding it down to the side of his face. It was just as she had suspected, she discovered. His skin was hot—unnaturally so—and a film of moisture had broken out on his brow. He gave every indication of a man running a fever. "You would seem to be in some distress," she said in no little concern.

"That does not begin to describe what I am," growled the Devil's Cub. Closing strong fingers about her wrist, he pulled her hand down and held it captive between them. "I suggest, madam, that you take your precious herbs and flee from here— now! Just as fast and as far as your horse will take you."

Not in the least inclined to take his advice, Theodora studied his eyes. They were regarding her now with a distinct ferocity of concentration, which unaccountably caused her breath to quicken and her mouth to become most inexplicably dry. It occurred to her that what she was experiencing was not unlike what a lamb might have felt in the presence of a very large and hungry lion. How odd, then, that she was not in the least intimidated! She did, in fact, find the whole experience uncommonly stimulating. In unconscious response to the physiological peculiarities she was experiencing, she ran the tip of her pink tongue between her suddenly parched lips. Interestingly, she felt his grip on her hand perceptibly tighten. "Why, sir, should I wish to do that?" she asked quite reasonably.

"Especially as I am certain I can be of some little help in relieving your symptoms."

A harsh laugh seemed forced from him. "Oh, you may be sure of it, madam. But not, I think, with your bloody potions." Abruptly he released her. "Now go, unless you wish to discover just exactly how you may be of use to me."

"But I have no intention of leaving you," Theodora declared flatly. "Perhaps you are unaware that I am a person of acute empathic powers of perception. As such, I am perfectly aware that you are a man of strong passions and, furthermore, that you are in the throes of some great torment. As a witch dedicated to the healing arts, I cannot, in all conscience, abandon you."

Styles stared at her. *Abandon* him! Good God, she did not have the sense of a three-year-old. Or perhaps she was convinced that once he took her at her word and relieved himself of his symptoms, his conscience would not allow *him* to abandon *her*, he speculated darkly. Obviously, she had not the least inkling of whom she was dealing with.

Deliberately he cupped his hand beneath her breast. "Very well, madam," he murmured dangerously, "since you feel yourself obligated to help me. I find I am of a mind to put your sense of dedication to the test."

Theodora did not budge an inch as his thumb began to describe slow, sensual circles around her nipple. Indeed, she could not have moved had she wanted to. She was utterly immobilized by her acute empathic powers of perception.

"My lord." She shuddered.

"Quite so, my dear," smiled the Devil's Cub. Closing his other hand in her hair at the back of her head, he covered her mouth with his.

Theodora, her lips parted on the point of uttering a sigh, received a startling demonstration of the pleasurable possibilities in this sort of physiological research. A low groan burst from her depths as his lordship's tongue thrust between her teeth.

She suffered a sensation not unlike what one might feel upon having a shock wave course through one's body in an electrical reanimation experiment. Certainly it served to vitalize various parts of her anatomy.

The earl, too, it soon appeared, had been no less stimulated in a physiological sense, though it seemed to Theodora, upon being released, that it was not precisely a pleasurable thing to him. His breath came harsh in his throat, and his face had taken on a wooden expression, which was rendered all the more acute by the smoldering heat in his eyes.

"My lord," Theodora exclaimed in no little contrition, "you are in pain."

"I would not dream of disputing your judgment, madam," groaned the Devil's Cub. "Or your acute empathic powers of perception. Perhaps now you are ready to concede that this experiment has gone far enough."

"But I am not at all ready to concede any such thing, my lord," Theodora asserted, unable to hide her disappointment at the sudden curtailment of her pleasurable sensations. "I assure you my sense of dedication is not in the least shaken. On the contrary, I am perfectly ready and willing to continue."

"You amaze me," rumbled his lordship. "It would seem your dedication to the healing arts knows no limits. Are you often called upon to administer this sort of cure to your male patients?"

"On the contrary. You are the first, my lord. Which is why I am most anxious not to terminate the treatment. It is hardly likely, after all, that I shall ever have the opportunity to repeat the experiment, and I find that I have suddenly developed an interest in this particular aspect of male-female physiology."

"So, now it is an experiment in biology, is it?" queried the nobleman with an incredulous lift of an eyebrow. "With which of us, I cannot but wonder, the guinea pig? You will pardon me if I mistook your motives. I thought your purpose was to relieve me of the discomfort to which I find myself prey at the moment."

"But it is," Theodora hastened to assure him with utmost earnestness. "Surely you cannot expect me, however, to be able to render you what aid you need without feeling certain physiological responses myself? If so, sir, I daresay that would be asking the impossible."

"You might be surprised at some females' lack of physiological response," responded his lordship dryly. "In your case, however, I suspect you are in the right of it. You are undoubtedly a creature of extreme passions."

"As are you, sir," Theodora pointed out, delighted that he had so easily perceived the depth of her potential for primal emotions. "In which case, we would seem ideally suited for an exercise in mutual discovery."

"Ideally," agreed his lordship with only the barest hint of irony. "I wonder, however, if you have considered the ramifications of such a study. Has it occurred to you that, while no one would be in the least surprised to learn to what new depths of depravity I am willing to sink, you, my girl, will emerge from this exercise in mutual discovery a ruined woman without a shred of respectability?"

"Pooh," exclaimed Theodora, who had been anticipating a far more forceful argument. "My reputation is clearly of secondary importance in this matter."

"Secondary to what, madam? My dubious honor as a gentleman?" demanded his lordship.

"Dear, I *have* shocked your delicate sensibilities, have I not? And I'm sure I cannot blame you for putting the worst possible construction on my unmaidenly conduct. But the truth is I am far too old to be concerned over something which must clearly be insignificant when compared to all I shall be able to learn from this encounter. Even were I not on the shelf, it would make no difference. I am quite determined never to alter my single state. So we need not consider my reputation. And, besides, there is the matter of your cure, my lord. If we can achieve two aims with one endeavor, then surely there can be no excuse for letting the opportunity slip from our fingers."

"Your logic would seem infallible," applauded his lordship, who had been listening to this interesting exercise in discursive reasoning with a sense of unreality, "save for two salient facts. One, you haven't the least idea how exceedingly unpleasant it can be to be deprived of your reputation. And, two, you have overlooked the obvious. Very often experiments of this nature result in an unwelcome by-product."

He waited with a keen sense of expectancy for the obvious repercussions to sink in and was rewarded with a thoughtful moue from his surprising enchantress. Instead of the maidenly dismay he anticipated at the realization that she was inviting the possibility of a pregnancy, the unpredictable little wretch gave every indication of one involved in performing mathematical computations.

"Not unwelcome, my lord," she ventured at last. "It could never be that. I believe, however, that the possibility of our producing a child at this juncture is minimal at best. Naturally I do not rule out the possibility, but I am prepared to take that infinitesimal risk based on my monthly cycle."

"Well, then," remarked the earl with a distinct edge to his well-modulated tones. *She* was willing to take the risk. Good God! And he, by extension, must naturally relish the notion of fathering a bastard on an obvious innocent. For he knew, if she did not, that that was what came of relying on rhythms and cycles to avoid parenthood. One might as well depend on astrology and fortune-telling as the predictability of a woman's cycles. "Naturally we may discard that extreme unlikelihood."

"Indeed, sir," Theodora agreed, relieved that he was proving so amenable on the subject. "And as for your other objection, I should much rather be ruined than live my entire life in ignorance. Surely you, of all people, must understand how I feel. You, who are noted for your intellectual curiosity."

He was aware of her eyes on him and wondered suddenly if she could see into him, to the hell of darkness that was slowly devouring him. Savagely he thrust the thought from him, along with the last, small, lingering voice of conscience.

She was here, where she had no business to be, and she was perfectly amenable to being instructed in human physiology by no less a personage than the Devil's Cub. Good God! Who the devil was he to disappoint her?

Wordlessly, he picked her up in his arms and carried her to a bed of grass in the clearing.

"Does this mean you do intend to ravish me, my lord?" she queried, feeling a trifle breathless, a condition which she attributed to being clamped in arms of steel.

"In every rumor," he answered, laying her down and settling himself beside her, "there is always a *grain* of truth. As you, my dear, are about to discover for yourself."

Theodora was not given the opportunity to voice an answer to that wholly enthralling suggestion before he silenced her with his mouth on hers. In the spirit of cooperation she parted her lips to receive the full benefits of his instruction and was promptly rewarded with the thrust of his tongue between her teeth.

Theodora, shuddering in the throes of an exquisite physiological response, sank her fingernails into his shoulders and clung to him.

"Ah, that pleasures you, does it, my eager little pupil?" murmured his lordship, releasing her lips in order to seek out an incredibly sensitive area on her neck below her ear.

"Indeed," Theodora gasped, "I find it—most—enlightening, my lord." She did not even notice that his nimble fingers had unloosed the fastening of her cloak or that they were even now busy undoing the buttons down the front of her bodice. Eager for further instruction, she arched her back to him, a movement which bared her chest to him.

"You will find me an inspired instructor, I promise you," declared His Lordship, presented with the unobstructed view of her breasts pressed against the near transparency of her lawn chemise. By God, he had never felt so inspired! Lowering his head, he proceeded to introduce her to new physiological heights.

Theodora, quite forgetting herself, uttered a groan as his tongue through the thin fabric of her chemise caressed her nipple to a taut rigidity she had not thought possible. Squirming beneath him with a rising sense of urgency, it occurred to her that she wished nothing more than to be rid of the constricting confines of her clothing. Apparently the same thought occurred concurrently to His Lordship. Indeed, she wondered feverishly if he, too, were possessed of acute empathic powers of perception, for no sooner had the thought formulated itself within her mind than he began with singular purpose to free her of her dress, followed swiftly by her chemise, her drawers, her half-boots, her garters and her stockings.

She lay on her cloak completely naked to the world and most certainly to the Devil's Cub, who regarded her with undisguised appreciation of her physical attributes.

"Do you find me a worthy subject for experimentation, my lord?" queried Theodora, feeling a trifle uncertain now that she found herself poised, as it were, at the moment of truth.

She blushed pink from her toes to the top of her head at the look he bent upon her. "I believe, my dear, that I have seldom seen a finer specimen."

"Are you quite sure, my lord? I have never been certain I was the sort to excite a gentleman's primitive urges. I am, after all, built on rather diminutive lines. My papa was used to calling me a mere dab of a female."

"Your papa's judgment notwithstanding, my dear," uttered the Devil's Cub in a voice of hardly controlled passion, "you are exactly the sort to excite a gentleman's primitive urges." His Lordship groaned with the effort to contain his own physiological urge to sink his shaft into her without further delay. Instead he lowered his head to address the matter of a delightfully taut nipple, which seemed in need of his immediate attention, while with his hand he found the flesh of her inner thigh and began a wholly instructive journey of exploration upwards.

Theodora went suddenly rigid with shock as his quest led him to the source of the moist heat she had been experiencing since first he began his journey a seeming eternity before. "That is a most peculiar sensation, my lord," she gasped, as his fingers gently parted the soft petals of her flesh. "It would seem to me the experiment is progressing quite nicely, would it not?"

"In a truly exemplary manner," agreed his lordship, feeling his body painfully hard as he inhaled the musky scent of her arousal. "We are, in fact, on the point of making an earth-shaking discovery."

"I could not be more pleased, sir," Theodora responded, her voice rising to a keening pitch as he experimentally slipped a finger inside her. "Oh, yes, I begin to see what you are driving at," she gasped. In her eagerness to help the experiment along, she arched frantically against him. "Please, please. I beg you will not stop now."

"No, I believe nothing could stop me now. You are a most precocious student. You are already flowing in anticipation of our final probe into the mysteries of physiological research. How small and tight you are," he added, delving into her once more with his finger and slowly drawing it out. By God, she did not know what a magnificent creature she was! She was not even aware of her power to arouse him to what was tantamount to madness. Nor must she ever know. What she *was* about to discover was the power of her own body to transport her into a state of physiological rapture. That much at least she would have, he vowed, pressing his lips to the blond triangle of hair. And it was very close now. It needed only a tiny nudge to push her over the edge into bliss. If, that was, he did not perish before he could bring the bloody experiment to its inevitable culmination. He groaned, his muscles rigid with the impossible task he had set for himself.

Theodora writhed beneath him, feeling with a sense of shattering awe his finger caress the bud within the petals. Faith, what was he doing to her? She did indeed feel herself on the brink of a stupendous discovery. Surely she was about to explode or possibly ignite in a devastating conflagration. But it was not right. It was not at all the way she had imagined it. It was not the way she wanted it.

"Stop, my lord!" Theodora gasped, nearly overcome with the pleasurable sensations he was arousing in her. Her fingers lodged in his hair and attempted forcibly to gain his attention. "Stop it at once!"

The Devil's Cub, made painfully aware that his student was suddenly and most inexplicably in a state of revolt and misinterpreting the source of her frantic attempts to thwart what was very nearly a successful completion of the experiment upon which she herself had insisted, moved immediately to nip her rebellion in the bud.

"Softly, my dear. I promise you are about to have your intellectual curiosity amply satisfied. Trust me. You have nothing to fear in what I am doing."

"But I am not in the least afraid, my lord," Theodora declared indignantly. "It is only that this is not at all the sort of experiment upon which we agreed. I do not intend to make this journey alone, sir. Indeed, I cannot in all conscience allow it. Our primary purpose was to cure you of your indisposition, and I cannot think this will be achieved if you do not participate fully in the treatment. I tell you I will not have it, my lord. This is an endeavor we are meant to make together."

It took only a moment for him to realize she was perfectly in earnest and, further, that he was physically beyond the point of resisting her power to incite him to madness. Hellsfire, she did not know what she was doing to him! In another moment she would have him spilling his seed like the veriest untried adolescent. He doubted if the devil himself could have withstood her witchery.

"Very well, madam, if you insist." In short, savage gestures, he rid himself of his cloak, which he spread out beside her and which was followed swiftly by his coat and waistcoat. After an equally brief struggle, he divested himself of his boots and stockings.

Theodora stared entranced as his shirt came off over his

head to reveal a magnificent muscled chest bristling with a thick mat of hair. His torso, too, was a superb example of its kind. Intriguingly rippled in all the places that it rightfully should be, it narrowed exquisitely to a marvelously firm, flat belly. Theodora was quite sure she had never seen anything to equal the perfection of the Devil's Cub's upper body.

Faith, but even that paled before the enthralling sight of the Devil's Cub *sans-culotte!*

"My lord!" she exclaimed, her eyes wide and fixed as she beheld his erect male member.

"Exactly so, madam," growled the Devil's Cub with grim satisfaction. Spreading wide her thighs, he thrust his hips between them. "Now, my dear," he pronounced in a voice he hardly recognized as his own, "I hope you are pleased with yourself. You find me fully prepared to participate in my rehabilitation in a whole-hearted manner. I am, as a matter of fact, very nearly beyond the point of being able to do anything else, madam."

Theodora smiled encouragingly up at him. "You may be sure, my lord, that I am perfectly aware of your physiological condition."

"Ah, yes." The earl dropped his head as he uttered something between a groan and a laugh. "Your acute empathic powers of perception. I had almost forgot."

"You had a great many other things on your mind," Theodora magnanimously excused him. "Now, my lord," she added on a firmer note, which he doubted not was meant to inspire him with confidence, "I believe you need not be afraid to exert yourself fully. I'm sure you will see when it is all over that I was quite right to insist upon your complete cooperation in this matter. I feel strongly that it is bound to have a most beneficial effect upon you."

"I am glad that you think so," replied His Lordship humbly. "As it happens, I am of a similar opinion. Rest assured that I shall strive to make it a mutually beneficial experience. You have only to trust me to help you through rough waters."

"Never doubt it, my lord." Theodora, greatly moved by his concern for her, cradled his face between her hands. "You have always had my complete trust. I have always known you would never do anything to hurt me."

The Devil's Cub stared at her grimly. "Then we are lost before ever we begin," he said, and, inserting the tip of his shaft into her body's unguarded lips, he slowly, but inexorably, drove himself into her.

Theodora gave vent to a strangled cry and went rigid with surprise.

Instantly the earl stilled, his entire body tensed with concentration. "My poor enchantress. You are no doubt angry at me now, but soon, I promise you, you will forgive my betrayal of your trust." Cautiously, he began to move inside her. "We are on the threshold of a physiological breakthrough which will make you forget the pain I have caused you."

"Threshold?" Theodora blinked, brought to an awareness that they had already achieved what she had secretly believed was impossible. It had occurred to her when she first beheld his lordship's superbly erect manhood that her dainty proportions might prove an insurmountable hindrance. But no sooner had she been convinced of it, than she had found herself suddenly filled with him. It was unbelievable! He was inside her and her body seemed quite capable of accommodating him. More than that, his slow movements in and out were arousing a whole new range of exciting possibilities.

Digging her fingernails into his shoulders, she arched herself frantically against him. "Oh, yes. Please, my lord. Please. I begin to see it!"

"The devil!" groaned his lordship, who was a great deal closer to achieving revelation than she.

Theodora reached for it, knowing she had never wanted anything quite so much.

"Soon, my sweet," gasped the Devil's Cub. "Yes, I feel you are upon the threshold."

Upon the threshold? Faith, she thought furiously, she was a

bloody dam ready to burst. And just when she knew she could not bear it anymore, incredibly she felt his lordship draw out and back. Her lips parted to voice a protest, but before she could utter it, the heel of his hand found the swelling bud between her legs.

Faith, it was too much. She exploded in a shuddering wave of release at the very moment that his lordship plunged his shaft ruthlessly into her. She felt him tense, and his mouth covered hers with a groan of triumph as his seed spilled gloriously into her.

Then with a last shudder of pleasure, he collapsed on top of her.

Theodora lay limp beneath him. She had never dreamed that scientific research could be so utterly exhausting or so marvelously exhilarating. Nothing could compare to what she had discovered with the Devil's Cub.

It was not only the purely pleasurable sensations she had experienced at the startling intimacy to which she had been subjected, but the revelation that she had had upon its culmination. The one had communicated to her a raw, savage need in his lordship and a great deal more that he undoubtedly would not have wished her to know, and the other had taught her that there was a great deal about the human anatomy of which she had never even dreamed before.

Tenderly she ran her hands over his sweat-moistened back. The years in foreign parts had not healed her dear Devil's Cub, she realized. Indeed, there was some new affliction, some added torment, which was taxing even his iron strength. She had known almost from the first moment she had laid eyes on him. He was ill, and she was determined to do anything it might take to lead him back to health.

No sooner had that thought wedged itself firmly in her mind, than he stirred and lifted his head to gaze at her from beneath heavily drooping eyelids.

Theodora smiled gravely up at him. "I believe, my lord, that you are feeling much better."

"Witch," grumbled his lordship, dropping a kiss on the tip of her nose. He rolled off her on to his cloak, still stretched out beside her, and pulled on his breeches and shirt. "I am worn to a state of utter exhaustion." Concern reflected in his marvelous eyes, he paused in the middle of tugging on his stockings and boots to study her gravely. "And you, Enchantress. How are you feeling?"

"Considerably enlightened, my lord," Theodora replied lightly. "A service for which I can never repay you."

The Devil's Cub lowered his head to hers. "I shouldn't be too sure of that, were I you," he warned, then, kissing her, he wrapped her in her cloak and drew her to his side. "One should never bargain with the devil," he murmured thickly. The next moment he was sound asleep.

Three

Theodora stirred, teased to awareness by the persistent two-noted call of a chiffchaff somewhere overhead and what, curiously, sounded like the tattoo of a woodpecker attempting to peck a hole in a post of her four-poster bed. A furrow etched itself in her brow as the musky aromas of moldering leaves and rich, damp earth filled her nostrils instead of the rosemary and lavender scents of sheets to which she was accustomed to awakening. Even more puzzling, she could feel the cool kiss of mist against her face and hear the chuckle of a stream close by, she was sure of it—and, instead of the plump softness of her pillow, something firm, warm, and strangely comforting beneath her cheek. Things, she reflected, were not what they should be.

Her eyes flew open to be met with the sight of a rumpled white linen shirt at exceedingly close range and an undeniably masculine chest, intriguingly covered with bristling, black hair.

Theodora went very still, thoroughly awake and totally cognizant of where she was and exactly whose chest resided beneath her cheek.

The soft thrill that went through the entire length of her she attributed to the chill in the air. It was, after all, the twilight before dawn, and a thick veil of mist hung in the air. Grateful for the earl's warmth, Theodora hesitated; then, reasoning that she might never again have the opportunity to explore this new and curiously delectable sensation of awakening next to a firm muscular body, she snuggled closer. A whimsical smile touched her lips as it occurred to her that perhaps she should have felt some embarrassment at finding herself clasped in a man's arms while she lay stark naked beneath the folds of her cloak, especially this man's arms. But the truth was she felt nothing of the kind. Quite the contrary, she liked it where she was. Unfortunately, she was reasonably certain her dear Devil's Cub would not be equally sanguine upon awakening to find himself in compromising circumstances with a female whose name he did not even know. One, moreover, she reminded herself with an irrepressible grin, who was a self-proclaimed witch. She doubted not that he would be in a devil of a taking.

Folding her cloak around her, she carefully pushed herself up so as not to wake him. Tenderly she covered his bared chest with his coat and deliberately studied the strong, manly features.

Even relaxed in sleep, Styles, with his lean, stubborn jaw intriguingly shadowed with beard, presented a formidable presence. Her previous mirth gave way to a thoughtful purse of the lips as it occurred to her that he was undoubtedly going to prove troublesome in the extreme. A shame he could not be depended upon to be reasonable, she reflected, mulling over the difficulties she envisioned before her.

Styles was clearly not himself. She had sensed that almost from the very moment she laid eyes on him, and further contact had made it exceedingly plain that his pride would never allow him to admit to anyone, and least of all to a woman, that anything was in the least the matter with him. That same pride would hardly permit him to accept the help of a female, especially one who had placed him in what he must soon come to consider an untenable situation.

Theodora hardly needed to be told she was no common healer. She had a gift for it. Not even a witch with her acute empathic powers of perception could help Styles, however, if she were not given free access to him, and, to that, she very strongly suspected he must find more than a few objections.

How very bothersome it was, to be sure, she reflected, ever

of a practical nature. All she required was time to observe and determine the precise cause of his malady (perhaps no more than a few days, if he were completely cooperative and she was lucky) and to discover the right formula of herbs and roots to treat it. Then, keeping him under close observation, a few weeks' regimen of proper food and rest, and she doubted not that she would soon have him right as a trivet again. She would have done, that was, if he could have been brought to set aside the proprieties and his sense of honor in order to allow her to run tame in his castle.

She might be a provincial who had never had a come-out in London, but she had not been a student of human nature for as long as she could remember without having learned a great deal about the male gender. And all of her considerable powers of observation, not to mention her acute empathic powers of perception, had told her from the very beginning that Styles would not willingly agree to anything that violated his gentleman's code of ethics. Briefly she dismissed their experiment in shared human physiology as an incident outside the realm of social covenant. After all, they had agreed she was acting as a healer in his behalf. Furthermore, he had been in the throes of whatever was ailing him and had, as a consequence, been rendered somewhat vulnerable to suggestion. Allowing her to watch over him day and night for the length of time it would take to insure his health and well-being was another matter altogether. His reputation, after all, would be at stake, and he would undoubtedly balk at the prospect of incurring the scandal that consorting with an unmarried female who just happened to be a witch must inevitably bring.

Briefly, she wished her papa had not taken himself off to Scotland on a sudden notion to study under Sir Charles Bell, who was making significant discoveries in the area of anatomy. She might have laid the whole before him and trusted him to deal with the matter. On the other hand, she could not think he would have looked at all favorably on the news that his daughter had spent the night in the woods with the infamous

Devil's Cub. Very likely he would have done something positively Medieval, like insisting that Styles do right by her and
wed her, and that would not have done at all. She much preferred an agreement, based on mutual intellectual inquiry without the complication of marriage. The notion of two equals,
willingly joined on a mission of discovery, had ever so much
more appeal, after all, than a forced marriage that would have
placed her in the unenviable position of being an unwanted
wife. If only Styles could be made to see it that way.

Hell and the devil confound it. There must be a way. His
well-being, after all, would appear to depend on it, if she was
right in her assessment of the symptoms she had already been
given to note.

Theodora sighed philosophically and, rising quietly, swiftly
dressed.

Normally she might have tried bringing Styles to reason
through persuasion and logic as well as a demonstration of her
healing arts. In this instance, however, there simply was not
the time for anything so direct as that must be. Her every
instinct warned her that every moment was critical, and the
truth was, she had nothing solid to offer as evidence that his
health and well-being were imperiled. She had only her highly
developed intuition in such matters, her experience and skill
in diagnosing illnesses, and her knowledge of plants and drugs,
which was undeniably extensive. Still, it was not enough, she
decided, not with a man like Styles, who prided himself on
his analytical abilities. He would require more than a witch's
empathic powers of perception to convince him he was in need
of her particular services. She had learned from years of experience, after all, that what women seemed able to grasp in-
tuitively, men tended more often than not to find curiously
incomprehensible.

What a devil of a toil she found herself in. No doubt her
papa would have said she was guilty of having committed the
worst kind of folly. And, indeed, she could not deny that she
perhaps had been wiser to choose a less unorthodox method

of treatment for the Devil's Cub. Still, as a witch dedicated to the healing arts, she could not regret the beneficial results to her unwitting patient.

He had responded better than even she had expected to the after effects of their physiological exertions. A sweat bath could not have done better to cleanse his system of unhealthy toxins or done more to relieve him of his obvious tension. And certainly she could have found no better way to divert him from what she sensed was a brooding preoccupation with something that afforded him no little discomfort. *Something* had driven him out in the middle of the night, she reflected, frowning as she recalled the look of revulsion on his face when she had risen up suddenly almost beneath his horse's hooves. She did not think it was the headache from which he had been obviously suffering and which had left him in the wake of venting his passions in a manner she judged greatly beneficial. He had exerted himself to the point of exhaustion and fallen into a healthy slumber, which was always a good sign. Sleep very often was a healer's greatest ally in fighting illness. And if she herself had derived no little enjoyment from the experience, surely she could be forgiven for it. She was only a woman, after all, and her motives had at least been altruistic in nature.

Besides, she could hardly have done nothing, she told herself. It simply was not in her nature to turn her back on anyone in need. How much less could she walk away from the Devil's Cub! It simply was not an option that would ever have occurred to her. If he could not be persuaded by reason, then she really had no choice, she told herself as she tied her bag of freshly gathered herbs to Ginger's saddle. She must simply employ somewhat devious tactics to achieve what might otherwise have been accomplished in a straightforward manner.

Catching up the reins, she cast one last, lingering look at the sleeping nobleman. It did not seem quite right, leaving him like this. On the other hand, she could not see what else she might have done. At last telling herself that he would come to no harm where he was and that it would never do to have him awaken and find her still there, she knelt to lay a sprig of lady's mantle across his breast to invoke its protection over him. Then leading her mare down the ravine until they were safely out of earshot, she mounted.

Seeing no one, but Tom Dickson, turning in the lane to Cliff House, a shovel over one burly shoulder, Theodora accomplished the ride home without incident. The sun had hardly penetrated the curtain of mist, turning it the color of mother-of-pearl, before she had settled the mare in its stall, made her way through the herbal garden to the house, and, entering by the back way, stolen quickly upstairs to her study, cluttered with books and journals and her own, hand-drawn charts of various aspects of the human anatomy.

Sifting through a stack of carefully dated journals in which she had made it a practice to record the observed symptoms and treatments of each of her patients, she came at last to the one she most in particularly wanted. "I know it is here someplace," she murmured to herself as she thumbed through the pages. "It was six years ago, I am sure of it. Ah, yes, here it is. Mary Ellen Ellard. A female of four years of age, taken suddenly ill." Theodora sank down on the only chair in the small study, her eyes scanning the pages of the journal. "But of course," she exclaimed moments later. Closing the journal, she came to her feet. "That must be it. But who would do such a thing and why?"

Returning the journal to its stack on the table, Theodora left the study and, mulling over the extreme seriousness of what she had begun to suspect, trod on tiptoe past her aunt's room till she came to her own.

As she slipped inside, she was greeted by Percival, the single offspring of the kitchen feline that Theodora had saved from a disreputable life filching fish from the dockyards, and by the musky scent of potted geraniums mingled with the sweetness of dried rose petals.

"Not now," laughed Theodora, bending down to pick up the small mass of white fur that was energetically attacking the hem of her skirt. "I haven't time to play. You see, I am expecting a very important visitor, and I must be sure not to be here when he arrives." Holding the kitten up, she gazed into unwinking green eyes that looked back at her for all the world as if they comprehended every word. "Yes, I know that makes very little sense, but I'm afraid I haven't time to explain it to you."

"Then perhaps you could explain it to me," suggested a voice from the doorway. "After all, I am your aunt, and Thaddeus depends upon me to look out for you. If we are to have a very important visitor we wish to avoid seeing, Theodora, I think I should know about it."

"Dear," exclaimed Theodora, coming about to view the attractive middle-aged woman attired in a rumpled nightdress designed rather on the lines of an ungirded Greek peplos. Her short blond curls were disheveled and her eyes heavy with sleep. "Aunt Philippa, I'm sorry. Did I wake you?"

Philippa Havelock smothered a yawn. "Actually, I had only just gone to bed when I heard you come in. You have no idea how difficult it is to divorce oneself from all the goings on in this house. I daresay Uncle Pervis and Aunt Edna kept me up most of the night. Uncle Pervis has yet to forgive Aunt Edna for cooking up mushroom ketchup in August, when she never could tell the difference between panther cap and common morel, and I must say I can hardly blame him. It could not have been pleasant suffering from severe gastrointestinal irritation, vomiting, and loose bowels. And then to be forced to witness hallucinations of Grandmother Beatty railing at him over the chamber pot for having wed poor Edna against his mama's wishes right up until the moment he succumbed to a coma— well, it cannot be the easiest manner to quit this plane of existence. Is it any wonder that he absolutely refuses to cross over so long as his mama is there, waiting for him on the other side?" Philippa gave a slight shudder. "I daresay, faced with a similar welcoming committee, I should insist on an immediate transmigration. Grandmother Beatty, I regret to say, always was an absolute terror."

"Poor Aunt Philippa. It cannot be easy being in contact with all the dead spirits that inhabit Cliff House. I can only be grateful that my empathic powers of perception do not extend to those who have already passed on. It is quite enough to sense when the living are ill or in pain."

The older woman sighed fatalistically. "Yes, well, it cannot be helped. We cannot cavil over the gifts we have been given, and I'm afraid it would seriously distort our karma not to use those gifts for the good of those with whom we come in contact. One must strive to be true to the Universal Self."

"If only it were that simple, Aunt," Theodora reflected, absently rubbing the purring kitten behind its ears. "It is not always exactly clear, after all, how one should proceed. Especially when the person in need of help is not likely to believe in the diagnosis. And then there are all the complications of silly conventions that only muddle what should otherwise be patently straightforward. I'm afraid I am in the devil of a quandary."

"I thought I detected an aberrance in your normally vivid chromatic emanations. You are troubled, Theodora. Perhaps you should tell me about this visitor you have no wish to see."

"But I do wish to see him," declared Theodora, who should have known she could hide nothing from her Aunt Philippa. The woman had an uncanny ability to read people's spiritual emanations perceived in a halo of colors surrounding the head and shoulders. "In fact, it is imperative. I very much fear that his life depends on his finding me. Which is why I must not be here when he comes looking for me."

"I'm sure that makes perfect sense," sighed Philippa, dropping down on the green dimity sofa. "No doubt it is only that it is too early in the morning for me to perfectly comprehend it. Perhaps, Theodora, you would not mind elucidating a little."

Theodora wrinkled her brow. "I'm not sure that I can, Aunt Philippa. It is, you see, a matter of the strictest confidence between patient and healer. Suffice it to say that the subject is a man of extreme pride and integrity and will most certainly insist on adhering to the conventions. I, unfortunately, am ethically bound to thwart him in his honorable intentions."

Philippa, who might be a trifle eccentric in her intellectual pursuits, was yet hardly a slow-top. Instantly she snapped to attention. "Theodora, he means to offer for you. And you intend to turn him down. By all that is marvelous, *why*—if he is eligible?"

"I daresay there is none more eminently eligible. But I told you," Theodora gestured impatiently. "It is a matter of ethics. Besides, I have a distinct aversion to the idea of marrying for reasons other than mutual affection. All of which is beside the point. The man is in peril of his life, and I'm afraid I am the only one who can save him."

"Then save him, you must," replied Philippa, who had complete confidence in her niece's curative abilities. "I fail to see the difficulty."

"The problem is he is a man of powerful intellect who is skeptical of anything that cannot be demonstrated in a precise, scientific manner. Can you imagine what he will say when I tell him I believe he is the victim of an insidious plot, first, to convince him he is losing his reason, but, ultimately, to foully murder him—by slow, deliberate poisoning?"

"Good heavens!" Philippa gaped at Theodora. "I should think, after his initial shock, he would be interested to know how you came to such a conclusion."

"Precisely. And what am I to tell him? That I sensed his pain and, based on my empathic powers of perception, I immediately began to analyze his symptoms, all of which led me to conclude that he has been made for some little time to ingest a potentially deadly agent that manifests itself in hallucinations?"

"Why not? It is only the truth, after all. Unless—" Philippa's brow furrowed. "Theodora, you did not. Oh, but you did. You told him you are a witch. As if I haven't warned you often enough. It is far better to stick to the bare essentials of truth. You are an herbalist. People are far less likely to object to being told you practice the ancient art of healing with herbs than they are to accept you are a practicing witch. After all, you do not dabble in spells or make compacts with the devil."

"Do I not, Aunt?" Theodora smiled ruefully. "As it happens, my difficult patient is none other than the Earl of Styles, and I very much fear that I now have the devil by the horns."

Philippa sank heavily against the settee back. "Faith, Theodora, do not tell me you have compromised yourself with the Devil's Cub."

"But I am afraid that is exactly what I have done, and now I see no other course but to avoid him. It is the only way I can think of at the moment to keep him intrigued enough to come in pursuit of me, for, if you must know, I have observed that there is nothing so desirable as that which we cannot have and nothing that palls so quickly as having something that has been too easily obtained. If I am to be allowed to come close enough to him to determine the nature of the poison and the manner in which it is administered, I have no choice but to make sure I stay at least one step ahead of His Lordship."

"Just be sure you do not end up stepping off the edge of a cliff, Theodora," Philippa warned, dragging herself up from the sofa with the intent of returning to her bed to recoup her strength. It appeared she would need to have her wits about her in the very near future if she was to be of the least use to Theodora.

"That is not in the least fair," objected Theodora, leaping swiftly to the earl's defense. "Styles had nothing to do with his tutor's unfortunate demise. It was an accident. You would know that if you ever met him."

"That may be as may be, Theodora," Aunt Philippa replied. "Nevertheless I suggest you think this thing through carefully. Styles, you may be sure, did not get his reputation for being the most dangerous man in England because he is easily duped or manipulated."

"I know that, Aunt," Theodora replied, grateful that the interview was come to an end. Aunt Philippa might be more

attuned to the next world than this one, but she had a disconcerting habit of seeing straight to the heart of a matter. "You
must simply trust that I know what I am about."

When Philippa thankfully had gone, Theodora set the kitten
on the bed with a ball of string to keep him entertained. Then,
thinking of all that she must do to prepare for the inevitable
confrontation with the lord of Devil's Keep, she hastily
stripped and washed.

If Styles awakened with the first shafts of sunlight through
the trees, she might expect him to arrive back at the keep as
soon as midmorning, she reasoned as she donned a fresh gown
of muslin, which had once been the blue of harebells, but, having since seen a great deal of service, was faded to the purplish
hue of the heather-covered moors. Then, an hour to bathe and
dress and fortify himself with breakfast before he began to make
inquiries among the servants, she continued with her line of
reasoning. It would not take long for him to learn the pertinent
details concerning the Witch of Weycombe Mere, she reflected
with a wry quirk of her lips. There was not a soul in the village
and roundabout who did not know Theodora Havelock. She was
a mite peculiar. Teched in the head, she was, always poring over
dusty old books when she wasn't shut away in the ramshackle
shed what she was fond of calling her herbarium. And heaven
only knew what she was about in there, what with her brewing
and concocting of potions. A regular witch's den, it was, what
no one would go near, did they know what was good for them,
Theodora grinned to herself.

He would take time to consider, she doubted not. He was,
after all, a man of strong intellect, one, moreover, who had
learned to distrust his emotions. In the sobering light of day,
he would find a great deal to question in the previous night's
events, not the least of which were her motives. By the time he
came to the conclusion that he could not make a rational judgment until he had confronted the perpetrator of his present pre-
dicament, the morning would be well advanced, perhaps even
drawing well nigh on to noon. Mounted, he could reach Wey-

combe Mere in twenty minutes. Going around the long way by carriage, forty-five. Either way, she might expect him no earlier than afternoon tea, which would give her time enough to lay out her herbs to dry and to prepare a bottle of elixir for Mrs. Fennelworth before she herself must be gone from home.

But first, a bite of breakfast, she decided, haphazardly pinning her hair in a loose knot on top of her head. Having missed her supper, she was devilishly sharp set.

The sprawling stone cottage overlooking the bay had been in the family for five generations of Havelocks and wore a homey look, rather like a comfortable, well-used shoe, Theodora was wont to reflect. Despite the well-worn carpets and sunbleached wall hangings, the somewhat threadbare furniture and faded drapes, Theodora had managed to infuse a rarefied atmosphere into the old house with potted plants, dried herbal arrangements, and flowers in strategically placed baskets and earthenware vases. The house exuded light and life and a pervasive sense of health and well-being, which was only as it should be for one whose inhabitants were dedicated to the healing arts. With the result that what might otherwise have appeared shabby genteel took on an aspect of earthy charm and beauty. Not that Theodora consciously thought of the old house in such terms, any more than she would have been given to consider her own remarkable beauty as wholly natural and unaffected. The cottage was simply an extension of herself. Its vitality was an outward manifestation of her own and therefore to be taken for granted.

The breakfast nook was no exception. On the ground floor, which placed it conveniently near the kitchens below stairs, it had the added charm of being bounded on two sides by a solid front of windows that overlooked the herbal garden and the bay. Theodora and her father, who were little given to entertaining, were wont to take their two daylight meals there in the warmer summer and fall months when, that was, they were not away on their separate professional calls, which occurred

all too often—to Mrs. Tibbet's way of thinking. The elderly
housekeeper, hearing Theodora's light footfall on the stairs,
clucked her tongue in disapproval and retreated to the kitchens
to fetch a fresh plate of toast.

The old housekeeper had been with the Havelocks since the
master was a boy and had watched over the motherless Theodora
as if she were her own. Not that Theodora had required all that
much mothering. Of a naturally independent disposition, she had
early on demonstrated a precociousness that had rendered unnecessary much of the sort of care her mother might have given had
the poor missus not succumbed to an untimely demise giving
birth to a stillborn son when Theodora was only three. Still, Mrs.
Tibbets had done her best by the child, teaching her what was
expected of a lady of a proud and ancient lineage. Nor had she
ever reconciled herself to the fact that the last of the Havelocks
had fallen on impoverished times of late, a circumstance that had
precluded a proper come-out for Theodora. The child had deserved better than to end up a spinster with a reputation for ec-
centricity, but there was nothing for it. The good doctor might
have earned a more-than-respectable living had he not seen fit to
practice his calling in the country where he might be paid more
often than not in kind instead of in good hard English brass.

No doubt Theodora might have looked forward to a curtain
lecture from Mrs. Tibbets on the inadvisability of hiring Tom
Dickson to enlarge the herbal garden that didn't need being
made bigger when there was little enough in the household
budget for the grocer and the butcher. She might have, that
was, had not the housekeeper already been occupied below-
stairs with scolding Sadie for wool gathering when the child
had ought to be scrubbing out the pots and pans.

Smiling to herself at the familiar sounds issuing from the
kitchen quarters, Theodora poured cream in a saucer for Percival and set it and the kitten on the floor. Then she filled her
plate with ham and scrambled eggs and poured a cup of
chamomile tea. As she carried these to the table, she saw Tom
Dickson, already at work in the garden, and smiled again. Mrs.

Tibbits might complain about Theodora's propensity for hiring work done that might have been put off till later, but she was every whit as softhearted as her employers. The housekeeper had set him to work as if she had been expecting him all along. It was only what Theodora had known the old dear would do.

Whimsically she wondered how the housekeeper would react when she found another male on her doorstep later that day, one who was not only very large, but extremely commanding in appearance.

She was not allowed to dwell on the possibilities, however, as Mrs. Tibbits, still muttering to herself something about empty-headed scullery maids, entered the breakfast room, carrying a fresh plate of saffron bread slices, toasted to a golden brown.

"So you're up and about, are you, miss, when you should be abed getting your beauty rest," scolded the elderly housekeeper, sapiently eyeing her mistress. "You can't come home with the rooster's crow and expect to look fresh as a posy without so much as an hour of repose. You, of all people, should know that."

"Am I so very fagged, dear Mrs. Tibbets?" replied Theodora, who might have known she could not pull the wool over her housekeeper's eyes. "I promise I feel quite up to trig. Indeed, I have seldom been better."

"Now that you mention it, you would seem to have a kind of glow about you," observed the housekeeper, the expression on her plump, round face instantly alert. "Just what might you be up to, Miss Theodora? And don't try to deny it. You've the look of a fox that's been at the henhouse."

"Do I?" Theodora laughed. "As a matter of fact, I have had a simply glorious night gathering herbs. I fell asleep in a meadow while gazing at the moon and am consequently well rested. Which reminds me. I promised to send Sadie to Millie Dickson for a few days. It is imperative that Millie remain in her bed. Would you be so good as to see to it for me? I have a few things to do, then I am off to Squire Meeks to beg his forbearance for Millie."

"Humph," grunted the housekeeper, frowning her disapproval. "A lot of good it will do you. I expect we'll have Millie Dickson here at Cliff House before all's said and done. And as for your sleeping out beneath the moon, miss, I'll not say a word, save only that you had ought to know better. It's neither safe nor seemly for a lady. You're not a child anymore, Miss Theodora. It's time you stopped all this moon-gazing before something bad comes of it."

Theodora patted her mouth with the linen napkin. "Nothing bad can come of it, Mrs. Tibbets, I promise you," she said, rising from the table preparatory to leaving, "but only good. Everything depends on it, you see. Tell Aunt Philippa I shall be at Mrs. Fennelworth's and then the squire's, should she inquire. I should be home in time for supper."

Snatching up her cloak, which she had earlier deposited on a peg by the back door, Theodora fled the house before Mrs. Tibbets could voice the multitude of questions which must certainly have risen to her tongue in the wake of Theodora's undeniably cryptic utterance.

She spent the next hour and a half laying out her herbs to dry and brewing the elixir she had promised Mrs. Fennelworth, so that the morning was well advanced when she was at last able to call for her mare.

The ride to Squire Meeks's took her past the junction of the village high road and the track to Devil's Gill, where only ten hours earlier she had sat her mare in indecision. Well, she had her herbs now, and a great deal more besides, she reflected with a wry quirk of her lips. Indeed, she doubted not that her life had taken a course from which there would be no turning back, she decided and, lifting the reins, sent Ginger past the fateful track.

"Renfield!"

The earl's resonant shout reverberated through the halls and corridors of Devil's Keep, a harsh reminder that the master had returned to the castle in a devil of a mood. Indeed, the entire household had taken to treading on tiptoe, a wary eye cast over one shoulder lest they be the next to fall victim to his displeasure. Renfield, who had borne the brunt of his master's black mood, morosely shook his head and bent his creaking limbs toward the earl's study.

Styles, clad in an ebony coat and buff riding breeches tucked into the tops of gleaming black military long boots, glared at the gentleman seated across the writing table from him.

"I informed your superiors before I left London that I was through taking an active part in business," announced the earl, who made no attempt to hide his displeasure at finding himself in the presence of an unexpected caller, especially one who chose to begin the unlooked-for interview with a blatant reference to His Lordship's duty as a gentleman of no little influence. "It had better be a matter of no little importance which brings you here."

"Naturally, my lord, I should not have intruded on your privacy were it otherwise," replied the gentleman, careful to school his rather sharp features to reveal nothing of his inner musings. His peculiar eyes, so pale as to be of an indiscriminate color, however, did not fail to take in every minute detail of His Lordship's appearance to be filed away for future reference. "You were involved in some extremely delicate negotiations when you made your announcement, a circumstance that aroused the concern of not a few of the principals."

"You mean the principal beneficiaries," Styles uttered coldly. "You may return to London and inform Their Lordships that they shall not lose by my retirement. The negotiations to which you refer were finalized before I made my departure. There remained only a few insignificant details to iron out, matters which I left in Franklidge's capable hands. You may be sure everything will be in position and fully operational before the summer commences. I have given my word on that. I should not like to think," he added in soft, meaningful tones, "that Their Lordships hold my word in doubt."

The gentleman visibly paled. "But you mistake me, my lord. It was not concern for the—er—business arrangements that prompted my employers to send me here, but concern for your welfare. You will admit that your decision to withdraw from active life came wholly unexpectedly and at a time when you are more indispensable than perhaps you are aware."

"No one is indispensable, Mr. Whitfill," observed the Devil's Cub. Wishing the man without remorse to the devil, Styles rose to his feet. "And now that you have reassured yourself both as to my well-being and that of your employers' enterprise, I fear I must ask you to excuse me. My servants will see that you are refreshed before you leave."

Whitfill, who had known better than to expect more from a man of the earl's reputation for unpredictability and who, further, was not exactly displeased at the prospect of being given free run of the place for an hour or two without His Lordship's being in attendance, likewise came to his feet. "Very kind of you, my lord. I believe I should not be averse to a spot of breakfast before I take to the road again. May I say that I am relieved to find you in better health than rumor had it."

The devil he was, thought Styles. Hell and damnation! He had taken every precaution to keep his condition a secret. No one, save for the doctors, could possibly have known for a certainty that he was in anything but excellent heath. And, still, it was being whispered all over London that the Earl of Styles was suffering some unknown ailment, which had precipitated his retirement to the country. He would have given a great deal to know who had instigated the rumor and to what purpose.

"You *have* said it, Mr. Whitfill," Styles observed coldly. Then, at the butler's entrance, "And now good day, sir. Renfield, see our visitor to the breakfast room. And have Erebus brought around. I shall be going out directly."

"Very good, my lord," replied Renfield, his morose features studiously impassive. "Mr. Whitfill, if you please . . . ?"

Styles waited for the door to close before giving vent to the

spleen that had been steadily building since his rather rude
awakening that morning to the discovery that his mysterious
enchantress had gone without a word. So thorough was her
vanishing that he might have believed he had dreamed the
entire affair, had there not been certain incontrovertible evidence to the contrary, not the least of which was the sprig of
lady's mantle left residing on his chest.

"Damn the chit!" he pronounced to the empty room at large.

He had had more than enough time during the ride back to
Devil's Keep to analyze the night's events and his ungentle-
manly conduct toward an innocent who should have had every
right to expect something quite different from him. His conclusion that he must have been either a deal more than bright
in the eye or utterly mad offered little in the way of comfort
and nothing toward a solution to the damnable coil in which
he now found himself. In the true tradition of his forebears,
he had set aside every precept by which he had previously
ruled his life and sunk so low as to ravish a virgin! Good God,
it did not bear thinking on. And yet he had thought of it;
indeed, he could think of nothing else.

Caleb Dameron, Devil's Cub and the Earl of Styles, had
allowed himself to be seduced by a self-proclaimed witch with
the analytical manner of a scientist, the charms of a siren, and
the sweetness of a ministering angel. Good God, it confounded
every tenet of reason! Who the devil was she? And, more importantly, what was she about?

Not since his salad days when he had succumbed to the
charms of a scheming widow, even going so far as to imagine
he had lost his heart as well as his virginity to the deceitful
baggage, had he allowed himself to be manipulated by a
woman—until last night, that was. What he had not expected
was to discover when it was all over that he was, for the first
time in weeks, marvelously free of pain and quite totally and
blissfully relaxed. She was in truth a witch with the power to
incite him to an intoxicating madness. But even more significant than her proven ability to arouse him to a passion the

likes of which inspired certain parts of his anatomy all over again merely at the thought of it, was the unsettling realization that his mysterious enchantress could dispel the gnawing darkness in a manner that he had not thought possible.

Damn the woman! At the advice of his numerous doctors, who could offer him no other consolation or hope, he had long since abandoned himself to his deplorable fate. Now even that had been taken from him by a meddling female who should have had better sense than to tempt the devil. Not for the first time he told himself that, by all rights, he should banish her from his thoughts and leave her to her fate. The fact remained, however, that he had for the first time in weeks found something upon which to focus his considerable intellect other than his encroaching madness and ignominious death. He could no more banish her from his mind than he could dispute the one irrefutable logic: could she indeed stand between himself and the devil's curse, if only for a little while, he would be a fool not to take her to his bed, and the devil be damned.

All of which left him on the horns of a dilemma.

If she was a female of gentle birth, as seemed evidenced by both her speech and her manner, he could not in all conscience pursue an illicit alliance with her purely for his own therapeutic benefit. How much less could he ask her to live as wife to a man on the road to destruction? The thought of having her as witness to his own final degradation and descent into madness was beyond contemplation. And yet he could not ignore the indisputable fact that he was honor-bound to wed her. Hellsfire and damnation! He had made a devil of a coil for himself.

The solution to the problem had come to him as he stood peering at his face in the mirror while shaving off the day-old growth of beard. If circumstance dictated a wedding, then a wedding there would be. His enchantress was a woman of extreme passion with acute empathic powers of perception, he reminded himself with a smile that was rather more grim than whimsical. No doubt she would balk at the notion of what would in the end become little more than a marriage of convenience, especially one with marriage settlements that would make her a wealthy widow. He was, however, as the dolt Whitfill had so clumsily pointed out, a man of considerable influence, and he was not averse to employing whatever means might be necessary to achieve his ends. The enchantress would be brought to marry him, he had not the least doubt of it.

She would, that was, if she was indeed what she appeared to be, he reminded himself. Nor would she come to regret it, he promised himself, contemplating the lengthy honeymoon he envisioned, enlivened by frequent experiments in shared male-female physiology. She would come away from the honeymoon well educated in the finer aspects of human biology. And when it was over, he would leave her at Devil's Keep, none the worse for her experience, while he pursued his own path to destruction alone in London.

It had been Renfield who solved the problem of her identity. Everyone in the vicinity was familiar with the Witch of Weycombe Mere, the butler replied in answer to his master's carefully worded inquiry. She was the only daughter of Dr. Thaddeus Havelock of Cliff House, the last of the Somerset Havelocks, a genteel family of the lesser nobility, and her name was Theodora.

Theodora. The name had a pleasing melodic quality about it and a certain exotic flavor fitting for one who styled herself a witch. It suited her, he had decided the moment he heard it. Still, it had not been the name that had suddenly sparked his memory, but the additional information concerning her family background.

Her father was a physician of long-standing in the area, and she was his only daughter. Fifteen years ago, she would have been ten, a precocious imp of a girl who very likely already showed promise of an unusual gift for compassion and analytical reasoning, as had the little pixie who, braving the churchyard in a rainstorm on a dare, had stopped to minister to a stranger's grief. The pixie had seemed just such a one who might in womanhood conduct an experiment in male-female physiology out of pity and an intellectual curiosity. Bloody hell, it would be just what one might expect of her! Surely there could not have been another like her in a community the size of Weycombe Mere.

"Well, Miss Theodora Havelock. We shall know soon enough." Abruptly, he strode out of the study.

Four

Not since Bishop Arundale had arrived unannounced on his way to Bristol, complaining with a stomach ailment, had the old stone cottage rung with such excitement as it did that afternoon when the Earl of Styles made his appearance at Cliff House.

Mrs. Tibbets, who opened the door to the imposing figure, towering well above her meager five feet three inches in height, remained undaunted at discovering the Devil's Cub on her doorstep—until, that was, he asked to be announced to the mistress of the house.

It was one thing to have the Earl of Styles call on the local doctor (after all, even earls fell ill and required the services of a physician, and no doubt His Lordship wasn't aware the master was off to Scotland), but quite another for the infamous nobleman to request an interview with Miss Havelock, and to what purpose, the devil only knew. Mrs. Tibbets was not made easier when, inquiring if His Lordship was expected, she was treated to a disconcerting glitter from demon black eyes and a smile that boded ill for someone, she doubted not.

"You may be sure Miss Havelock has fully anticipated my arrival," replied His Lordship with a forbidding grimness. "It is more than probable she made sure I should come. If not, however, no doubt her peculiar powers of comprehension have by now made her aware I am here. It remains only for you to go through the formality of announcing me."

Clearly His Lordship was pixilated, thought Mrs. Tibbets, dropping a reluctant curtsy and, muttering to herself something about the devil's proxy, grudgingly left the earl in the downstairs parlor while she went to inform Miss Havelock that she had a gentleman caller.

The grey stone house on the side of the hill overlooking the bay was just as Styles remembered it. He had found it easily enough, starting at the churchyard and following his remembered footsteps from that other time straight to the pixie's doorstep. Content, of course, merely to see the child to safety, he had not then entered the house. Nevertheless, he found the interior just as he might have expected it to be. Strangely pleasing and wholly without pretension, it was a far cry from the luxurious, but gloomy, environs of Devil's Keep. The obvious contrast, in fact, caused him to suffer sudden grave misgivings as to his purpose in coming there.

Not even a pixie or an enchantress was immune to the unsavory influences of Devil's Keep. Theodora would be in danger of succumbing to the curse of the House of Dameron, just as the beautiful Lady Gwendolyn had done, he reflected bitterly. Indeed, just as everyone did sooner or later. He smiled cynically, as it came to him to reflect that his enchantress might be better served were he to simply walk away—now, before she was made a victim of his own private hell. But then, she would be well paid for her services, he reminded himself—an earl's coronet and the fortune that went with it. As a wealthy widow, she would hardly find it necessary to linger in the gloomy confines of the family pile.

"Forgive me for keeping you waiting, my lord," announced a throaty feminine voice from the doorway. "I'm afraid, however, if you've come for a reading, I must warn you. Not everyone is prepared . . ."

The voice abruptly ceased as Styles swung about to be met by the sight of what he might easily have taken for one of his blasted apparitions, had it not been accompanied by the distinct aromas of burnt resin and a peculiar mixture of honey, wine, and bitumen that he recognized from his travels in Asia Minor. Whatever the case, this tall, exotically attractive middle-aged woman, wearing a shoulder-length black wig in the style of a Cleopatra and garbed fantastically in a white linen robe, gilded collar, headdress, and bracelets, her feet bare in Egyptian sandals, most definitely was not his enchantress. Furthermore, she appeared to be staring with riveted fascination, not at him, but, annoyingly, at a point beyond his right earlobe. Now, what the devil?

"I beg your pardon, madam?" he drawled dangerously, sternly quashing the urge to glance over his shoulder.

The apparition appeared to arouse herself from her momentary fit of abstraction. "—For the metaphysical journey of discovery," she finished her interrupted statement. "My lord, I apprehend perfectly why you have come."

Styles's eyebrow rose quellingly toward his hairline. "Do you? How very fortunate. No doubt that shall save us endless time in pointless explanations."

"Pointless, indeed," she agreed. "Pray do not move, my lord!" Still staring at him in that most peculiarly unfocused manner, she proceeded to wave her hands through the air around and about his head and shoulders rather in the manner of the proverbial tailor intent on taking his measurements for emperor's clothing. "How does one explain the ineffable, after all? One seeks to penetrate the curtain of unknowing to that which can be experienced but never described—the Essence and the union of the self with the Self," she informed him, as, still performing her peculiar rite, she stepped round in back of the astounded figure of the earl. "But then, I perceive that there is no need to tell *you,* my lord."

"You cannot know how relieved I am to hear it," replied Styles, who, far from desiring a lecture on metaphysics from

an exotic facsimile of the Queen of the Nile, was close to
wishing his hostess to the devil.

"But I do know," she insisted. "And more. It is all there to
read for one who has the eyes to see. No, no, my lord. I beg
you, do not move. You will distort the emanations at this, the
most crucial point in my reading."

Styles, who little liked the idea of having a female of questionable sanity hovering at his back, stopped in the midst of
making an about face. "Naturally, that must be the last thing
I should wish."

"Clearly, you are one of the enlightened ones," applauded
his companion. "You are, furthermore, a man of great intellect
and strong passion with a profound capacity for love. The
woman you marry will be blessed indeed."

"Shall she?" queried His Lordship, a dangerous glint in his
eye. It would seem his enchantress was not so reluctant to
embrace the wedded state as he had previously imagined.
Briefly, he wondered where she had come up with the idea of
employing a fortune-teller to bring him up to scratch. Theodora
was, if nothing else, creative in her capitulation.

"She will, my lord, if she is of a compatible spectrum,"
temporized the fortune-teller, no doubt realizing she had been
a trifle too blunt. "A predomination of rose, yellow, and deep
green, I should think, with, perhaps, a pale shade of blue and
purple would blend nicely with your own hues, which, you
must know, are particularly brilliant. I have only once before
beheld an aura of such intensity as yours."

"I have no doubt I am a veritable peacock, as it were,"
Styles commented dryly, considerably enlightened. Until that
moment, he had not had the smallest clue to what the woman
was referring.

"You jest, my lord," chuckled the lady. "As a matter of fact,
I should better describe your spectrum as demonstrating the
colors of the sunset. The dusky red of passion and sensuality,
the yellow of strong intellect, and the rose of deep affection."

She frowned, studying him with sudden compassion. "There is, however, an inconsistency, which troubles me."

"An inconsistency. Ah," nodded his lordship, disposed to be entertained, at least for the moment.

"Your aura displays the vividness of good health, and yet I perceive distinct aberrations, shadows in the midst of brightness. These are signs of an affliction, which, while it has yet to impair your health, is causing you no little discomfort. It is fortunate that you came to me. You will naturally wish to examine your past lives. Therein may lie the clue to your karma. I shall be only too glad to serve as your guide. Together we shall find the means of restoring you to *dharma*. Only then, when you are in conformity with your true nature, will you come to know peace."

Styles went suddenly still, no longer even remotely amused. The rumors, it would seem, had penetrated even to the far reaches of Weycombe Mere. He no more believed in auras and spiritual emanations than he believed in goblins and bogeymen. Obviously, the woman was a skilled flim-flam artist, who was about to discover she had grossly misjudged her mark.

"Enough, madam. No doubt I am sorry to disappoint you, but I have not the least intention of delving into my lives with you, past or otherwise." He gave a mirthless bark of laughter. "Egad, what a singularly fruitless exercise that must prove."

"On the contrary, my lord, I have been witness to just such a journey of discovery. I assure you the subject was greatly relieved to learn that her abhorrence for white linen tablecloths was due to her having in a past life served as a laundry maid. And it is, after all, why you are here, is it not? Because you felt the need to consult one who has devoted her life to a study of the nonphysical realm of being."

"I doubt you will find anyone less inclined to an interest in the nonphysical ream of being," growled His Lordship. "You must know very well why I am here, madam."

"Indeed, I told you I did, the moment I laid eyes on you, my lord. You needn't go into a rage, and pray don't deny that

Sara Blayne

is what you are doing. Your spectrum is positively radiating crimson, and everyone knows what that means."

"In my case, I believe I must require a translation, madam," responded His Lordship, eyeing his interlocutor with a grim wariness. "My crimson radiations notwithstanding, I am not, madam, feeling either passionate or in the least sensually inclined."

"Don't be absurd. I know perfectly well what you are feeling. Having studied for many years in the Orient, I am an experienced hermeneut of metaphysical radiance. The deeper red of passion and sensuality is distinctly different from the brilliant crimson of rage. I am not likely to mistake one for the other, I assure you."

"You comfort me, madam," Styles said shortly.

"That is my *dharmic* purpose in life—to comfort the metaphysically afflicted. I feel compelled to advise you, moreover, since you obviously have no faith in a remedy employing metaphysical means, that you consult one versed in the healing arts without delay. I cannot impress on you too strongly that to fail to do so may very well put you in grave peril of your life. I shall even go so far as to suggest you could do no better than to trust yourself to my niece Theodora, who, besides being knowledgeable in herbology, demonstrates a strong emanation of pale blue in her spectrum."

Her niece! Good God, he might have known it. The aunt went beyond what was original to being very nearly daft. But then, he himself could find very little about which to boast in his family tree, Styles cynically reminded himself. "How very fortunate, then, that I have come for the express purpose of seeing Miss Havelock," he stated pointedly. "I believe she is expecting me."

Miss Philippa Havelock, for so he had surmised she must be, gave what could only be construed as a nervous flutter of the hand and turned away with what would seem a suspicious suddenness. "Oh, but you must be mistaken. I'm afraid Theodora is away for the day. To the squire's, I believe she said.

Surely if she had known you would be calling for one of her elixirs, she would have let me know."

The earl's eyebrows snapped together. She was lying. Why? "As it happens, I did not come for one of Miss Havelock's potions, delightful as that must be," Styles replied with only a hint of irony. "My purpose is of a more personal nature."

"Dear." The elder Miss Havelock shook her head in sudden perplexity. "Personal, did you say. I'm afraid Theodora is not at all inclined to look favorably on calls of a personal nature from gentlemen. She is fond of saying she hasn't the time for such nonsense as chit-chat in the parlor when she might be better employed with her experiments in the curative properties of herbs."

"Does she, now," murmured Styles, appearing anything but amused at that revealing insight into Theodora's views on courtship. If anything, he suffered a twinge of conscience that was as unfamiliar as it was distasteful. It was becoming increasingly clear to him that his enchantress, mortified by the night's events, had made sure to be gone from the house no doubt to avoid having ever to lay eyes on him again.

"Indeed, my lord," the middle-aged spinster was saying. "Theodora is quite devoted to the practice of herbology, you understand."

"Quite so," replied his lordship, who understood exactly to what lengths Miss Havelock's dedication might take her.

"She is compiling for publication a new and updated herbal of medicinal plants found in and around Exmoor," added Theodora's aunt. "I believe it consumes all of her time when she is not making house calls on various of the poorer families of the neighborhood who prefer her sort of healing to that of, let us say, more accepted medical practices. You might be surprised to learn that there are people who think a physician like my dear brother is good only for treating broken bones and things of a traumatic nature."

"You will find that I am seldom surprised by anything," replied the earl, who had his own reasons for entertaining a distrust of modern medicine and its practitioners. "Does your niece share such a view?"

"Theodora?" trilled her aunt. "Heavens, no. I daresay she knows more about medicine than most doctors. I believe one might say her views are eclectic. I doubt there is a theory, modern or otherwise, that she has not studied."

"It would seem a pity she was born a female," speculated His Lordship, aware of a vague surprise at this new insight into the undeniably intriguing Theodora. "If what you say is true, she would undoubtedly have made an excellent doctor."

Miss Havelock smiled mirthlessly. "Rather say, my lord, that it is a pity a female with my niece's gift for healing is banned by society's precepts from joining the ranks of her male peers. As a doctor, she might very well be at the forefront of her profession. As an herbalist, I fear she is looked upon as something of an oddity."

Styles, who did not doubt that for a moment, indeed, could comprehend better than anyone what it was to be considered outside the pale, smiled cynically. "In London, you may be sure she would be viewed as an Original," he commented, thinking that his enchantress would discover that a title and a fortune the size of his could render an "oddity" all the rage overnight. It occurred to him that he would have taken no little satisfaction in seeing such a triumph as that must be.

"I am sorry you missed Theodora," the aunt said, studying him through improbably long and exceedingly black eyelashes. "Shall I tell her that you will be calling again, my lord?"

"No, Miss Havelock," Styles replied, with a hard gleam of a smile. "I believe I shall perform that office for myself. You did mention Squire Meeks, did you not." Then, before Philippa could utter a protest, he bowed ironically at the waist. "A pleasure, madam. No doubt we shall meet again."

"Indeed, my lord, I shall look forward to it," said Miss Havelock, but it was directed at Styles's retreating back.

* * *

"They say he's come back to pay the devil his dues," declared Mrs. Fennelworth to Theodora over tea and ginger biscuits. "And him without an heir to carry on the title when he's gone." Mrs. Fennelworth shook her grey head. "I never thought to see the day when there would not be a Devil's Cub at the keep. In spite of all that's said of him, it just doesn't seem right somehow."

"Yes, but then, it will never happen—not in our day, you may be sure of it," Theodora stated emphatically. "Nor for a great many years to come. I daresay the earl will be setting up his nursery before very much longer, and then all this nonsense about devil's dues and curses will be seen for what they are—a parcel of nonsense made up by a lot of people who should know better."

Mrs. Fennelworth, a widow well past her middle years, eyed the younger woman askance. "You seem awfully sure, Theodora, for one who's never even met the earl."

"I am sure. And, as it happens, I have spoken with his lordship—on more than one occasion," Theodora replied with what she hoped was a casual air. "I found him to be as fine a gentleman as one could hope to meet."

"Aye, he was used to be a fine, bright lad when I knew him. Of course, that was before they sent him off to school."

Theodora leaned forward in her chair. "You were acquainted with Styles in his youth?"

Mrs. Fennelworth nodded her head over her cup of tea. "He was Lord Fitzjohn then. I was used to do a bit of sewing for the countess. I don't look it now," said the woman, ruefully holding up gnarled, arthritic hands, "but I was once clever with a needle, and the countess took a liking to me. For all that he was heir to a title and a fortune, I always felt a mite sorry for young Fitzjohn. What chance did he have with a father who, no sooner than he had got himself an heir, was away, wenching and gambling and the Lord only knows what else? And that mother of his. Faith, if ever there was a woman unsuited for motherhood, it was Lady Gwendolyn. A strange, wild creature, she was, who, like the rest of the Underwoods, cared for naught but her own pleasures. Her brother, Lord Harry, ran tame about the place, a bad influence, if ever there was one. And Lady Damaris Gale that was Lady Gwendolyn's bosom bow was little better. If you were to ask me, I'd say she had no little part in alienating the earl's affections, if ever there were any, from his wife. Everyone knew the earl wed Lady Gwendolyn for the fortune her maiden Aunt Louisa settled on her. It was certain sure Lady Gwendolyn knew it. I daresay neither the earl nor the countess cared a whit about one another or the poor lad they brought into the world."

Theodora felt a small wrench at the memory of the youthful Styles at the graveyard. He had confessed at the time that there was little love lost between his mother and himself, but Theodora had pitied him nonetheless. She had seen the bitter anguish behind the cynical mask he had already taken to wearing, even at twenty. *"I* did not know," Theodora said quietly. "What a very unhappy family they must have been."

"Harumph," Mrs. Fennelworth snorted. "A cursed family, if ever there was one. You know the tales told of the Damerons, and the Underwoods were hardly better. In the end, Lady Gwendolyn was as mad as her father and those others that came before her. Certainly, no woman with any natural feelings would have put her own child in the hands of a tutor the likes of Josiah Fix. Why, he was master of his own school, until he was run out for nigh beating one of his pupils to death. 'Discipline,' he called it. But he was a cruel man with a relish for punishing them that couldn't fight back. Little wonder that they found him at the bottom of the cliffs. It was only what he deserved, no matter how it came about," Mrs. Fennelworth ended darkly.

"You mean even if Caleb Dameron pushed him to his death, but you are wrong, Mrs. Fennelworth," Theodora declared, her lovely eyes sparkling with utter conviction. "It was an accident. I know it as well as I know that Caleb Dameron is innocent of all the other terrible things that are said of him."

"And how could you know that, Theodora? Unless you can see into crystal balls now and read tea leaves along with everything else that's said about you," scoffed the old woman. "I hope you haven't taken to paying heed to your Aunt Philippa's ravings. Miss Philippa was always flighty as a gel, but that was nothing to what she is now. It's all that traveling in the Orient and other foreign places that did it, mark my words. Such doings aren't seemly for a woman, even if she was a paid companion to that wealthy countess."

Theodora bit her tongue to keep from uttering a sharp retort to the kindly Mrs. Fennelworth. Aunt Philippa might be a little eccentric, but then, she had reason to be. After all, how many people had transcended the plane of unknowing to glimpse the Universal Truth? Such an experience was bound to have an unsettling effect on one, especially in light of everything else that had happened to the poor dear. "The countess of Windemere was a noted scholar of ancient philosophy and Eastern religions," Theodora pointed out, carefully setting her cup in its saucer on the cherrywood sofa table. "Her loss will be deeply felt by the intellectual community for a long time to come, but most of all by Aunt Philippa. Lady Lavinia and she were the dearest of friends for over twenty years. If she seems a trifle strange in the wake of this untimely separation, it is perhaps only to be expected."

Mrs. Fennelworth, who could only think that the word "trifle" understated the matter more than a little, refrained from arguing the point out of deference to Theodora. The gel herself was something out of the ordinary and likely failed to notice that her Aunt Philippa was notional at best.

"You've finished your tea," she pointed out instead, reaching for the tea server. "Come, child. Have another biscuit."

Theodora smiled and shook her head. "Thank you, Mrs. Fennelworth, but no. I really must be going if I am to speak to the squire before the evening milking." She got up from the sofa. "I shall depend on you to take your elixir. I believe it will afford you no little relief from your rheumatism. And don't forget the poultices in the evenings. With any luck we shall soon have the swelling down."

"I'm depending on it, my dear. Oh, and, Theodora, one thing more before you go. There is something I want you to have." Mrs. Fennelworth drew forth a small wooden box, which resided on the table, and, opening the lid, took out, dangling from a silver chain, a translucent gemstone of green with curious glints of red. "It isn't much, but I've always thought it was pretty to look on."

"Oh, but I couldn't," Theodora exclaimed, staring at the gemstone the size of a robin's egg. No doubt it was the only thing of any material value the woman possessed.

"But of course you can. I insist on it," Mrs. Fennelworth said, closing Theodora's fingers around the stone. "I found it on the beach one day years ago when I was watching for Captain Fennelworth's ship to come in. At the foot of the cliffs, it was, with Devil's Keep hunkered on the top of the cliff above me. I expect it was lost by some lady, but no one ever came to claim it. I've kept it all these years. You remember Professor Wilkes, who used to live in the old Kitteredge cottage. It was him who told me it was a heliotrope. Those spots in it, he called jasper. I daresay it is not worth very much, but I would like you to have it."

"It's exquisite," Theodora murmured. "And quite special for more reasons than one. You should keep it, Mrs. Fennelworth."

"Nonsense. I've no one to leave it to. The captain and I never had any children. For many years it brought me luck. The captain always came back to me, till the ague took him, here, in this very house. Perhaps it will be lucky for you, my dear."

Theodora shook her head doubtfully. "You are very kind, but . . ."

"Now, none of that." Mrs. Fennelworth firmly took the gemstone and slipped the chain over Theodora's head. "I want you to have it, in the way of payment for all the many times you've nursed me through my aches and pains without ever asking for anything. It would make me feel better, knowing I had given you something back in return, no matter how small."

Theodora smiled, one hand clasped on the stone that now hung on its chain around her neck. "Thank you, Mrs. Fennelworth. I shall keep it always and remember you whenever I wear it."

"But of course you will. And now off with you," Mrs. Fennelworth said, shooing the other woman from the room, "though what good you think you'll do with the squire is beyond me. He'll more likely show you the door than prove in the least charitable. I daresay he would sell his own mother down the River Tick if it served his purposes."

"No, how can you say so," Theodora laughed, "when you have just given me your lucky stone. Thanks to you, I daresay I shall have Squire Meeks eating out of my hand."

Theodora was not so confident, however, when, some thirty minutes later, she was ushered to the squire's downstairs parlor, where, she was informed, the squire was already with a visitor. Indeed, the truth be known, she was not in the least certain in what manner she would be received. She had had past dealings with the squire, who, a noted trencherman and an inveterate huntsman, had required her father's professional services more than a few times for the treatment of gout and minor fractures, cuts and abrasions. On one particular occasion, the squire, in his cups, had mistaken her for a housemaid and, thinking to satisfy his more primitive urges, of which he had many, he had cornered her with the intention of taking undue liberties with her person. She had had to dissuade him with a porcelain pitcher applied tellingly against his bald pate, with the result that he had learned to treat her with a wariness for which, until now, she could only be grateful.

"Well," she told herself, unconsciously laying her hand over the stone, residing for safety underneath her bodice, "there is no point in anticipating the worst. He has at least agreed to see me."

Whatever she had expected upon stepping into the parlor,

it certainly was not to have the squire stride forward to meet
her, his hand outstretched in welcome and his heavily jowled
face positively radiating pleasure at her presence.

"Miss Havelock," he exclaimed, his stays creaking as he
bowed his considerable bulk over her hand. "And as welcome
as a ray of sunshine. Come in, my dear. Come in." Jovially he
turned her to face the room. "I was just telling my very good
friend the earl, here, that we do not see enough of you at Moor
Hall. And suddenly you appear, just as he promised that you
would." He chuckled and favored her with a sidelong wink.
"Perhaps it was not entirely by coincidence, eh, my dear?"

"No, Squire, I daresay it was not," answered Theodora, who
was not certain what astounded her more—the squire's exceedingly odd behavior or finding herself suddenly and quite unexpectedly face to face with the man she had taken great pains to
avoid. One arm propped carelessly on the mantelpiece, Styles
loomed, a very large and quite unmistakably formidable presence. "I did not come, however, with the expectation of finding
the Earl of Styles here." Indeed, she had obviously miscalculated the earl's timetable. By all rights, she should have been
gone from Moor Hall long before Styles made his appearance.

Styles smiled ironically. By God, the pixie was even more
beautiful in the clear light of day than in moonlight—and more
obviously stubborn, mettlesome, and self-willed. It could not
have been plainer that Miss Havelock intended to lead him a
merry chase. She would soon discover, however, that he knew
all there was to know about games of hide and seek. "Did
you not, Miss Havelock? I had thought, given your peculiar
gifts for extraordinary perception, you would have had certain
foreknowledge of my intent to visit the squire. I, on the other
hand, was apparently mistaken in believing you would make
sure to be at home today to receive me."

"I never claimed I could see into the future, my lord," retorted Theodora, uncommonly irritated by this unforeseen
hitch in her plans. She must be more careful henceforth not
to underestimate what would seem to be Styles's propensity

for acting with despatch on matters that concerned him. "I cannot think of a single reason why I should be expected to know what you might choose to do, my lord."

"No, can you not?" Styles elevated an incredulous eyebrow. "I thought we had agreed you are a female of uncommon intellect. Simple logic might have served you in the absence of foresight. Am I to believe it never occurred to you that I might wish to see you after our momentous previous encounter?"

Theodora choked on an unwitting burble of laughter. The devil, to tease her so! He knew very well she had been purposely evading him. But then, she had been counting on that very thing. Her entire plan depended on it. "On the contrary, my lord. I thought it a distinct possibility. Unfortunately, I had matters to attend that could not wait. I am glad, however," she added, anxiously scrutinizing his harsh features, "to see you are looking much more the thing than the last time I saw you."

"I have observed that scientific research very often has a salubrious effect on persons of an inquisitive bent," drawled His Lordship. Quizzically, he studied her. "Has that been your experience, Miss Havelock?"

"You must know very well that it has, my lord," Theodora replied, meeting him look for look. "There is nothing so stimulating as conducting a scientific experiment or so exquisitely pleasurable as crossing the threshold of discovery. I should think the effect must of necessity be beneficial to the entire constitution."

"Scientific experiments—poppycock," interjected the squire. "Give me a good horse, a pack of dogs, and a fox on the run any day. Now, there's something that invigorates the constitution. That and maybe a woman now and then, what, my lord?" he said, jabbing an elbow at the earl's ribs. "We were just about to have a spot of brandy, Miss Havelock. Would you care for some tea or ratafia?"

"Neither, thank you, Squire. I have only just taken tea with Mrs. Fennelworth. And the business that brought me here will take only a moment or two of your time. I wished to speak to you on behalf of Millie Dickson, who, you must know, has only recently gone through a difficult lying-in."

"Then I'm afraid you've come to the wrong place, Miss Havelock. The Dickson woman no longer works for me. Now, now. You needn't look daggers at me," said the squire, glancing up from pouring brandy in two glasses. "I cannot be blamed for what cannot be helped. Cows must be milked. They cannot wait for milkmaids who cannot be bothered to come to work."

"But that is hardly fair. I ordered Millie Dickson to stay in her bed."

Shrugging, the squire turned, a glass in either hand. "Then I daresay it is your fault that she is now unemployed, not mine. *I* had no wish to let her go. I should even go so far as to say I shall not soon find someone as clever as Millie Dickson at coaxing milk from a reluctant cow."

Theodora's fingers pressed against the gem at her bosom as though by that she might still her outrage at the man's callous indifference to a woman with six children, all of whom depended on him for a livelihood. "Then surely it would be to your advantage to wait the week or so Millie needs to recuperate rather than lose so valuable a retainer."

Squire Meeks gave Theodora an oily smile. "As it happens, I have already replaced her, much to my regret, of course. Naturally, being a woman, it is difficult for you to grasp the necessity for such harsh measures. I'm sure *you* understand, my lord."

"Perfectly," murmured Styles, who had been observing the peculiar manner in which Theodora's eyes sparkled green when she was in the throes of righteous indignation. Previously jade, they had assumed the brilliant intensity of emeralds, the full force of which he found turned on himself at that moment with telling effects on his anatomy. It was time, he decided, smiling grimly to himself, to be rid of his tiresome host. "The woman is obviously a valuable asset, whom I shall be pleased to add to my staff. Perhaps, Miss Havelock, you would not mind informing Mrs. Dickson for me that she may report to my agent whenever she is sufficiently recovered."

Theodora, who had been wishing both of her masculine companions without remorse to the devil, was forced to hastily revise her opinion of at least one of the gentlemen. The rogue, she thought, to deliberately bait her! She should have known Styles would see to the heart of the matter. He, was, after all, a man of powerful intellect. She flashed her wholly irresistible smile at him. "I should be only too happy to, my lord. As a matter of fact, the Dickson cottage was to be my next stop."

"Excellent, Miss Havelock. In that case, I shall accompany you."

"But—but, my lord. I—" blustered the squire, gesturing with a glass-filled hand.

"Quite so," drawled Styles, and, relieving the sputtering Meeks of a brandy, lifted the glass in salutation. "To my gain, sir," he said, emptying the glass and replacing it in the squire's hapless grasp. "And your loss. And, now, Miss Havelock, if your business is concluded?" Taking her arm and inclining his head to his host, he murmured, "Squire," and ushered Theodora from the room.

Five

"That was kindly done, my lord," Theodora said a few moments later, as they descended the steps to their waiting mounts. "However, I feel obligated to point out that you do not presently have any milch cows at Devil's Keep and consequently can have little use for a milkmaid."

"Then no doubt Mrs. Dickson will be obliged to learn a new trade," shrugged the earl, whose interest in his newly acquired retainer was rapidly waning. "And I never do anything out of kindness. I am a man who acquired a fortune in business, Miss Havelock. If the woman is as industrious as you say she is, then it is clearly to my advantage to hire her for whatever duties my agent sees fit to assign her."

"I see," murmured Theodora, a decided gleam of mischief in her witch's eyes. "If that is the case, then I must suggest that it would be equally advantageous for you were you to employ Mr. Dickson at some capacity as well. Tom is a strong, able-bodied man, who is honest and hard-working." Reflectively, she tapped a forefinger against her chin. "I daresay he would make an excellent groom for you."

Styles cocked a sapient eyebrow at Theodora. No doubt Miss Havelock had no end of needy supplicants, all of whom would, unless he put a stop to it, be destined for employment at Devil's Keep. "I already have a groom, Miss Havelock," he said repressively. "A man who has been with me since I first put my hands to the reins."

"How wonderful to command such loyalty," Theodora applauded, allowing Styles to lift her to the saddle. "But then, he must be near the age at which he might look kindly on someone younger to relieve him of some of his duties. A protégé, perhaps, whom he might take pride in training and molding into a man worthy to succeed him upon his retirement?"

Whimsically, Styles contemplated a mental image of his groom, Hodges, a man, who, in his early forties and, weighing in at one hundred seventy pounds of lean muscularity, was not only the very picture of robust health, but was fiercely jealous of his duties and position as well. A wry grimace twisted briefly at his lips as he gazed up into green, witch's eyes. Mentally he shrugged. "I should not be at all surprised, Miss Havelock," he said. Hodges, Styles reflected somberly, would be the very devil to placate when he learned of his newly acquired protégé.

"There, you see?" Theodora said cheerfully. "I knew good things would come from your return to Devil's Keep. You have no idea what a generous thing you have done."

"I am not noted for my generosity, Miss Havelock, but for something quite different. It remains to be seen whether your Dicksons will even wish to brave Devil's Keep."

"Gammon. Very naturally you have some doubts as to your reception among the people of Weycombe Mere and roundabout, but I assure you, you have only to show yourself among them from time to time and they shall soon be made to see you for what you are."

"A hideous prospect," contemplated His Lordship. "I am, in fact, a bogeyman to frighten children."

"You would like to think so, of course," Theodora said, the dimple peeping forth at the corner of her mouth. "You have, after all, become used to enjoying your reputation as someone sinister and marvelously dangerous. I certainly should were I in your shoes. You are nonetheless the Earl of Styles. Do you not think it is time you dispelled all the silly rumors?"

"No, why the devil should I?" Turning away from Theodora, Styles mounted Erebus in a single, effortless movement. "What people choose to think is not of the slightest concern to me."

"But of course it is not, anymore than it is of concern to me." Theodora lifted Ginger into a walk along the drive that led to the village high road, which would, in turn, take them to the Dickson cottage. "We are, after all, persons of intellect to whom gossip must naturally seem insignificant in the grand scheme of things. Still," she reflected, glancing at the earl out of the corner of her eye, "it would seem rather selfish to deliberately barricade oneself away from those who could benefit so much from one's active participation in the community. And as the master of Devil's Keep, there is a great deal you could do for those who might look to the House of Dameron for a livelihood."

"I have never claimed to be anything but exceedingly selfish, Miss Havelock," countered His Lordship, anything but amused to find himself being lectured to by an impertinent female whose sole distinctions were her claim to witchery and an uncanny ability to arouse his primitive male urges to the point that he had acquired both a milkmaid and a groom's assistant he neither wished for nor needed. "Nor have I ever neglected my responsibilities to my various estates or my people. I am not such a fool, I assure you."

"I wish you will not be absurd, my lord," Theodora retorted, her temper flaring at his unreasonable leap to conclusions. "I never thought you were."

"You relieve my mind, Miss Havelock," said Styles with sardonic appreciation of Theodora's indignantly heaving breasts. He experienced a distinct physiological urge to pull her from her horse then and there in order to give her further instruction in male-female biology.

"But then, I was not referring to your estates," Theodora

continued as if she had not been rudely interrupted. "If you had been listening, you would know that I was talking about Weycombe Mere and those who have suffered most from this ceaseless war—the families of those who have lost husbands and sons to the press gangs, for example. The British Navy calls at port on a regular basis for that purpose."

"The British Navy has an insatiable need for sailors and calls at every English port on a regular basis for that purpose. It is a harsh reality, Miss Havelock, one over which I have no control."

"No, of course you do not, my lord." Theodora's eyes flashed. Faith, the man was being deliberately obtuse. But then, he had little reason to love Weycombe Mere or to feel the least compassion for people who persisted in believing the very worst of him, she reminded herself. Deliberately, she drew a long, deep breath and forced herself to relax her viselike grip on the reins. Styles, she realized, was going to take a deal of patience. "It is not the men," she added reasonably, when she had got herself in hand again, "but their families who concern me. If you were here for any length of time, you would see what it has done to them."

Good God, thought Styles, she was a reformer. And the very worst kind, at that—a provincial who knew nothing of the world. Well, she would find other things to occupy her when she was his wife. He would make sure of that. "I have seen it, Miss Havelock. And, still, there is nothing I can do to change it. Even I do not have the resources to employ all the poor of Somerset. I suggest you keep that in mind when it comes to you suddenly that I must surely require a valet's apprentice or an assistant to the underfootman in training. And you will," he added grimly, seeing her lips part on what was undoubtedly a protest. "I find I am fast developing an acute empathic sense about these things."

Theodora's lips clamped shut, and a decided tinge of color pervaded her cheeks. He was right of course. The devil! She *was* guilty of rushing her fences, but with time and tact, she doubted not she could bring him to view the matter in a different light.

"Quite so," murmured Styles with a gleam of satisfaction. "And now, Miss Havelock, that we understand one another, enough said on the subject. I believe we have more pertinent matters to discuss. Why, for example, you disappeared this morning without a word and why you have been actively seeking to avoid me ever since."

"I should think the reasons are obvious, my lord," answered Theodora, who had been mentally trying to prepare herself for those very questions. "Why do you think I should have done it?"

"You disappoint me, Enchantress," Styles said quietly, studying her averted profile. "I had not expected you to employ evasive tactics. Until now, you have been admirably direct. But, very well, since you ask, I confess it had occurred to me that you are feeling some little regret at what happened between us."

Instantly Theodora's head came around. "But I do not regret it in the least, my lord. Indeed, why should I? It was possibly the most illuminating experience of my life. I daresay, however, that *you* thought better of it the moment you awakened. Indeed, I am certain of it. And now you wish to complicate something that was not in the least complicated before, and all because of your silly sense of honor. Well, I will not have it, my lord."

"Will you not?" Styles looked at her, an odd expression in his hard black eyes. She had found it illuminating, had she. The thought gave him a distinct feeling of satisfaction. And now she was determined to excuse him from any responsibility for the act. This was hardly the sort of explanation he had expected to hear from her, and yet no doubt he should have done. After all, Theodora was like no other woman he had ever known. "And *that* is the reason for this elaborate attempt to avoid me? Because you wished to save me the embarrassment of making an offer you could not bring yourself to accept?"

"I wish you will not be absurd," Theodora snapped. "It is

not that I could not bring myself to accept an offer of marriage from you, my lord. It is the motivating factors for which you would make such an offer that I find totally unacceptable. After all, we are rational adults, you and I. It is incomprehensible to me why we should allow convention to dictate our course, when it is so completely unnecessary."

"No doubt you are in the right of it," the earl said reflectively. At least she had not ruled out the possibility of marriage. And if she had enjoyed her first excursion into love-making, then surely it was not an aversion to further such experiments that deterred her now from accepting his offer. Or was it? he wondered, studying her narrowly. "I should tell you, however, that I have developed a sudden keen interest in human biology, which I have every wish to pursue to its fullest. I had thought it was an interest we shared in common. I had, in fact, entertained the notion that you would wish to assist me in conducting further research along the same lines."

"But that is exactly my own notion, my lord," exclaimed Theodora, delighted that he was proving a deal more reasonable than she had ever imagined he would.

"Excellent," Styles applauded, bemused at having so easily hurtled what he had thought to be the greatest obstacle in his path. "Obviously we are fully empathetic to one another, at least in that regard. In which case, what course do you see us pursuing, Miss Havelock—if, that is, we are to continue the scientific research we have begun?"

Theodora straightened unconsciously in the saddle as she found herself at last at the crux of the matter. "A course dictated by reason and logic, my lord," she said.

"Naturally, Miss Havelock. I never thought otherwise."

"Indeed, my lord?" Theodora queried, eyeing him sharply. "You will pardon me if I believed you were acting out of a compulsion to satisfy your gentleman's code of honor."

Styles grinned satirically. "You will find, Miss Havelock," he said, "that I never act out of compulsion, and my gentleman's code of honor is questionable at best."

"Now, you are doing it much too brown, my lord," Theodora insisted, her eyes dancing. "You know very well you are a man of rare integrity. I'm afraid I can find no other explanation for your proposal of marriage. Especially in light of the fact that we had agreed my services were of a purely professional nature—healer to patient. A service that I am fully prepared to continue," she added judiciously, "until you are completely restored to health. In which case, marriage is clearly out of the question. I do not make it a practice, my lord, to marry my patients."

"But then, you will agree that ours is a unique case," Styles did not hesitate to point out. "You did say, did you not, that I am your only male patient ever to require this particular form of treatment?"

"You know very well that I did." Theodora furiously blushed. How dared he fling her words in her face! "That, however, has little to say to the matter. It does not alter the fact that I should be acting wholly unethically to accept such an offer. It would, in fact, be taking undue advantage."

Undue advantage, good God! mused the most dangerous man in England. "What advantage, Miss Havelock?"

"It is not unusual," Theodora explained kindly, "for a patient to form a certain emotional attachment for the healer. It is, however, only a temporary condition, which passes in time. When that time comes, my lord, you will undoubtedly be grateful that I refused your generous offer of marriage."

"And if I could give you assurance your fears are unfounded and a reason that has nothing to do with a gentleman's code of honor?" He leaned suddenly near, his hand closing over hers on the reins. "What then, Miss Havelock?"

The docile mare came obediently to a halt along with the snorting stallion. Theodora sat stiffly in the saddle, her heart behaving in a most erratic manner. Things were not going at all as she had planned them, she realized, but then, she was not thinking precisely rationally at the moment. She was, in fact, prey to an entire panoply of physiological disturbances occasioned by the warmth of his hand on hers and his unmistakable air of strong purpose.

"I should think it would depend, my lord—" She swallowed and lifted her eyes to his. "—On the reason, would it not?"

"Indubitably, Miss Havelock," murmured His Lordship, kneeing the stallion closer to the mare. "It occurs to me that two persons of an inquisitive disposition—" Lightly, he brushed a loose strand of hair from her cheek and curled it behind her ear. "—With a strong proclivity for passion—" Theodora sat perfectly still, held immobilized by her acute empathic powers of perception. "—Would do no better than to marry."

"Indeed?" Theodora whispered, and, closing her eyes, instinctively turned her cheek into the palm of his hand. "And why is that, my lord?"

Styles gazed at her, his eyes glittery beneath heavily drooping eyelids. By God, he had never known a woman who responded so readily to his touch. He no longer marveled that he had so far forgotten himself as to make love to her, a virgin of obviously gentle birth, in the very crassest of fashions—on his cloak spread on a bed of grass in the woods. Hell and the devil confound it! He wanted to take her in a similar manner now. "In answer to your first objection, I never fall in love and therefore am not in the least danger of forming an unwise emotional attachment to my physician. And because," he added thickly, his arm going about her waist, "secondly and more importantly—" He drew her to his chest. "—It would facilitate our scientific research."

Theodora had hardly time enough to digest the less-than-consoling assurance that her ethical considerations were unfounded because he could not love her, before Styles closed his mouth over hers in a kiss that significantly raised her temperature even as it caused dramatic changes in her pulse rate, her respiration, and—she strongly suspected—her blood circulation. The peculiar effects, in fact, were not unlike what she had observed in a patient who foolishly had drunk a par-

ticularly strong port in conjunction with eating *Coprinus atra-
mentarius,* a mushroom, more commonly known as inkcap.
Indeed, she doubted not her face was just as flushed as had
been her patient's and her limbs every whit as weak, when at
last Styles released her and allowed her to settle somewhat
unsteadily back in her saddle.

"Well, Miss Havelock?"

The question came as something of an irrelevance in the
context of what had just preceded it.

Theodora blinked. "Well, what, my lord?"

An amused smile touched his lips at sight of her. She was
undeniably adorable with her hair falling in disarray from its
wholly ineffectual pins and her green eyes as bewildered as a
child's. But she was no child, by God. She was the most desirable woman he had ever met, and he wanted her for his
wife, if only for the few weeks of sanity that were left him.
More than that, she would bloody well have the protection that
his name would give her, whether she liked it or not. He was
damned if his final act on this earth would be to dishonor an
innocent and leave her to face the world penniless and unprotected.

"Have I provided sufficient reason for you to set aside your
scruples and accept my proposal of marriage?" he asked.

Theodora frowned, brought rudely back to reality.

"This is not at all what I had planned, my lord. Indeed, I
cannot but think you are taking unfair advantage of my primitive passions. And while I can see that being married would
make it easier for us to conduct an extensive study of male-
female physiology, I am not convinced it is reason enough to
go through with a marriage ceremony. You know nothing about
me."

"On the contrary, I know you are a witch with acute empathic powers of perception, which should tell you that I shall
require the sort of intensive therapy that you can provide only
if you are married to me."

"They tell me a deal more than that, my lord," Theodora

confessed soberly. "Which is why I cannot think you would truly wish to be leg-shackled to a self-avowed witch. Think what it would do to your reputation."

"Yes, of course. There is always that." The earl's lips twisted in startled bemusement. Good God! The pixie was worried about *his* reputation. He found the notions not a little novel. He had never known anyone before to be concerned about his tarnished name.

"There, you see," Theodora said with an air of vindication. "I knew you had overlooked the practical considerations. Very likely you allowed your primitive male urges to override your intellect."

"You may be sure of it," agreed His Lordship, whose primitive male urges were even then making themselves felt in a taut bulge at the front of his breeches. "However, I think perhaps you have overlooked a pertinent point as well, Miss Havelock."

"Really?" Theodora wrinkled her brow in concentration. "I cannot think what it would be. I assure you I have thought this matter over quite thoroughly."

"Yes, I was sure you had," agreed His Lordship, much struck at her failure to take into account the one glaring detail that no one else would have failed to consider. "You would seem to forget, however, that I am the Devil's Cub. I have had any number of unsavory misdeeds attached to that name, not the least of which is the suspicion that I have caused the death of everyone who was ever close to me. Far from sustaining any damage, I daresay my reputation would only be enhanced by my wedding a witch."

Styles watched, fascinated, as Theodora irrepressibly dimpled. "Yes, put in that light, I daresay we would make a pair to draw to. We should probably provide a source of speculation for a considerable length of time for any number of people. But it is too bad of you, my lord. I believe you are vastly entertained at the prospect."

"Then you are mistaken," Styles said, oddly not in the least amused. His eyes glittered coldly. "I should take no pleasure in hearing my wife was a subject for gossip mongers. But then, the matter will not arise. London is not Weycombe Mere. As my wife, you will command both respect and influence, you may be sure of it. No door will be closed to you. You will be inundated with invitations and surrounded by admirers eager to court your favors. The countess of Styles will set the fashion, wherever she is. It could not be otherwise."

"No, I don't suppose it could," Theodora reflected soberly. A great deal would be forgiven the wife of the most dangerous man in England. More importantly, however, the wife of the most dangerous man in England would be in the most advantageous position to discover just who was attempting to poison her husband.

It was a point that had not occurred to her before. One that clearly overshadowed her own selfish concerns. If Styles could not bring himself to love her, at least she loved him. She could admit it to herself now. She loved him, indeed, had known deep down all along that she did, even as she had instinctively known as a child of ten that there could never be anyone for her but the Devil's Cub. In which case, it was patently absurd to cling to scruples that made little sense in the face of this greater concern. If she must be an unwanted wife, she would be one who did so, not out of some meaningless convention, but because she had a very good cause—the preservation of the man she would marry.

"You make a very strong case, my lord," she said slowly, feeling her way.

"That was my intention, Miss Havelock."

"Yes, and you are used to having your own way. I am well aware of that. Which is why, before I agree to become your wife, I must insist on certain conditions."

A single black eyebrow swept upward toward the earl's hairline. "Conditions, Miss Havelock?"

"Indeed, my lord. After all, I shall be giving up my independence, which, you must know, is dear to me. Before we launch ourselves on a course from which there will be no turning back, it would seem only reasonable that we understand one another."

"I am not a tyrant, Miss Havelock," Styles pointed out. He wished Theodora would look at him. Bloody hell! She need not make it seem as if she were sacrificing herself on the altar of matrimony. She would be free of him soon enough. "You will discover that, far from depriving you of your independence, I shall rather be inclined to be lenient with you."

"Yes, my lord," Theodora said, at last lifting her eyes to his. "After all, you are a man of reason and innate generosity. However, should I become your wife, you cannot deny that I should be placing myself under your authority. It is intrinsic in the very leniency that you would so generously grant me."

Hell and the devil confound it, of course he could not deny it. It was the way of the world. A wife respected her husband's wishes, and, in return, she was provided for and protected. "And if I concede that you are right, I believe that so long as you conduct yourself with a modicum of common sense, you will find my authority rests lightly on you."

"You may be sure that I intend to make you a good wife, my lord," Theodora assured him, a suspicious gleam in her witch's eyes. "Indeed, I believe that, if you will only keep an open mind, you will find my conditions will occasion you little difficulty."

"Little devil," Styles said feelingly, keenly aware that she had given him back some of his own. "Very well, tell me these conditions of yours. I find I am overcome with curiosity."

"First, my lord, I shall wish to continue my work, unhindered by my new position. With my father away in Scotland, the people of Weycombe Mere depend on me more than ever to see to their ills. And after he returns, there is still my research on the herbs of Exmoor and their medicinal uses, which I plan to have published upon its completion."

"So long as you agree to having an escort when you make your calls, I have no objection," replied the earl, who could only be grateful she would have something to occupy her when the time came for him to leave her. "And as for your research, I should never stand in the way of a scientist and her work. When the time comes, you will discover that I have any number of valuable contacts that will facilitate the publication of your findings. Is there anything else, Miss Havelock?"

"As a matter of fact, I have four more conditions, my lord," Theodora answered, relieved at having so easily surmounted the first obstacle to an understanding between them. "The second one is relatively minor and should not pose a difficulty—unless, my lord, you have some objection to cats. You are not allergic to cat hair, are you? Because, if you are, I'm afraid it shall prove something of a problem. For if you must know, I should feel rather lost without a cat, especially Percival, who promises one day to be a gifted mouser. There is nothing so comforting when one is feeling the least out of frame than having a cat to stroke and hold in one's lap. And, besides, no respectable witch, even a white one of the healing arts, would be without one. It would be tantamount to depriving her of her spells and potions."

"Then no doubt it is fortunate that I am not allergic to the creatures," said his lordship, envisioning his exquisitely tailored coats and unmentionables made hirsute with cat fur. "I confess I have no particular fondness for felines. So long as Percival confines himself to your rooms, however, I see no reason why we should not rub along well enough."

"You may be sure that he will, my lord," Theodora exclaimed, rewarding him with a smile for which even an avowed cat-hater would have welcomed any number of the wretched beasts into his domicile. "We are making very good progress, are we not?"

"Excellent progress, Miss Havelock. I begin to have hopes of satisfactorily meeting all of your conditions. You did say there were to be five in all?"

"Yes, my lord. Five." Theodora gazed studiously down at Ginger's mane, a sure sign, noted his lordship grimly, that the third condition was of an entirely different order from the first two. No doubt she was having second thoughts about placing herself at the mercy of the Devil's Cub, who, after all, was rumored to be responsible for the deaths of everyone close to him. "Third and fourth, my lord," Theodora ventured on a surprisingly firm note. "I should like you to procure me a trousseau from Bristol—I shall provide you a list of the things I require—and to give your promise that, after we are married, you will not absent yourself from me in the next two months longer than a few hours at a time." Theodora's eyes flew to his. "Oh, I know they seem rather odd requests, but I'm afraid I really must have your word on both. They are of the greatest importance to me."

Styles, who had prepared himself for something quite different, wondered if he had heard her correctly. "I shall gladly provide you the trousseau, Miss Havelock. Indeed, the thought had already occurred to me—rather in the nature of a wedding present. And I am flattered that you would seem to entertain so great an affinity for my company. Or can it be that you are uneasy at the prospect of removing yourself to Devil's Keep? I promise you will find little, in spite of the prevalent rumors to the contrary, to fear in the castle itself."

"I wish you will not be absurd, my lord," Theodora declared impatiently. "I am far too analytically minded to be afraid of ghosts and haunted castles or even the most shocking of devil's curses. My Aunt Philippa assures me that Cliff House is full of dead souls with whom she communes on a regular basis, but I have yet to be bothered by a single one of them. No doubt I am far too practical to be pervious to their sort of influence. I am sorry to disappoint you, but I'm afraid you will find I am totally lacking in the delicate sensibilities. Or had you forgotten, my lord? *I* am a witch."

Styles regarded her with no little bemusement. The devil, she was. If she was not afraid of the castle, then what did frighten her enough to demand his constant attendance? Much as he found the notion thought-provoking, somehow he could not bring himself to believe that she was motivated by a sin-glemost desire to pursue their experiments in mutual discovery for a full two months on a twenty-four-hour basis. Not even he was prepared for so rigorous a schedule as that must be. "I beg your pardon," he said. "I confess I had not taken into account a witch's lack of delicate sensibilities. But if that is not the reason for your request, Theodora, then what is?"

Theodora, hearing her given name on his lips for the first time, glanced up at him in startled surprise. Far from being offended at the familiarity, she found that she liked it very well. "Perhaps it is because I believe two people entering into the state of matrimony should be given time to come to know one another. I have observed, my lord, that very often in the normal course of events, life tends to intervene just when two people are joined in marriage so that they wake up one day to find they are strangers to one another." She was thinking of his own parents and what a pity it was his father had not stayed home long enough to come to know his beautiful young wife and the son she had given him. Perhaps things would have worked out quite differently for them had it been other-wise.

"I'm afraid that such an agreement is out of the question" Styles replied oppressively. He could not be certain in the cir-cumstances that he could keep such a promise. He was no doubt mad even to contemplate taking a bride whom he must inevitably abandon. "I have a great many business concerns, any one of which might call me away at a moment's notice."

"Then you must give your word to take me with you, my lord," Theodora calmly insisted. "I am only asking for two months, after all. And they may be necessary for you to fulfill the final condition. You must promise to give me a child."

"A child." Good God. A successor to carry on the line of Dameron was possibly the last thing he had considered, espe-cially in light of the fact that he had already reconciled himself to the doctors' prognosis. He was the last of the Devil's Cubs. Considering the less-than-illustrious history of his line, it had not seemed wrong that it should come to an end with his demise.

"I am not, after all, growing any younger, my lord," Theodora continued. "I have to take into consideration the fact that I have only so many child-bearing years left to me. If I am to be married, I do not intend to waste the opportunity afforded me to experience the most intriguing biological function given to the female of the species to perform. As a man of intellectual curiosity, you must surely, of all people, understand how I feel."

"Perfectly," murmured the Devil's Cub, who was still battling with the idea of deliberately attempting to father a new line of Damerons. Somehow he found the notion of being considered little better than a stud to provide his prospective wife with an offspring more than a little unsettling. But then, who was he to cavil at the opportunity fate had set before him? Certainly the process of getting Theodora with child could not but offer intriguing possibilities. And if he could not fulfill her cursed conditions, what did it really matter? At least he would have accomplished what he had set out to do. Theodora would have his name to protect her and his fortune to provide for her future.

Theodora gazed at Styles uncertainly. "Does that mean you agree to my final conditions, my lord?" she asked.

"In so far as I have the power to satisfy them, I see no reason why not. So long as you agree to mine. We shall be married by special license no later than three days from tomorrow. Quietly, in the chapel at Devil's Keep, or at Cliff House, if you prefer."

"I infinitely prefer Cliff House," Theodora did not hesitate to assert. "Mrs. Tibbets and the rest of the household would never forgive me if they did not have a hand in the wedding preparations. Besides, I have always thought that, in the unlikely event I should ever succumb to parson's mousetrap, I should like to have the ceremony in the Rose Salon. It would be rather like having my mother with me, since her portrait presides over the room."

"Then Cliff House it must be," Styles readily agreed. "No doubt you will want your aunt to attend you. I regret," he added quietly, his eyes never leaving her face, "there will not be time to send for your father, Theodora. Naturally, I shall see that he is notified. And you will want to write him, too, I have no doubt. You may be sure there will be nothing in the marriage settlements to which he may find objection."

"No, I don't suppose there will be," Theodora answered, feeling a trifle weak, now that the thing was settled. "Knowing my father, the marriage settlements will be the very least of his concerns. When he hears from me, however, that I am well content with the course I have chosen, you may be sure we shall have his blessings. If, that is, he can be persuaded to leave his work long enough to send them."

"He sounds a remarkably understanding parent."

"He is, in fact, a selfish parent who, though he loves me dearly in his own way, has always preferred never to have to interfere in his daughter's life or to have his daughter interfere in his. It has been, therefore, a mutually satisfactory arrangement. No doubt you will like him exceedingly when you finally have the opportunity to meet him. I always have," she added, aware as she did so, that she had never wished for her lamentably absent-minded, but undeniably fond, parent more than she did at that moment when she found herself so unexpectedly betrothed to the Devil's Cub.

Six

"You are mistaken, Renfield," Styles said to his butler, who was studiously adjusting the already flawlessly arranged glassware on the grog tray. "The countess cannot possibly be roaming about the dungeons. She retired to her rooms half an hour ago to rest before dinner."

The normally impassive superior servant appeared distinctly uncomfortable. He even so far forgot himself as to nervously clear his throat. "Yes, my lord. I'm sure I should not wish to dispute your word. However, Her Ladyship did summon me in order to request the keys to the wine cellars. I'm afraid I directed her to the cellar stairs as well. I hope I did nothing wrong, my lord. She did say, as she was mistress of the house now, she wished to familiarize herself with every inch of it—from bottom to top, as it were."

"Apparently the countess takes her new role seriously," observed Justin Villiers, who, thirty-five, fair-haired, slender, and of average height, was not only the earl's oldest friend, but had, only a few hours earlier, stood up with Styles at his wedding. "Indeed, I should say she was a paragon among wives. What bride on her wedding day, after all, would concern herself with the state of her lord's wine cellars?"

"You have yet to know my wife," Styles pointed out. "Theodora is given to original thinking. Upon our very first meeting, she did not hesitate to inform me that she was a witch and, as such, was perfectly capable of looking out for herself. Still, I dislike the idea of her alone in the dungeons."

"Begging your pardon, my lord, but Her Ladyship is not alone," Renfield humbly interjected. "I should have gone with her myself, but she did not wish to take me from my duties. She insisted her page was sufficient company."

"Ah, one of the many Dicksons, one must presume," Villiers humorously supplied, flopping his elegant person down on one of the overstuffed leather chairs that occupied the earl's study. "They seem to be sprouting up around the Keep like turnips."

Styles, unamused, reached for the decanter of port. The Dicksons, ejected from their cottage by their landlord, the squire, had been induced to take over a sizable portion of the servants' quarters until other arrangements could be made. In the meantime, the earl's staff had been enlarged by the addition of a prepubescent scullery maid, an eleven-year-old stableboy, and a diminutive page, all bearing the distinctive flaming red hair and freckles bequeathed to them, presumably, by their mama—Millie Dickson, the countess's new abigail. Tom Dickson, the countess's new personal groom, after all, had brown hair.

"Mrs. Dickson is, if nothing else, a prolific breeder," Styles observed drily. "I daresay we shall not experience a dearth of candidates for employment at Devil's Keep for some time to come." Filling two glasses from the decanter, he crossed leisurely to Villiers. "I can only hope that my wife's familiar, unlike her brood of protégés, does not turn out to be the progenitor of a long line of felines. I believe I should object to having the castle overrun with cats."

"Cats, egads." Villiers favored the earl with a quizzical glance. "She must be a singular woman, your countess. You were never so indulgent with your numerous paramours, old friend, admit it."

His face coldly impassive, Styles casually lifted his glass to the spill of sunlight through the window. "You are not, I trust, drawing a comparison between my wife and the women with whom I have enjoyed occasional brief friendships," he murmured, studying the tawny color of the liquid.

Villiers gave a deprecatory wave of an elegantly turned hand. "No, of course not. I should not dream of placing your countess in the same category as your lights of love. It was, perhaps, a poor choice of words."

"Yes, hardly up to your usual style." Styles lowered the glass to sample the wine's bouquet. A frown touched his brow. "I am singularly fortunate," he said—an odd gleam flickered in the demon black eyes at thought of the profoundly singular trousseau his bride had requested of him—"to have met a woman who, far from catering to me or my purse for favors, does not bore me." Experimentally, he drank from the glass, swirling the liquid around in his mouth and over his tongue before swallowing.

"Ah, I begin to see. Fancies you, does she," observed Villiers, his handsome face cynically amused. "You will admit, however, that your lovely bride is cut of a different fabric. I mean, a witch, Caleb. She was roasting you, was she not?"

"On the contrary, my dear Justin. She could not have been more serious. . . . Renfield." Turning, Styles regarded his butler with penetrating eyes. "This is undoubtedly the seventy-nine."

Renfield, who had been rather nervously observing his master go through the ritual of judging the first sampling of a bottle of wine, swallowed, sending his Adam's apple bobbing above his high-pointed collar. "Yes, my lord," he agreed in the accents of one in anticipation of being precipitously condemned to the guillotine.

"The seventy-nine was not to be decanted for another year at best. You will kindly explain yourself."

"It-it was by order of the countess, my lord," Renfield supplied on quavery notes. "Until Her Ladyship has had the opportunity to inspect the potable wines, she informed me."

"No, did she?" queried his lordship. "For which, you have ruined a vintage port. You surprise me, Renfield."

"Yes, my lord," the butler acknowledged miserably. "I beg your pardon, my lord."

"Yes, no doubt. With what other instructions has Her Ladyship favored you?"

"She requires me in future to submit every bottle to her for approval before it is served, my lord. She took the precaution of sampling this one. A swallow, my lord. No more. I believe," he added, his cadaverous face utterly impassive, "that she did not find it exactly to her taste."

"No, I don't suppose she would," submitted Villiers, apparently much struck by the countess's exceedingly odd behavior. "An immature vintage port does not exactly commend itself to the palate."

"No, sir." Renfield drew his thin lips together, an expression that passed in the butler for a grimace. "I am deeply sorry, my lord. Shall I in future disregard Her Ladyship's instructions?"

"No." Styles, who had been staring thoughtfully into the depths of his glass, raised his eyes to Renfield. "She is chatelaine of Devil's Keep. You will treat the countess's orders as you would mine. Now, bring Mr. Villiers a bottle of the seventy-five. I believe in this instance it will not be necessary to submit it to the countess for testing."

"Never mind, Renfield," Villiers smoothly interjected. "No need to go to all that trouble. I shall be satisfied with the sherry." Rising, he crossed to the sideboard upon which a decanter of oloroso was kept as a morning reviver for the earl.

"Very good, sir." Renfield, bowing, backed gratefully from the room.

"Well," commented Villiers, his hazel eyes amused. Pouring out a glass of sherry, he returned to his chair. "I begin to see why she intrigues you, old man. A bit medieval though, wouldn't you say? Employing a taster? Hardly the normal duties for a countess, what?"

"I should not refine on it, if I were you, Justin," replied the earl, setting aside the wineglass. "Theodora is a female of uncommon intellectual curiosity. No doubt she has developed an interest in a scientific study of wines. And now I believe I must beg your indulgence. I am experiencing a sudden, irresistible impulse to discover how her research progresses."

Villiers, sampling the sherry, eyed his friend curiously. "Think nothing of it. I shall be on my way directly at any rate. I am a man of sudden impulses myself, you see. One of which brought me to Devil's Keep just in the nick of time to witness an event I had thought never to see—the Devil's Cub submitting to parson's mousetrap."

Styles paused at the door. "That reminds me. Precisely what did bring you to Exmoor, Justin? No doubt you will pardon my somewhat belated curiosity. I had thought you would be occupied in your usual pursuits. There was, I believe, a wealthy widow ripe for the plucking."

"Ah, the delightful Lady Corinne. As it happens, the lovely widow took it in her head to remove herself to Bath for the off season. I have allowed her a fortnight to discover how little she can bear life without me and am even now on my way to relieve her of what must by this time be a crushing ennui. I thought perhaps you would not mind putting me in the way of a small loan, old man. Devil of a nuisance. It would seem I find myself in the damnable position of being pockets to let at the moment."

"Let us rather call it a gift—on the occasion of my wedding, as it were," murmured the earl, drawing forth his purse. "Loans can be so very tedious between friends. Shall we say five hundred?"

"I should never say no to a man on his wedding day," Villiers submitted, rising with alacrity from his chair to accept the five one-hundred-pound notes from the earl. "Devilish good of you, Caleb. Always knew I could depend on you."

Styles cocked a speculative eyebrow. "I suggest you put the sum to good use. You may not always find me in a generous mood. I shall tender your regards to Lady Theodora and your regrets that you are unable to remain for dinner."

"Naturally. I am decidedly *de trop,* after all, and the beautiful Lady Corinne awaits. I shall just stay to finish this excellent oloroso, and then, thanks to you, I shall be off. In spite of your unparalleled wine cellar, I confess I was not overly fond of the idea of rusticating for any great length of time in the wilds of Exmoor."

"Yes, I was almost certain that was the case," murmured Styles, replacing his purse in an inner coat pocket. "Give my regards to Lady Damaris and Lord Harry when you apprise them of my new marital status. No, do not promise to keep mum. On the contrary, view it as an economy measure. You will no doubt eat out for a month on such a scintillating *on dit* as that will be."

Villiers bowed with a flourish. "You are all heart, *mon ami.* And, as ever, so exceedingly foresighted. Congratulations on your lovely bride. You may be sure that I wish you both happy."

Styles, having, with a single stroke, insured a sudden halt to the rumors concerning the uncertain state of his health, was congratulating himself as he proceeded downstairs to the dungeon where he anticipated a wholly stimulating verbal exchange with his unpredictable bride. A man in the throes of a serious illness would hardly be expected to take himself a wife, after all, he reasoned. And Justin Villiers, who lived by his wits and his undeniable charm, would make certain before the week was out that everyone in Bath who was anyone was aware the Devil's Cub had at last taken incontrovertible steps to set up his nursery.

The news would provide food for thought for a great many speculators who might have been anticipating the failure of any of his many business enterprises, not the least of which was his newest project in the Balkans. He frowned. Nothing must be allowed to interfere with the delicate agreements he had only recently negotiated at great personal risk to himself. He was all too aware how much depended on making sure

Black George and his Serb rebels continued to believe in the Earl of Styles's complete invulnerability. It was why Styles had removed himself from the public eye.

His handsome lips thinned to a grim line as it came to him, not for the first time, that someone had deliberately started the potentially dangerous rumors for the very purpose of destroying his credibility. But who? Obviously someone who had something to gain from seeing the Balkan agreements rendered null and void. One of his competitors then? One who counted personal gain above loyalty to king and country? Bloody hell, it was not impossible. Nor was it inconceivable that it was a personal enemy, one who would like nothing better than to see the Earl of Styles fail. A man in his position had enemies too numerous to count. There was one possibility even more plausible, however, than either of the other two, and that was that the villain was an enemy of England.

His eyes glittered coldly at the thought. A French spy privy to state secrets was an exceedingly dangerous proposition, one that would require his immediate attention at a time when he distinctly wished to divorce himself from public concerns. For the first time in his life he was not sure he could maintain the rigid control that had made him what he was in the eyes of others—ruthless and untouchable, a man above other men's rules. And yet somehow he must at least give the appearance he was unchanged. No one, other than himself, had ever been witness to his recent mental aberrations, and no one must— not, at least, until what he had set in motion in the Balkans was fully operational. Only then could he allow himself the luxury of succumbing to the weaknesses to which other men were prey—rage, regret, and the inevitability of his own mortality.

A grim smile thinned his lips. At least, thanks to his wholly bewitching enchantress and to Justin Villiers's habitual need for funds, he had bought himself a little time. He was aware of a quickening of his blood at the thought of Theodora, and

a resurgence of curiosity at this new start of hers to involve
herself with his wine cellar.

Bloody hell! The spy could wait awhile longer. Styles was
damned if he would spend his honeymoon, trying to ferret out
a bloody French agent. He could leave that for the time being
to Their Lordships in London. At the moment, he had more
pressing concerns.

Theodora viewed the row upon row of carefully stowed bottles and pipes of wine with a sinking heart. Faith, where the
devil was one to begin? she pondered, feeling hopelessly
daunted at the task she had set herself.

Immediately she chided herself for a faint-hearted fool. All
that was needed, after all, was a carefully reasoned plan. Having quelled panic in favor of rationality, she quickly eliminated
the pipes and all but the potable wines from consideration.
After all, the poisoner would hardly choose to corrupt an entire
cask when his evil intent was directed at a single individual,
and it would have been pointless to induce the poison into a
spirit that would not be judged suitable for consumption for
another several months or longer.

Even when she had narrowed the suspect beverages to those
ready for immediate consumption, however, she found herself
faced with the formidable task of deciding how to determine
which of those among them might be contaminated. At last,
logic prompted her to begin with the numerous bottles of vintage port.

It was only reasonable to suppose, after all, that those wines
with the reputation for the fullest body must prove the most
effective in disguising an adulterating influence. She counted
it as extremely fortunate that her papa liked nothing better
than a good bottle of port on a chill evening since it had given
her a rather more intimate knowledge of that particular bev-
erage than she might otherwise have enjoyed. She could not,
as a consequence, have failed to identify on the momentous

occasion of her midnight encounter with Styles the distinct aroma of that vintage wine on his person. Nor would she have known otherwise that every vintage bottle of port was marked with white paint to insure that, if ever it had to be moved, it would always be kept lying with the same side uppermost. Otherwise, the crucial crust that formed during its long years of maturation must inevitably come dislodged and have to be allowed to form all over again.

It was that which drew Theodora's sudden attention—a bottle, lying with its telltale mark slightly off-center, the crust obviously disturbed. Her fingers shook ever so slightly as she reached out to touch the anomaly in the long line of perfectly set bottles. This was not the sort of error a butler like Renfield would make. Unless she was very much mistaken, someone else had been in the wine cellar.

She was aware of a chill along her spine, coupled with a tingle of excitement, as she withdrew a magnifying glass from the placket pocket in her dress and bent to examine the cork stopper. Injecting poison through the stopper directly into an unopened bottle of wine was hardly a novel way to rid oneself of one's enemies. It was rumored the Medicis of Florence had not been averse to the practice as far back as the fifteenth century. She hardly knew what she felt when she found it—a flaw that gave every appearance of being a minuscule puncture mark at the center of the cork.

"What is it, Miss Theodora?" queried an eager young voice at her elbow. "Did you find something?"

"Perhaps, Tommy," Theodora answered without looking at Millie Dickson's oldest boy. "I cannot be certain until I have tested the contents." At last she lifted her head as she sensed her other two companions gather around her and Tommy.

"I must have my herbarium moved to Devil's Keep at once, Tom," she said, a frown marring the purity of her brow. "Everything must be set up and ready for my immediate use. Can you manage it, do you think?"

"Aye, Miss Theodora—er—m'lady," Tom Dickson replied.

Sheepishly he grinned at his lapse in decorum. "I expect, with little Tommy's help, I can do the thing quick enough."

Impulsively Theodora laid a hand on Dickson's coatsleeve of brown homespun. "Thank you, my friend," she said simply. "I cannot express too strongly how very important this is. I fear it is very possibly a matter of life and death."

Her words had the immediate effect of planting an expression of grim determination on the man's plain, rugged features. "Then it's as good as done, m'lady. You can depend on Tom Dickson."

"I know I can—on all of you," she added, glancing around at her three cohorts, who, besides Tom Dickson and Tommy, included nine-year-old Will, her page. "You shall be my eyes and ears."

Moments later, having dispersed her small company of archplotters to their various duties, she carefully hid the bottle of port among the wines of immature vintage.

"There." Satisfied that no one would interfere with the potentially dangerous vessel in its new location, she put away her magnifying glass and, picking up the lantern she had brought with her, made her way down the long aisle between stacked wooden barrels to the door. With any luck she would soon isolate and identify the poisonous agent, she told herself, stepping through and pulling the door to. But more importantly, perhaps, she would have the proof she needed to convince Styles he was in deadly peril.

In the meantime, she would be curious to know who, besides Renfield and Styles himself, could have gained access to the wine cellar, she reflected, weighing the heavy ring of keys in her hand. In the norm, the butler would never allow the keys out of his possession. She had made sure of that much at least. Renfield had been most reluctant to trust them to her care. Styles, of course, would have his own key. It would not hurt, she decided, turning the key in the lock, to inquire if there had been any visitors to the castle since His Lordship had taken up residence.

Theodora had already discarded the servants as possible candidates for suspicion, save for Thistlewaite, the earl's gentleman's gentleman. After all, the symptoms had most certainly begun while Styles was in London; and only Hodges, the groom, and Thistlewaite, the valet, among the servants at the Keep would have been in attendance on their master away from the castle. While not impossible, it certainly was far-fetched to think the groom, confined for the most part to the stables, would have access to the earl's various beverages in Town. Thistlewaite, on the other hand, would have both access and opportunity.

Mentally she added an interview with the gentleman's gentleman to her growing list of things to do and, turning away from the door, nearly collided with the one person whom, in her preoccupation, she had quite utterly forgotten.

"Styles! Good God," she exclaimed, clapping a hand to her bosom. "You startled me."

"Then naturally I must beg your pardon," murmured the Devil's Cub. Taking the lantern from her, he turned to escort her up the curving stone stairway. "As you, no doubt, will pardon my curiosity. I am afraid I cannot but wonder, Theodora, about this sudden interest of yours in my wines."

"But it is not in the least sudden," Theodora objected. "Or at least my interest in wines in general is not. As an herbalist and a healer, I have spent no little time studying the subject. Did you know that certain spirits imbibed with certain mushrooms at a particular time of the year can lead to dire consequences, sometimes even death?"

"It has been my experience that in the company of mushrooms, the imbibing of spirits is the only way to avoid death from the sheer onset of boredom at any time of the year," whimsically reflected his lordship.

Theodora choked on a startled burble of laughter. "That was too bad of you. You know very well I was not referring to the kind of mushroom that walks about on two legs."

"Then I must confess that, though I occasionally enjoy the

edible variety, mushrooms of the class Basidiomycetes are, strictly speaking, outside my area of expertise. Which still does not answer my question. I had thought to find you resting in your rooms, but I am informed that you are instead in the dungeon. Why, Theodora?"

"But I told you. I have a professional interest in wines. And you, you will admit, have a superb collection. I simply could not resist the opportunity to further my education. Besides, I am chatelaine of Devil's Keep. I have to start familiarizing myself with my new home sometime."

"At the risk of sounding somewhat less than appreciative of your wifely zeal, Theodora, I fear I must object to submitting to have my countess sample every bottle of wine before it is brought to me. One would almost imagine you are afraid I am in danger of being poisoned." He paused as he studied her profile, illuminated in the glow of lanternlight. "You are not, are you, afraid I am being poisoned?"

"On the contrary, Styles," Theodora retorted, her eyes coming up to meet his. "I think it is a more than distinct possibility. I am not, after all, unversed in the signs and symptoms of such an ailment."

Good God. And she had thought to protect him by serving as his taster? The thought both unnerved and appalled him. She could not have known, after all, that his was a poison bequeathed to him by his mother. And he would make sure she did not know, not before it was absolutely necessary. "Then I am afraid I really must insist that you do not sample my wine before me. It would seem, after all, an extreme measure, even for a witch dedicated to the healing arts. I will not have you risking your life for mine, Theodora. Even if, as in this case, there was never any real danger."

"Really, Styles, I am not such a fool. Giving my life to save yours might serve in a novel of Gothic romance, but it would hardly be the intelligent solution. I was, in fact, following the dictates of logic. If the poisoner's intent had been to kill you outright, you would hardly have survived this long. It was obvious to me, therefore, that, while I might learn something of the nature of the poison, I should be in no great peril from imbibing a single swallow. Indeed, you may be sure I should have followed a different course had I thought there was the least danger of a lethal dose."

"No doubt you relieve my mind," murmured Styles, exceedingly grim. "You will, nevertheless, obey me in this. It is not the effects of poison I am feeling at this moment, Theodora, but something quite on a different order, I assure you."

"You cannot know how pleased I am to hear it," Theodora said, turning to give him a frankly assessing glance. Styles certainly did not appear in the least ill, she noted, aware, as she did so, of a sudden rush of heat through her veins. If anything, he had never looked fitter or more marvelously formidable than he did at that very moment. "But then," she added reflectively, "I did make certain you were away from Devil's Keep and the most likely source of the poison until I should be here to conduct a thorough investigation into the matter. Though it is true my wardrobe was sadly lacking, I am not, I promise you, in the norm greatly concerned about fashion."

"Little witch," pronounced Styles with obvious feeling. He might have known she had sent him to Bristol for an ulterior purpose. To say the items she had commissioned him to buy were, for a female of refinement, eccentric would be to put it mildly. Bloody hell, he had had the devil of a time even finding them, which, no doubt, had been her intent all along. She had obviously expended a deal of thought on her undeniably unique list and no little literary research, for, unless he was vastly mistaken in her character, he doubted that she possessed an intimate knowledge of things that clearly fell into the category of exotic. He had complied with her requests only because his curiosity had been keenly aroused and because he had assumed she, in her naïveté, had thought of the items in the nature of apparatus to aid in their scientific research, a notion which, he could not deny, he had found intriguing, to say the least.

Obviously he had misjudged her motives. And what of her other conditions? His black eyebrows snapped sharply together. Aside from the continuation of her work and the introduction of a cat into his household, might not they be similarly motivated?

It was time, he decided grimly, that his meddlesome and overimaginative young bride was made to understand she could not manipulate him, no matter how altruistic her motives. It was, in short, time she was taught a lesson.

Theodora, noting her lord's distinctly satyric expression, could not but wonder if she had been better to keep her tongue between her teeth. And yet, how very disobliging of him to open the door to her only to slam it shut again! Obviously he had never any intention of treating her diagnosis of his condition with the seriousness it deserved. Hell and the devil confound it! She had vastly preferred to wait until she had incontrovertible evidence to support her contentions, but when he had so conveniently asked her opinion, what could she do but tell him the truth? Well, there was nothing for it now, but to make the best of the mull she had made of things. In the circumstances, there was little she could do but brazen her way through. "I did warn you what I am, Styles," she did not hesitate to remind him. "And there is no point in trying to deny that you have been ill. That is not the sort of thing you can hide from a witch with acute empathic powers of perception."

"So I have been informed by your inimitable aunt, who sees flecks of shadow in my otherwise brilliant emanations. It is not, however, something with which you need concern yourself, Theodora. In fact, I fear I must insist that you do not."

"Naturally you would say that," Theodora retorted, out of all patience with him. "I knew there was not the least use in telling you the truth. After all, you have made it plain that you are in no danger of forming an emotional attachment for me, in which case, you could hardly be expected to understand that I should, on the contrary, be exceedingly concerned that my husband is being poisoned and wish to do something about it." Having reached the kitchens, Theodora took the lamp from Styles and set it on a table before coming around to face that recalcitrant husband. "I am well aware that you cannot bring yourself to love me, Styles, but you should know that that does not mean I am of a similar disposition."

Styles stared at her, a curious glint in his eye at this new and seemingly irrelevant turn in subject.

"You will no doubt pardon me if I seem a trifle obtuse, Theodora," he said, firmly leading her out of the kitchens and away from the curious eyes of the staff at work preparing the evening meal. "I should not, however, wish to misunderstand you. Are you by any chance saying that you are in love with me?"

"I wish you will not be absurd, Styles." Theodora gave a wry grimace as they emerged in the dining room. "Being in love so very often leads to being out of love, does it not? I was in love with Billy Wickers when I was eight and with Peter Ainsworthy two months later. I am saying I am of a different disposition from you and, therefore, it is not inconceivable that I might love you, which is not at all the same thing as being in love with you."

"Is it not? You intrigue me, Theodora. I believe I have never before had occasion to make the distinction."

"Yes, I know, which is very sad indeed," replied Theodora, reflecting how different was her own case. Thanks to Papa and Mrs. Tibbets and Aunt Philippa, she knew very well what it was to be surrounded by love. "Love is hardly a temporary condition, which comes and goes, rather like a cold or a bout with dyspepsia. It is a deal hardier than that. If I loved you, Styles, you may be sure nothing could ever induce me to cease to do so."

"Then do not make the mistake of loving me, Theodora," Styles uttered harshly, wishing they were not two stories down from his private quarters. Theodora, her modish, new morning dress of aquamarine unfashionably covered with a bibbed

apron and her delightful nose sporting a smear of dirt from
her recent stint in the cellar, had never looked more desirable
than she did at that moment when she had all but declared
that she loved him. He was experiencing an overpowering urge
to crush her to his chest and take her in a most unseemly
manner—without preamble, there, in the middle of the dining
room. Instead, he took the hem of her apron and wiped the
absurd smudge off the tip of her nose. "You are far too young
to condemn yourself to so lengthy and unrewarding a sentence
as that must be."

Prey to a host of sensations aroused by the Devil's Cub's
black, glittery orbs at exceedingly close range, Theodora did
not make an immediate answer. Instead, to the earl's fascination, she swayed irresistibly toward him, her beautiful eyes
partially closed and her lips invitingly parted. Like a man
caught up in a spell, Styles lowered his head toward hers.

It was at that most unpropitious moment that Renfield, bearing the newly polished silver for the table, backed through the
serving door into the dining room.

"Bloody hell!" Styles cursed, the moment broken, and drew
Theodora through the double doors into the adjoining withdrawing room.

"You are mistaken, my lord," Theodora, jarred from her momentary abstraction and unreasonably vexed at what she perceived to have been an untimely interruption, at last found the
wit to answer him. "You may be sure I should not regard
loving you in the light of a sentence. Really, Styles, you must
get over this notion that because you are the Devil's Cub, you
must live up to the stupid things that are said of you." In her
agitation, she paced two steps forward then back again, while,
behind her, Styles purposefully pulled the doors closed. "I see
nothing in the least disagreeable at the thought of loving a
man of intelligence, generosity, wit, intellectual curiosity,
and—and—"

She was not allowed to finish her list of the earl's agreeable
attributes, as Styles, unable to resist the primitive urges her

naïve and unexpected championship inspired, pulled her strongly into his arms and covered her mouth with his.

Startled, but agreeably so, Theodora reacted with a whole-hearted, natural fervor. Lifting her arms about the back of his neck, she melted against him.

"Ah, Theodora," murmured Styles no little time later, releasing her lips in order to begin a wholly instructive exploration of the slender column of her neck. "You respond so sweetly to me. I have never known a woman like you."

"No, I daresay you haven't," Theodora answered practically, if a trifle unsteadily. With a shuddering sigh, she leaned her head to one side to facilitate his exploratory quest. "I'm sure it is not everyday that you meet a witch. The prevailing attitude toward women of my vocation over the centuries has tended to deplete our numbers drastically."

Perhaps it was true that association with Theodora had served to enhance His Lordship's latent powers of apprehension or perhaps he detected a subtle movement beyond the hall exit. Whatever the case, Styles, in the process of nibbling at her earlobe, suddenly stiffened. Slowly he lifted his eyes to behold an exceedingly self-conscious underfootman, standing rigidly at his assigned station in the entryhall in a direct line with the gaping doorway at the far end of the room.

Deliberately Styles straightened. "The world is unfortunately severe on those who do not conform to the accepted mode. A pity, if it has denied itself even one such as you." By God, he doubted that there could ever have been another like his enchantress. She had only to be near him to inflame his senses. Without warning he bent down and swooped her up in his arms. Purposefully, he carried her out of the withdrawing room, past the absurdly grinning underfootman, and up the gracefully curved stairway. "You are a delectable change from the usual run of young beauties."

"Yes, well, I have benefited from an unusual education, which in the norm is denied to women," replied Theodora, who had instinctively clasped an arm about his neck. She had been rendered intriguingly breathless and not a little dizzy by his unexpected move. Indeed, the source of the colloquialism, "being swept off one's feet," was not only made suddenly quite clear to her, but its every facet of meaning was indelibly impressed on her reeling mind.

Styles inhaled deeply, intoxicated by the sweet scent of her hair, which, in spite of her aunt's gallant efforts to subdue the unruly mass in a fashionable coiffure, had slipped from its pins. Theodora was unbelievably beautiful.

The three days and nights preceding this, their wedding day, had been bloody interminable. His excursion to Bristol to purchase her trousseau had been maddeningly fraught with visions of Theodora, bewitching in an indecently transparent green silk peignoir trimmed in swansdown or devastatingly fetching in an equally provocative black negligee of chantilly lace, both of which he had purchased against his better judgment. Nor had it helped to be tantalized by an image of her, her arms, neck and shoulders bare in an evening dress of Persian silk, slit up the side to the thigh and shot through with silver threads. Where, he had wondered, did Theodora think to wear such a creation? Certainly not where any but his eyes would behold her, he had vowed, driven nearly to distraction with any number of creative possibilities for so intimate an evening as that must prove.

While it had been a relief to find his thoughts distracted from what had been fast becoming a morbid fascination with his encroaching madness, he had taken little comfort in the realization that Theodora exercised so powerful an influence over him. Had he not entertained a healthy skepticism of anything even remotely suggestive of the supernatural, he might have been tempted to believe she had indeed cast a spell over him.

Hell and the devil confound it! He had governed his life under the precept that a man was a fool to grant anyone even a modicum of power over him—especially a female. Women were to be appreciated for what they could provide in the way of diversion from a man's weightier existence. Beyond that, they were kept separate and at a distance, protected, as it were, from the real world, which men ruled. But, more than that, women were never to be trusted.

Females, after all, were, with rare exceptions, flighty, unpredictable creatures, prey to emotional upheavals and absurd starts of sentimentality. Powerless themselves, they took power in the only way they could—from men foolish enough to allow themselves to be ruled from their beds. Styles had never committed his father's supreme folly, and he did not intend to start now with Theodora, no matter how bewitching he found his new bride. What happened in the bedroom had nothing to do with what transpired outside of it.

Theodora, he vowed, would learn that he was master at Devil's Keep, until circumstances dictated otherwise. And now that she was in his arms, her small, lissome form conforming so readily to his embrace, he was filled with an overwhelming need to have her. First, however, she must be impressed with the fact that she could not employ womanly wiles against him.

"Forgive me, Theodora," he said, coming to a halt outside her door, "but I believe I cannot wait any longer to further your admittedly excellent education."

Theodora smiled and reached up to touch his face. "How very fortunate, since I find I, too, am all eagerness to renew our experimentation."

A smile flickered at the corners of his lips as Styles bent his head to taste the tender flesh beneath one delicately rounded earlobe. "Yes, I sensed that you were. That is one of the things I find most delightful in you—your unaffected enthusiasm for scientific research."

Theodora, noting that her temperature would seem to have begun sharply to rise and that his lordship's lips at her throat would seem to be having a peculiar effect on her nether regions, wondered deliriously why he did not proceed immediately into her chamber. She was even more bewildered and not a little disoriented when he set her on her feet.

"I believe we shall not wish to go down to supper," he said. His fingertips lightly caressed her cheek. "If you are agreeable, I shall order it sent up. An hour or so, do you think? That should give you time enough to prepare yourself. You will find everything you require has already been laid out."

"H-has it?" faltered Theodora, wondering why she should be experiencing a sudden frisson of uneasiness. "How very thoughtful, but what of Mr. Villiers? It would seem something of a rudeness to leave him to dine alone while we immerse ourselves in scientific inquiry."

"Just so, my sweet. However, as it happens, Justin has asked me to tender his regrets. He has found it necessary to make an early departure and will not be dining at Devil's Keep after all."

"I see." Theodora eyed the earl doubtfully. "I do hope it was nothing in the way of unwelcome news that drew him so suddenly away."

"Only a widow in need of consoling, I have been assured." Styles dropped a kiss on the tip of Theodora's nose before opening her door for her. "An hour, Enchantress. I promise I am looking eagerly forward to it."

"Indeed, so am I," Theodora answered. Stepping past Styles into the chamber, she only just remembered to smile at him as she closed the door. "Or at least I think I am," she added, staring at the carved oaken barrier with a quizzical expression. Aside from his strong passions, kept rigidly in check, she had sensed something else in her dearest Devil's Cub. Indeed, she had had the oddest sensation.

Styles was up to something, she was sure of it. But what? she wondered, turning to find Millie Dickson staring at her with a distinct look of horror.

"Miss, he's a devil, he is. Only say the word, and I'll not abandon you to him, no matter if it means Tom and all of us must go to the workhouse, I promise you."

"Nonsense, Millie. I wish you will not speak such twaddle.

The earl is my husband now." Quickly Theodora crossed to the distraught woman. "Now, tell me. What is the matter?"

"Begging your pardon, m'lady, for so you are, and I daresay there's no calling a halt to it now. Not but what we wouldn't take you home to Cliff House, was you of a mind to go. My Tom would see to it, never you fear."

"Enough, Millie. I have not the least wish to return to my father's house. Devil's Keep is my home, and if you wish it to be yours, you will calm yourself and tell me what has caused you to kick up a dust."

"It's in here, m'lady. All laid out and ready for you," said Millie. Drawing her mistress into the bedchamber in the manner of one entering a serpent's lair, she pointed to the bed. "Your trousseau, Miss Theodora. Just look what he has sent in for your bridal clothes."

Theodora stared, her mouth agape. Then suddenly her shoulders began to shake. "Good God," she gasped, her face convulsed in mirth. "I never dreamed he would actually find them. The devil! I never believed such things truly existed. And now it would seem I must wear them!"

Seven

Theodora stared in mute fascination at her reflection in the ormolu looking glass. She was not sure whether to laugh or to blush at her image clad in an exceedingly skimpy white silk chemise that reached a point midway above the knees and from beneath which protruded short ruffled silk drawers of a hue that could only be described as blushing rose. White stockings, embroidered with red rosebuds down the outside of each leg from below the knee to the ankle and held in place by beribboned garters, called indecent attention to her legs, and on her feet were white embroidered shoes with recessed French heels. Over the whole exceedingly exotic costume, she wore a flowing white negligee of gauze trimmed with feathers.

To say her attire was immodest was a gross understatement. Her appearance was positively wicked. At least she had flatly refused the absurdity of a white leather bust improver, which, secured about her torso in such a manner as to lift her breasts to a wholly unnatural elevation, had had more the flavor of a medieval instrument of torture than something that belonged in a woman's drawer of unmentionables.

"Are you quite sure this is all there is to it?" she asked a scandalized Millie Dickson, who stood watching her in thin-lipped disapproval. "It would seem to be a trifle brief."

"It's an abomination," Millie declared without round-aboutation. "Beggin' your pardon, m'lady, but you can't gammon me into believing this is the sort of thing a gently bred female would wear on her wedding night."

"Heavens, no, Millie," Theodora replied with a gurgle of laughter. "I daresay it is clearly in the style of a lady bird. How perfectly delectable. I have always entertained a great curiosity about those ladies of the evening. What a very gay sort of life they must lead, free of convention."

"Uncertain is more like, m'lady," Millie supplied dourly. "Not, but what a woman's life is anything else. But at least them that's got themselves a good husband is a sight better off than them that don't."

"Then I am indeed fortunate, and you may all cease to worry about me. I could not ask a better husband than Styles, I promise you. After all, what other man would procure so wicked a trousseau at his bride's request? Very likely a less understanding man would have seen it as just cause to cry off."

"Not to cry off, surely, Enchantress," murmured a thrillingly masculine voice from behind Theodora. "You may be certain that even a man of lesser understanding must apprehend the unique potentialities in such a bride."

Theodora came about with a swirl of feathers and white gauze. Her heartbeat perceptibly quickened at the sight of Styles, his tousled, windswept hair shining blue-black in the lamplight, his long, powerful frame intriguingly clad in a splendid example of the ankle-length deshabille. Belted at the waist, the black brocade dressing gown set off his broad shoulders and narrow torso to perfection. What was more, she was reasonably certain he wore nothing beneath it. The realization brought a blush to her cheeks, which she told herself was perfectly ridiculous. After all, it was not as if she had not already seen him in all his masculine perfection. It was only that she was suddenly struck with the significance of two pertinent facts. First, she was quite certain there could not be a more magnificent specimen of the male gender than the Devil's Cub; and, second, he was her husband. To her mortification, she felt her limbs go suddenly weak at that sublime realization.

Styles, attributing her frozen aspect to something altogether different, smiled faintly. Even attired in the garb of a lady bird, Theodora could not be mistaken for other than what she was— an unsophisticate clearly in the throes of embarrassment. She need not have felt chagrined. In spite of the fact that he preferred his lights of love tastefully attired, his bride at that moment presented an undeniably charming aspect. Indeed, he was filled with a sudden, overwhelming impatience to be rid of the abigail.

It was at that moment that Theodora's eyes met the Devil's Cub's black, glittery orbs and held. "That will be all, Millie. Thank you," she said, without looking at the lady's maid. "Go to bed. I shan't be needing you again tonight."

"M'lady." Millie curtsied and, avoiding the earl's eyes, slipped past his tall figure into the sitting room. Casting a last, uncertain glance at her mistress, Millie reluctantly slipped out the hall door, taking care to close it behind her.

"I fear your Mrs. Dickson does not approve of your bridal clothes," Styles observed, breaking the silence that had fallen over them with the woman's withdrawal.

In answer, Theodora dimpled naughtily. "No, how could she? I present an altogether disreputable appearance. Do you like it?" Holding the negligee out at her sides, she pirouetted before him. "I have never felt so deliciously wicked. And how very clever of you to choose white." Stopping, she scooped Percival off the bed where he had been curled in a little ball, asleep. "Percival and I make a perfect match."

The devil, thought Styles. That did not begin to describe the picture they made together. Theodora, in pristine white, the snow-white kitten held to her cheek, presented an image of youthful beauty and innocence, which was as disarming as it was utterly seductive. He experienced an unsettling urge to fling a blanket around her shoulders to cover her scantily clad form.

"Oh, dear," exclaimed Theodora, staring at him with sudden awareness. "I have embarrassed you. Is it really so indecent?"

"Indisputably," remarked Styles, cynically amused at her assessment of his reaction. "I believe I have never beheld anything quite so conducive to arousing a man's more primitive passions. You are breathtaking, Theodora."

"Am I?" Lowering her gaze to Percival, whom she held nestled contentedly against her breast, Theodora absently ran her hand over his soft kitten fur. That was not precisely the impression she had gotten from Styles. Quite the contrary, in fact. It had seemed to her that the sudden searing leap of his eyes had been meant to burn holes through her. But how very mortifying. *The Rangers' Magazine* as well as Mr. Harris's annual register describing the Covent Garden Ladies who had been used to entertain gentlemen in his tavern in Drury Lane had been most explicit. But then, both periodicals had been in vogue in the latter part of the previous century. Perhaps their information was outdated. Or perhaps it was only that she was not suited for a lady bird's plumage, she thought, willing to consider every possibility. Hell and the devil confound it. It seemed perfectly clear that Styles, who was well-versed in such matters, found her less than appealing.

"You needn't employ Spanish coin with me, Styles," she said, striving for a lightness of tone. "Though I confess I am disappointed in your reaction. Especially in light of what I had to go through to obtain a catalogue of a Cyprian's unmentionables. I had the devil of a time persuading Aunt Philippa to inquire of my dearly departed Great Uncle Pervis where he was used to hide his copies of Mr. Harris's register and *The Rangers' Magazine* from my equally departed Great-Aunt Edna. Even then, it was deucedly hard to discover just the right trunk. Have you any notion how much raff and rubble can accumulate in an attic over five generations?"

"I believe I may have some vague idea," replied Styles, whose family holdings went back a great deal further than five generations.

Theodora flashed him an uncertain glance, quickly averted again. "Yes, well, then, you can no doubt imagine the formidable task of recovering a single item in the midst of chaos. I daresay I might still be looking—" Her breath caught as she felt Styles loom suddenly behind her, the warmth of his hands coming to rest lightly on her shoulders. How absurd that her mouth should go inexplicably dry. "—had Great-Aunt Edna not intervened by sending a brass birdcage toppling down on top of it." Theodora uttered what was meant to be a trill of laughter, but which came out sounding absurdly breathless. "Apparently she had known all along about his secret cache of oddities. Poor Uncle Pervis. He was never able to—"

Deliberately Styles turned her to face him.

"To pull the wool over her eyes," Theodora ended on a fading note as she found herself staring close-up into the earl's compelling orbs.

Smiling slightly, Styles ran the tip of an index finger lightly down her cheek. "She sounds an astute woman, your Aunt Edna." Theodora's eyelids drifted partially closed as she succumbed to a shiver of pleasure. "Like her grandniece, no doubt." His touch wandered along the delicate contour of her jaw, found the pulsating throb of her throat, and passed on, traveling tantalizingly slowly down the valley between her breasts.

Theodora, her entire being focused on the progress of his trailing fingertip, lost the threads of his words. She was immersed in the purely physical sensations he was arousing. How curious that a touch, so feathery light, should have the effect of sending penetrating thrills pulsating down the entire length of her body, she thought. Indeed, she scarcely breathed as she waited with keen anticipation for further developments. She had not long to wait. His quest took him to the swelling bud of her nipple. Taking it between his fingertips, he lightly squeezed.

She was wholly unprepared to experience a melting pang of pleasure that communicated itself to a corresponding burst of moist heat in the region of her intimate parts.

With a gasp, Theodora opened her eyes.

"She killed him, you know," she blurted. "With poisoned mushroom."

Styles stared at Theodora in startled surprise. Mortified, Theodora stared back at him. "How very unkind of her," remarked the Devil's Cub. The devil, he thought. Somehow he had not expected a nervous bride on his wedding night. Not with Theodora, who had given herself to him so sweetly only a few nights before.

Theodora caught her bottom lip between her teeth. Good God, what had possessed her to reveal that particular tidbit about her deceased kinsmen, now, of all times? "It was an accident, of course," she hastened to explain, "but the results were still the same. They both succumbed in the most dreadful manner. Aunt Edna, you see, could never tell the difference between panther cap and common morel, and she would insist on making mushroom ketchup in August when, as everyone knows, panther cap is turned quite deadly."

An amused smile touched the Devil's Cub's lips. "How very unfortunate for your uncle. You, I trust, are not similarly motivated to concoct mushroom ketchup at any time of the year. It sounds abominable stuff. I'm afraid I should unequivocally have to refuse such a treat, even from you."

Theodora choked on an unwitting burble of laughter, which caused her eyes to light up like gems.

"Yes, that's more like," commented Styles, drawing her to him. "There is not the slightest need for you to be nervous, Theodora. I promise you." His hand moved over her hair, which she had instructed Millie to leave down, since the newly recruited abigail had not the least notion how to put it up in a fashionable coiffure. "You will find that I am never embarrassed. And most certainly not by a beautiful woman who, besides having gone to a great deal of trouble on my behalf, has the distinction of being my wife. You may believe I am not employing Spanish coin when I tell you I find you irresistible, Theodora."

"You cannot know how relieved I am to hear it," Theodora replied candidly. "For if you must know, you had not the look of a man inordinately pleased at finding his bride attired in the manner of a Cyprian. Not that it signifies. When you insisted I should find everything laid out for me, I was given no choice but to dress accordingly. I did, after all, promise to be a conformable wife, my lord, and, besides, I confess to having entertained a certain curiosity. I wished to understand why gentlemen seem to prefer their mistresses to their wives, and this seemed as good a time as any to put a theory of mine to the test."

The devil it did, thought Styles. She was perfectly aware his intent had been to teach her never again to use him to her own purposes. He might have known she would find a practical application for the experience.

"I see," he said dryly. "You thought to discover if a wife who assumed the role of her husband's mistress would be rendered more attractive in his eyes, is that it?"

"Well, it does occur to me that a wife who fails to employ every means available to her to hold her husband's interest, let alone his affections, must be sadly lacking in initiative. And what better way for her to achieve such a purpose than to imitate the sort of woman to whom he is naturally attracted? At the very least, I daresay it would go a long way to alleviate the boredom that must inevitably come with long-term familiarity."

"Oh, at the very least," agreed Styles, who doubted that any man married to Theodora could ever come to be bored, even if he had the time to reach a state of long-term familiarity. "I'm afraid, however, that you have failed to consider two salient points." Firmly, he removed the kitten from its cozy resting place and, despite its protestations, set it in the cushioned window seat, conveniently near at hand. "First of all, far from being in danger either of feeling familiar or bored," he said, pulling her deliberately into his arms, "we find ourselves at the very threshold of discovery. It is, after all, our wedding day. And, secondly, I do not have a mistress."

"Y-you don't?" queried Theodora, who had not been at all sure where the wind lay in that quarter. "But you have had, Styles. You know very well that you have. You are noted for the beautiful women with whom you have kept company. I daresay you have experienced any number of adventures of a romantic nature and participated in not a few orgies, which you found vastly entertaining. And why should you not?"

The Devil's Cub's head went back in a startled bark of laughter. "Oh, any number of orgies, all of which you may be sure I enjoyed immensely," he replied, his harsh features transformed with mirth. "And, truth to tell, I cannot think of a single reason why I should not. Is it an orgy that you wish, Enchantress?" he asked, a slow, smoldering fire igniting in his eyes as he pulled her close. "I believe I should enjoy such an event as that must be."

"Then you may be sure that I, too, shall derive great pleasure from it," Theodora answered, her heart going out to him. She suspected, in spite of all the rumors to the contrary, that her dear Devil's Cub had found very little to bring laughter and joy into his life. Indeed, he bore every aspect of a man who had seen a great deal to make him cynical in what the world had had to teach him. She smiled brightly up at him. "And I, after all, am dressed for the occasion. Where shall we begin? With food and wine? Shall I peel a grape for you and feed it to you while you lie in depraved abandon on the bed? Or perhaps you would have me dance for you while you play the flute?"

"I have not the least desire to play the flute at this moment," Styles growled, lifting her high in his arms. "And the thought of peeled grapes fills me with revulsion. I have better things to do with you than lie in bed, in depraved abandon or otherwise, while you poke fruit down my throat."

"Well, how am I to know?" Theodora demanded, a dimple irrepressibly peeping forth. "I'm not the one who is experienced in decadent pursuits. I rely wholly on you to teach me how to go on."

"You may be certain of it," replied Styles, keenly aware of his already fully aroused state. Good God, the last thing Theodora required was instruction in the art of seduction. She was an enchantress cloaked in innocence, a witch with the power to inflame his senses with her mere presence.

Purposefully, he carried Theodora to the bed.

"The food and wine will come later," he dutifully informed her. "After we lie, spent, our passions sated."

"I suppose that would seem the logical progression," Theodora sensibly reflected. "I shouldn't think I should feel at all like sating my passions if I were already engorged with food and muddled with drink. Very likely I should simply wish to fall asleep."

Styles uttered a laugh that had more the sound of a groan. "Exactly so, my sweet. You are a most precocious pupil. A surfeit of spirits not only dulls the senses, but very often has a detrimental effect on a man's performance."

"In that case, I should vastly prefer that you do not make indentures before we have drunk fully of Eros' sensual pleasures. Though I cannot but think you must be an exception to the rule, Styles," she added, her brow puckered in retrospection. "Our first experiment in mutual discovery, you were three sheets to the wind."

"Witch," declared the Devil's Cub with obvious feeling and covered her mouth with his.

The instant he did so, he felt her witch's power ignite in a flame of passion. Her mouth parted beneath his with a readiness that had nothing to do with art or seduction. She was earth and sweetness and life. God, how he wanted her. He had never wanted anything so much in his life as he wanted Theodora. With a groan, he thrust his tongue into the moist depths of her mouth and, holding her with one arm, allowed her feet to slip to the floor until she stood, leaning against him. His hands moved over her shoulders and down her arms, relieving her of the negligee, which drifted to a pile at her feet.

By God, she was beautiful. Her breasts peaked beneath the thin chemise, the nipples already firm, like berries ripe for the plucking. Cradling a rounded breast in his palm, he caressed a delectably taut nub with his thumb. As a gusty sigh breathed from her depths, he bent his head to her lips.

He unloosed a storm of sensations within her, a frenzy of emotions more intense than anything she had ever known before.

Theodora quivered. Her arms clung to him. Her fingers clutched in the fabric of his dressing gown, only to unloose their grasp in order to seek the hard chest beneath. She felt herself shaken by a dark wind. Styles wanted her. Her dear Devil's Cub needed her in a way that he would never admit to her or himself. She felt small and slight clasped against his great strength, but she was not in the least afraid. Molding herself to him, she bent with the wind, riding it, more than willing to give herself to it. After all, he was her Devil's Cub. She was perfectly safe in his hands. But, oh, God, what was he doing to her?

It would seem that an orgy was on quite a different order from a mere experiment in shared mutual discovery. Things were moving at a much swifter pace for one thing, due, no doubt, to what she sensed was a driving urgency in her dear Devil's Cub. The contact of his strong, hard body against hers communicated a wealth of information, not the least of which was the fact that every muscle in his powerful frame was strained to an alarming rigidity, rather as if he anticipated at any moment to be struck down by a paralyzing blow.

"Styles?" she queried, experiencing a sudden check in her riot of emotions. Anxiously, she lifted her eyes to look at him.

Grimly, Styles shook his head. Beads of sweat stood out on his forehead, and his eyes burned with a dark, feverish intensity. "I'm afraid you would seem to have a powerful effect on me, Enchantress. Bloody hell, Theodora. This is not going to go at all as I planned it."

"Dear." Her breasts pressed against his chest as, tenderly, Theodora reached up to brush a damp lock of hair from his forehead. Styles drew a sharp breath, his face a rigid mask of control. "I sensed something was not quite right. Very likely it is all my fault. If it is these wretched clothes, Styles, I shall gladly take them off."

Something like a smile, but which was more of a grimace, twisted at the Devil's Cub's lips. "I shall take them off for you very shortly. Be certain of it." Bloody hell, he was dangerously close to being forced to rip the cursed things off her. He drew in a painful breath. Not since his extreme youth had he been so close to utterly losing control. "Egad, you haven't the least notion what you are doing to me." His hands on her firm, rounded posterior drew her hard against him. "Tell me you want me, Theodora," he commanded thickly.

Theodora gasped as she encountered the sizable bulge of his erect manhood. "Oh, but I do want you, Styles," she said. "I have been able to think of little else since our first excursion into human biology. It was the most sublime moment of my life," she assured him.

"Was it, Enchantress? And you may be sure there will be others just as sublime. This, however," he ground out between his teeth, "may not prove to be one of them."

Bending down, he lifted her without preamble on to the bed. He did not bother to remove her satin heels, embroidered stockings, or beribboned garters, with which he was beyond coping in his precarious state, but instead quickly stripped her of her bloomers. He flung off his dressing gown and inserted himself between her thighs.

Theodora gasped as she felt his manhood press against the swollen petals of her body.

"Styles?" she queried, her eyes wide on his, questioning. This was not at all like that other time. Indeed, while she felt herself on fire with a wild, feverish excitement, she was not quite sure she was ready for the inevitable culmination of events. Everything was happening so swiftly.

"Trust me, Enchantress," Styles uttered on an agonized breath. "You are a most apt pupil. You are already moist with anticipation. Your sweet nectar flows so readily for me. And I—hell and the devil confound it—I cannot wait any longer!"

With as much care as he could manage in his straitened circumstances, Styles drove himself into Theodora.

Instantly, he went still, sweat pouring over his body. His head down, he fought to contain the overpowering urge to complete what he had started.

"Bloody hell," Theodora gasped, startled at finding herself so suddenly filled with him. Still, her body seemed perfectly designed to accommodate itself to him, she realized, just as it had that other time. And just like that other time, she was awakened to a slow, aching sense of urgency. Indeed, she could not bear it. Faith, what the devil was he waiting for? Why did he not *do* something?

"Styles," she pleaded. Wriggling beneath him, she clasped her legs around him and, thinking to help him out of his seemingly frozen state, lifted herself to him.

"No, Theodora, *don't*—!" Styles's anguished cry came too late. She broke his control. Driven beyond even the devil's endurance, Styles thrust again and again, until at last, arching his back, he drove himself hard into her one final time.

A surge of elation welled up from deep within him as he spilled his seed into her. By God, he had never felt so wondrously depleted. He collapsed, dragging in deep ragged breaths, and lay still on top of her.

Theodora lay bewildered beneath him. She ached, her body's needs unsated. He had yelled at her. Obviously, she had done something terribly wrong. But then, how was she to know the proper manner in which to conduct an orgy? she thought, mortification changing to resentment. He might at least have taken the time to instruct her.

To her dismay, she felt tears of hurt and frustration well up behind her eyelids. Disgusted at such a feminine display, she turned her head away.

Styles, feeling her move, roused himself from his lethargy enough to lift himself on his elbows. Tenderly, he kissed her cheek, followed by the corner of her eye. Encountering the dampness of tears, he went suddenly still.

"The devil," he exclaimed sharply, cursing himself for a heartless blackguard. "Did I hurt you, Theodora?"

"No." Theodora sniffed. Impatiently, she brushed at the tears with her fingertips. "Of course you did not hurt me. Indeed, how could you."

"Very easily, I'm afraid." Grimly, he studied Theodora's averted profile, aware that he wished she would look at him.

Now, what the devil? It had been four days since she had given him the gift of her virginity. Surely that was sufficient time to ward against any tenderness she may have experienced in the wake of that momentous occasion. Still, Theodora was inordinately small and delicately wrought. He suffered a pang of remorse that was as sharp as it was unexpected. No doubt he had been an unfeeling boor to force himself on her. "I beg your pardon, Theodora. I never meant to take you in so brutish a manner. I fear it may have been too soon for you."

At that, Theodora did look at him. "I wish you will not be absurd, Styles," she said irritably. "There is nothing physically wrong with me, I promise you. It was not the occasion that was too soon."

"Not the occasion—?" Styles stopped and stared at her. Then, with sudden, dawning realization, he burst into laughter.

Instantly, Theodora stiffened in resentment. "I am naturally sorry if I failed to perform my part in an exemplary manner, but you will admit that I informed you beforehand I was not up to snuff in the matter of orgies. It really is too bad of you, Styles, to laugh at what could not be helped."

"Peagoose," he retorted, the lingering mirth in his eyes quite taking her breath away. "If the culmination of our orgy came too soon, it is precisely because you performed your part only too well, Theodora. But you are right to feel disappointed. You are, after all, a woman of extreme passion, who deserves better than to be left less than satisfied." Lowering his head, he kissed the corner of her mouth. "A circumstance which I shall take immediate steps to remedy."

It was on Theodora's tongue to retort that it was not at all necessary to exert himself on her account, but his mouth silenced hers in a slow, sensuous caress that utterly banished the thought. Nor was that all or the least of it. Freeing her of the silk chemise and her other things, he moved his hands over her body in such a manner as to totally scatter her thoughts. With a long sigh, she gave in to the melting warmth that his hands and his lips aroused in her.

Carried on a delirious wave of pleasure, she was only vaguely aware when Styles parted her legs and lowered his head to her. The moist warmth of his caress on her tender bud was not only unexpected but quite took her breath away.

"Styles?" she uttered on a keening gasp. Her eyes widened with shock and a wholly exquisite pleasure.

"Trust me, Theodora," Styles murmured thickly. With his tongue, he caressed her. "Soon you will have your orgy."

"Yes, Styles." Theodora shuddered, thinking she must surely die from the pleasurable sensations he was arousing in her. "Please! Please do not stop."

Nothing could stop him now. Nothing, that was, but his own untimely demise, Styles reflected with something of a wry sense of wonder at himself. Theodora wielded a witch's power. Having inflamed him to a point of losing his self-control, she now inspired him to new and greater heights. Where only a few minutes earlier he had felt impossibly drained and heavy with lethargy, he now found himself once again hard with need. And Theodora was very close to reaching the orgy of pleasure earlier denied her.

Feeling her arch in a frantic attempt to capture that which seemed just beyond her reach, he moved quickly to grasp the moment.

Theodora uttered a bewildered cry as Styles, counter to her pleas, abruptly ceased what he had been doing. Flinging himself down on his back, he drew her to him, lifting her as she came until she straddled his thighs.

"Now, Enchantress," he breathed, his eyes mere slits of fire. "You have brought us to this. If it is an orgy you wish, you must make it happen."

Theodora stared at him in flustered uncertainty. "I?" she queried. "But, Styles, I cannot think this is at all fair. I don't know how—"

"You are a scientist with all the apparatus you need before you." Styles gasped and gritted his teeth as Theodora's belly came into contact with his swollen member. "You *know*, Theodora. For God's sake, do not delay overlong in indecision."

Theodora, faced with a problem in logic, was not slow to see its solution or the unique possibilities inherent in its execution. Lifting herself with her hands braced against his chest, she fitted the head of his magnificent shaft to her woman's opening.

"Are you quite certain this is the proper manner to conduct an orgy, my lord?" she asked, a wicked gleam in her green witch's eyes. "It would seem to confer a certain advantage not normally conferred on the female of the species."

A decided thrill shot through her at the leap of fire in his eyes.

"An advantage which is a double-edged sword at best," growled the Devil's Cub. Clasping her waist with his hands, he held her poised at the pinnacle of his manhood. "And at the very least illusory." He pulled her down and thrust sharply upward, burying his shaft in her.

Theodora's mouth parted on a gasp of pleasure as her flesh closed around him, snug and warm and intensely exciting. "But it is not at all illusory," she informed him. Her eyes glowed with the wonder of a woman's knowledge. She lifted herself off him, arching her back, then deliberately lowered herself. A shudder shook the Devil's Cub's powerful frame, sending waves of delirious joy through Theodora. "We are a perfect fit, you and I."

"Witch," uttered Styles, grimly aware that Theodora was the only woman who had ever breached his formidable defenses, the only person who had ever glimpsed behind the mask he wore for all the rest of the world. It was not something he would normally have risked. And yet, Theodora held the darkness at bay. With Theodora he was not alone. By God, that was worth any risk, he thought, thrusting himself into her.

Theodora gave a low cry. Her flesh clenched on his in a bursting shudder of release. Styles rode the wave with her, marveling at her generosity. She was an enchantress who had yet to learn the full extent of her power over him—or what she gave so freely to him. A pity she would never come to love him or know the empty void she had filled, he thought with a sudden pang of regret as he thrust powerfully one last time and spilled his seed into her.

The supper that had been laid out for them was forgotten as, with the last of his strength, Styles drew Theodora down to his side. Pulling the sheet up over their nakedness, he wrapped an arm around her waist.

"Theodora," he murmured after a moment, his voice thick with sated passion, "about this afternoon's excursion to the wine cellar."

"Yes, Styles?" queried Theodora, her head pillowed most satisfyingly against Styles's shoulder.

"Though I applaud your enthusiasm for your new duties, I should prefer you stay clear of the tower."

"The tower?" Theodora, even in her state of utter content-ment, experienced a sharp pang of dismay. She had been look-ing most in particularly forward to exploring the most ancient part of the castle. "But why?"

"It is enough that I wish it," Styles replied, in no state for an argument. "And that I have no desire to discuss it," he added judiciously, feeling himself slipping into a gloriously exhausted slumber.

"Very well, Styles," Theodora responded. "I promise I shall give your request my careful consideration."

She was answered by a faint, but unmistakable snore.

Smiling Theodora lay still, listening to Styles's slow, measured breathing. Not in her wildest flights of fancy had she ever come close to imagining what it would be like to lie, her passions utterly sated, in the arms of the Devil's Cub. Never had she felt so blissfully contented before, she mused, smiling in wonder at herself. Orgies, she decided, were truly magnificent events, which should be celebrated on a regular basis—every couple of months or so. She doubted not that to do so much more often than that must surely serve to dangerously deplete one's inner resources. But then, making love with the Devil's Cub must always be an orgy—a wonderful, glorious orgy. She, after all, loved him unreservedly; and one day, no matter how long it might take, she would bring Styles to love her, she told herself, as she hovered blissfully between wakefulness and sleep.

The candle by the bedside had guttered and gone out when Theodora was thoroughly aroused to awareness by Styles, shifting his weight on the bed. With a bewildered sense of loss, she felt him rise, heard him swiftly donning his dressing gown. He was leaving. Why? No doubt she had been a fool to allow fancy to conjure a picture of herself awakening in the morning to Styles with rumpled hair and sleep-filled eyes. Indeed, she told herself she had hoped for too much to think he might be moved to kiss her awake or that that might be the first step in initiating something even more intimate. He, after all, was the Devil's Cub, who had experienced any number of orgies with women of far greater allure and experience than anything to which she could lay claim. And he had made it plain that he could not love her. It was patently absurd to expect him to wish to linger in her bed.

Theodora experienced an ache in her throat as she sensed Styles come to the bedside to stand for a long moment gazing down at her. Prompted by some instinct she did not fully understand, she feigned sleep, wondering that he was oblivious to the furious pounding of her heart. When at last she heard his soft footfalls retreat across the room, followed by the click of the latch as the door opened and closed, she sat up in the bed. The bed covers pulled to her breast, she listened to the muffled sounds issuing from his room, adjoined to hers. Only then did she realize that his leaving had little or nothing to do with her.

He was pacing, prowling about the room with the restlessness of a caged animal. It was the lingering effects of the malady. Anxiety-induced insomnia would not be uncommon in cases of this kind. After all, he was convinced he was going mad. Then, too, with certain agents that precipitated hallucinations and delirium, one could expect recurring symptoms days, sometimes even weeks, after ingestion. Theodora recalled reported cases in which subjects who had survived particularly strong doses of extract of morning glory seeds had demonstrated fits of madness as long as two years after apparent recovery.

Theodora went suddenly rigid with apprehension at the sound of a door opening and closing. Heedless of her natural state, she slipped out of bed and flew to her door. Opening it enough to peer around the corner, she was in time to see Styles, dressed in riding clothes, a black cloak billowing around his tall figure, stride down the hall to the staircase.

Damn the man's obstinacy! fumed Theodora, retracing her steps to the bedroom. She did not doubt for a moment that, driven by his own cursed demons, he meant to ride Erebus in reckless abandon across the moors until he had exhausted both himself and his horse. It was very likely something she might choose to do were she in his shoes. It was, however, so patently unnecessary.

"If he could only bring himself to trust me!" she declared to Percival, who was valiantly attempting to distract her by rubbing against her ankle. Bending down, she picked the kitten up. "He might have saved himself a great deal of grief, Percival. You know very well that he might," she said sternly to the kitten, who, hanging loosely in her grasp, purred happily back at her. "And me a thankless night spent worrying about him." Really, it was too much, she fretted, plopping down on the bed. She and Styles could have been ever so much more comfortable snuggled cozily together beneath the bedcovers.

"It is up to us to remedy the situation, Percival." Laying her head down, she set the kitten on the empty pillow beside her. "I am exceedingly fond of you, Percival. You know that I am. But if you think I am content to spend my nights alone in your company, you are very much mistaken. I am a witch, and I am not averse to employing whatever means I deem necessary to achieve my ends. It is only for Styles's own good, after all."

At last, pulling the counterpane up over her against the chill in the room, Theodora began to plot her strategy.

Eight

Styles descended one side of the two identical curving staircases that converged in the New Hall, part of the additions made to the castle by the twenty-second Earl of Styles in the seventeenth century. Met with the mingled scents of lilacs, roses and something vaguely resembling cinnamon, he smiled faintly to himself. It would seem the twenty-seventh Countess of Styles had been busy again at making her own additions to Devil's Keep.

Theodora's first action as chatelaine of the keep had been to have removed all the more unsightly mementos of past ages. The George I silver épergne, standing three feet in height and dubiously depicting a pack of dogs savaging a wild boar, and a prized stuffed grizzly that evoked memories of a previous earl's sojourn in the Americas, among other items of questionable taste, had found their way to the attics. The red damask drapes in the hall had suffered a similar fate. Substituting a flowered drape of cream-colored caffoy had lent an atmosphere of light and air to the formerly oppressive elegance of the great room. She had, in fact, through the vehicle of wild flowers arranged in vases, plants in pots, and a varied assortment of dried herbs in wicker baskets of various sizes and shapes, brought an unmistakable flavor of Cliff House with her into her new home with dramatic results. The keep had begun to exude an air of domesticity that he had thought never to see in the gloomy old pile in which he had spent his boyhood.

Theodora, it seemed had the faculty for banishing gloom wherever she went. She had unmistakably worked her influence over the household staff. Gaspard, the French chef, not only exerted himself to incorporate an endless variety of herbs into recipes designed for the sole purpose of delighting his new mistress, but had taken as well to sending up to the countess's familiar on a daily basis a plate of choice delicacies meant to please the most fastidious of feline tastes. Mrs. Gill had been heard to declare to Mrs. Dickson that a new day had dawned at Devil's Keep when the master had taken himself Lady Theodora to wed. Even Renfield, reflected Styles in sardonic amusement—the venerable butler positively beamed whenever Theodora breezed into his presence, nor could Styles mistake the decided improvement in his old retainer's appearance. The scraggly wisps of hair that sprouted from the bald pate had been noticeably cut close to the head and further subdued with a judicious application of pomade, an alteration that Styles doubted not could be laid at Theodora's door. It appeared that everyone from the plethora of freckled, redhaired Dicksons to the lowliest scullery maid positively doted on the new young countess.

The truth was that Theodora's influence permeated the castle, transforming it until it hardly bore a resemblance to the formerly dreary house of Dameron. Styles would not have been surprised had Aunt Philippa come forward to pronounce the ancient ghosts of the keep quite utterly banished.

Theodora's influence over himself, he found just as remarkable and not a little thought-provoking. Not only had he become resigned to sharing his wife's bed with a feline that had unaccountably formed a bias for sleeping on Styles's feet, but he was becoming daily more inured to discovering adulterating substances in his morning cup of coffee. Beyond these previously unimaginable changes in his life, he was finding that he actually liked to listen to Theodora pratter on over breakfast about the Hemphill twins' odd penchant for developing spots at the least little thing, or Mrs. Fennelworth's discovery of what gave every evidence of having been a prowler in the vicinity of her henhouse.

No doubt his tolerance for topics for which he had never previously entertained the remotest interest was a clear indication that he was indeed losing a grip on his sanity, Styles reflected ironically as he exited the keep and swung astride his waiting mount. Certainly he found himself questioning his own rationale as he departed the bailey and deliberately took the little-used track that would take him by way of Devil's Gill to Weycombe Mere. He had, after all, been content never again to have to set foot in the village. He had, that was, until he had fallen under the spell of a white witch of the healing arts who had not hesitated to disrupt his ordered existence and divert him from other, more melancholy preoccupations.

Lifting Erebus into a canter, he resigned himself to what promised to be a less than gratifying morning revisiting the village that had taken no little pleasure in damning the last of the Devil's Cubs.

Humming softly, Theodora poured a teaspoonful of hazelnut oil into a bottle already containing a like amount of wheat germ oil, after which, she filled the bottle nearly to the top with oil of grapeseed. To this she added neroli, basil, lavender, and chamomile and gently stirred with a glass rod until the ingredients were thoroughly blended. Dropping a glass stopper in the mouth of the bottle, she carefully labeled and dated the blend before setting the bottle aside.

A smile touched her lips as she considered the unexpected benefits to be derived from nightly applications of the aromatic oils. Initially, it was true, Styles had not been exactly receptive to the idea of submitting himself to her hands. But then, she had to admit in all fairness that he had not precisely been prepared, when he rose from his bath, to discover his wife instead of Thistlewaite standing, ready and waiting with a towel in hand.

Strange, she mused whimsically. She had never considered the possibility that the Devil's Cub might be discomposed at having the privacy of his bath invaded by a woman, especially a woman who was his wife. His sentiments, however, had been made all too obvious.

"Theodora, good God," he had growled, ignoring the towel in favor of his dressing gown. "You will kindly explain what the devil you are doing here. And where the bloody hell is Thistlewaite?"

"It is very simple, really." Theodora favored him with quizzically arched eyebrows. "I sent Thistlewaite away. After all, I could not think his presence would be required, since I intend to give you a rubdown. However, if you want him back—?"

To describe his look as dumbfounded might, she reflected, have been putting it rather too mildly. "A rubdown. Good God. Is that what you informed Thistlewaite was your purpose?"

It had come to her then that he was unsettled at what his austere gentleman's gentleman might construe as a flagrant breach of conduct. The relationship between a gentleman and his valet, after all, was not one to be lightly trifled with.

"There is not the slightest reason for you to be concerned, Styles," she hastened to assure him. "Thistlewaite, after all, is a grown man. No doubt he understands perfectly."

"Oh, you may be sure of it. You, however, it appears, do not. Bloody hell, Theodora, a woman does not come barging in on her husband's bath uninvited and unannounced. Not unless she wishes to apprise the entire household of what does not concern them."

"I wish you will not be absurd, Styles. Thistlewaite is the very soul of discretion. He will not breathe a word of this to anyone, I promise. Now, do stop ripping up at me. You will only bring to nothing all the good that your bath has done for you," she had added, noting the ominous bulge of muscle along the lean line of his jaw. "In order to benefit fully from the treatment, one should ideally be relaxed."

A strong, masculine arm closed without warning about Theodora's waist and pulled her irresistibly close. "Then I suggest that ideally," Styles murmured, lowering his head to sample the exquisitely sensitive flesh of her neck below her ear, "the subject should be given the opportunity beforehand to determine whether or not he wishes to undergo the treatment."

Smiling, Theodora tilted her head back. "Not in this case, my lord. I, after all, am your very own personal healer," she did not hesitate to remind him. "It was, if you recall, one of the reasons I agreed to marry you. This," she said, firmly disengaging herself from him, "can wait until after. Right now, I want you to come and lie down. I promise not to eat you. You might even find the experience to your liking before we are through."

Even after playing her trump card, however, it had still taken all Theodora's patience and not a little feminine persuasion to overcome Styles's resistance to the idea of submitting himself totally into her hands. After all, to lie naked and vulnerable while giving oneself over to the physical manipulations of another was not the sort of thing that came easily to a man like the Devil's Cub. It had been an act of the greatest sort of trust, Theodora saw now, as, alone in her herbarium, she looked back over the incident. He had given in with poor grace and only after grimly extracting from Theodora a promise of reciprocal treatment at his hands, to which she had subsequently given herself wholeheartedly.

Theodora's smile deepened. The Devil's Cub had soon changed his tune. The oils, chosen for their soothing as well as their therapeutic properties, had worked wonders. They had not only served to reduce certain disruptive elements in the harmonic balance of the Devil's Cub's humors, but they had proven to be uncommonly stimulating in purely pleasurable pursuits as well. The past four weeks of nightly applications had been attended almost without exception by subsequent, enthusiastic research in applied areas of human biology—and with truly remarkable results.

Styles, she had come to suspect, might very well have met her fifth and final condition. It was very possible she was increasing.

The thought suffused Theodora with happiness and not a little awe. Indeed, she could not imagine how she managed to keep her secret from Styles, who, she doubted not, would do better to remain in ignorance of it, at least until there was no longer any question she was right. It seemed to her that he need only look to see the happiness radiating from her. But then, men tended to be blinded to such things by their preoccupation with purely masculine pursuits, and certainly Styles was no exception to the rule, mused Theodora with a whimsical twist of her lips.

In spite of the indisputable fact that the weeks had brought them closer together than she had ever dared to imagine, she could not but sense that Styles persisted in maintaining a barrier of aloofness between them. It was, she suspected, his way of protecting her from things he considered unsuitable for a female to know. After all, it was the same sort of absurd masculine logic that, maintaining a woman's sensibilities were too delicate for the less than pleasant environs of the sickroom, had barred her from becoming a doctor.

It had not, however, prevented her from pursuing her own carefully prescribed treatment with Styles with the utmost confidence of achieving his full recovery. And while she was not completely dissatisfied with the results, she found herself baffled by her most significant failure. In spite of everything, she had not as yet found a way to dispel the disruptive influences that disturbed the Devil's Cub's dreams and robbed him of his sleep.

From the very beginning, she had been acutely sensitive of the brooding restlessness that drove him night after night from her bed to seek solace on the moors or in the study with a decanter of brandy. In time, however, it had become increasingly obvious to her that the black moods owed their source to something other than the effects of the poison, which, after all, had long since been expelled from his system.

His, she very much feared, was a torment of the soul, and while herbs alone would go a long way toward returning him to a harmonic balance, they might not be enough to free him of his own, personal demons.

It had come to her only the night before, as she lay watching Styles drift into a dream that made him twitch and break into a sweat, that the final solution lay in discovering the mysterious source of the Devil's Cub's torment, the clue to which—since he had not, presumably, been troubled in a like manner before he returned to Devil's Keep—must surely reside in the castle itself. It was only logical that she had thought immediately of employing the aid of her Aunt Philippa. After all, she had reasoned, who better than one well versed in the nonphysical realm of being to determine the root cause of the Devil's Cub's personal nightmares?

To that end, she had not hesitated to send Tom Dickson to Cliff House that very morning with an invitation for Aunt Philippa to come for a visit. It was unfortunate that her aunt had been away from home, a circumstance that Theodora found extremely odd, to say the least. Philippa, in her six months' sojourn at her brother's house, had categorically refused to call on her neighbors, claiming that to do so would be far too fatiguing for one of her delicately honed sensibilities.

"You know how I should be besieged, Theodora," she was used to say, inevitably with a shudder. "If only Lavinia had not passed beyond the veil, I should perhaps have learned in time how to erect protective barriers around myself. As it is, I cannot bear to be exposed willy-nilly to the spiritual emanations of everyone, living and dead, with whom I come in contact, Theodora. You know that I cannot. I should soon find myself a candidate for Bedlam."

Theodora had not pressed the matter then. Philippa needed time to adjust to her new state, she had told herself. It could not be easy for her aunt to pick up the threads of her life after the loss of her dearest friend and companion of twenty years. Now, in spite of the fact that she could not but be disappointed at being denied Philippa's help when she most wanted it, she was pleased that the older woman had found the courage to at least leave the house.

Theodora consoled herself with the knowledge that Styles was making progress in his recovery. He was doing so well, in fact, that she must soon reduce the amounts of his daily doses of ginseng, blended with a mixture of other rejuvenating herbs, which she slipped in his morning coffee, she reflected, turning back to her work. Retrieving from a shelf a sealed container of dried roots, leaves, and flowers, she began to distribute the mixture in wooden bowls while she continued to assess the Devil's Cub's recuperation. The improvements in Styles were not precisely of a medical nature, she realized of course. Indeed, they had little to do with symptoms one might record in a medical journal. They were, nevertheless, quite real and tangible to one blessed with acute empathic powers of perception.

Her fingers, moving through the dried herbs, releasing the fragrance of rose petals, lavender, sweet myrtle, bay and bergamot into the air, suddenly stilled. Styles had begun to laugh, that same rich, wonderfully vibrant sound the memory of which had haunted her since she was a child of ten. In addition, he was showing a distinct tendency to linger in her company after meals and the intimacy of love-making. And the brooding look she had glimpsed all too often for her own peace of mind seemed rather less pronounced of late.

Perhaps most significant of all, however, the previous night he had not left her, as was his usual custom when he judged she was safely asleep, but had remained in her bed until well after midnight.

It was all very curious, the strange notions that went through one's mind, Theodora reflected. As she had watched over Styles in slumber, sleep and the spill of moonlight through the window had seemed to transform him, softening the harsh lines of his face. For a few moments he had seemed more the youth who had captured her childish imagination and stolen her heart long ago in the churchyard and less the cynical man of the world. To her dismay, she had felt a painful lump swell in her throat at all that had been taken from him—his youthful illusions, the idealism that must once have been so much a part of him, his very trust in people and his own emotions. But how absurd, she had instantly scolded herself even as she resisted the urge to brush a stray lock of hair from his forehead for fear that she might awaken him. Nothing had been taken from him. Whatever he had been made to suffer had only served to make him the man he was, and that was all that really mattered, when one went to the heart of the matter.

The youthful Caleb Dameron might indeed have won her heart, but it was the Devil's Cub who had initiated her into the mysteries of love. Aside from her determination to return him to health and in spite of his damnably stubborn pride which prevented him from placing his trust in her, she would not have had him the least whit different.

Nevertheless she sighed, thinking things would be a deal simpler if only he could be made to accept that his life was in danger. As it was, he was proving uncommonly resistant to the idea that someone had tried to poison him. He refused, in fact, even to discuss the possibility with Theodora, who lived in constant dread that her vigilance would not be enough to save him should the poisoner strike again.

Blast his stubbornness! she fumed. For a man of strong intellect, he was behaving in a remarkably irrational manner. It was almost as if he believed in all the silly nonsense about being cursed by the devil. Theodora, however, did not believe in it. She was far too practical minded ever to accept anything so preposterous. Furthermore, she was damned if she would let him go to the devil in a handbasket. If he would do nothing to save himself, he left her no alternative, but to take matters into her own hands. Unfortunately, she had made little headway in discovering who had tried to poison him, she conceded with a troubled frown. Indeed, the culprit would seem to be diabolically clever.

Still, what she had accomplished in just four weeks' time was not insignificant. She had managed, after all, to discover three additional contaminated bottles of port; and, though she could not determine the exact poison they contained, she had eliminated the possibilities of strychnine, arsenic, and potassium cyanide and narrowed the field down through logic and careful experimentation to a handful of poisonous herbs whose symptoms included a high fever, headache, and mental aberrations on the order of hallucinations. She had, as a result, instituted a therapeutic regimen of herbs designed to counteract the poison's harmful effects and to build Styles's resistance to foreign substances of a toxic nature. Whether he knew it or not, he was completely recovered from his last bout. It was the possibility of a next one that worried Theodora. Unfortunately, when one got right down to it, there was little to offer in the way of protection against a lethal dose of poison, save to prevent the poisoning itself. And the only certain way to achieve that end was to expose and apprehend the guilty party before the villain could make another attempt.

It always came round to that, thought Theodora with a sigh as she began to gather up the finished bowls of potpourri for the keep. So far as she had been able to discover, Styles had had only three visitors since his return, and only one of these, Mr. Johnathan Franklidge, the earl's man of affairs, had called before her fateful encounter with Styles in Devil's Gill. Logically, that would seem to eliminate Justin Villiers, she reasoned, as well as the mysterious Mr. Jerome Whitfill, who, in spite of the fact that he had apparently failed to make a favorable impression on the earl's staff, had clearly arrived after the fact.

Still, Theodora mused, it would not hurt to discover what she could about Mr. Whitfill's background and his association with Styles. Thus far the only thing she had been able to learn about the man was that he apparently served in the capacity of some sort of agent in various of the earl's business transactions. That, and the fact that Renfield had stumbled on Mr. Whitfill snooping about the kitchen larder, she added, with a thoughtful purse of the lips. It would seem rather farfetched to suppose anyone would choose to contaminate the castle's foodstuffs in an attempt to poison one man. Very likely, such a ploy would succeed only in killing off the cook and any of the members of the kitchen staff unfortunate enough to sample the various dishes for the proper seasoning. Not only would he have failed in his purpose, but such an event would be sure to invite a deal of unwelcome speculation. No, it was far more logical to suppose that Mr. Whitfill's purpose had been to gain access to the wine cellar, the stairs to which were in the same general vicinity as the larder. Perhaps he had managed the thing before, using a duplicate key or even a lock pick. Whatever the case, his name, along with those of Franklidge and Thistlewaite, the earl's valet, comprised Theodora's slender list of candidates.

Johnathan Franklidge, she had yet to meet and had, consequently, formed only the vaguest impression of the man. The youngest son of an impoverished nobleman, he had attended Eton contemporaneously with the earl and was apparently as near as anyone had ever come to gaining a position of trust with his employer. Not the sort, one would think, to wish to put a period to the Devil's Cub, Theodora reflected, placing the blend of oils and bowls of pot pourri into a wicker basket. And as for Thistlewaite, she had discovered one might as well fling oneself against a brick wall as to try and breach the impregnable facade of one of those vastly superior beings known as a "gentleman's gentleman."

Barricaded behind a veritable fortress of civility and circumspection, he had confessed to having been with the earl from the time Styles left his shortcoats and to being, as a consequence, greatly attached to his lordship. Other than that tidbit of information, he had parried her every attempt to break past his formidable guard with the finesse of a seasoned dueller.

Theodora was, consequently, more than a little surprised to look up from her worktable to find the valet poised uncertainly in the open door to her herbarium.

"Mr. Thistlewaite," she exclaimed, nearly upsetting the basket. "Faith, but you startled me."

"I beg your pardon, my lady," intoned Thistlewaite, a slightly built man past middle age with thinning grey hair combed straight back from the forehead. He was, furthermore, immaculately clad in the subdued coat and trousers that identified him as one of those august personages, a gentleman's gentleman. "It was not my intent to take you unawares. The—er—door was open."

"Yes, of course." Theodora favored the valet with an understanding smile. "I often leave the door open when I am working. At Cliff House my herbarium looks out over the sea. Here, I sometimes feel I have taken up residence in a gloomy old cavern."

"Still, perhaps you would not mind my saying that you have done wonders with the tower room, my lady," replied Thistlewaite, his gaze wandering over the roomy chamber made both colorful and fragrant by herbs hanging from the ceiling to dry and by potted plants thriving in the late afternoon sunshine. He seemed peculiarly fascinated by the shelves filled with glass containers of roots, stems, flowers, and seeds, Theodora noted in amusement, and perhaps a trifle wary of her cauldron, which, when suspended in the fireplace, was used in making up potions and elixirs. He looked askance at her great wooden worktable littered with glass crucibles, bottles, and all the other accoutrements that made up an herbalist's workshop. No doubt he, like so many others, had expected to find her, bent over the cauldron, chanting spells over a noxious concoction of toads, bat dung, and any number of other unspeakable ingredients.

"Was there something about which you wished to speak to

me, Mr. Thistlewaite?" she gently prodded, when it seemed he might be tempted to bolt from her presence.

Thistlewaite nervously cleared his throat. "I—as a matter of fact, my lady, there was a small matter I wished to discuss with you in the hopes that you would not take exception to what might be considered by some as an impertinence on my part."

"You have my assurance that I shall not think any such thing," Theodora answered, aware of a small tingle of excitement at this unexpected visit. "Pray do not be afraid to open the budget, Mr. Thistlewaite. Won't you come in and have a seat?"

Bowing, Thistlewaite entered, but did not take the seat on the bench to which Theodora waved him. "You are, as I have come to note, exceedingly gracious, my lady. Indeed, I have come to note many things since you came to Devil's Keep, not the least of which is the beneficial effect you have had on His Lordship. Dare I go so far as to confess that I have observed you administer certain drops in his lordship's morning coffee?"

"You are, to say the least, keen-sighted, Mr. Thistlewaite," Theodora observed dryly, wondering if the man had been intentionally spying on her.

Thistlewaite's expression remained maddeningly unaltered. "I have," he said, "taken it upon myself to keep my eyes open, since I first began to suspect His Lordship was in perilous waters, my lady. I have come to the conclusion that your intentions toward His Lordship are clearly to his good. It is the reason I have dared to approach you. To offer you my services in any way that will benefit His Lordship. I believe you are not unaware of the troubles he has suffered lately."

"Styles has been ill," Theodora stated quietly. "But then, you know that better than I. You have seen him in the throes of the malady, haven't you, Mr. Thistlewaite."

Mr. Thistlewaite had, he confessed, been deeply troubled by a radical change in the earl's mental state, which he had perceived as coming on suddenly in the form of fits of delirium.

"The first incident occurred on the third Friday of January, my lady," Thistlewaite confided in his ponderous manner. "Following Lady Gale's dinner party. I remember because His Lordship had been away for some time on one of his—er—extended absences. It occurred to me at the time that his sojourn from home could not have been a particularly easy one for His Lordship."

"Indeed?" murmured Theodora, sensing a significance in the fact that Styles not only made it a practice to vanish for lengthy periods of time, but that he apparently chose to do so unaccompanied by his valet. "What do you mean by 'easy,' Mr. Thistlewaite?"

"I believe I can say without undue pride that I have been the envy of many a gentleman's gentleman for my service to His Lordship, who, as I am certain you have noted, is a splendid figure of a man. Indeed, I could not ask for a better gentleman to dress. Upon his return, however, I could not but remark that the fit of his clothing lacked something of its previous perfection."

"Styles had lost weight," Theodora was quick to interpolate.

"He had the appearance of a man who had been subjected to a rigorous physical regimen," agreed Thistlewaite, his narrow somewhat pinched features expressive of disapproval.

"And who had had neither the time nor the inclination to indulge in regular meals, one must presume," speculated Theodora in tacit sympathy with the manservant.

"He has ever been the sort who, once his interest is engaged, immerses himself wholly in whatever project he undertakes."

"Indeed," Theodora nodded sagely, "he is a man of strong inclinations and unshakable dedication."

"I see you apprehend perfectly His Lordship's singular nature, my lady. In any case, I recall the specific day of Lady Gale's dinner party because it was on the evening of His Lordship's arrival home, and it was obvious to anyone who knows him as I do that he was not overly pleased at the thought of going out. Indeed, I am of the opinion that he would have cried off had he not anticipated the presence of someone at Lady Gale's table whom he wished particularly to engage in conversation."

"A woman?" queried Theodora perhaps too sharply. She was conscious of a peculiar stab near the vicinity of her breastbone.

"As to that, I'm afraid I couldn't say, my lady," Thistlewaite replied circumspectly. "He returned home at precisely twelve past eleven. I was waiting up as I always do. I perceived at once that His Lordship was out of frame, though at the time I attributed his condition to his having made indentures."

"A natural supposition in the circumstances," Theodora commented. "Had it been His Lordship's custom to dip deeply?"

Thistlewaite answered stiffly. "Until recently, I had seldom known His Lordship to go beyond his limits. He is a man who knows how to hold his drink. On this particular occasion, I took into consideration the fatigue I had earlier noted."

Theodora nodded, liking the man for his loyalty to his master. "Something subsequently happened, however, which changed your mind."

"Indeed, my lady," Thistlewaite responded with something vaguely resembling a pained expression. "He informed me in terms quite unlike his customary manner that my services were not required."

"He consigned you to the devil, in other words," interpreted Theodora with a faint, understanding smile.

"I'm afraid I dare not repeat his exact words," confessed Thistlewaite. "It was obvious he was not himself. Indeed, he appeared to be suffering the headache and I am almost certain he was in a high fever. I should even go so far as to say he was delirious. He seemed obsessed with the notion that there was someone else in the room. I confess I was uncertain how to proceed."

"You were understandably alarmed. After all, even under the best of circumstances, you are hardly up to His Lordship's weight. Naturally, you did the sensible thing. You adhered to his demands."

Thistlewaite spread wide his hands in a helpless gesture. "I left him, my lady. What else could I do?"

"Nothing, Mr. Thistlewaite, except what you did do. You sent for the doctor, did you not?"

"Not then," the valet confessed. "I knew His Lordship could not wish to be seen in such a state. I waited outside the door until I heard the demise of the brandy decanter."

"His Lordship broke it."

"He flung it against the wall. It was empty, you see."

"Perfectly, Mr. Thistlewaite," Theodora assured him, walking a pace before turning back again. "After which, you waited until all activity had ceased in His Lordship's chamber."

"Yes, my lady. When everything was quiet, I entered the room to find him, fully dressed and stretched across the bed, asleep."

"Unconscious, I should think," Theodora corrected grimly. "And then what did you do?"

"I made His Lordship as comfortable as I could in the circumstances. Upon which, I remained at his bedside until morning."

"I see. Very commendable, Mr. Thistlewaite," Theodora applauded. "And what were his symptoms upon awakening?"

"Not a great deal different from those of one suffering the after effects of an overindulgence of wine. He is hardly the sort to wear his emotions for others to see, but I could tell he was troubled."

"And was His Lordship never examined by a doctor?"

"His Lordship would not have it. Not then. It was not until after the second such incident three nights later that he at last consulted a physician under the strictest secrecy."

"And what was the diagnosis? Pray do not be afraid to confide in me, Mr. Thistlewaite," she added, when the valet noticeably hesitated. "I am His Lordship's wife. I must know everything if I am to be of help to him. And I can help him,

I promise you. I am very good at making people well. Now. You do know what the doctor told His Lordship, Mr. Thistlewaite. Don't you."

"He said it was an accumulation of humors on the brain, my lady, for which he deemed surgery was necessary to alleviate the condition. Indeed, he was most insistent. He stated he would not be held responsible for the consequences in the event His Lordship failed to do the sensible thing."

"The devil he did!" exclaimed Theodora in such a manner as to cause a distinct crack in the valet's normally unshakable composure. Furiously she began to pace. "Accumulation of humors indeed. Needless to say His Lordship expressed his refusal in no uncertain terms. And now he has *that* burden to carry around with him along with everything else. Good God, what a parcel of nonsense!"

"Begging your pardon, my lady," Thistlewaite interjected, "but am I wrong in thinking that you do not concur with the doctor's diagnosis?"

Theodora turned with flashing eyes on the manservant. "You are not in the least wrong, Mr. Thistlewaite," she declared with fierce and utter conviction. "His Lordship is in perfect health and will remain so with our help. Styles was suffering the ill-effects of drinking wine that had been deliberately poisoned."

"Poisoned, my lady?" echoed the manservant, showing a distinct tendency to give way to a sudden weakness in the knees. "Are you certain?"

"I am most definitely, Mr. Thistlewaite. Which is why I have been taking certain precautions to insure that it does not happen again. You could be of immeasurable help to me in my endeavors."

Thistlewaite, who was still struggling with the news that his employer was the victim of a dire plot, withdrew a linen handkerchief and mopped his brow. "Naturally I should do whatever I can, my lady, though I confess I am not quite certain of what use I might be."

"But it is obvious, is it not? You have only to continue to keep your eyes and ears open. I know I can count on you to come to me if you should happen to notice anything suspicious or unusual."

Squaring his shoulders with an air of firm resolve, Thistlewaite looked Theodora straightly in the eye. "You may be certain of it, my lady. I shall watch over His Lordship with the greatest dedication. However," he added, his glance never wavering, "as you cannot have failed to notice, His Lordship is often away from the house. It is then, I fear, that he may be in the greatest danger."

Theodora frowned, sensing that there was more to that gentle reminder than lay on the surface. Could it be that she had drawn the wrong conclusions concerning Styles's midnight rides on the moors? Obviously the valet either knew or suspected a deal more about His Lordship's activities than he was willing to divulge.

Biting her tongue to keep from quizzing the man further, Theodora allowed Thistlewaite to take his leave. Very likely she would only lose what ground she had gained did she try to press him about His Lordship's private affairs. It was enough for now that she had succeeded not only in eliminating Styles's valet from her list of those who fell under the heading of suspicious, but that she had won the manservant over to her small company of archplotters. Not an insignificant achievement, any way one chose to look at it, she decided, especially in light of what the valet had had to tell her.

The devil! she thought. No wonder Styles refused to discuss his condition with her, convinced, as he apparently was, that he was suffering a terminal condition that could only be alleviated by having someone bore through his skull. Good God, no doubt he deserved an extraneous hole in the head for believing anything so patently ridiculous. How dared he to accept willy-nilly the diagnosis of an obvious quack over hers! She no longer marveled that he was bothered by nightmares. She could only wonder if he had planned ever to tell her that he had married her in all expectation of leaving her a widow!

Cynically amused at the stir he was causing, Styles stepped out of the tobacco shop, which carried his favorite blend of snuff, and, strolling past Mrs. Wickerly, the parson's wife, who was engaged in a whispered dialogue with the two Misses Ledbetter, both aging spinsters, touched the brim of his hat.

"Good morning, ladies."

"Indeed, my lord," stammered Mrs. Wickerly, blushing a rosy hue as she dipped a curtsy. "A fine morning," she added. Her plump face, framed in blond curls peeping out from beneath a beehive bonnet of straw trimmed in pink ribbon, turned to follow the earl's tall, elegantly clad form. Styles, mounting his prime bit of blood in a single, effortless movement, was privileged to overhear that he was "undeniably a gentleman of no little distinction, even quite well to look upon if one discounted the harshness of the features." No doubt he took after Lady Gwendolyn, his mama, Miss Penelope Ledbetter postulated, for he had not the look of his father, not with that hair and those eyes. Styles detected a distinct shudder in the spinster's spare frame. Indeed, agreed Miss Agatha, Penelope's sister, the late earl had been fair-haired and quite utterly charming.

Styles, noting numerous heads turn his way, reflected dryly that he rated somewhat below the traveling circus as an object of interest and perhaps a little above the daily arrival of the Bristol ferry at the Weycombe dock. With a faint, ironic smile on his lips, he lifted Erebus into a walk along the Village High Road with its jumble of small, quaint shops clustered on one side and the village green on the other.

He had come on a whim, whose birth, he did not doubt, he owed to his wife's insistence that he would be welcomed in Weycombe Mere in the manner of some long lost prodigal son. While he had not been received precisely with open arms, aside from the predictable buzz of conversations, quickly cut off at his approach, and the wary, speculative glances that might be expected for one of his repute who had been away for fifteen years, he had not as yet caused any females to swoon or children to flee in fright at the mere sight of him. Mr. Silas Mudd, the tobacconist, had even gone so far as to express the opinion that Miss Theodora had done the village proud. Not a soul, it seemed, had ever thought to see one of their own accorded the distinction of being wed to the Devil's Cub.

No doubt he owed it to Theodora that the villagers appeared to have awarded him what amounted to at least a temporary reprieve for his past, alleged crimes. He found the notion revealing and not a little amusing. Obviously, in spite of her eccentricities, Theodora's credit was sufficient in Weycombe Mere to carry even the Devil's Cub.

Considering the number of calls she made to treat the various ills of the local inhabitants and the fact that she exacted nothing in payment, it would have been surprising had it been otherwise, Styles could not but reflect. The new Countess of Styles was so greatly in demand, that he had been forced to curtail her house calls to the hours of daylight. Far from being gratified at her popularity, he would gladly have wished her entire clientele to the devil or, barring that extremity, had come to the point of contemplating removing with her to London for the Season.

He smiled sardonically at the thought. Only a month ago he would have considered such a possibility inconceivable. But then, that was before Theodora had worked her magic. He had not once in the past four weeks been visited by the spectres that had previously attended his nights and driven him to accept in spite of his highly developed intellect and skeptical nature that he was the inheritor of the curse that lay on the House of Dameron. Even more importantly, however, Theodora had provided him with a more palatable alternative explanation for his symptoms other than accumulated humors on the brain or inherited madness, either of which had left him with little to look forward to, save an unrewarding end.

A poisoner, good God. What a blind fool he had been not to see it for himself! But then, he had had his own, all too obvious explanation for his fits of madness. After all, he was, as Miss Ledbetter had so aptly pointed out, patterned in the image of his mother. It had taken Theodora's discerning eye and acute empathic powers of perception to see beyond the seemingly obvious.

The possibility that he was the victim of poisoning loomed ever more plausible the longer he remained free of the malady. What was more, such a theory was entirely consistent with certain other accumulating evidence that pointed to the existence of a traitor among his acquaintanceship.

He no longer doubted that someone wanted the Balkan agreements to fail, and obviously that someone was willing to go to any lengths to achieve that end. Which was why Styles could not give Theodora the credit she deserved for pinpointing the most likely cause of his recent ailment. To do so would only serve to involve her in matters about which she was better off remaining in ignorance.

He had come to know his enchantress far too well to suppose she would be content to sit idly by while trusting him to see the thing through to a satisfactory end. She was far more likely to fling herself into reckless pursuit of the culprit's identity without the least knowledge of the dangers inherent in such an undertaking. Which was one more reason to launch her into London Society, he reflected. With Theodora occupied in an endless round of gaieties, he would be free to pursue his own course of action. She should be safe enough, he reasoned, so long as he made certain she did not meddle in matters that did not concern her.

Preoccupied with his own thoughts, Styles failed to notice a slight figure dart into the street from between two carts until he was almost upon the urchin.

"M'lord," said the boy, thrusting a grubby hand up at the

earl. "Someone wishes a private word wi' you. A lady, m'lord, what said to give you this."

Styles, taking the note, twisted in a screw, flipped the boy a coin for his trouble. "What's your name, lad?"

The boy snatched the coin out of the air. "Freddy. Much obliged, m'lord. Knew you was a right 'un the moment I laid eyes on you." Flashing a grin over a scrawny shoulder, the boy spun on his heel and dashed down an alley, leaving Styles to peruse the terse and undoubtedly hastily scrawled message.

"It is imperative we talk," he was informed. "The village crossroads. Pray do not fail me."

"The devil," muttered Styles in no mood for a rendezvous of a questionable nature with a female who would seem to have a penchant for high drama. Impatiently, he quelled a feeling of foreboding to which such a cryptic message must naturally give rise and, lifting the reins, sent the stallion down the street at a trot.

Nine

The crossroads near the village limits skirted the corner of Potter's Field on one side and a wood on the other and lay only a short walk from the tree-bordered drive to Cliff House. Styles should not have been unprepared, in consequence, to discover Theodora's Aunt Philippa, dressed in a sari with an Indian veil of blue silk gauze draped over her head, waiting in fretful anticipation of his arrival.

The devil, he thought.

"My lord," Philippa exclaimed, "thank heavens! I had nearly convinced myself the boy must have missed you, and that would never have done. I am quite certain I could not have borne another five minutes alone in this dreadful place, for if you must know, I had quite forgotten what lay over there," she said, indicating with a shudder the unkempt grounds reserved for the remains of beggars and criminals. "You cannot imagine the clamor I have been made to endure this past thirty minutes. Poor, lost souls. I'm sure I could not be mistaken in thinking my Great-Uncle Clarence was among them. He was hanged, you know, for something so trivial as dabbling in the pirate trade."

"My condolences, ma'am," drawled Styles, stepping down from his horse.

"Not at all." Philippa waved a deprecatory hand. "It was

before my time. I never really knew the man. But it did cause a dreadful fuss in the family."

"Families tend to frown at having their dirty linen hung out before the village green," Styles drawled in sardonic appreciation. Taking the lady's arm in one hand and the reins in the other, he drew Philippa and his mount into the safety of a cover of trees in time to avoid a passing wagon. "No doubt you will pardon my curiosity, ma'am, but I cannot but wonder why you should choose a meeting at the crossroads. You must know I should not have been averse to calling on my wife's aunt at home."

"I know it must seem odd," Philippa conceded, peering out at Styles through the obscuring veil of gauze. "But when I saw you pass the house on your way to the village this morning, I realized I simply had to see you. I could not be certain the boy would find you, and I really could not risk missing you. It seemed the sensible thing, in the circumstances, to wait for you here. What I have to tell you, you see, is of the utmost importance."

"I was sure it was," murmured Styles, thinking "odd" did not begin to describe this tête-à-tête. Unaccountably, he experienced a sudden tautness in the pit of his stomach. "Something concerning Theodora? I should be happy to deliver to her any message you might have for her."

"No. I cannot think that would do at all. What I had in mind was in more of a confidential nature. I'm not precisely certain I should tell even you, but you must see I have to do something. If anything happened to Theodora while I held my tongue, I should never forgive myself."

Styles, who had been disposed until that moment to treat Theodora's eccentric aunt in a tolerant humor, suddenly lost all sense of amusement at the implied threat to Theodora's well-being.

"Perhaps, madam," he suggested in measured accents, "you should allow me to judge what is best for my wife. You may begin by telling me whatever it is that is troubling you."

Philippa, who could not have missed the introduction of a steely edge to her nephew-in-law's soft-spoken manner, gave an uncertain flutter of the hand. "Yes, of course. That would seem to be the most sensible course—since I have got you here." She paused as though reluctant to go on, then, squaring her shoulders, took the plunge. "The thing is I have been in communication with an entity."

"An entity," repeated Styles carefully.

"Yes. A rather persistent essence, who speaks to me in my sleep. Indeed, I cannot tell you how very distressing it has been. To be visited night after night until one cannot look forward to bed with the smallest degree of pleasurable anticipation. You cannot imagine how I have been made to suffer."

"Yes, no doubt," replied Styles, his features assuming a rather ominous wooden expression. "I suggest, however, that we shall both feel a great deal better if you simply tell me straight out what you brought me here to say. You did say it concerned Theodora, did you not."

"You know very well that I did. But then, what you really meant was that I should come directly to the point. Very well, the truth is, I have been made to see that a cloud hangs over Theodora."

"Why, I wonder, am I not surprised?" said Styles, marveling that he had somehow expected something cogent from a woman who chose to appear in public in the guise of an Oriental snake charmer. A cloud, good God. "Is that all?"

Philippa visibly bristled. "But of course it is not all. Though," she paused to reflect, "a cloud in itself is a very serious matter, never to be taken lightly. It is almost always a portent of danger of some sort. The entity, however, was a deal more explicit. I have been visited with images of a most unpleasant nature. Just last night, for instance, I saw myself seated at the table for dinner, only to have Mrs. Tibbets spill a perfectly delightful cooked pheasant off the tray. It lands in a bowl of Bombay punch. Naturally I am upset. After all, she has managed to ruin my dinner, the tablecloth, and my white silk in a most unforgivable manner. Surely I cannot be blamed for bringing her to task for her clumsiness. She, however, has the temerity to claim she was shoved, when there is not another soul in the room. What do you think of that, my lord?"

"How very disobliging of her," Styles was moved to comment in caustic tones. "I fail to see, however, how this concerns Theodora."

"But it is obvious, is it not?" demanded Philippa. "The pheasant was dressed in its feathers. They were blue, the predominant hue in Theodora's aura, which is only as it should be. She is, after all, a gifted healer." She gazed at Styles with an air of expectancy. "Well? Do you see now?"

With an effort Styles held on to his temper. "See what? That the ill-fated bird represents my wife because it is wearing blue feathers?"

"Dear. It sounds all rather silly when you say it," confessed Philippa. "But then, that is the nature of signs and portents. They are never perfectly clear, are they? Which is why I could not go to Theodora herself. Whenever one tries to avoid something glimpsed in one's future, one nearly always does the very thing that brings that future upon one, which must be dreadfully annoying. And though I feel certain Theodora is in no immediate danger of being served up on a platter, I do wish I could bring you to believe me when I say she is even now, at this very moment, in some sort of peril, I feel it."

"But I do believe you," replied Styles, thinking he must truly be losing his mind. Nevertheless, he could not dismiss the distinct feeling of unease that had come over him the past several minutes, the cause for which could probably be as easily attributed to the oncoming headache he had contracted during his dialogue with Theodora's maddeningly eccentric Aunt Philippa as to anything of a supernatural origin. Whatever the case, he was suddenly filled with a cold sense of dread which communicated itself in an overwhelming impatience to be on his way. "You may be equally certain," he assured Philippa, "that I intend to let nothing harm your niece."

Philippa, meeting the cold glitter of demon's eyes, could not doubt it. Indeed, she was very nearly comforted when, a few moments later, Styles, springing to the saddle, left her at her doorstep in a cloud of dust.

Picking up a lighted lantern and her basket, Theodora let herself out of the herbarium, careful to shut and lock the door behind her.

The tower chamber she had taken over for her workroom resided in a section of the keep, which being the oldest, was for the most part unused and seldom visited. These very attributes had attracted Theodora to it in spite of the fact that Styles had all but forbidden her to set foot in the place. Save for Tom Dickson and his son Tommy, and now Thistlewaite, no one else had ever disturbed her in her lonely retreat.

The reasons were obvious. The ancient stone fortress positively exuded an aura of moldering decay. Theodora would not have been in the least surprised to discover it was haunted by a host of dead ancestors of the House of Dameron. She never ceased to expect to encounter around each bend in the spiral staircase a phantom, resplendent in the full regalia of a medieval knight—or perhaps, she reflected soberly, the ghastly spectre of Lady Gwendolyn Dameron, who, confined against her will in the tower room, had affected an escape and flung herself to her death off the gallery on to the paved floor of the Great Hall. Theodora shivered, a reaction she attributed to the chill draughts that ceaselessly prowled the staircase and passageways.

In spite of the fact that March had long since given way to April, the tower remained impervious to the burgeoning influence of spring. The cheerless stone walls and deeply recessed windows seemed to repulse sunlight and warmth as effectively as they had once repelled invaders, reflected Theodora, thinking wistfully of the light and airy environs of Cliff House. She knew why she herself had chosen the less than congenial environs of this part of the keep in which to install her herbarium. It had practically insured that no one would be tempted to bother either her or her work. But why, she could not but wonder, had Lady Gwendolyn apparently favored it, even going so far as to establish her living quarters in the rooms once inhabited by the ancient lords of the keep?

Theodora paused, as she almost never failed to do, on the third-story landing. Lifting the lantern high, she stepped out on to the open gallery and peered down over the balustrade into the great hall a full two stories below. The lantern, swaying from her hand, caused shadows to writhe and dance over the far wall and its muraled stairway like spirits scrambling to escape the light. No doubt they ducked behind the wall-hangings, Theodora reflected humorously at the subtle movement of tapestries, touched by invisible draughts.

Her attention was caught by the dance and shimmer of the lantern light off the rippled surface of water—a Roman fountain Lady Gwendolyn had caused to be installed in the Great Hall in honor of Bacchus, the god of wine. A good ten feet in diameter and perhaps knee-deep, it was not only perfectly hideous in its medieval surroundings, but, fed perpetually by an ingenious system of pipes, was a superlative example of Lady Gwendolyn's extravagance at her son's expense.

Quelling another shiver, Theodora found it difficult to believe that Lady Gwendolyn had liked to entertain guests here, of all places. A less inviting atmosphere for an evening of social intercourse could hardly be imagined. But then, Lady Gwendolyn's notions of entertainment had been something out of the ordinary, Theodora had been informed by no less a personage than Mrs. Gill, the earl's housekeeper of long-standing. The late countess had, as a matter of fact, apparently been in the habit of indulging herself in all manner of excess and vice, very often in the company of a select number of intimates who, in addition to thinking nothing of living lavishly off her at her son's expense, had shared her tastes for the exotic.

It was little wonder that Styles entertained an aversion to

the tower, reflected Theodora, stepping back from the balustrade. Lady Gwendolyn and her friends, besides doing their best to ruin him, could not have been the most ideal company for a youth on the verge of entering manhood. It would have been marvelous indeed had he not been disgusted at his mama's excesses. And then to have her come to an untimely demise under both tragic and uncertain circumstances! Viewed in such a light, it would have been asking a deal too much to expect Styles to have fond feelings for Devil's Keep in general and the tower most in particularly.

In a mood to indulge what Theodora feared was a morbid curiosity, she continued on toward the sharply arched portal at the end of the gallery, which led into what initially had been the living quarters of the lord and lady of the keep. Successive lords of Dameron had long since built on to the original structure various additions that afforded the inhabitants greater luxury and comfort than could ever have been had in the tower, which, after all, had been designed for the purpose of fortification. Nevertheless, Lady Gwendolyn had caused a small fortune to be expended on modernizing and refurbishing the master chambers before she took them for her own.

Why? wondered Theodora, coming to a halt before the massive oak barrier behind which lay what had once been Lady Gwendolyn's private sanctuary. Theodora's hand went out to touch the ornately carved rosettes that adorned the door nearly in its entirety. Unaccountably, she suffered a sudden chill, as if somewhere in the shadows there were eyes, watching her. But how absurd, she told herself, deliberately dismissing the feeling as a natural reaction to her less than cheerful surrounds. No one other than herself ever came to the tower. Knowing that it was of no use, she nevertheless gave into the irresistible impulse to try the door handle. She was hardly surprised to discover the door refused absolutely to budge. Indeed, she would have been surprised only had it been otherwise.

The Devil's Cub, after all, had ordered the door locked fifteen years ago, and not a living soul had stepped over its threshold since.

With a wry grin at herself, Theodora let her hand drop. No doubt it was a perversity of character that caused the locked door to loom irresistibly in her imagination. She had been drawn to it since Renfield had inadvertently revealed its existence to her. The butler had even unbent enough to suggest that the locked door was not a subject that his lordship ever discussed, which was why she, with no little effort on her part, had forborne from bringing the matter up to Styles.

Perhaps it was time, however, that she threw caution to the wind, Theodora speculated. Somehow, she could not rid herself of the notion that something in Lady Gwendolyn's chambers might shed light on the pall that hung over Styles. There might even be a clue to the identity of the poisoner, thought Theodora. She had nothing logical on which to base such a premise. It was only what her papa would have called "one of her empathic presentiments." Still, she would have given a great deal to gain admittance to the chambers.

Thought of her papa brought a wistful smile to Theodora's lips. She had been greatly moved and not a little surprised to receive the single, hastily scrawled missive from her absent parent, which assured her that he did not doubt, in spite of what might appear strong evidence to the contrary, her course had been based on logic and sound reason. He had, she had even noted, given his blessings to the marriage *before* launching into extensive praise of Sir John Bell as an enlightened man of science whose study of anatomy from a surgeon's point of view was proving as edifying as it was innovative. He had ended by promising to give her upon his return a detailed account of the Scottish surgeon's procedures, which looked to advance medicine not insignificantly.

How very like her papa not to mention Styles or the marriage settlements or to inquire about her new life, she reflected, smiling as she began to retrace her steps. A lump arose unexpectedly in her throat as it came to her that she would have liked nothing better than to have her papa installed once more at Cliff House, if only for the purpose of convincing Styles he was not in the remotest danger of suffering an immediate demise from anything. Anything, that was, but the possibility of ingesting a lethal dose of poison, she reflected dourly, as she stepped beneath the arched portal.

The flutter of the lantern flame and a chill draught at the nape of her neck brought Theodora to a halt, her heart pounding absurdly beneath her breast. It came to her that a door had been opened behind her. But how absurd. There was only the locked door at her back. Feeling foolish, she turned to look over her shoulder—and felt a sudden rush, like a strong wind at her back.

The blow took her unawares, knocking the lantern from her hand and sending the basket flying. Theodora struck the balustrade, felt a scream rise to her throat as the wood gave way beneath her. And then she was falling, her face turned up to the gallery above her and her eyes fixed on the gaping hole in the balustrade.

Styles, cursing himself for a bloody fool, rode his lathered mount through the castle gates and slid to a plunging halt in the courtyard. Leaping from the saddle, he thrust the reins into the hands of a stable lad and, with the terse order to walk the stallion until it was well cooled, strode with long strides into the hall.

He did not pause longer than it took to discover that, while everyone was fairly certain the countess had not gone out, no one knew precisely where she might be found. Inexplicably, he felt a hard clamp, like a vise, tighten on his vitals.

"Then search for her. Summon the entire household, if necessary. She must be here somewhere."

It was at that point that Thistlewaite, attracted no doubt by the hubbub, appeared at the far end of the hall through an arched doorway.

"Begging your pardon, my lord," he said. "But if it's the countess you want, I believe she is in her workshop in the old tower room. If you like, I should be glad to—"

The sentence was left hanging, unfinished, as Styles snatched up a candelabra and strode grimly past Thistlewaite into the Long Gallery. He walked swiftly, aware of an unwonted pressure in his chest.

The tower! Bloody hell, he should have known it. Cursing the tower and Theodora's impetuous nature, which had led her to set up housekeeping in the one place he had made clear he wished her to avoid, Styles lengthened his stride.

At least he could count himself fortunate that, intimately acquainted with his family pile, he knew all of its secrets. The circular staircase, which belonged to the original structure and gave access to the parapet, neither suited his mood nor his purposes. He chose a shorter route through a movable panel behind which lay a secret escape passage, the genius of his great-great-grandfather, who had indulged in questionable political intrigues. The passage skirted the original entrance to emerge by means of a revolving stone slab at the foot of the mural stairway that descended from the entryway into the Great Hall.

Panting from his exertions, Styles shoved the slab open and stepped through—to be met with the less than comforting sight of Theodora, poised almost directly above him, her head and body partially turned to look back over her shoulder.

Styles felt his blood, suddenly cold in his veins. It was like being trapped in the grips of a recurring nightmare—Lady Gwendolyn, poised in the archway, only moments before she had flung herself to her death over the balustrade. Only this time it was Theodora. The devil, he thought, setting the fluttering candelabra aside and, skirting the cursed Roman fountain, strode grimly forward.

The words were on his tongue to demand Theodora come down at once, when, to his horror, he saw her hurtle suddenly forward, the lantern and basket flying from her hands.

"What the devil—!" Theodora plunged through the balustrade. Styles, with a desperate lunge, reached for her—and was in the nick of time to catch her in strong arms. Carried off balance by the force of Theodora's fall, he staggered back a step and toppled—Theodora still clutched in his arms—full-length into the pool with its spouting representative of Bacchus.

They came up together, gasping and sputtering, from the icy shock of the water.

"Hellsfire!" uttered Styles, emerging with his head beneath the jet spewing from an unspeakable part of the god of wine's anatomy. The cold clamp of fear gave way only slightly at discovering Theodora alive and astraddle his hips in a most unseemly manner.

"Styles?" Theodora blinked with startled surprise into her husband's thunder-stricken countenance. "G-good heavens, how do you come to be here?"

"Do not think—" Styles replied, heaving himself out of the water and pulling a wet and bedraggled Theodora after him, "—I have not been asking myself that very question since a tête-à-tête with your aunt that was, at the very least, extraordinary. I found myself repeatedly questioning my own rationality all the way here, a condition to which I have been peculiarly prone of late. Suffice it to say that I have apparently been summoned to your rescue by the offices of an entity for whom your aunt serves as some sort of intermediary." He clasped her by the arms and fiercely gazed down into her face. "The devil, Theodora. Are you all right?"

"Y-yes. Or at least I think so." Theodora gave him a twisted smile. "I seem to be all in one piece, thanks to you and, it would seem, Aunt Philippa. It was one of her visions, was it not?" she asked, striving for a lightness of tone. Faith, she had never seen Styles so grim before. "By all that is marvelous, she actually foresaw what was to befall me today and hastened to warn you so that you might ride *ventre à terre* to my rescue?"

"She envisioned you in the form of a pheasant served up on a platter, but I see no reason to cavil," Styles supplied, his temper fraying in the wake of his initial relief at having Theodora unhurt and alive. By God, how dared she behave as if she were accustomed to falling off any number of galleries nearly to her death! By all rights, she should be in the grips of a lengthy swoon instead of appearing remarkably beautiful in spite of her streaming hair and gown, which, in its sodden state, had been rendered disturbingly transparent. The muscle leaped spasmodically along the lean line of his jaw. "I arrived in time, and you are fortunately alive—at least for the present. I may yet give into the impulse to throttle you for subjecting me to such a moment as I have just been given to experience."

"Dear," said Theodora, drawing away so that Styles would not see just how tenuous was her own composure. She had never in her life before succumbed to anything so lowering as a feminine display of hysterics, and she certainly did not mean to start now in the Devil's Cub's presence "You are in a rare taking. I suppose it is my fault I was made to catapult over the rail."

"On the contrary," Styles declared acidly. "The fault is undoubtedly mine. It is, in fact, what has come of my allowing you a free rein, Theodora. You will agree that the entire episode might have been avoided if you had not been where you had no business to be."

"F-fiddle," Theodora retorted, glancing up from trying to wring out her skirts, an attempt that was proving wholly ineffectual. "The fact that the episode, as you call it, occurred in the tower is purely coincidental. It might just as easily have taken place anywhere in the castle. I daresay, on retrospect, that something like this was bound to happen sooner or later."

Styles stared at her. Clearly her wits were affected by her near fatal mishap. Certainly, she had begun to shake uncontrollably, and her lips were assuming an unbecoming tinge of blue. "Bloody hell!" pronounced the Devil's Cub. "Obviously, this is not the time to discuss things in a rational manner."

Theodora stiffened in resentment. Her lips parted to assure him that she, at least, had never been more rational, when without warning Styles bent down and, clasping her behind the knees, slung her unceremoniously over his shoulder as if she were no better than a sack of laundry.

"Styles!" she gasped instead, on a pitch mortifyingly resembling a purely feminine shriek. "Put me down at once. I have not finished the point I was about to make."

"The point," Styles informed her, carrying her to the gaping door to the secret passage, "is that, having been subjected to a quarter of an hour in your Aunt Philippa's less-than-elucidating company, a harrowing ride home at a breakneck pace, spurred on by any number of visions of my wife poised on the threshold of disaster, none of which remotely compared to the dubious privilege of actually witnessing her plunge from the third-story gallery, I am in no mood to indulge you at the moment. I should even go so far as to suggest you do not say another word."

Theodora, judging that Styles was in no case to be reasonable and that consequently there was little use in arguing, firmly clamped her lips shut.

"God in heaven," exclaimed Millie Dickson in horrified accents some time later, as Styles burst into Theodora's bedchamber, the bedraggled form of his wife, her hair and clothing streaming water, slung indignantly over his shoulder. "Miss Theodora! What in heaven's name—?"

"Not now, Mrs. Dickson," Styles grimly interrupted. "Your mistress has had an accident. By some trick of fate, it appears she has not broken anything. Nevertheless, you will divest her of these wet clothes at once, after which she will go straight to bed."

"I w-will do no such thing," Theodora said through teeth that chattered. "I am p-perfectly all right, Millie. Fortunately the f-former countess was R-roman in her pursuits. If not for her s-silly fountain, I should most c-certainly be dead now."

"Dead? Lord help us," gasped Millie, her face turning an ashen hue.

"You, my girl, are lucky you did not lose what few brains you have," growled Styles, setting Theodora on her feet before the fire to which Millie had already hastened to add a sizable log.

"Hell and the devil confound it, Theodora. You were well aware I did not want you anywhere near the tower. Now perhaps you see why." In a fury at himself for having failed to take better care to insure her safety, Styles turned and paced a step. "For your own good, Theodora, you will swear never to set foot again in that part of the castle. Is that perfectly understood?"

"Pooh!" sniffed Theodora.

Styles came sharply about. "I beg your pardon, madam?"

" 'Twas only a sneeze, my lord," Millie hastened to assure him as she made a show of handing her mistress a handkerchief.

"Nonsense." Theodora waved the handkerchief aside. "I said, pooh. And I shall say it again if I please. Pray let me decide what is for my own good, Styles. I am a grown woman well used to thinking for myself."

"Yes, so you have informed me on any number of occasions, but you will pardon me if thus far I fail to see any evidence of it. I warned you about the tower and specifically requested that you stay out of it. Your independent thinking nearly brought you to a disastrous conclusion, Theodora."

"Gammon," pronounced Theodora, as close as she had ever been to being angry with Styles. "I have been perfectly safe in the tower until today. The structure is old, but basically sound, as you would realize if you had ever troubled to examine it. Lady Gwendolyn, in case you had forgotten, had a great portion of it redone."

"I am well aware of the extent of my mother's efforts to restore the keep to its former glory," Styles replied, looking as if he might yet give into the impulse to throttle Theodora.

"Her expenditures almost ruined me. That does not alter th
fact that you fell through the balustrade nearly to your death.

"But then, that is *not* the fact," Theodora countered, obliv
ous to the pool of water forming at her feet. "I did not fa
through the balustrade, Styles. I thought you must have rea
ized that. I was shoved, probably by the same villain who po
soned your vintage port. Not that I shall ever bring you t
believe that," she added bitterly, and, feeling perilously clos
to tears of pure frustration, turned and marched toward th
screen, which, designed for the purpose of allowing a lady t
dress in the company of her cicisbeos, she had thought singu
larly amusing and not a little extraneous until that very mc
ment. "And now I believe I must ask you to excuse me, Style
I find I am grown uncommonly weary of this wretched gown.

Styles stared after her, unamused to discover he was grinc
ing his teeth together. "Bloody hell," he uttered harshly, mor
shaken than he could ever have thought possible. But then, h
could hardly be expected to accept with equanimity the ci
cumstance of just having witnessed Theodora reenact hi
mama's fatal fall from the tower gallery.

Millie, who had sprung to her mistress's assistance, checke
for the briefest instant at the sight of his lordship. Faith, b
she had never thought to see such an expression in the blac
demon eyes as she saw then.

"I'll tend to her, m'lord," she was moved to offer kindl
"You might want to send for a bath and a hot drink for he
ladyship. Belike she'll need more'n the fire to warm her. An
it wouldn't hurt for you to see to yourself, m'lord. You're ever
bit as wet as she is, if you don't mind my saying so."

The earl's eyes flashed to Millie's and held. For an instar
the harsh features relaxed ever so slightly. "You are a goo
friend to her, Millie. The countess is fortunate to have you.
Styles glanced again at the screen, his face resuming the gri
mask of the Devil's Cub. "I have a few matters to attend t
but I shall be within call. Send for me if there is any need fc
my presence."

"Yes, m'lord. And don't you worry. Your lady might be no biggern' a mite, but she has a lion's heart. She'll come through this little the worse for wear. I'll take good care of her, never you fear."

Styles nodded. "I shall depend on it, Millie." At last he turned on his heel and strode with long strides to the door.

Pausing only long enough to order bathwater to be sent up to the countess along with a cup of hot chocolate, Styles made swift work of divesting himself of his ruined clothing. No sooner was he dressed again than he took up an oil lantern and made his way through the murky passages to the tower staircase.

As a boy, the ancient keep with its narrow fissured windows, like crosses of light hewn through the rock, and the deliberately uneven steps designed to trip up any would-be invaders, had held a certain adventurous fascination for Styles. He had taken advantage of every opportunity to escape his tutors to explore the tower fortress, until he knew every inch of it from the gloomy environs of the dungeons to the dizzying heights of the parapets. Whatever charm it had once held for him, however, had been forever blighted soon after the death of his father.

She had defiled it, his dearest mama, just as she had everything that was Dameron.

Styles did not doubt that his loving mama, knowing of her son's fondness for his family pile, had deliberately chosen to make over the ancient hall in the tasteless image of a Roman pleasure house. She had derived a perverse satisfaction in summoning him to her when she held court surrounded by her intimates, and therein lay the final irony.

Even then, in the throes of humiliation at finding himself the object of their sport, he had not ceased to look to her for some spark of motherly affection—or to despise her for what she was become.

She had not always been obsessed with hatred of everything
Dameron. There had been a time when he was very young that
she had treated him with gentleness, even fondness. Nor could
he forget that it had been at her insistence that he was sent
away to school against his father's wishes. Styles smiled cynically to himself. Even the cold discipline of boarding school
had been preferable to the uncongenial surrounds of his family
pile. It was, in fact, the one good to chalk up against all the
bad: At school and in the broader world far removed from
Devil's Keep, he had almost been able to forget he was one
of a cursed line or that death dogged the heels of the Devil's
Cub.

This day, like no other, had irrevocably and forcibly brought
it all back to him. This day he had almost lost Theodora.

Styles entertained a particular aversion to anything that reminded him of his boyhood and in the months since his return
had not deigned to set foot in the one place most certain to
bring those memories flooding back to him. He had, consequently, not been pleased to discover upon his return from the
village and his unsettling encounter with Philippa Havelock
that Theodora was nowhere to be found. Nor had he been made
easier to learn from his normally reticent gentleman's gentleman that his wife had chosen to set up her workshop in the
very room in which Lady Gwendolyn had spent the last days
of her unhappy existence. He had, in fact, been overcome with
a sudden and unreasoning sense of foreboding—the result, no
doubt, of being wed to a witch, he speculated humorlessly.

It was logic, however, and an intimate knowledge of his
wife's maddeningly independent nature that now led him to
the one irrefutable conclusion: He was a fool to believe Theodora would stay out of the tower simply because he ordered
her to. She would naturally be attracted to it precisely because
it was forbidden to her. Bloody hell, how irresistible must she
find the wholly intriguing locked door, especially as she must
have heard by now an account of Lady Gwendolyn's exotic
history!

We'd Like to Invite You to Subscribe to Zebra's Regency Romance Book Club and Give You a Gift of 4 Free Books as Your Introduction! *(Worth $18.49!)*

If you're a Regency lover, imagine the joy of getting 4 FREE Zebra Regency Romances and then the chance to have these lovely stories delivered to your home each month at the lowest prices available! Well, that's our offer to you and here's how you benefit by becoming a Zebra Home Subscription Service subscriber:

- 4 FREE Introductory Regency Romances are delivered to your doorstep

- 4 BRAND NEW Regencies are then delivered each month (usually before they're available in bookstores)

- Subscribers save almost $4.00 every month

- Home delivery is always FREE

- You also receive a FREE monthly newsletter, *Zebra/ Pinnacle Romance News* which features author profiles, contests, subscriber benefits, book previews and more

- No risks or obligations...in other words you can cancel whenever you wish with no questions asked

Join the thousands of readers who enjoy the savings and convenience offered to Regency Romance subscribers. After your initial introductory shipment, you receive 4 brand-new Zebra Regency Romances each month to examine for 10 days. Then, if you decide to keep the books, you'll pay the preferred subscriber's price of just $3.65 per title. That's only $14.60 for all 4 books and there's never an extra charge for shipping and handling.

It's a no-lose proposition, so return the FREE BOOK CERTIFICATE today!

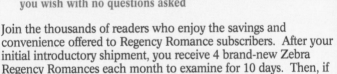

FREE BOOK CERTIFICATE

YES! Please rush me 4 Zebra Regency Romances without cost or obligation. I understand that each month thereafter I will be able to preview 4 brand-new Regency Romances FREE for 10 days. Then, if I should decide to keep them, I will pay the money-saving preferred subscriber's price of just $14.60 for all 4...that's a savings of almost $4 off the publisher's price with no additional charge for shipping and handling. I may return any shipment within 10 days and owe nothing, and I may cancel this subscription at any time. My 4 FREE books will be mine to keep in any case.

Name _____

Address _____ Apt. _____

City _____ State _____ Zip _____

Telephone ( ) _____

Signature _____
(if under 18, parent or guardian must sign.)

RF0996

**COMPLETE AND RETURN
THE ORDER CARD TO
RECEIVE THIS $18.49 VALUE,
ABSOLUTELY FREE!**

**Say Yes
to 4 Free
Books!**

(If the certificate is missing below, write to:
Zebra Home Subscription Service, Inc.,
120 Brighton Road, P.O. Box 5214, Clifton, New Jersey 07015-5214)

Earlier, Styles had been oblivious to the whispers and groans natural to the tower. For once he had even forgotten his aversion to the cursed place and all the memories it evoked. He had been consumed instead with the utter certainty that Theodora was where she had no business to be. His one thought had been to find her. This time they intruded on his grim mood, like echoes of his unsavory past. One of a superstitious persuasion might be tempted to believe they mocked his arrogance in thinking he could protect Theodora from them.

Styles gave vent to a bitter oath. The death of his young countess would have been the final jest. In such an event, he would not have hesitated to have the tower razed until not a stone stood to remind him of the curse that dogged the Devil's Cub.

Cynically amused at his macabre thoughts, Styles took the mural staircase to the gallery two steps at a time. If what Theodora had claimed was true, then the afternoon's events owed nothing to the supernatural. Whatever hand had nearly sent her to her death was made of flesh and blood.

The gallery and the broken balustrade loomed before him, grim reminders of the scene he had witnessed earlier. His blood curdled at the memory of beholding his enchantress, like Lady Gwendolyn before her, hurtle from the heights into the hall below. Hell and the devil take him before he had ever to live through such a moment as that again!

Deliberately, he dispelled the image, and, stepping past Theodora's spilled basket and the shattered lamp, knelt to examine the floor beyond the arched portal.

"Depend on Theodora to keep her wits about her," he murmured with a mirthless smile. "Ghosts do not leave bootprints behind."

The telltale marks left in the dust led Styles unerringly to Lady Gwendolyn's door, where they abruptly ended. He was not greatly surprised to find the door locked. Whoever had tried to murder Theodora in a manner that could only have been meant to resemble Lady Gwendolyn's end would not have failed to overlook such a relevant detail. Obviously the intruder was in possession of a key.

It did not take a great deal of logic to arrive at the conclusion that the possessor of the key was one of Lady Gwendolyn's former intimates, who would naturally be familiar, not only with the events surrounding the death of the countess, but with the secrets that lay on the other side of the cursed door.

Grimly Styles straightened. At least the day's events had served some purpose. The traitor, whoever it might be, had made a grave error in making Theodora a target. It would seem obvious Styles needed to look no farther for the villain than to his mama's former intimates, but more than that, it had been made clear to him that any thought of taking Theodora to London for the Season was out of the question.

Theodora had almost died today because of him. Furthermore, she would continue to be in danger as long as she posed an obstacle to what were undoubtedly the traitor's true designs—to destroy the architect of the Balkan agreements and through him, the arrangements with the Serb rebels. Bloody hell. It was the only explanation that made any sense.

No doubt Theodora had first attracted the assassin's notice when she had had the temerity to diagnose the Devil's Cub's madness as the inevitable result of poisoning. How disappointed the villain must have been to discover that Styles, far from succumbing to his mama's supposed legacy of madness, had so far recovered as to take himself a wife, a wife, who not only had thwarted any further attempts at poisoning, but had dispelled, by her mere existence, the rumors that the most dangerous man in England was suffering from anything more debilitating than a legshackling.

A faint smile touched the Devil's Cub's lips. He did not doubt that the latest *on-dit* in London was that the infamous Styles had at last fallen a victim to love. What other reason could there be, after all, for one to suffer self-imposed exile in the barren wilds of Exmoor?

The smile thinned to a grim hardness as it came to him that

the prospect of London without his new countess loomed as a far less appealing prospect than he could ever have thought possible.

Ten

Theodora sat on the high poster bed, her back propped against a mound of pillows and Percival stretched out on her lap in an attitude of blissful abandonment.

"This is a fine kettle of fish," she announced to the lanky half-grown kitten, who gazed up at her with droopy eyes. "Here we are, alone and abandoned, just when everything looked to be going so well. Styles has taken a notion in his head, you may be sure of it, Percival. And all because of what happened today. Very likely he attributes my mishap to the curse of Dameron or some such silly thing and is even now in the study blaming himself for it. Oh, you are perfectly right," she added, as Percival sympathetically displayed all his teeth in a wide yawn. "It is all a parcel of nonsense. He *should* be here with me, pursuing a logical examination of the facts instead of indulging himself in stupid self-recriminations. And now I suppose you intend to ask what I am going to do about it, when, really, Percival, I wish that you wouldn't!"

Theodora flopped back against the bedpillows, not at all certain how to answer that troublesome question. How very unfair of Styles not to at least afford her the courtesy to allow she knew when she had been pushed. But then to confine her to her chamber in isolation the rest of the day and the entire evening as if she were some frail creature who must take to her bed, really it was too much.

She could forgive his high-handed manner only because she understood it. After all, it was only what one might expect from a strong man of great passion and no little pride, who had been made to feel he had failed in the most primal of male instincts—the instinct to protect his mate. No doubt she might have reacted in a similar fashion had their situations been reversed, Theodora conceded in a practical vein. She could not, however, similarly excuse him for not having come to her when he had had time to return to a state of rationality. Indeed, she was very close to giving into vexation at his childish behavior.

Blast it all! Shaken at having only just escaped by a hairsbreadth being literally dashed to death on the Great Hall's parquetry tiled floor, she had hardly been in a condition earlier to state her case with any degree of lucidity. She had, instead, reacted in the manner of an hysterical female, when, unfortunately, what the situation had required was calm rationality. And now Styles was off somewhere by himself, indulging in what she doubted not was a brooding orgy of guilt.

How like a man to think only of himself at such a time. As if there were anything he *could* have done to prevent what had clearly been an attempt to murder his wife, especially when he had had no reason to suppose anyone even remotely entertained an evil intention toward her. Unless, of course, he actually did adhere to the preposterous notion that a ghost or the devil had done it, she reflected ill-humoredly, and that possibility she would not allow for a moment. Styles was far too analytically minded ever to lend himself to a superstitious interpretation of events.

No, she very much feared his reasons for not coming to her bed when she most particularly wished him to have done had little or nothing to do with any alleged curses that might hang over the House of Dameron. It was far more likely that he had formed a disgust of her. After all, she could not deny that she was perfectly aware he would not be pleased to learn she had set up her herbarium in the one place he would least wish her to have done. And though it was quite true the tower room had offered a well-ventilated, dust-free environment favorable to drying and preserving herbs, it did seem, in retrospect, singularly foolish to believe Styles would be inclined to accept the flimsy rationale that had prompted her to go against his obvious wishes. She had chosen it, after all, simply because it appealed to her to be removed from the rest of the castle and all its inhabitants.

She could not dispute the truth, however, that, in Styles's inevitable view, she had not only flouted his wishes, but had caused him a great deal of trouble. In the circumstances, he could hardly be blamed if he wished to have nothing more to do with her until he got over being vexed with her, Theodora acknowledged with an involuntary hollow sensation in the pit of her stomach, a hollowness that gave way almost instantly before a sudden, mounting heat of purely feminine indignation.

How dared Styles assert his authority over her at the first little unpleasantness! It did not matter a whit that he had made it perfectly clear he could never bring himself to love her. He was the one who had insisted on marriage. And now that she was his wife, the least he could do was listen to what she had to say on the subject of the insidious plot that threatened him and had come perilously close to cutting her stick for her. And, indeed, she *would* make him listen—now, this very night. Furthermore, if he would not come to her, she would go to him!

Firmly setting Percival aside, she flung herself off the bed and bent in search of her slippers, which, upon having realized Styles did not mean to come to her that night, she had earlier hurtled blindly across the room.

"You needn't wait up for me, Percival," she announced, draping a serviceable if somewhat less than fashionable shawl around her in lieu of her dressing gown, which, having suffered a fate similar to her slippers, had had the misfortune to knock over her pitcher and even now lay, unmourned, in a puddle of water. "I expect I shall be late."

Candle in hand and her jaw set with unshakable determination, Theodora let herself out of her chamber and made her way straight to the earl's study.

"I believe I have tried to be patient, Styles," she announced, flinging the door open and marching in without bothering to knock. "I have something to say to you, however, and this time I do not intend to be put—off."

Theodora's voice broke and abruptly stopped—indeed, she was furiously aware that her face must be flaming—at the unsettling discovery that Styles was not alone. A gentleman, wearing a distinctly startled expression on his rather indistinguishable, but not unpleasing features, sat in conference with her husband.

"Dear, I beg your pardon! I had no idea—" exclaimed Theodora, prevented by the necessity of holding her shawl in place from clapping hands to her overheated cheeks.

"Theodora, what is it?" Styles rose to his feet, followed swiftly by his gentleman caller.

A stunned silence resonated through the room, upon which, Theodora, hastily recalled to a sense of her own tattered dignity, summoned a beatific smile and drew herself up to her full five feet two inches in height. "Nothing that cannot wait, Styles. I apologize, gentlemen, for this intrusion and beg you will continue as you were. In the meantime, I bid you both a good night."

Her back held regally straight, Theodora turned, congratulating herself on having managed a strategic retreat. Consequently, she did not see the sudden twitch of sardonic amusement at the corners of Styles's lips.

"A moment, my dear," drawled a voice, unmistakably the Devil's Cub's.

Theodora gave a capital imitation of one who had abruptly met with an invisible barrier.

"Surely you cannot expect me to allow you to withdraw without first making you acquainted with our visitor."

The devil, she thought, at the approach of a slow, thrilling step at her back. She might expect a lot of things from Styles, but making her remain for an introduction in a humiliating state of deshabille was hardly one of them. A hand closed on her arm, and Theodora shot a dagger-filled look up at Styles. Odiously, he smiled imperturbably back at her.

"Mr. Johnathan Franklidge," he announced, turning Theodora to face the gentleman, "my wife, Lady Theodora Dameron."

Theodora momentarily forgot both her embarrassment and her vexation at Styles. This was Franklidge, after all, one of her most likely candidates for having poisoned the earl.

Modestly, but passably, dressed in a double-breasted cutaway coat and breeches of an identical hue in the manner of a French suit and with a neckcloth and collar that did not aspire to unseemly heights, he would not seem, at first glance, to look the part of a cold-blooded assassin, Theodora mused. Indeed, though there might seem a hint of strain about the pleasant mouth and though she would seem to sense something of disquietude in the otherwise mild blue eyes, he would appear to be not so much unpersonable as stolid. But then, one never knew about appearances and she, after all, had never before met a cold-blooded murderer, she told herself, gliding forward with what was meant to be a disarming smile.

"Mr. Franklidge. You cannot know how I have looked forward to meeting you." Extending her hand, she gave him a singularly penetrating glance that might have disconcerted even the most hardened of criminals. Franklidge gave the impression of a man who suddenly felt his collar was too tight. "Styles has mentioned you often."

Franklidge retained sufficient composure to do the niceties, Theodora noted as he took her hand. And his touch would seem to convey a surprisingly sincere warmth she would not have expected of a would-be murderer. "Lady Theodora. It is both an honor and a privilege. May I—er—say you are even more lovely than rumor had it."

Theodora frowned.

"You may say anything you wish, Mr. Franklidge. Indeed,

you are too kind," Theodora answered, thinking that *something* was bothering the man. She had not the feeling, however, that it was the discomfort of a would-be assassin finding himself suddenly and unexpectedly face to face with his intended victim. It was something else, she was sure of it. Imperceptibly she relaxed. "Unfortunately," she added, sending a fulminating glance at Styles before turning back to Franklidge with a dazzlingly sympathetic smile, "I fear I am not precisely at my best at the moment. Which is why I must beg you to excuse me with the hopes that we shall have the opportunity to become better acquainted in the near future. Indeed, Mr. Franklidge, should you ever feel the need to talk to someone, please keep in mind that I should be only too happy to listen."

Franklidge gave her a startled look, only imperfectly concealed behind a sudden cough, meant presumably to clear his throat. "I shall, my lady. Er—thank you."

"Not at all, Mr. Franklidge," Theodora said kindly, acutely aware of the Devil's Cub's narrowed gaze boring a hole midway between her shoulderblades. "And, now, perhaps you would excuse me. I really should leave you to finish your business with my husband."

Franklidge, who had been evincing every appearance of a man who found himself in deep waters without precisely knowing how or the reason why, gave vent to an immediate expression of unutterable relief. "But I have finished, my lady. As a matter of fact, I was just on the point of leaving. Unless, my lord," he added, favoring Styles with a glance that seemed to Theodora to be fraught with unspoken meaning, "there was something else you required?"

Styles, Theodora noted, was as maddeningly impenetrable as ever. "Not at the present, Johnathan. As far as I am concerned, there is nothing more to be said on the subject. As I myself am leaving in the morning for London—"

"London!" Theodora exclaimed involuntarily.

"—I shall take care of it," Styles smoothly continued, as though Theodora had not even spoken. The devil, she thought.

"Anything further we might need to discuss can wait until your return from Cornwall."

"I don't know what to say, my lord," Franklidge replied, extending his hand, "except thank you. And it will not happen again, you may be sure of it."

Styles met the other man's hand in a firm grip. "I *am* sure of it. You needn't concern yourself further with matters that are for all practical purposes over and forgotten. I want your entire concentration on your present assignment."

"You may depend on it, my lord. The matter rests in capable hands." Retrieving a black leather valise from the earl's great oak desk, Franklidge bowed to Theodora. "Lady Dameron, a pleasure."

"Mr. Franklidge," Theodora managed with what she was sure must have been a simpering facsimile of a smile.

Styles, with a hand on the other man's shoulder, conducted Franklidge toward the door. "You will find your customary rooms are ready for you, as always, should you change your mind about continuing on tonight."

"It is kind of you, my lord, but I am become well accustomed to sleeping in the coach. And I am of the opinion that time is of the essence. I shall look forward to seeing you in London."

Theodora, preoccupied with more pressing concerns of her own, turned away from the men. Her brow creased in a frown, as she began to pace, as was her custom when presented with a problem requiring a solution. She heard no more of what passed between the two men. Her only coherent thought was that Styles must indeed have formed a disgust of her.

Good God, he had determined to abandon her at Devil's Keep for more pleasurable pursuits in London, just as his father had done to his mother before him! But then, *she* was not Lady Gwendolyn, and he was not his father, Theodora reminded herself, lifting her head in an unconscious gesture of defiance. She was a witch with acute empathic powers of perception, which told her that Styles could not possibly be completely devoid of feeling for her. It simply was not logical, when one took into account their shared experiments in mutual discovery. No, there was something else behind this unheralded decision, she was sure of it. It required only a cool head and the simple application of reason to discover Styles's real motivation.

Abruptly, she stopped her pacing.

"Of *course,*" she declared, her face suddenly brightening with intelligence. "What an idiot I have been not to see it from the very first!"

"Come, my dear. You are far too harsh on yourself," came in Styles's inimitable accents. "An idiot, Theodora?"

"Yes, an idiot," retorted Theodora, belatedly aware that Franklidge had apparently departed some time ago and that, in consequence, Styles, one broad shoulder propped against the closed door, had been observing her perambulations with no little interest. "And it is all a parcel of nonsense, Styles."

"I could not agree with you more." Maddeningly, Styles straightened. "Whatever you are, Enchantress," he expanded, crossing leisurely to the grog tray and reaching for a decanter of brandy, "it is hardly a person of impaired intelligence."

"No, and you know perfectly well that is not to what I was referring. It is the absurd notion to which you have come. You think I am in danger because of you and that by flying off to London, you can remove any further threat to my well-being."

"I did tell you you could never be accused of diminished mental capacity," Styles replied. Ironically, he lifted the glass in salute to her.

"Naturally I am flattered that you think so." With an effort, Theodora restrained herself from picking something up and flinging it across the room at him. "Unfortunately, I am not inclined to return the compliment."

No, she was, in fact, on the point of accusing him of having a lamentably faulty memory, reflected Styles wryly. Unfortunately, he could not tell her how much he regretted that he could not live up to her fourth condition. Theodora was far too likely to take any such admission as an excuse to follow him to London.

"Whatever you think of my intellectual abilities, you are my wife, Theodora, and you will submit to my judgment in this matter. You will be better off at Devil's Keep without me until I have found and dealt with whoever was desperate enough to turn a hand against you today."

Theodora's eyes flew to Styles with sudden dawning comprehension. "Styles, you have found something to convince you I was right about my unfortunate incident. What? Tell me at once."

An amused smile played at the corners of the Devil's Cub's mouth. "It should be fairly obvious to one of your acute mental abilities. There were footprints in the dust coming and going from—"

"The locked room!" Pressing the knuckles of her clasped hands to her lips, Theodora whirled and began energetically to pace again. "I knew it. I felt the draft on the back of my neck. Whoever it was was hiding in Lady Gwendolyn's chambers." Coming to a halt with a sudden thought, Theodora frowned. "But I do not understand. No one could possibly have known I would come there at that particular time. I, after all, was ruled by nothing more than an impulse."

There were a great many things Theodora did not understand, reflected Styles, watching the animated show of emotions play over her face. Unfortunately, he was ruefully aware that she would not rest until she had come to understand every one of them. There was, in fact, very little point in trying to keep her any longer in the dark. "It is conceivable," he suggested, swirling the brandy in the glass, "the villain was in the room for some other purpose, and you unfortunately happened along at the wrong time."

"Yes, but what other purpose?" Theodora felt a tingle down her back, as she lifted searching eyes to Styles. "Something in the room? Something the villain was after? Styles, what is in that room?"

Shrugging, Styles took a drink from the glass. "Save for the removal of the Dameron jewels, I ordered the room left as it was. It still contains Lady Gwendolyn's personal things— clothing, toiletries, books, various objets d'art. Some of which are of considerable value. I never cared to make an inventory."

No, Theodora did not suppose he had, not in the circumstances. He must have wished anything to oblivion that might even remotely remind him of his mother. But a burglary? "I'm afraid, Styles, I cannot accept robbery as an explanation for today's events. It is not in the least logical. A common burglar would have had no reason to shove me off the gallery. I, after all, did not pose a danger to him. Whoever was in that room went deliberately out of the way to try to cut my stick for me." Theodora lifted her eyes to Styles's. "I daresay the villain was waiting for the chance to do that very thing, and please do not deny it."

Save for a faint hardening of his eyes, Styles appeared remarkably unmoved at such an eventuality. "I have no intention of denying it," he replied, having come to a similar conclusion some hours before. "That does not alter the fact that the opportunity may have been fortuitous rather than deliberate. It would have been a simple matter for someone inside the room to determine it was you on the other side of the door. There happens to be a peephole concealed in one of the door's rosette carvings."

"A peephole! Faith, I might have known." Theodora gave an involuntary shudder. "I think I did know it. I had the most curious feeling that someone was spying on me in the dark."

"Your acute empathic powers of perception in action, one must presume," Styles commented grimly. Setting his glass on the mantelpiece, he drew Theodora to the fire and folded her in his arms. "You are trembling, Theodora. And little wonder. Would I be presumptuous to point out that your dressing gown would provide you with greater warmth than that indisputably intriguing wrap you have affected for receiving callers?"

Theodora choked on a helpless gurgle of laughter. "I did

not affect the shawl, as you must know perfectly well. I'm afraid my dressing gown was the victim of an unfortunate incident—not dissimilar from my own, when one stops to think about it." Instinctively, she nestled her cheek against the comfort of Styles's chest. "Styles," she said after a moment, "you have come to accept my diagnosis of your recent indisposition, haven't you. You might as well admit it. You cannot pull the wool over my eyes. I am a witch, if you recall."

Styles ran his hand over Theodora's tousled hair. "I assure you I am not in the least likely to forget it, Theodora. It is one of the things I find most irresistible in you."

"Do you?" Theodora bent her head back to look up at Styles with green, startled eyes. "I was not aware you found anything irresistible about me. I was, on the contrary, afraid you had come to think of me as being rather too independent, stubborn, and not a little bothersome, when I have tried to be a conformable wife, Styles. Truly I have."

Styles returned her look with a glint of amusement. "You *are* independent, Theodora. And stubborn, and I should venture to say even troublesome at times. On the other hand, I never asked you to be anything other than you are and most in particularly not a conformable wife. I can, as a matter of fact, conceive of few things more disagreeable than the thought of being wed to such a creature as that must be."

Such an avowal from her dear Devil's Cub infused a delicious warmth through Theodora. With a sigh, she returned her cheek to its former resting place against his chest. "I am exceedingly glad to hear it, Styles. Especially as I am about to assert my independent nature."

Theodora felt Styles stiffen. "I said I could not wish a conformable wife, Theodora. Which is not to say I shall countenance one who is blatantly disobedient or headstrong."

"I understand the meaning of the word *conformable* perfectly, Styles," Theodora assured him. "What I am about to propose is an exercise in logic."

"Why, I wonder, do I find that a vastly more disturbing

prospect than mere disobedience?" mused Styles with an air of resignation.

Theodora irrepressibly grinned. "I trust it will be painless. You do know now, don't you, that you were never on the point of going mad as your mama did. I surmised almost from the very beginning you had been poisoned, and you will be interested to learn that I have since uncovered evidence of it. Four bottles of port, all of them contaminated with a particularly strong hallucination-causing herb. Now, will you admit that I was right in my diagnosis?"

Strong hands closed on her arms and held her away from Styles. "Good God, four bottles, Theodora? And how the devil did you arrive at your analysis? If you did so by testing them in any manner whatsoever on yourself, I shall most assuredly consign you to the castle dungeon for an indefinite length of time."

"Then rest assured that I used other means at my disposal," Theodora hastened to inform him. Briefly she toyed with the temptation to tell him *why* she had deemed using herself as a subject for experimentation patently out of the question, a reason that might very well have proved more than a little justified. She, after all, had not dared put at risk the possibility of any future heirs. Reluctantly she decided it was hardly the time for a revelation that would, by its very nature, put them off the subject at hand. She did not intend to allow anything, even something so marvelously significant as the possibility that she was breeding, to interrupt this particular exercise in logic.

"I suppose that answers my question," she added, accurately assessing the emotions only beginning to recede from Styles's glittering orbs. "It must follow, then, that you have come to realize that there is a plot against you. In which case, you will no doubt have come to the conclusion that the two incidents—the poisonings and the attempt against my life—must of necessity be connected. After all, to say they are the products of coincidence must surely defy the bounds of imagination."

"Having come to accept your diagnosis quite some time

ago, I assure you the same line of reasoning has already oc-
curred to me," Styles freely admitted. "Which is precisely why,
Theodora, I am not taking you with me when I depart for
London in the morning.

"But that is exactly where your logic is unsound, Styles."
Theodora pulled away in order to look Styles in the eye. "Do
not think I am not perfectly aware why you insisted on intro-
ducing me to Franklidge. You did it deliberately in order to
observe his reaction to meeting one who had just escaped being murdered only a few hours previously. Furthermore, you
were interested to know what my impressions of Franklidge
would be. Oh, do not deny it. You may not *trust* me, but you
have come to believe in my acute empathic powers of perception, you know very well you have."

"I should never argue with a witch, Theodora," admitted
Styles with suspicious casualness. "What, by the way, were
your impressions of Franklidge?"

"Oh, it is all very fine for you to ask—now, when you have
been noticeably uncommunicative with me these past few
weeks," declared Theodora, beginning to pace in sudden,
dawning awareness. "You might at least have told me you accepted my diagnosis of poisoning. You cannot imagine what
has been going through my head. All this time, I actually believed you were living in dread of going mad or succumbing
to an accumulation of humors on the brain. I have been in an
agony of fear, wondering when the poisoner would strike
again. And you may be sure that he will, Styles. In London,
where I will not be around to prevent it from happening."
Suddenly she came to a halt. "Good God," she said, rounding
on the Devil's Cub in the manner of one who has had the
scales lifted from her eyes. "Why *have* you been stealing out
at night if not to escape your own, personal demons? Styles,
if you are keeping a mistress, you might at least have had the
decency to let me know."

Styles, who had been observing Theodora's wild perambulations with a keen sense of expectation, was hardly prepared

for that particular interpretation of events. His dark head went back in an unwitting bark of laughter.

"If ever I should take a mistress, Enchantress," he observed, his marvelous eyes most disarmingly brimful of mirth, "you may be sure you will be the first to know."

Theodora favored Styles with a doubtful look. "You are laughing at me. How dare you, Styles, when you are perfectly aware I am trying to be serious. Pray credit me with sense enough to know that husbands do not in the norm tell their wives about their mistresses. We, however, have agreed to a marriage based on reason and mutual intellectual discovery. I should not like to think you would keep something like that from me."

"No, I don't suppose you would," said Styles, no longer laughing. With a sigh, he reached out and drew her irresistibly into his arms. "But then, I was not laughing at you, Enchantress. And I most definitely do not have a mistress hidden away on the moors. Good God, perish the thought. It is more than enough to bed a witch of extreme passions, not to mention acute empathic powers of perception. I fear more than that would be an orgy beyond even my powers of endurance."

Theodora, aware of a sharp pang of relief, dimpled naughtily. "Now you *are* roasting me, Styles. And do not imagine for one moment I do not know the reason why. You wish to know my impressions of Franklidge."

"You are mistaken, Theodora." Styles, inhaling the sweet fragrance of her hair, slipped the hideous shawl off her shoulders. "I believe I could not possibly be less interested in Franklidge at the moment."

Theodora gave utterance to a low gasp as Styles, pressing his lips to the throbbing pulsebeat at the base of her throat, began to undo the lacing down the front of her gown. "You may be sure that I am in perfect empathy with your present feelings, Styles. "However—" Baring her breasts, Styles molded the palms of his hands to her firm, soft flesh. Theodora's voice rose sharply in pitch. "—I had not finished my logical line of reasoning."

"Pray don't allow me to stop you." Smiling faintly, Styles kissed the corner of her mouth, while at the same time running a thumb over one of Theodora's delightfully hardening nipples. "You may be sure you have my complete attention."

"Yes, and it is very gratifying to be sure," admitted Theodora, who was ruefully aware her primitive urges were fast gaining ascendancy over her powers of reason. "Especially after being abandoned in my room for six hours and twenty-three minutes when I particularly wished to talk to you."

"I beg your pardon—for what may have seemed—a gross—dereliction—on my part," Styles murmured, between planting small, tantalizing kisses down the side of her neck. "I was initiating an investigation into the identity of our culprit."

"An investigation, but—" Styles, running his hand with practiced familiarity down the inside of her open gown, found the moist heat between her thighs. A long, "O-o-oh," burst in a keening sigh from Theodora, interrupting not only what had begun as a peremptory question, but her entire thought process.

"Bloody hell, Styles," groaned Theodora, abandoning any further attempts at logic.

"Quite so, my love," Styles replied sympathetically. "It is all very disconcerting." It was, in fact, a non-ending delight, one at which he would never cease to marvel—Theodora's profound generosity. Already, she was flowing in anticipation of him. Closing strong hands about her waist, he lifted her to him and carried her a short distance across the room.

"Styles?" Theodora blinked in startled surprise at finding herself unexpectedly perched on the writing table, her gown gathered in a most unladylike fashion around her waist.

"I beg your pardon, Enchantress," murmured Styles, who was busy undoing the fastenings at the front of his breeches. "A writing table would not in the normal course of events be my first choice for tasting your delights. On the other hand, I am in no case to carry you up two flights of stairs to more congenial surrounds."

"No, I daresay you are not." Theodora dimpled irresistibly at sight of the Devil's Cub's magnificently erect manhood. "In which case, I suggest we might view the experience in the light of academic research."

"Witch," pronounced Styles feelingly, glancing up into green, impish eyes.

"Devil's Cub," Theodora chided back at him.

At the soft timbre of her voice, Styles came to stand over her. His demon eyes burned into hers with a fierce intensity that quite took her breath away. "Hell and the devil confound it, Theodora," he uttered harshly. "You are my wife, and I nearly lost you. And that is something I will not permit to happen. Do you understand me?"

Not feeling in the least foolish, Theodora smiled up at him through a wholly absurd mist of tears. "But of course I understand," she answered. Tenderly, she framed his face with the palms of her hands. "It would be strange if I did not." Understanding, however, did not change anything. She, after all, was every bit as determined to do all in her power to see that no one did away with her Devil's Cub. And for that, she must be with him in London.

She did not say that, however. Indeed, she could not have said it even had she been foolish enough to wish to have done.

Styles, bending ruthlessly over her, covered her mouth with his.

Even experiments in the finer aspects of orgies did not compare with the novelty of making love on the writing table in Styles's private study, Theodora decided somewhat deliriously, as the Devil's Cub, spreading wide her thighs, inserted himself between them. There was something deliciously wicked in having one's gown around one's waist, leaving one bare above and below it. And Styles had not even taken time to so much as undress. But more than that, his touch conveyed a fierce tenderness that she had never felt in him before.

Clearly, he was in the throes of strong emotions, which
aroused her in a manner that was totally new to her. She hardly
knew how she came to be suddenly lying on her back, her
legs supported on the Devil's Cub's shoulders. She felt borne
on the wings of what must surely be a driving passion. Certainly, her dear Devil's Cub needed her dreadfully. The fleeting
thought came to her that she wished he could love her, too, if
only a little. Then even that thought fled before the tingling
warmth of Styles's hands on her belly. At last it came to her
to wonder what he would do if he knew his seed was growing
there, inside her. She experienced a wave of tenderness for
Styles at the thought, followed swiftly by purely physical sensations as his lips found the tender flesh of her inner thigh.
Then his hands on her waist were pulling her to him.

Styles, leaning over her, maneuvered her to the edge of the
table. Theodora gazed up at him with eyes like green, glowing
gems. She was beautiful, his sweet enchantress, and he had
almost lost her. The realization was a spike driven deep into
his chest. Parting the petals of her woman's body, he pressed
his manhood against her. Hell and the devil confound it. The
thought of life without Theodora was a madness far worse
than any he had ever imagined. He needed to thrust himself
into her, if only to banish the lingering horror, like a fist in
the pit of his stomach. His hands beneath her buttocks, he
drove himself deep into her.

Theodora's reaction was hardly what he expected. His name
breathed through her lips on a long keening sigh. "Styles. God,
I do love you. I cannot help myself."

A fierce stab of elation shot unexpectedly through the
Devil's Cub. *Theodora loved him.* Driven beyond any thought
of control, Styles drew back and plunged into her with a savage, mounting need. Again and again, until he heard Theodora
cry out and felt a melting burst of pleasure shudder through
her. With a groan of triumph, Styles gave a final thrust and
spilled his seed into her.

Styles stood, his arms braced against the writing table on

either side of Theodora, his breath coming in great heaving gasps.

By God, she was a witch with a witch's powers. And she had said she loved him. Surely he could not have imagined that. But then, she had been in the grips of powerful primitive urges, he reminded himself, smiling twistedly. She had not known what she was saying. Still, he could not deny that it had sounded sweet upon her lips.

With a grimace of loss, he withdrew from her and quickly set himself to rights again.

When he turned back to her, Theodora was curled on her side on the table. An arm folded beneath her head, she watched him out of emerald eyes. A wry smile played about his lips as it came to him that she resembled nothing so much as a blissfully contented kitten.

Styles held out a hand to her. "Come, you will soon be chilled if you stay like that."

Theodora, he noted, gave no discernible sign of moving. "Little do you care. I daresay I could take a chill, and you would not think twice about riding off to London without me. Styles, you gave me your word."

A frisson of warning went through Styles, even as he experienced a fierce stab of possession. Theodora was his wife, and the sooner she accepted the fact that he would never again allow anything to place her in harm's way, the better off she would be.

"And if I did, I am now forced to take it back again. Just as I shall be forced to drastic measures to prevent anything so unfortuitous as allowing you to contract an inflammation of the lungs." His large palm fell significantly on her bare hip. "Just now you are not only exceedingly vulnerable, but you present an almost irresistible temptation."

The devil, thought Theodora. He meant it. He would beat her. She could see it in the stern cast of his mouth. Reluctantly, she placed her hand in his and, allowing him to pull her up, swung her legs over the side of the writing table. "You might at least tell me why you were out on the moors at night," she suggested as she slipped her arms through the sleeves of her gown. "If you were not seeing a mistress, then what were you doing?"

"Seeing a man," replied Styles, relacing the front of Theodora's gown for her. "A gentleman of the free trade whom I employ to keep his eyes open and his ear to the wind. You may have heard of him. Mr. Elias Pendergraft. I believe he has a certain reputation in these parts."

"A reputation for ruthlessness. Good God, Styles, is that how you made your fortune? Smuggling illicit goods?"

Theodora, he noted, appeared rather more thrilled than dismayed at the prospect that her husband might be numbered among that august fraternity of gentlemen, who were reputed to be perfectly willing to cut the throats of anyone who even so much as whispered a word against them.

"No doubt I am sorry to disappoint you, Enchantress," he answered dryly, flinging the shawl around her shoulders. "The reputation of my forebears notwithstanding, I am not now, nor have I ever been, a smuggler."

"A pity," Theodora commented with an air of innocence. "I have often wondered how the free traders manage to conceal their crops of goods without being caught. They must be familiar with every inch of the coast and every ravine. I daresay they could show me any number of hidden places where wild herbs thrive. No doubt they could be of invaluable aid to me in the compilation of my herbal."

"I strongly suggest you make no attempt to enlist their aid," Styles said, alarmed at this new turn of subject. "In fact, I insist that you do not. They would sooner cut your stick for you, Theodora."

"Do not say so, Styles. How very ironic. It would seem life at Devil's Keep is fraught with its own perils, even without the Devil's Cub in residence. At least your mind may be at rest in regard to your Mr. Franklidge. You may be interested to learn I was not given the feeling that he is the sort to go about killing people. Especially the wife of his employer. Quite the contrary. I believe he took sincere pleasure in what he conceived to be your happiness."

"You cannot know how relieved I am to hear it," replied the Devil's Cub, eyeing her warily.

"On the other hand," Theodora continued, "it occurs to me that perhaps you should talk to him in order to give him the opportunity to unburden himself. It was my impression he is an honest man in the grips of some sort of trouble."

"The devil," said Styles. "You could not have been closer to the truth had you been privy to our private discussion."

An indignant blush flooded Theodora's cheeks. "I am not in the habit of listening at keyholes, I assure you."

"No, I did not suppose you were," countered the Devil's Cub with a wry laugh. "As it happens, Franklidge confessed to having made a number of unwise personal investments. Rather than come to me, he has been foolish enough to allow a cent-per-cent to sink his clutches in him. I had just refused to accept his resignation from my employ, when you made your dramatic entrance."

"The poor man," Theodora murmured, discarding with reluctance her most promising candidate for cold-blooded murder. "Naturally you informed him before he left that you would bail him out. And where, pray, does that leave us?"

"Where we were before you began this new tack in logic. Far from caving into the notion that my countess is contemplating throwing in with smugglers, I have no intention of changing my mind. You, my dear, will be content to remain at Devil's Keep, while I see to this matter in London."

"But that is not in the least reasonable, Styles," objected Theodora, who, quite the contrary, was absolutely certain she would never content at so arbitrary a decision. "Two heads are better than one in solving a problem, and I have the advantage, after all, of being possessed of acute empathic powers of perception. I can be of no little help to you in London."

Good God. He must suppose she expected him to relish the

thought of his wife, in the company, no doubt, of her eccentric Aunt Philippa, embarked on a mission to discover the villain desperate enough to attempt to cold-bloodedly murder her. In point of fact, he found such a prospect more than a little unnerving. "The only help you can give me, Theodora, is to remain here at Devil's Keep. In London, you would be a dangerous distraction. And now let there be no more said on the subject. Far from being in the mood for a pointless discussion, I find I am uncommonly weary. I suggest it is time I escorted you to bed."

It was on Theodora's lips to point out that he was not so weary only a few moments earlier, when she was silenced by the germ of an idea that had not previously occurred to her. Perhaps it suited her purposes very well for Styles to go on without her—at least for the day or two it would take her to make a thorough search of Lady Gwendolyn's former living quarters. Then, too, there were any number of things she must do—arrangements to be made for her patients to see the doctor in the next village in the event of any emergency, elixirs to be concocted ahead of time, and an afternoon to persuade her Aunt Philippa that the poor dear would enjoy nothing so well as a few weeks away from Great Uncle Pervis and Great-Aunt Edna—all before she followed Styles to London.

"Very well, Styles. I have never been one to beat a dead horse. And now that you mention it, it has been rather a long day. I suppose I am just a little tired myself." Prettily, she smothered a yawn before placing her hand in the crook of his arm. "No doubt we shall both see things a deal more clearly after a good night's sleep."

The Devil's Cub's gaze narrowed sharply on Theodora's sublimely innocent profile. "I shouldn't be at all surprised," he agreed, leading her from the room. And, indeed, surprise was the least of his reactions to her unexpectedly easy capitulation. More to the point, he suffered an immediate and distinct sense of foreboding.

Eleven

Styles was made to feel a little easier the next morning when he descended to the breakfast room at the wholly uncivilized hour of seven to discover, waiting for him, Theodora, becomingly gowned in a morning dress of sprig muslin, her hair done up in a creditable facsimile of a Greek chignon from which silken strands had already begun to escape. He paused in the doorway, struck by the thought that he preferred his unpredictable countess in the faded, but serviceable, "work" gowns in which she customarily made her morning appearance to this vision of fashion, who, while undeniably lovely was an unknown quantity.

"Good morning, Styles," cheerfully pronounced this new Theodora, setting a fresh cup of coffee before his customary place at the head of the table. "I trust that you slept well," she had the further audacity to add in what could only be described as lilting accents.

The Devil's Cub arched a single arrogant eyebrow. Theodora, it would seem, had yet to give up the notion of accompanying him to London. Why else, after all, would she go to such lengths to turn herself into a female of fashion? Relaxing ever so slightly, Styles prepared himself for an unusually stimulating breakfast.

"Well enough, thank you, my dear." Smiling, he kissed Theodora on the forehead. "You are looking particularly fetching this morning," he observed, crossing to the sideboard and generously filling a plate with steak, eggs, and toast, liberally buttered.

Theodora beamed at him. After all, it had been no easy matter, rising an hour before dawn in order to give Millie plenty of time to try her hand at the new hair style she had been working to master. "Do you like my gown?" Holding her skirts out at her sides, Theodora performed a gay pirouette. "It is one of the new ones I had made up."

"On you, my dear, it is everything that is lovely," Styles replied, graciously pulling Theodora's chair out and waiting for her to be seated. "I cannot but wonder, however, what special occasion has prompted you to wear it."

"Why, your leaving, of course." As if it were not perfectly obvious, Theodora thought in no little amazement to herself. "I could hardly wish your parting image to be of your wife dressed in an old gown with her hair falling out of its pins."

"I believe I like my wife with her hair falling out of its pins," Styles remarked, thinking how greatly he would miss these little duels of wit with his enchantress. Still, he reminded himself, it could not be helped. Curling one of those rebellious locks behind her ear, he kissed her lightly at the nape of her neck. Then seating himself, he shook out his napkin and laid it across his lap. "Are you sure that is the only reason for the gown this morning?"

Theodora glanced up at him out of wide, questioning eyes. Inside, she felt her heart leap in alarm at the sudden suspicion that Styles had somehow surmised her intentions. He was, after all, a man of powerful intellect, and as little as she looked forward to a week without him, she was keenly aware that she might soon be wishing him to the devil. "But of course. Styles," she managed with what she hoped was a convincingly guileless air. "What other reason could there be?"

"Why, none that I know of." The little minx, Styles noted with wry appreciation. She was playing her role to perfection. He was almost tempted to give into her. After all, he had the men and the resources at his command to provide her with a formidable safeguard. Perhaps he had been too hasty in condemning her to exile in Somerset. On the other hand, he had made it a rule never to go back on a decision once it was made. Experience had taught him long ago that his first instincts were generally right. No, for her own sake, it would be better to let her play out her charade and then firmly, but gently remind her that as his wife, she was bound to honor his judgment in such matters.

Styles picked up his knife and fork and began to explore the food on his plate with a keen sense of anticipation. Theodora, he doubted not, would eventually make her real intentions known.

Though Theodora conversed freely about any number of topics concerning her work and the running of the household, however, she made no attempt to bring up the subject that should have been by all rights uppermost in her mind. If anything, she gave every impression of a woman perfectly content to send her husband off for an indefinite length of time, reflected Styles with the sudden birth of annoyance.

His mood was not improved, when a quarter of an hour later, he pushed back his chair and rose preparatory to leaving. Theodora had still to make a single reference to her being left behind or to employ even the smallest of feminine ploys to change his mind. The devil, he thought. But then, no doubt she was leaving it for a tearful last plea before he boarded the waiting coach, he decided, as Renfield helped him on with his many-caped greatcoat. He steeled himself to let her down easily.

"I shall miss you, Styles," Theodora said with perfect equanimity a few moments later, as she accompanied her husband down the steps into the paved courtyard. "Now, do have a care for yourself. You know very well I shall not be content until we are together again."

"Shall you not?" Egad, if he did not know better, he would swear the little baggage could not be rid of him soon enough.

"You may be sure I shall be home as soon as the culprit is apprehended," he added, annoyed at himself for giving her a chaste buss on the cheek she turned up to him for that very purpose, when he had fully anticipated for that moment an entirely different scenario of tearful expostulations. "I have every reason to believe we shall be reunited in a very short time."

"Indeed, Styles. I am sure of it," Theodora replied, doing her best to conceal a small prick of conscience at deceiving him, a ploy, which appeared, perversely, to the Devil's Cub to betray an unnerving lack of concern. "And now had you not better be on your way? I daresay it is a long drive to London."

The Devil's Cub's black, arrogant eyebrows snapped together over the bridge of his nose. "Theodora—"

"Yes, Styles?" The face Theodora lifted to him was the very picture of innocence.

Indeed, she was a deal too innocent, reflected the Devil's Cub, coming suddenly to his senses. Hell and the devil confound it. He had been on the verge of ordering her into the coach with instructions for Millie Dickson to follow with what few things Theodora would need for the journey. The little devil. He should have known his enchantress would never resort to tears and feminine pleas. Obviously she had planned to breach his defenses with a pretense of indifference. And by God, she had almost succeeded! A wry smile tugged at his lips as it came to him that he would never be bored with Theodora.

"Nothing," he said, thinking wryly of the merry chase Theodora would have led him in London. "Save only that I believe I have not expressed how deeply I regret the interruption of our honeymoon. You will have your fling in Town, Theodora, I promise."

"You may be sure that I shall hold you to that," smiled Theodora, who was looking forward to that event far sooner than he could possibly have anticipated. "Be sure to give my regards to Mr. Franklidge," she added as Styles, congratulating himself on having taught Theodora a valuable lesson in wifely deportment, kissed her lightly on the lips and stepped into the coach.

He was to feel a deal less sure of his analysis of the situation a few seconds later as Theodora, smiling prettily, gaily blew him a kiss at the very moment the coach lurched into motion. Styles's brow darkened in a frown.

Theodora breathed a sigh of relief.

Styles, she was certain, had been evincing every manifestation of a husband who was suspicious of his wife. Indeed, she could not be mistaken in such a thing. She had been in dread that at any moment he would spoil everything by absolutely forbidding her to follow him to London, which was quite different from merely refusing to allow her to accompany him to that destination. After having reasoned the matter through, she could could not see that, strictly speaking, she could be considered either rebellious or disobedient for doing something he had not specifically forbidden, after all.

It was all Theodora could do to stand waving until the coach had at last disappeared around the curve in the drive. She had a great deal to do and very little time in which to do it. No sooner had the conveyance passed out of sight, than she turned to the first business at hand.

"Renfield," she pronounced without preamble, holding out her hand. "I will have the key to the locked door if you please. And pray do not pretend you do not know to which door I am referring. I haven't the time to argue."

The aroma of dust and stale air greeted Theodora as she shoved open the previously locked door and boldly entered Lady Gwendolyn's chambers. A cold draught followed her into the room, ruffling the cobwebs draped in a macabre fashion

from the furniture, lamps, and ceiling, and there was the distinct scutter of tiny feet in the gloom.

"Rats!" exclaimed Millie Dickson in no little disgust. "Are
you certain you want to go through with this, Miss Theodora?"

"I have never been more certain of anything, Millie," Theodora replied, grateful, nonetheless that she had thought to
change into an old woolen gown. Lighting one of the lamps
off her candle, she glanced sympathetically up at Millie
"There is not the least reason for you to stay, however, if you
had rather not. I promise I am perfectly safe."

"I'll not let you do it alone, m'lady," Millie declared
roundly, planting her buxom figure squarely in the center of
the room. "I'd rather be eaten by rats than leave you here by
yourself. Miss Theodora—faith, you're not locking the door
are you?"

"I most certainly am," declared Theodora, not only turning
the key in the lock, but wedging a chair beneath the doorhan-
dle. "Purely as a precautionary measure. I find that I dislike
the notion of having someone sneak up behind me."

"But the ghost of Lady Gwendolyn, Miss Theodora. Everyone knows these rooms are haunted. Mrs. Gill says . . ."

"Mrs. Gill says a lot of things that you should know better
than to believe. She is an old woman with an overactive imagination. Now," she concluded, dusting her hands off as she surveyed the sitting room, "where shall we begin?"

"You might start by telling me what we're looking for
m'lady," Millie suggested, staring doubtfully at the luxuriously
furnished apartment as if expecting to be set upon at any moment by Lady Gwendolyn's ghost.

Theodora's wry chuckle sounded incongruously in the
brooding silence. "I haven't the remotest idea, but you may
be sure I shall know it as soon as I find it. Books, papers
anything that might lead someone to risk stealing in here to
look for it."

Millie shifted uneasily. "I'm afraid I'm not much for read

ing, Miss Theodora," she confessed. "Belike I couldn't tell what was important from what wasn't."

No, of course she could not, the poor dear, thought Theodora, chiding herself for her thoughtlessness. Millie and Tom, like others of their station, would hardly have had the opportunity to learn how to read or write. It was a circumstance Theodora had long deplored, and now that she was a countess, perhaps she could do something about it.

"Never mind, Millie," she said, mentally adding a school for the tenants and retainers to her list of future projects. "You don't have to read them. Any papers you find, simply lay aside in a pile. I suggest you start, here, in the sitting room, while I look in the bedchamber."

Leaving the light for Millie, Theodora carried the candle into the other room and pulling the cobwebs off a lamp, lit the wick.

"Good heavens!" exclaimed Theodora, as a circular bed of generous proportions draped in cobwebs and red velvet curtains leaped into view. It came to her to wonder how one slept in a round bed and found herself imagining any number of difficulties, not the least of which would be the tendency to end up with one's head or feet hanging off the edge, unless, of course, one were a sound sleeper content to remain on or near the diameter of the circle. The problems in logistics, however, would seem to pale before the greater challenge of being remotely able to sleep under the picture that dominated the wall at what was presumably the head of the bed.

The picture was an oversized portrait of a woman in exceedingly scanty attire and poised in what could only be described as a most peculiar attitude. She lay with her neck bared to a comely youth who appeared, if anything, a deal overzealous in his ardor. Not only did he have a hand on her bared and voluptuously rendered breast, but he gave every evidence of being on the point of sinking his teeth into her flesh.

Not one to judge the tastes of others, no matter how greatly they might differ from her own, Theodora yet could not but think the thing was badly done. After all, who had ever seen a youth with protruding fangs that more clearly resembled the dentition of a canine than that of a *Homo sapiens,* or at least a cross between the two, something which she doubted not was scientifically impossible? Furthermore, she could not imagine that anyone, not even an obvious bohemian such as Lady Gwendolyn was reputed to have been, would be moved to display a pleasurable anticipation at so horrendous a prospect. Clearly it was all a parcel of nonsense.

Having such a thing looming over one's bed, Theodora decided, would surely be conducive to nightmares or, at the very least, would contribute to a chronic state of dyspepsia. Clearly Mrs. Gill had not exaggerated when she claimed the former countess leaned to an originality in her thinking.

As if to add further proof of the pudding, a glimmer of light overhead drew Theodora's attention. In mute fascination, she stared at her own image reflected back at her from a ceiling of mirrors. In addition to her other peculiarities, Lady Gwendolyn would seem to have been inordinately enamored of herself, marveled Theodora, who could not think why anyone would wish to lie in bed admiring oneself. Obviously the former countess had been given to more than disturbing dreams, she mused, as she turned away to survey the rest of the chamber.

Clothes presses of cedar, lining one wall, revealed a stunning array of apparel that, while costly and undeniably elegant, could not have been described as being precisely in the first stare of fashion. It seemed to Theodora, holding up a gown of transparent black gauze with a neckline that must have plunged very nearly to the countess's waistline, that they would seem to be a bit overly revealing. Certainly Theodora's bridal trousseau paled in comparison to the curious items she discovered in Lady Gwendolyn's dresser drawers, not the least of which was a diamond-studded collar bearing a leash which ended in a golden manacle, complete with a jeweled key. Still, though undeniably intriguing, the dressers' contents would not seem to be on the order of anything that would warrant a daring break-in by someone capable of calculated acts of violence.

With a sigh of disappointment, Theodora plopped down on the edge of the bed amidst a cloud of dust.

"It must be here somewhere," she mused aloud. "If only I knew what it was and where Lady Gwendolyn would have chosen to conceal it."

A draught, like the chill touch of a hand, against her cheek brought Theodora hastily to her feet. Faith, she had had, for the briefest instant, the most disconcerting feeling that someone or something took a malevolent exception to her presence on the bed. But how absurd. As if she had the least interest in something so hideous. She would sooner sleep on the meanest bug-infested pallet on the floor than avail herself of the dubious pleasure of Lady Gwendolyn's bed, she told herself, backing away from the monstrosity.

The sudden touch of something cold and hard between her shoulder blades brought her up short, a hand to her throat. She turned with a gasp to discover her retreat had brought her back up against the fireplace. "The devil," she laughed, albeit a trifle shakily, and nearly sagged with relief. Obviously she was allowing fancy to run away with reason. She was a witch of the healing arts, she reminded herself, and far too analytically minded to be afraid of a draughty old room. It was time she got a grip on herself. A pity she dared not order a fire laid. There was nothing like the cheerful crackle of wood burning on a grate to banish the gloom from a place. After fifteen years of disuse, however, it would be remarkable if the chimney were not blocked by rats' or birds' nests or any number of loathsome things.

At least she could light the candles, she decided, and, tipping toward her a brass candlestick ensconced in a niche at the side of the mantle, reached up to light the candle's wick.

Instantly, to Theodora's amazement, the interior and back of the fireplace swiveled, presenting an identical representation of the original, and in it—a tall, sinister figure cloaked in black and glaring at her with hard, glittery eyes.

"Lady Dameron," he announced, bending his head to step through the fireplace into the room. "Curious as it may seem, I thought I might find you here."

"Styles!" exclaimed Theodora, a hand clasped over her heart.

"As you see, madam," said the Devil's Cub, straightening and dusting the cobwebs from his greatcoat. "Obviously I cannot turn my back on you for an instant." He had been, in fact, little more than half a mile from home before it came to him— the real purpose behind Theodora's odd behavior that morning. He had wasted little time in turning back to Devil's Keep.

"Faith, I might have known," Theodora exclaimed, her eyes lit with rueful laughter. "So this is how the burglar slipped away with no one the wiser. And you knew of it all along. For shame on you. You might at least have told me."

"I did not consider it pertinent for you to know. Any more than it is pertinent for you to be in these chambers. I believe I left clear instructions that you were not to come again into the tower."

"Pooh! You might as well have ordered me to stop breathing. At least, now that we are here, you might as well tell me where the passage leads."

Styles eyed her with grim humor. She was right, of course. Having become intimately acquainted with Theodora's inquisitive nature, he had been telling himself that very thing for the past twenty minutes. "Most significantly, to a cave at the foot of the cliffs. As it happens, it was excavated by the fifteenth Earl of Styles, who dabbled in piracy and smuggling whenever he felt the need to replenish his depleted coffers, which was more often than not. Fortunately, he disliked the notion of being trapped like a rat in its hole. He added escape routes, which gave him a direct access to the stables, among other strategic locations. And, no, you are not going to explore the tunnels. Not now or ever, Theodora. At least not without me along. I will have your promise on that. Even if, by some miracle, you did not lose yourself in that bloody warren of passages, it is doubtful you would escape the numerous pitfalls designed to discourage intruders."

Far from being daunted at such a prospect, Theodora, he noted, did not even attempt to conceal her disappointment. "Oh, very well. I suppose I must. But only if you promise *me* there is nothing in them that would help us find our burglar."

"You may be sure of it," Styles did not hesitate to inform her. "The only clue they might provide is in knowing who would be intimately acquainted enough with Devil's Keep to be aware of their existence."

"And how to safely navigate them," added Theodora thoughtfully. "Which leads me back where I began. I am certain the clue to his identity lies in these chambers. A diary perhaps. Or letters. Something the burglar was most keen to recover. Where would Lady Gwendolyn have kept her most intimate papers?"

"But that is easy, Theodora," said a dear, familiar voice from the doorway. "Let me see. I have an image of a hidden compartment somewhere . . ."

Theodora turned, a grin of welcome starting on her face. "Aunt Philippa, by all that is marvelous. Where in the world did you spring from?"

"It's my doing, Miss Theodora," Millie confessed, shamefaced. "I couldn't bear having the door locked. Not when Mrs. Gill told me how sometimes at night, Lady Gwendolyn can be heard moaning and carrying on up here. I opened the door in case we might need to get out in a hurry, and there was Miss Philippa. You could have knocked me over with a feather, I was that surprised."

"Not now, Mrs. Dickson," Philippa admonished, holding up a hand. "I am in contact with my entity, who assures me Lady Gwendolyn is most anxious to communicate an important mes-

sage. I'm not sure, but I believe there is something about a
bed and people who think nothing of invading other people's
privacy whether they are invited to or not. There is most certainly a journal, hidden . . . dear, I am not at all certain, but
I think it is over—"

"Here, perhaps?" murmured the Devil's Cub at Aunt Philippa's back. He pulled a decorative cord suspended from the
ceiling. Instantly the, at least in Aunt Philippa's opinion, less
than flattering portrait of the unknown woman slid upward
along the wall to reveal a cleverly concealed wall safe. This,
Styles proceeded to open.

"Oh," exclaimed Aunt Philippa, in obvious delight. "It is
just as I visualized it. Only I was sure it would be over there,"
she said, pointing vaguely in the direction of the huge Gothic
fireplace. "I must say it is very curious. The emanations are
most powerful."

"But of course they are," Theodora was quick to reassure
her. "No doubt it was the secret passage that you detected.
Styles, how did you know?"

"Lady Gwendolyn, as far as I am aware, was careful never
to reveal the existence of the safe to anyone, a privilege she
could hardly deny me. I, after all, was made to foot the bill
for its installation." Reaching inside, he extracted a small journal bound in red satin.

"Here," he said, handing the thing to Theodora. "Take it
with my blessing. Somehow I cannot think you will find it all
that enlightening. Still, it will no doubt make for scintillating
reading for you on the journey to London."

Theodora's eyes flew to the stern face, which wore at the
moment an expression of sardonic expectation. "London!" She
flew into his arms. "Do you mean it, Styles? You will take
me with you?"

"It has occurred to me that I shall be less prey to worry
with you near me than with you away from me. And, besides,
my acute empathic powers of perception tell me that you would
not have been far behind me at any rate. I suggest you send

Millie to pack a trunk for you. Aunt Philippa, I trust, is already packed."

"Now that you mention it, I did have a dream about Cleopatra en route to Alexandria," supplied Aunt Philippa. "I thought it was most peculiar that she had what was most certainly Percival perched on a pillow beside her."

"A clear indication that Theodora was destined for a momentous journey," submitted the Devil's Cub. "Which, one must suppose," he added dryly, "was only corroborated by the note Tom Dickson delivered to you this morning."

Theodora's face lit with—accusing laughter. "You met Tom on the road and guessed where he had been."

"I'm afraid it was the most obvious conclusion," he admitted with a humble air that did not fool her in the least. "Especially in light of what I had already surmised. You have cost me a deal of trouble, Theodora, which might have been avoided if you had simply confided in me. I believe I am not an unreasonable man. Faced with the prospect of having you find your way into the secret passages that catacomb the hill and castle, you may be sure I should have seen the wisdom of taking you with me to London, where I might at least keep an eye on you."

"I have always said you are a man of powerful intellect," Theodora said, nearly dazzling him with her smile. "Millie, did you hear?" Theodora called out, her eyes shining up at Styles. "You may stop searching and go and pack. We found what I was after, and His Lordship is taking me to London."

"I'm fast on my way, m'lady," came Millie's voice, pregnant with relief. "I can't say I'll be sorry if I never have to set foot in here again. It's no fit place for a living soul."

"I could not agree with you more, Mrs. Dickson," said Aunt Philippa, clearly ill at ease now that her services were no longer required. "I shall just go along with you. Theodora, I advise you not to tarry long. I cannot like the spiritual emanations here. I should even go so far as to say the *dharma* is in utter disharmony."

"I daresay she is right," Theodora said to Styles when they were alone. She could feel the chill in the room even through the old woolen gown. Her glance went involuntarily to the portrait. "On the other hand, there is a certain fascination to the place. With a good cleaning and certain significant alterations, it might be made rather charming."

"It will be no such thing, Theodora," Styles said warningly. "I am prepared to allow you a great deal of latitude in renovating the keep to your liking. But these rooms you will leave to Lady Gwendolyn's ghost, or the devil. I care not which."

"Yes, of course, Styles," Theodora answered vaguely.

Styles snapped to attention. Now what the devil? Theodora's gaze was riveted on the portrait, her lovely brow puckered in a frown. And little wonder. It was a loathsome thing, a hideous representation of the sort of visions that had come to his mama in her madness. He should have taken it down and burned it long ago had he not preferred never to have to lay eyes on it again.

"Styles. It was not your fault, you know."

Startled, Styles glanced down at Theodora. His lips twisted in a wry smile.

"No doubt I am gratified you think so. If you are referring to my mother's suicide, however, I feel compelled to point out that you know nothing about it."

"I know that you blame yourself for it. And you shouldn't. I believe there was little you could do to prevent it. It's all there, somehow, in the portrait, if only I can make sense of it."

"Then you will only be wasting your time, Theodora," Styles said coldly, his face masked with cynicism. "The portrait is a fanciful creation by one of my mother's intimates. And rather badly done, at that. It was all a game to them, one of the many in which they delighted. Unfortunately, they did not take into account my mother's uncertain mental state. She began to believe in the fantasy."

"What fantasy, Styles? I don't understand."

No, of course she did not, Styles reflected, berating himself for a fool. How could she? Unfortunately, she would not rest until she did understand it, or until she at least had all the sordid details. He shrugged. "It was nonsense," he said dismissively. "All of it. Something Lady Damaris dreamed up. A game with all the medieval trappings of a treasure hunt."

Wryly, he saw Theodora's interest quicken. "A treasure hunt. For what, Styles?"

"Nothing, Theodora. It was over and done with a long time ago. I see little point in dredging it up all over again. It has nothing to do with the things that have happened in the past weeks, you may be sure of it."

Theodora drew back to look at him with that intensity of expression that never failed to set him on his guard. "Dear, I have upset you, haven't I?" Theodora said ruefully. "When truly that is the last thing I should wish to do. I'm afraid it is my impetuous nature. Papa was used to say I was like a cat worrying a mouse to death. Not a very flattering assessment of my character, is it, especially since it is so very close to the truth."

Styles stared at her, a peculiar, stricken look in his black demon eyes.

"Styles?" queried Theodora, her face clouding with uncertainty.

Abruptly he threw back his head and laughed.

Theodora, her hair falling from its fashionable coiffure and her face smudged with dirt, had never looked more adorable. Good God, she had not the least idea what she was; and had they been anywhere, but there, he would not have hesitated to show her exactly how he felt about her.

"Styles, you are laughing at me," Theodora scolded, her own eyes filling uncertainly with shared mirth.

Instantly, Styles pulled her close. "If I am, Enchantress, it is all your own fault. It is, in point of fact, one of your greatest attributes."

Theodora stared doubtfully back at her beloved Devil's Cub, his face still alight with humor. "Making people laugh?"

"Putting everything in a wholly practical perspective. The truth is, I don't really know what the treasure was. The game was kept closely shrouded in secrecy. I have only my own conclusions, based on theory and a knowledge of my mother's particular obsessions. Lady Gwendolyn hated the thought of growing old, but more than that, she was morbidly afraid of dying. I can only surmise that the object of her quest was . . ."

"The secret of immortality," Theodora finished for him. Her eyes widened in sudden understanding. "Good heavens, how perfectly dreadful. It was one of the things I stumbled across when I was doing my research for my trousseau—in a very old issue of the *Gentleman's Magazine*, which was flung in with the others. A story about a Mr. Arnold Paul, who was thought to be able to rise from his grave. But, no. I do not believe it. I mean, even if your mother believed in the silly old wives' tale that suicides become like this Arnold Paul, I cannot think she would actually attempt such an experiment. It simply is not logical. After all, she could not be certain of the results and once accomplished, there would be no turning back again. She certainly would consider the possibility that it was all a parcel of nonsense, and if your mama was so afraid of dying, well—! I am sorry, Styles, but such a theory simply would not seem to conform to the facts."

"You are undoubtedly correct in your assessment, my dear," murmured the Devil's Cub, who, perfectly willing to consign the entire matter to the past where it belonged, did not bother to point out the one fallacy in her line of reason. Lady Gwendolyn had been quite mad at the time of her death and, consequently, could hardly have been expected to pursue either a logical or a rational course.

Theodora, who was once again staring at the poorly, if graphically, rendered portrait, frowned and shook her head. "Vampires, really, Styles. Why would anyone choose to play at such a game? I'm afraid their lives must have been dreadfully empty and wholly without purpose. I cannot but think it was a terrible waste."

Whatever they were, it is over now, and I find I am damnably weary of these surrounds." Styles took her arm and, turning her away from the portrait, firmly led her out of Lady Gwendolyn's bechamber.

Theodora, clasping the journal to her breast, made no objections. Indeed, she was in perfect agreement with his sentiments.

Twelve

Styles, in the company of Johnathan Franklidge left the Ship Tavern near the Admiralty in Whitehall and, ordering Hodges to take them to Lady Harrington's, climbed into the waiting carriage.

"At least that is done with," he observed dryly, as he sank back against the squabs. "Their Lordships are assured the rumors concerning my uncertain health are unfounded; and, thanks to the dispatches you brought with you from the Balkans, they are satisfied their agreements are well on the way to being made a reality. It's good to have you back, Johnathan."

"Thank you, my lord. I'm glad to be home. And you were right about Cornwall, my lord," Franklidge said as the carriage lurched into motion. "Mr. Pendergraft's information was sound. It seems one of the Cornish boats did rendezvous with a Frenchman. Only instead of French brandy, the cargo was an English gentleman—identity unknown, I might add. He wore a mask. It all happened close to a week before you yourself arrived back in England."

"Yes, it would have to be. He made his way from Belgrade to France, sold what information he had, and crossed the channel. It should not have been too difficult with a writ of safe passage guaranteed by the emperor. A short detour to Exmoor to plant the poison in my vintage port, and then by post chaise to London in time to welcome me at Lady Damaris's dinner party. Lady Dameron was right. The intent was not to kill me outright, but to make it appear I was going mad, like my mother before me. It was all so much safer that way. The question is which of my mother's cicisbeos was behind it? In addition to the other guests, they were all at Lady Damaris's that evening—Westfall, who claimed to have returned from taking the cure at Bath, Moreland, who I have little doubt was, as he claimed, at his hunting box with his latest favorite, and Maheux, who made no claims at all, save that he had been away on a matter concerning the Crown. Then, too, there is my inestimable uncle, Lord Harry, pockets to let and hoping for a few hundred to tide him over until his next quarterly allowance. He had the look of a man who had been lost for weeks in the pursuit of his favorite vice. Still, I should not dismiss him until we can account for his whereabouts. And one must not forget Lady Damaris."

"A woman, my lord?" queried the man of affairs, frankly disbelieving. "Surely that would be stretching things a bit. I mean if we are right in assuming the spy, in order to protect his identity, could not afford to trust the mission to an accomplice."

"Where Lady Damaris is concerned, anything is possible." Styles's eyes glittered beneath the brim of his hat. "While I agree it is hardly likely she trailed us to the rendezvous with Black George, I suggest it would be unwise to discount her too quickly. She would not be above lending aid to a traitor, if the rewards were ample enough."

"I see," said Franklidge. "Then no doubt it would not hurt to put a man on her, my lord, as we have already done with the others. Merely to discover whom she sees, where she goes, that sort of thing."

"You are, as usual, up to every rig, Johnathan," observed Styles as the carriage drew up before Lady Harrington's. "See to it, will you. In the meantime, keep me informed. I have a lead of my own, which I intend to pursue. Will you be coming in?" he added, as a footman opened the carriage door. "Or shall I have Hodges drop you somewhere?"

"Thank you, my lord, but I should prefer to take a hackney."

Nodding, Styles stepped down from the carriage and, wishing Franklidge a good evening, strolled up the steps to Lady Harrington's. He was ironically aware that his step had quickened with anticipation at the mere thought of being soon with Theodora. Thanks to his investigation into the matter of the French agent and Theodora's into Lady Gwendolyn's journal, he had not seen as much of his enchantress of late as he could wish to have done. He experienced a swift surge of impatience to be done with the entire affair that he might turn his attentions to the more important business of taking up his honeymoon where he had left it.

Instantly a wry smile twisted at the stern lips as it came to him that he would like nothing better than to fling his wife over his shoulder and haul her off to Exmoor with all despatch—Their Lordships and the bloody French agent be damned. Unfortunately, Theodora would likely take a dim view of being whisked away before she had identified the mysterious "M" who figured so prominently in his mama's diary. There were times, he reflected, when he almost regretted having taken advantage of the diary's existence to distract Theodora from his own investigation.

Still, the ploy had worked. He viewed it as extremely unlikely that his meddlesome countess could land herself in trouble doing research into the existence of vampires in England, which was the reason he had not hesitated to give her the journal. He, after all, had scanned sections of it before the event of his mother's death and had dismissed it as the ravings of a woman in the throes of a serious illness. It was in fact all a red herring designed to keep Theodora occupied until he could set a trap to catch a traitor.

It was not that he had lied about anything, he assured himself as he surrendered his greatcoat and hat to a footman. Everything he had told Theodora was all perfectly true. It was only that he considered it highly unlikely the events that had occurred fifteen years before could be remotely connected with a French agent intent on sabotaging England's war effort. It was unfortunate, but true that Lady Gwendolyn had taken her own life. He had been the unwitting witness to that.

Styles paused at the head of the gallery to gaze down into the ballroom in search of his wife. He was hardly surprised to discover her surrounded by a bevy of admirers—both male and female alike. Theodora, from the moment she had made her appearance at her first ball, had been an undeniable *succès fou*. Given the circumstances, it could hardly have been otherwise, he reflected, conscious of a quickening of his pulse at the mere sight of his enchantress, gowned to stunning effect in white, her hair dressed in spring flowers. She was beautiful, quick of wit, and charming—and she was his wife. Still, he could not but admit that he had failed to foresee the full extent to which she would be embraced by the first stare of Society.

The most immediate evidence had been forthcoming in a flood of invitations, which was hardly surprising. Styles had been counting on that very thing—to keep Theodora occupied during her stay in London. He had not been prepared, however, to discover his wife had become the arbiter of fashion, dictating by example that the ladies eschew all but the most unobtrusive beauty aids, wear the scents of cloves and Rosemary, and dress their hair *au naturel*—without the benefits of curls. The latter, since the Countess of Styles had tresses that hung perfectly straight, had led some of her imitators to attempt any number of methods to achieve the desired effect. The most common of these—the attempt to iron the hair straight—had led in at least one case to disastrous results. Lady Hortense Bellows, after singeing her tresses beyond redemption, had been forced to the extreme measures of cutting her hair to within an inch of her scalp and adopting the expediency of a wig.

Rumor had it that only Theodora's tactful avowal that a lady should wear her hair in the style that afforded her the greatest pleasure with the least effort had saved what might have become an open rebellion among the ranks of the ladies' abigails. A faint gleam of a smile flickered at the corners of the earl's lips. Though the preference for flowers instead of tiaras could still be seen in evidence around him, all further attempts to imitate Lady Dameron's uncurled coiffures of braids and knots would seem to have been thankfully abandoned.

Styles's eyes narrowed sharply, the humor vanished from their depths, as he observed the arrival of two newcomers to the group surrounding Theodora.

The man was slender and elegantly clad with lace cuffs of an earlier generation, and his dark hair was touched with silver over the temples. On his arm was a woman who, dressed in a gown better suited to a female of more tender years, comported herself in the fluttering manner of an aging ingenue.

The Devil's Cub's lips thinned to a hard line. Viscount Maheux and Lady Damaris Gale—the wolf and the spider, he thought.

Absently adjusting his cuffs, Styles straightened and descended the curving stairway into the crowded ballroom.

Since Styles made it a practice never to arrive before the second intermission, Theodora had early on grown used to attending galas in the sole company of her aunt, who, aided apparently in her endeavors by the entity that had taken up with her, made it a practice to spend her time at the card tables. Strangely enough, Theodora felt neither slighted nor neglected in Styles's absence. On the contrary, being much sought after for her knowledge of the healing arts, she had quickly established a loyal following who demonstrated almost as keen an interest in herbs and their curative powers as did she.

She was, in fact, occupied with explaining to Mr. Edward Willingham and Sir Anthony Westfall the beneficial effects of clematis on absentmindedness when Styles created a stir in the ballroom by putting in his appearance.

"While clematis will serve to stimulate the brain and aid in memory function," she said, unaware of the parting of the sea of dancers, "one must be careful in whatever cure one attempts. The purpose of any treatment, after all, must be to restore balance to the body's humors, which cannot be achieved by the application of any single herb."

"If you're an example of the benefits of herbal treatments, Countess, I recommend you bottle it," commented Sir Anthony Westfall, dabbing at his red, perspiring face with a linen handkerchief. "Devil of a thing, middle age. Daresay there'd be no end of demand for a cure for the rheumatism or the gout, not to mention discontinuity and loss of manly vigor."

Theodora, who had been taken aback upon being presented earlier to the aging dandy, could appreciate the sentiment behind the words. It was difficult to conceive of Sir Anthony Westfall as once having been a dashing young blood in hot pursuit of the beautiful Lady Gwendolyn. At sixty, he had succumbed to the inevitable results of a lifetime spent in indulging his tastes for port and French cuisine. Having long since given way to corpulence, he had lost what once must have been a suppleness of body and limb; and what might have been a comeliness of face was now heavy-jowled and spidery with veins.

"My recommendation, Sir Anthony, would be a balanced regimen of herbs, a sensible diet, a daily brisk walk in the air, and proper rest. And time, I might add, spent in peaceful meditation."

"What a charming notion," observed a feminine voice with a gay lilt of amusement. "And so very novel. Why, I daresay, Lady Dameron, instead of fetes and balls, you will soon have everyone sitting about in quiet contemplation of . . . Pardon me, my dear, what exactly is it one is supposed to contemplate while sitting about doing nothing?"

Theodora knew before she turned to whom that lilting voice belonged. She had had occasion in the past two weeks to become well acquainted with Lady Damaris Gale's barbed wit.

She had, in fact, formed a positive dislike of Lady Gwendolyn's erstwhile bosom bow. The woman might present an image of coy beauty and worldly charm, but Theodora had not since her earliest childhood been fooled by appearances. Underneath, Lady Damaris was a viper. The question was, reflected Theodora, was she a murderess?

"That, Lady Damaris, would depend on the meditator," Theodora replied reasonably. "I myself find the contemplation of earth and sky or perhaps a still pool of water relaxing. The object of meditation is not the image, after all, but the emptying of the mind of practical considerations in order to achieve a state of perfect tranquility."

"An excellent summation, Lady Theodora," applauded Willingham, whose perspiring bald head would seem to belie the determination stamped on his round face to remain Theodora's steadfast champion, come what may. He was, in fact, a shy, quiet sort, without the least pretension to fashion, but with excellent connections, which insured that he was invited to all the best houses whether he really wished it or not. He had discovered in Theodora a shared interest in Shakespearean herbal gardens. That, in turn, had led to a burgeoning friendship, which had proven mutually beneficial. While she had considerably enlarged his knowledge of herbs, he had helped to guide her through the pitfalls of High Society.

Theodora awarded Willingham a warm smile, which was not lost on Lady Damaris.

"Tranquility, indeed," said she, gently waving her feather fan before her face, whose artfully applied paint could not hide the telltale signs of aging any more than the elegant gown of rose silk could camouflage the perceptible thickening of her waist. She was a woman obviously in her late forties whose principal charm had once been an aspect of childlike innocence. In middle age, the china blue eyes had taken on a brittle hardness and the guinea gold hair more the color of brass. Indeed, in her desperation to cling to that earlier girlish image, she was, had she but known it, made to appear more fatuous than engaging. Theodora felt almost sorry for her. "What a very quaint notion," pronounced Lady Damaris. "And so utterly boring. Is this how Styles occupies himself these days? If so, he has changed considerably from the man I knew. Does it strike you, Sir Anthony, that perhaps the rumors concerning the Devil's Cub have an element of truth in them?"

"I beg your pardon?" Theodora's green eyes sparkled, suddenly dangerous. "What rumors?" she demanded before the gentleman could offer an answer.

"Why, the rumors that he is, shall we say, somewhat unbalanced of late," simpered Lady Damaris. "Not that he was ever the most stable of boys when he was growing up. There was that incident concerning his tutor—what was his name? Oh, yes, Fix, or some such thing."

Theodora felt her hands clench into fists at her sides at the sudden startled flutter of fans around her, not to mention the noticeable turning of heads in her direction. Lady Damaris was beginning to attract a deal of attention, which no doubt suited her purposes very well, whatever they were. Deliberately Theodora unclenched her hands. What was required to avert the scandalous scene Lady Damaris was intentionally inviting was calm rationality.

"Styles had nothing to do with his tutor's unfortunate end," she replied in clear, distinct tones, "as you must very well know. The man was given to excessive drink. He had the misfortune to stumble off the cliffs to his death."

"Dear, is that what Styles told you?" Lady Damaris gave a twitter of pitying laughter. "Can you believe it, Maheux? The child is obviously blindly infatuated with her husband."

"I suppose anything is possible, my dear," replied the nobleman with an unmistakable gleam of appreciation in the look he bent on Theodora. "Even that Lady Dameron is quite right about the tutor. As I recall the man was a disreputable boor. What is readily apparent is that Styles continues to be blessed with extraordinarily good fortune. May I say, Lady Dameron, you are as charming as you are beautiful."

"How very kind, my lord," murmured Theodora, lowering her eyes to hide their sudden flash of triumph. It was, after all, the reason she had come tonight—because she had learned the elusive Viscount Maheux was to be in attendance. Strange, she thought. A man in his middle to late fifties, Lord Maheux was a man who exuded an image of old world charm, and, while his almost aesthetic features displayed unmistakable signs of a life of dissipation, he presented not so much the appearance of depravity that she had expected as he did that of a man who had ceased to look forward in his life to anything surprising. He was, in fact, an engaging roué, whom she found herself resisting the urge to like. Smiling, she extended her hand. "I believe I have not previously had the pleasure."

The viscount's twinkling gaze held Theodora's while he gallantly saluted her knuckles. "It is my loss, my lady, to have been out of the country, when I might have had the pleasure of your company. One of the evils, I fear, of being one of His Majesty's emissaries."

"Very prettily done, Maheux," Lady Damaris observed with a brittle smile. "Beware of him, my dear. Where females are concerned, he is not to be trusted. But then, what man is? You, better than anyone, should know what I mean. I wonder that you can sleep a wink, married to Styles. Or haven't you heard? Things have a way of happening to those unfortunate enough to be overlong in his company."

Theodora's eyes narrowed amidst the sudden, frozen silence. She had the strangest impression that the entire ballroom was waiting with suspended breath for her answer. Certainly whatever pity she had earlier felt for the aging beauty had undergone a sudden eclipse. Lady Damaris Gale had come perilously close to going beyond what was acceptable.

"I believe you would not care to have me repeat what I have *heard* about those who have been close to my husband," she said in slow, measured accents. "Or read about them, for that matter," she added significantly. "I warn you: You may send as many barbs in my direction as you please, but you will *not* make my husband your target."

The feather fan quivered, as Lady Damaris gave a fair imitation of scandalized shock. Clearly she was enjoying being the cynosure of attention. "Or you will do what, my dear? Pray look around you. You have already made a spectacle of yourself. I suggest you would do well not to threaten me. It can hardly reflect well on either you or your husband, who, after all, is tolerated only because he happens to be wealthy as a nabob. I know what Styles is. I, after all, was like a daughter to his poor mama, whom he treated with a shameful disregard."

Theodora bridled with indignation. "Allowing Lady Gwendolyn to live lavishly at his expense may have been heedless," she retorted, making a flagging attempt to hang on to her temper. "It might even have led to what amounted to a shameful disregard—that of Lady Gwendolyn for anyone but herself. She was a spoiled and unhappy woman who demonstrated a total indifference to any but her own pleasures. Furthermore, if you were ever like a daughter to the countess, Lady Gale, then one can only presume Lady Gwendolyn was exceedingly precocious as a child. Why—why, it would be like saying I am like a daughter to Styles, and that, you will agree, is patently ridiculous."

"Patently. And not a little scandalous, my dear," came in Styles's inimitable, drawling accents. With a gasp, Theodora glanced up—straight into the eyes of the Devil's Cub. "My daughter? Really, Enchantress, I'm afraid I must object to your choice of inferential simile."

"Pooh." Irrepressibly, Theodora dimpled. "You know perfectly well what I meant."

"Indubitably. And so, I believe, does Lady Damaris, who, it would seem, does not know me nearly so well as she should. You, madam, are mistaken in at least one significant point, surely."

"I-I beg your pardon," Lady Damaris stammered, her gaze uncertain on the Devil's Cub's black, glittering orbs.

"If I am tolerated, madam," Styles obligingly answered her, "it is because it is considered dangerous to do otherwise."

"Softly, my dear Damaris," hastily interjected Maheux at sight of Lady Gale's expression of unadulterated loathing. "I fear you have said enough for one night."

Lady Damaris's face flushed and then paled beneath its layer of paint. "On the contrary, I have not said nearly enough," declared the lady, shaking off the viscount's restraining hand. "You do not frighten me, Styles. I am not afraid to say what everyone has always known. You drove her to it—your own poor mama. And the devil knows how many others are dead because of your devil's curse."

"Oh!" gasped Theodora, oblivious to the warning light in Styles's eyes or Maheux's gallant effort to draw Lady Damaris away. "You are a sad and deluded woman, and, worse, a very foolish one. And I am sure I feel very sorry for you, but I will not have you saying Styles is a murderer. Styles has no more killed anyone than I have, and the whole world will know it before very much longer. It is all in Lady Gwendolyn's diary."

Lady Gale went white as a sheet. "It's a lie! There was never any diary. It is only a poor attempt to fling dust in my eyes. The Devil's Cub killed Lady Gwendolyn. I know it as well as I know he will do the same for you one day!"

"Now you *have* gone too far!" declared Theodora, beside herself with indignation at the woman's absurd insistence that Styles was something he was not. "I am perilously close to losing all patience with you, and that, I promise you, will not do. Styles may be the Devil's Cub, but *I* am a witch. I should hate to think you might wake up one morning, my lady, bald as a billiard ball or covered from head to foot with hideous red splotches!"

As Styles was firmly ushering Theodora before him through the crowd and away from the scene of debacle, this last was flung defiantly around a broad, masculine shoulder. Indeed, Theodora's last view of the ballroom before Styles whisked her out on to the verandah was of Viscount Maheux hastily escorting Lady Damaris through the crowd of astonished on-lookers and of Mr. Willingham's red cherubic face wearing a twisted smile of thunderstricken awe.

"Styles," Theodora ventured a few moments later as they entered a garden of tall hedges and bordered flower beds. "I promise I am perfectly calm. I believe it would be safe to stop and talk now."

Styles, far from answering, maintained a silence that was hardly reassuring, especially since Theodora was beginning to suffer the first pangs of remorse for having so thoroughly abandoned all rationality as to make a public spectacle of her-self. Not that she regretted having set the record straight, she told herself, studying the back of Styles's dark head. Still, she could not but think that it might have been better to save her defense for a more propitious time and place. Very likely Styles would see no recourse but to send her back to Exmoor in disgrace.

"Styles," she said again, when she could no longer bear the silence, "I wish you would talk to me. Was it really so very bad that you cannot stand to discuss it calmly and rationally?"

Suddenly he halted and without preamble released her hand. It was only then that she realized in no little alarm that he had begun to shake all through his powerful frame.

"Dear, you *are* angry. Styles, I know it was a foolish thing to have done, but surely you must see I could not help myself. You cannot expect me to tolerate having people say such ab-surd things about you. I shall naturally beg Lady Harrington's pardon, if you say that I must, but pray do not ask me to apologize to Lady Damaris, for I am quite certain I should choke on the—"

Abruptly Theodora stopped as Styles gave forth with a curious strangled sound and, leaning with one hand against the trunk of a tree, stood with his shoulders still shaking and his head hanging down between them. Only then did it come to her that he was uncontrollably laughing.

"Styles! How could you!"

"The devil, Theodora," Styles gasped, dragging in deep draughts of air, "I could hardly do anything else. I believe I have never seen anything to equal what I have just been given to witness in Lady Harrington's ballroom." With a gasp, Styles went off into another helpless gale of laughter.

"Well, *I* was not similarly amused," declared Theodora, hard put to maintain a stern front in the face of the Devil's Cub's unbridled mirth. "I have never been so furious with anyone. I will not have you unjustly accused, Styles, especially by Lady Damaris Gale, of all people. It is time to have an end to it."

His mirth having subsided sufficiently to allow him to breathe rather more naturally, Styles took her firmly by the arms and bent his head to peer in her face. Theodora's heart nearly stopped at the strange, glittering warmth in the black demon eyes. "I could not care less what people think or say about me. There is only one person whose opinion matters to me other than my own, and, as it happens, she has just stood up for me in a manner that is certain to make a lasting impression." Bloody hell, it would be a topic of conversation for years to come. Lady Dameron had come to the Devil's Cub's defense like a lioness out to protect her own. He could not recall that anyone had ever done that before and certainly not with such unbridled passion. Recalling Theodora's final words to the lady, he wondered whimsically if Lady Damaris was even then taking the precaution of draping herself in cinquefoil and dill, not to mention elderberry gathered on the last day of April. "At least," he speculated wryly, "you may be sure it will be a long time before Lady Damaris attempts to use you again to get at me."

"No, I daresay she will come after me for my own sake next time, or at least after the diary," Theodora speculated with

an air of satisfaction that awakened Styles to a sudden chill
of apprehension. The devil, he thought, no longer even remotely amused. "Did you see her face when I brought the
diary up?" Theodora continued, intent on her own analysis of
the evening's events. "She was afraid. I could not be mistaken
in that. Oh, it really was too bad of her to insult you in so
outrageous a manner. I daresay I might have persuaded her to
tell me something about the Moravian Blood Stone with which
Lady Gwendolyn would seem to have been obsessed, or at
least who it was who was identified solely by the letter *M* in
her diary, if only she had not made me lose my temper."

"It is exceedingly doubtful she would ever have been
brought to confide in you," observed Styles, who had not until
that moment considered the possibility that the diary might
pose a threat to Theodora. "I can tell you, if you have not
already guessed, that the Moravian Blood Stone figured in
Lady Damaris's game. It was obviously a sham invented by
one of the gamesters to make the play more interesting. Theo-
retically it was invested with the power to confer eternal youth
and immortality on its possessor." Cynically he laughed. "Immortality. Good God. I was a fool not to realize what was
happening, but then I made sure not to be at the keep any
more than was necessary to see to the running of the estate."

Theodora nodded in perfect understanding. "I daresay it
could not have been terribly entertaining being made to witness
grown-up people behave in the manner of spoiled, unhappy
children with nothing better to do than make up games to fill
the emptiness of their hours. You were better off in London
doing whatever it is that one does in London."

Styles arched a single sardonic eyebrow. "One in London
pursues every available diversion," he observed in no little
amusement. "I thought by now you must have learned that,
Theodora."

"Then I hope you were excessively gay," Theodora firmly
retorted. "I should not like to think you wasted your time
brooding about things that had nothing to do with you. Indeed,

I should be exceedingly disappointed in you if you did not do a great many marvelously foolish things."

"You will be happy to know that that is exactly what I did. Unfortunately, if I had paid more attention to Lady Gwendolyn, I should no doubt have seen what the game was doing to her. She believed in it. No, she was obsessed with the belief in the stone's existence, which was undoubtedly her undoing. But then, there is a history of madness in her family." He shrugged. "Not that there is much of which to boast in the long line of Damerons." He looked at Theodora. "Yes, I know. I am a Dameron of many attributes, not the least of which has been to have the good sense to marry a witch. As for the mysterious M, I know only that he entered the game after I removed to London to pursue a life of dissipation." He smiled cynically. "It seemed preferable, after all, to witnessing the similar dissolution of my dear mama and her cicisbeos at Devil's Keep."

"How very far-sighted of you, Styles," applauded Theodora, thinking the countess and her friends deserved to have been taken out and horsewhipped for the senseless waste of their lives and what it had done to her Devil's Cub. "I daresay that was when you learned about orgies. And for that, I must be exceedingly grateful. It has, after all, contributed to the broadening of my education in a manner that I could not possibly have imagined before our experiments in male-female biology."

She was rewarded for her practical observations by a leap of amusement in the glittery orbs. "I could not have asked for a more precocious student," Styles said. A fingertip slowly traced the delicate contour of her jaw. "Are you sorry that I forced you to marry me?"

"No, how could I be?" she answered simply, smiling up at him gravely. "When I have loved you since I was ten years old. But that is neither here nor there at the moment. We *were* discussing the mysterious M."

Styles stared at her. Theodora had just declared for the second time that she loved him. This time he could not doubt that she not only knew what she was saying, but that she meant every word. Bloody hell! The last thing he wished at that moment was to explore the possible identity of M, mysterious or otherwise.

"Theodora—"

"I know exactly what you are going to say, Styles," Theodora interrupted, turning to pace a step before coming back again. "And you are undoubtedly right. M was very likely someone Lady Gwendolyn admitted into her confidence long after the game had begun. Which would seem to eliminate my entire list of candidates. I confess after tonight's unfortunate incident that I am leaning myself more to that line of reasoning, for although Maheux would have been one of the obvious choices, I am now convinced that it cannot be he." Mischievously, Theodora slipped her arms about Styles's waist. "He is delightfully charming, Styles, which is not at all what I had expected. Rather than believe him a desperate assassin, I am rather convinced I almost like him."

Styles, resisting the urge to throttle the little minx, pushed her away to gaze sternly into her face. "He is an aging wolf, Theodora, and you will have nothing further to do with him."

Theodora suffered a soft thrill at the realization that he was deadly serious. As delicious as it would be to tease him, however, she relented. After all, it was not often that she found him in the mood to talk about matters pertaining to Lady Gwendolyn and her diary.

"You needn't concern yourself. I have no intention of setting up a flirtation with Viscount Maheux. But neither can I picture him doing anything so ungallant as courting a beautiful woman for the sole purpose of cutting her stick for her. On the other hand, I *could* well believe Lady Damaris capable of it. I think she would have sunk her claws into you tonight had she dared."

"Or her fangs," observed Styles, his smile singularly mirthless. "For the first time in our long association, Lady Damaris has dared a deal more than she bargained for. I'm afraid you have an unsettling effect on her, Enchantress. Right now you may be sure she is wondering what possessed her to declare to my face what she has been hinting for years behind my back."

Theodora pulled away, struck by a sudden thought. "If that is the case, Styles, why the devil did you go to Lady Gale's dinner party that night? Did it not once occur to you that you might be putting yourself in deadly peril of your life?"

Styles, who was fast wearying of the subject of Lady Damaris, shrugged an indecently broad shoulder. "It would hardly occur to me that Lady Damaris might try to slip poison in my wine, nor does it now. It would make very little sense, after all. She asked me there that night in order to request a sizable sum to keep her creditors at bay. Suffice it to say that it suited my purposes to promise it to her. And, no, you may not ask. Thankfully, it no longer signifies."

Styles stared past Theodora, his expression exceedingly grim. "As long as Lady Damaris behaved herself, I was content to allow her to go her own way. Unfortunately, tonight, when she decided to turn her venom on you, she finally went too far." At last he looked once more at Theodora. "You will humor me, Theodora, by staying away from her. She would not hesitate to take you down with her if she could."

Theodora, however, was not listening. It had occurred to her that if Maheux was not M and if Lady Damaris had been too afraid of Styles to try anything so unwise as to poison him, at least before she got her hands on the money she required, then the list of possible poisoners was become limited indeed.

She was left with Mr. Andrew Moreland, Sir Anthony Westfall, and Harry Underwood, who, though he could hardly be the "young Adonis" who had apparently worshiped Lady Gwendolyn, still might have had reason to wish his sister dead. According to the diary, Lady Gwendolyn, having grown weary of his demands for money, had cheerfully consigned her only brother to the devil. There was, of course, one other possibility, which Theodora fully intended to explore on the morrow.

Styles, observing his enchantress's vacant expression, was

moved to more forceful means of gaining her attention. Taking her in his arms, he kissed her, long and quite thoroughly, until dazed, she sank limply against him.

A faint smile touched Styles's lips as it came to him the best way to make certain of Theodora's safety was undoubtedly to keep her in bed. Regrettably, he doubted that their lordships would accept that as sufficient excuse to allow a French agent to sabotage his country's war efforts. He cursed himself for a fool. Obviously, he had miscalculated in the matter of his mama's cursed diary, and it was time he rectified the error. Theodora was right, Lady Damaris *had* been afraid. In which case, until he could determine what lay in the rambling entries to cause concern, it would be better if Theodora confined her investigation to the nonexistent Moravian Blood Stone and mythological vampires.

It was at that point in his cogitations that Theodora stirred in his arms. Slowly opening her eyes, she gazed up at him.

"Styles?" she said.

Her voice was distant and dreamy, her cheeks flushed in the aftermath of his love-making. She appeared infinitely desirable. The Devil's Cub smiled, thinking perhaps it was time, now he finally had her attention, that they repaired to the carriage. Phelps could see Aunt Philippa home in Theodora's carriage.

"Do you think Sir Anthony Westfall could ever have been Lady Gwendolyn's Adonis?" Theodora queried in those same, dreamy accents. "I know it is hard to imagine, looking at him now, but I daresay at one time he might have been quite handsome. And then, of course, there is Mr. Andrew Moreland, whose name at least begins with an *M*."

"Hell and the devil confound it, Theodora!" exploded Styles, his mood considerably deflated. Taking her by the hand, he led her deeper into the shrubs. Then turning, he caught her in his arms and, covering her mouth with his, lowered her without preamble to a soft cushion of grass bordered by blue irises and white and purple delphiniums.

"Styles!—?" gasped Theodora, considerably surprised.

"Hush, Theodora," Styles silenced her. "At the moment I am not in the least interested in Lady Gwendolyn's Adonis, in whose role I could not even in the broadest stretch of the imagination picture Sir Anthony Westfall. And as for Moreland, when you meet him, you will understand for yourself that he could not possibly qualify, never mind that his name has the distinction of beginning with an *M*."

With that, he covered her breast with his hand and kissed her, forcefully, on the mouth, his tongue thrusting between her teeth.

Momentarily startled at her Devil's Cub's vehemence, Theodora nevertheless had the presence of mind to realize his passion was of no common order. There was a fierce possessiveness in the caress of his hands that awakened a melting heat in her veins. Just before her thoughts scattered on a rising tide of pleasurable sensations, it occurred to her that she was exceedingly fortunate to have married a man with Styles's inventive flair. Indeed, she doubted that any other man would have thought to fill the second intermission making love to his wife in his hostess's garden.

Releasing her mouth, Styles pressed his lips to the swell of Theodora's breast above the décolletage of her gown. The thought came to him that he had obviously lost his mind as simultaneously he slipped his hand beneath the hem of her dress and began to work his way upward along the silken smoothness of her inner thigh. But then, bedding his enchantress in Lady Harrington's flower bed would seem at the moment to make perfect sense, he reflected, acutely aware of the painful bulge at the front of his breeches. He doubted that there was the remotest possibility that he could postpone the inevitable for more genteel surrounds, especially as his quest revealed Theodora, already flowing with the honeyed nectar of arousal.

"Theodora, sweet love," he breathed, reaching for the fastenings at the front of his breeches.

"Please do hurry, Styles," Theodora whispered back at him. "I find it strangely exciting to experiment in new and unusual surrounds. Do you think perhaps I am sinking into a state of moral turpitude?"

The Devil's Cub uttered a laugh that was more in the nature of a groan. "I daresay you are hopelessly depraved." Theodora was all sweet magic, a witch who long ago had cast her spell over him. And by some benevolent trick of fate, she was his wife. Nothing could ever change that. Spreading wide her thighs, he fitted the head of his swollen manhood into the moist petals of her flesh.

Theodora's face shimmered up at him in the starlight, her eyes huge and dark, like deep glimmering pools. He found himself wishing she would say the words again. But then, she did not have to. It was all there for any fool to read in her face. Theodora loved him. She had loved him since she was a child of ten. He must have been blind not to see it from the very first. Then Theodora was lifting herself to him, and he plunged himself into her.

It seemed to Theodora that she was mounted on the glorious winds of a storm, a storm of her Devil's Cub's making. He was a magnificent specimen of manhood with his hard, muscular body, his hands and lips that carried her away into new realms of discovery. But more than that, he was the Devil's Cub, unguarded, passionate, fiercely tender. Theodora felt transported by all that he revealed of himself.

Then Styles was drawing up and back, and with a final, savage thrust, he spilled his seed into her. A keening gasp broke from Theodora as she felt a rippling explosion of release. The thought came to Theodora as Styles lowered his head to give her a long, lingering kiss, that she had never been so deliriously happy as she was at that moment with the Devil's Cub.

Thirteen

Styles lay with his weight propped on his elbows and his face turned into the soft curve of Theodora's neck, as he drew in great ragged breaths. Only as his heart began to slow to a more regular beat did the realization of what he had done strike him with its full significance. Good God, if anyone had told him just a few hours ago that he would be making love to his wife in someone else's garden while a ball was in full progress, he would have thought that individual either mad or a fool.

Belatedly aware of the picture they must make if anyone stumbled on their love nest, Styles heaved himself off his sated countess, who lay blissfully trailing one of Lady Harrington's severed purple delphiniums down her cheek.

"Promise me, Styles," she said languidly, "that we shall make love in a flower garden at least two or three times a year. Perhaps it is only something in the air, but I believe the experience has added a whole new dimension to our experiments in mutual understanding."

"I should say that was understating the matter," answered Styles dryly, who, having set himself to rights, reached a hand down to Theodora. "If you wish, we shall make it a tradition. Every thirtieth of April, we shall spend the second intermission of a ball in wanton abandon in a bed of prized delphiniums."

"Actually, I think I should prefer something more fragrant," Theodora said, dimpling naughtily, as Styles pulled her to her

feet. "Something in the family of orchids, perhaps, or hya-
cinths."

"Clearly roses would be most damned inconvenient," observed Styles, who, struck by his total lapse of what was due
his wife, was staring, dumbfounded, at Theodora.

Her hair in tangled disarray, the chaste garland of flowers
drooping wantonly over one eyebrow, she little resembled the
vision of fashion whom he had conducted forcefully from the
ballroom little more than half an hour before. Her white silk
gown, besides bearing evidence of grass stains, was creased
and hopelessly disheveled, and her white satin slippers were
soiled beyond redemption. In no little amazement at himself,
he felt his groin stir all over again at the sight of her. Egad,
he had never known a woman who could so utterly make him
forget himself as Theodora did.

"I'm afraid, my love," he said, attempting ineffectually to
adjust her fallen garland, "that we shall not be able to leave
Lady Harrington's ball in the accepted manner. While I myself
find you singularly ravishing, it does occur to me that to be
seen in your present state might seriously damage your standing as the reigning Arbiter of Ladies' Fashion."

In sudden belated awareness, Theodora's hands flew to her
hair and then to her ruined skirts. "Good heavens, I am a
frightful mess." To the Devil's Cub, who was expecting an
utterly different reaction, she lifted a face rosy with laughter.
"I am afraid I quite overlooked the obvious drawbacks to conducting scientific experiments in flower gardens. I don't suppose if we both concentrated very hard, we might persuade
Aunt Philippa's entity to summon her to our aid with a comb
and my wrap?"

"I'm afraid we are more likely to summon a deal of unwanted speculation," observed Styles, "when our prolonged
absence is finally noticed."

Taking Theodora's hand, Styles led her through the maze of
shrubs and flowerbeds to a point of concealment from behind
which they could obtain a view of the verandah. Styles, who

entertained little hope that Aunt Philippa's entity might be re-
lied upon to bring her to them, thought, on the contrary, they
had a better chance that Phelps, the man he had assigned to
act as Theodora's bodyguard, would be within calling range.
As it happened, it was neither Aunt Philippa nor Phelps who
came to their assistance, but Justin Villiers, who apparently
had stepped out to enjoy a cigar.

"Stay here, Theodora, out of sight," instructed Styles, brush-
ing bits of debris from his coat and breeches. "I shall be only
a moment."

Theodora, who had no intention in the circumstances of ex-
posing herself to public view, peered through the foliage at
Styles's retreating back. After the first exchange of greetings
between the two men, she could make out little of what was
said beyond an occasional phrase, such as "a little accident"
and "Miss Philippa Havelock." Theodora ducked behind cover
as Villiers shot a glance in her direction. The next moment,
he obligingly flipped his cigar stub into the yard and, clapping
a hand to Styles's back, disappeared into the ballroom.

"Villiers has agreed to fetch Aunt Philippa and your wrap to
the carriage," said Styles, rejoining Theodora. "Now, it only
remains for us to make our way out of here with no one the
wiser."

"Sneaking through the shrubs should make a perfect end to
an unusually stimulating evening," observed Theodora, stoop-
ing to remove her slippers and stockings. "Fortunately I have
had a deal of experience at it—looking for wild herbs," she
added, twinkling at Styles's inquisitively raised eyebrow. "Normally, however, such excursions are conducted under the light
of a full moon."

"In this instance, we may well be thankful for a moonless
night. It occurs to me we shall be bloody well lucky if we are
not taken for burglars before we are through," observed Styles,
leading Theodora back through the garden away from the house.

The strains of music issuing from the ballroom lent a certain
charm to the evening, reflected Theodora, who was savoring

the freedom of strolling barefooted through damp, freshly mown grass in the company of her husband. Indeed, her every sense seemed peculiarly heightened. It occurred to her, slipping her hand in Styles's, that now might be the perfect time to share her secret with him. After all, after three weeks of waiting for something that usually came as regular as clockwork, she was very nearly positive of her prognosis. Sometime in November Styles was almost certain to become a father, and at this moment, which seemed fraught with the magic of their love-making and her heightened awareness of the scents of dew and spring flowers on the music-laden breeze, she wanted more than anything to share that knowledge with him.

Glancing furtively up at Styles's stern profile, Theodora considered the best way to broach the subject. It would hardly do to simply blurt it out. A thing like this should be led up to gradually so that she could savor the moments of anticipation before she actually sprang it on him. After all, one was not afforded the opportunity to announce the pending arrival of a firstborn child more than once, she told herself. Perhaps she should begin by reminding him of the conditions under which she had accepted his proposal, not the least of which was the fifth and final one, she decided.

"Styles," she ventured, feeling her pulse quicken. Her lips parted to add that there was something she had been meaning to discuss with him, when she was met with a wholly disconcerting, blistering oath.

"Bloody hell! It needed only this." The Devil's Cub turned a darkly speculative look on Theodora. "How, my dear, are you at climbing fences?"

Only then did Theodora become aware that their way was barred by a brick wall, fully as tall as Styles. "I suppose there is no point in looking for a gate?" postulated Theodora, eyeing the obstacle doubtfully.

"Unless you number among your many talents the ability to pick a lock, I'm afraid a gate would be of less use to us than a ladder."

"Well, then." Bending down, Theodora slipped her feet in her shoes, then, rising, lifted her skirts. "It would seem we have little choice in the matter. I suggest, my lord," she said, handing Styles her stockings, "that you give me a boost to the top."

Styles, presented with a posterior view of his wife in less than a ladylike position, was struck with the thought that he had seen Theodora in many guises, but none so appealing as this, with her hair hanging in a disheveled mass down around her shoulders and her skirts hiked to her hips.

"Well?" queried Theodora, glancing back at Styles over her shoulder. "What are we waiting for?"

"As it happens, I was just admiring the view. The devil, Theodora, you take my breath away."

"I'm sure I am flattered, Styles," retorted Theodora, feeling her color rise. "However, I shall catch my death if I have to stand around like this very much longer."

"Witch," said Styles feelingly, stuffing her stockings in a pocket. "You have no appreciation of the finer things in life. You, my love, are a beautiful work of art. Promise me you will wait for me on the top. I want to keep you all in one piece."

"I will promise you anything, my lord, if only you will give me your undivided attention when we are safely away from here and in the carriage."

"Good God, Theodora, you may be sure you have that now." Bending down, he made a stirrup of his hands. "Promise you will wait for me."

"Very well. I will wait for you," said Theodora, placing her foot in his hands. "I don't see what else I should be doing."

Theodora lifted herself as Styles straightened, flinging her as easily as he would have a child to a seat on top.

It was then, as Theodora squirmed to a more secure position, that she glimpsed a figure detach itself from the shadows and hurtle toward Styles's unguarded back.

No doubt it was some primitive instinct which prompted her to cry out. "Styles, behind you! Look out!"

Styles, with the born instinct of the natural athlete, spun on his heel in time to meet his attacker. In horror Theodora glimpsed the flash of a knife. Styles uttered a curse. Out of the darkness came the sickening thud of a fist against bone. One of the men went down, then scrambling to his feet, lurched into a stumbling run. The other leaped in pursuit.

"Styles! Don't you dare go after him. I swear I shall jump if you do!"

Styles halted, his shoulders heaving from his recent exertions, then, turning, he came back again. "Bloody hell, Theodora, are you all right?"

"No, I am stranded on top of a wall, and I have lost one of my shoes, which I am very nearly certain I flung at your assailant, though I cannot in the least remember doing it. Who the devil was he?"

Two large hands planted themselves on the wall beside her, followed almost immediately by Styles, who, pulling himself up, vaulted over the top and dropped lightly to the ground on the other side. "We shall discuss it when we have you safely down. Unless you plan to stay the night up there."

Theodora required no urging. Swinging her legs over to the other side, she pushed off the wall into the Devil's Cub's waiting arms.

"Styles," she exclaimed, clinging to him as he set her on her feet. "He meant to kill you, and pray don't deny it. I saw the knife in his hand."

"Very well, I won't deny it," agreed Styles. Taking her arm, he began to lead her down the alley in which they had landed. "But it need not concern you. I have dealt with his kind before. At the moment, I am more concerned with getting you safely home before we have any more little misadventures."

Theodora limped after him in a bobbing gait occasioned by having one shoe on and one shoe off. "I wish you will not be absurd, Styles. It is perfectly obvious that *I* was never in any danger. The man was after *you.* Furthermore, I daresay he was no more than a hireling, some poor, desperate creature willing to do anything for a few shillings, else he would not have been made to run so easily. The real questions to which we should be applying ourselves are who sent him and why."

Styles came to an abrupt halt. "Not 'we,' Theodora," he said ominously. *"You* are not to involve yourself with this."

"I knew you were going to say that," declared Theodora.

"And how not? You are a witch with acute empathic powers of perception, are you not?" replied Styles in no mood to humor her. She had, with her usual acumen, struck far too close to the truth in the matter of his would-be assassin, which would undoubtedly lead her to even more dangerous conclusions.

"It is not that at all," Theodora retorted, hurt beyond reason by what she conceived to be his sarcasm. "It is only that you are so utterly predictable!"

She was rewarded with a cold glitter of demon eyes. Predictable, was he. And she, no doubt, preferred someone unpredictable and therefore exciting, someone like the mysterious M. Then so be it. At least he would make certain she was not harmed by her predilection for adventure.

"Then you will not be surprised to learn you are to have your wings clipped. Henceforth, you will confine yourself to the sole pursuit of those things proper to a young woman in London for her first Season, and only that. Lady Gwendolyn's diary is no longer your concern. Is that understood?"

Styles, Theodora reflected, could be damnably bull-headed at times. Obviously there was no point in reasoning with him in his present frame of mind. Indeed, there would seem very little point in talking to him at all.

"There is nothing wrong with my understanding, Styles," she assured him, and, turning on her shod heel, limped, bobbing, away with her head up and her back straight, leaving Styles to stare after her in wry appreciation of the fact that she had not answered his question.

In the street at the end of the alley, they found their carriages waiting, attended, in addition to the anxious coachmen, by

Phelps, who appeared to be nursing a headache, Aunt Philippa, who looked to be in deep consultation with her entity, and Villiers, who, after a single glance at the approaching couple, hastily flipped his cigar away and strode forward to meet them.

"Styles, old man. You took a deuced long time getting here. I was beginning to wonder if we should send for a Bow Street Runner," he said in concert with Aunt Philippa's cry of consternation.

"Theodora, good heavens!" Hastening down out of the carriage, she flung a pelisse of white sarcenet trimmed in swansdown around her niece's shoulders. "You look as if you have been set upon by footpads. Which would hardly be surprising, considering the fact that poor Mr. Phelps has already suffered a similar fate tonight."

"Phelps, is that true?" exclaimed Theodora, crossing in immediate concern to the bodyguard, who appeared rather more mortified than injured. "Here, let me see."

"Begging your pardon, m'lady, but it ain't nothing for you to be worried about. Only a lump where the blighter knocked me lantern out for me."

"I see," said Theodora, suppressing a grin. Phelps, who had led the uncertain life of a boxer until Styles had rescued him from a bout in which the aging pugilist had come close to being beaten within an inch of his life, presented the appearance of a lumbering behemoth, clad incongruously in a gentleman's evening attire. He had stood out among Lady Harrington's guests like a pit bull in a china shop, which probably had been Styles's intent all along. Anyone entertaining the wish to harm Theodora would naturally think twice before taking on Phelps.

Only someone had taken him on, from the rear, when he was not looking. From the looks of the lump at the back of his head, he had taken a blow that might have permanently disabled a less massively built man.

"It is my considered opinion that you will live, Mr. Phelps," said Theodora, smiling gravely. "I suggest, however, a cold compress of comfrey leaves for tonight. Come to me before you turn in, and I shall see to it."

"I'm obliged to you, m'lady, though I don't see why all the fuss. I've had worse and lived to tell of it."

"I'm sure you have," agreed Theodora, glancing over her shoulder at Styles in close conversation with Villiers. "Perhaps you would care to tell me how you came to receive this one."

"It was the work of a yellow-livered sneak, m'lady, or it'd be him with the lump, stead of me, and it wouldn't be at the back of the blighter's skull, but where his nose had used to be."

"I haven't the least doubt of it," said Theodora encouragingly. "But how did it happen?"

"It was like this, m'lady. It was some time after—well, after you and His Lordship went outside," declared Phelps, relieved, no doubt, to have gotten diplomatically past the countess's less than dignified exit from the ballroom. "I waited and watched, thinking you didn't need me when you was with His Lordship. But then, when you didn't come back again for the longest time, I began to get worried. Like, maybe I shouldn't't've let you out of me sight. I got as far as the bushes, when the blighter come up behind and took out me lights."

"My, my," said Aunt Philippa, "and to think it might have been any one of us unfortunate enough to wander outside. I daresay, Theodora, it could have been you."

"Yes, dearest, but fortunately it was not. What happened after that, Mr. Phelps?"

"It was Mr. Villiers what found me just when I was coming round. That's how I knew to come here, m' lady. And that's all there was to it, save to say how sorry I am I wasn't there when you needed me."

"Never mind, Phelps," Theodora said, laying a hand on the big man's sleeve. "It could not be avoided. And in a roundabout way you have been of no little help."

Reminding the bodyguard to come to her for his cold com-

press, she turned, then, in time to take her leave of Justin
Villiers, who had come up to the carriage with Styles.

"I believe, sir," she said, graciously extending her hand,
"that we have you to thank for my rescue. I can only say it
was exceedingly fortuitous for me that you happened to come
out for a smoke."

"Not at all, Lady Dameron." Straightening after saluting her
hand, Villiers regarded her with a suspicious gravity, belied by
a gleam in his eyes. "I am naturally pleased that I could be
of some small service. After all, it could have happened to
anyone. An unlighted garden can be a dangerous place, especially when garden tools are left carelessly in the path."

"Yes, I suppose it can," agreed Theodora, feeling herself
blush. She had not the smallest notion to what he was referring,
but she inferred from Styles's bland expression that she was
now guilty of being so fumblefooted as to have tripped over
a garden rake or some equally ridiculous thing. The devil.

"By the way, old man," Villiers said, turning to Styles, "I
took the liberty of expressing your regrets to Lady Harrington.
It seems Lady Dameron was suffering the headache. And, now,
I believe that covers everything. Unless there is something else,
I shall just be able to make it back for the supper dance, which,
you will be glad to hear, has been promised me by the delightfully charming Lady Margaret, who," he added with a
wink at Styles, "has only just laid off wearing black gloves."

"A bounder, if ever I saw one," muttered Philippa under her
breath to Theodora, as Villiers, after having wished them all
a good evening, left them, presumably to return to Lady Harrington's and the latest in a long line of well endowed young
widows.

"Yes, but an engaging one, one must presume," observed
Theodora as she took Styles's hand and prepared to follow her
aunt into the carriage.

"Theodora." Theodora's heart gave a leap as strong fingers
closed over hers.

Theodora drew a breath and lifted her eyes to the Devil's

Cub's. "My lord?" she said, aware of a flutter in the region of her stomach. "Was there something more you wished to say to me?"

She was rewarded with the distinct leap of the muscle along the firm line of her Devil's Cub's jaw.

"I believe it was you who wished to say something to me," Styles pointed out, keenly aware of Theodora's formality of address. The devil, he thought. "I did promise you would have my undivided attention."

"Yes, so you did, and you, naturally, are a man of your word. Unfortunately, I am afraid I cannot remember anymore what I wished to discuss with you."

Theodora glanced away from Styles's thunderous look of disbelief. He would just have to think of her what he wished. The magic of the evening had been irrevocably spoiled. Indeed, *he* had spoiled it with his arrogant male assumptions, chief of which was the notion that, because she was a woman, she could be treated with a total disregard for the fact that she was a highly intelligent, rational being who could never be content to be confined to pursuits considered suitable for a female of the species. She had thought Styles, of all people, would have understood she could never settle for anything less than the freedom to exercise to the full her ability to do and think for herself. Certainly, the last thing she wished at the moment was to reinforce his position by telling him she was breeding. She doubted not he would send her immediately home to Exmoor. Besides, the mood was hardly right for what should be a joyous moment of celebration. Not, now, when she was as close as she had ever been to being out of all patience with Styles.

Deliberately she stepped up on to the carriage mount, only to stop and look back at him. "I suppose it slipped my mind in all the confusion. I'm sorry, Styles. Truly I am. Perhaps it will come back to me when I have had time to consider the evening's events in a more rational manner. Right now, I simply wish to go home. I believe I have had my surfeit of fresh air for one night."

The devil she had, thought Styles, acutely aware as the carriage pulled away, that for the first time since that fateful night in Devil's Gill Theodora had deliberately erected a barrier between them. And little wonder. A quarter of an hour ago, she had been sparkling with excitement in the aftermath of her unlooked for adventure, and he had ruthlessly quashed that exuberance by relegating her to the role of a society fribble. Naturally she would be angry. Still, as little as he enjoyed hurting her, he could not see that he had had any choice in the matter.

Bloody hell! The truth was his hands were tied.

Theodora was a bloody innocent, wholly inexperienced in games of intrigue. She knew nothing of desperate men who would think nothing of putting a period to her existence. Good God, she would be little better than a lamb among wolves. And even if it had been possible to insure her safety, the fact of the matter was he could not have brought her into his confidence even if he wanted to. In a matter that concerned the welfare of England, he was bound to secrecy.

Uttering an oath, Styles stepped into his waiting carriage.

"To White's," he said curtly to Hodges.

"It is all here, Aunt Philippa," Theodora said sometime later that night, leafing through Lady Gwendolyn's diary. "If only I can reason it out. One must suppose the game began innocently enough. Unfortunately, it would seem to have gotten entirely out of hand sometime after the Mysterious M entered the picture. Here. January fifteenth. 'M is coming, my beautiful young Adonis. Tonight I shall dream beautiful dreams.' And here. January twenty-second. 'M was here. Damaris insisted he should be Lord of the Feast. Pray God Styles does not hear of it.' "

"How very curious. What do you suppose she meant by

that?" asked Philippa, occupied with winding a turban about her head. For the sake of appearances, she had taken to wearing proper English gowns whenever she was in the public eye. At night, in her own company, she catered to her preferences for costumes that suited her flare for the inventive.

"I wish I knew," Theodora confessed, frowning over the passage. "From what I have been able to gather, the Feast refers to a rite of passage in which newcomers were initiated into the game. I can only speculate that M, as Lord of the Feast, was the initiate and that either Lady Gwendolyn hoped Styles would not find out he had been brought into the game or she hoped he would not learn the ceremony had taken place."

"Or perhaps it was a simple matter of hoping Styles would not learn M had been to the castle," Philippa pointed out, smearing her face with a cream with the scents of cucumbers and strawberries. "Whatever the case, it would seem she was in some manner afraid of her own son."

Theodora pursed her lips in a frown. "I don't know, Aunt. Somehow I don't think that was it. Sometimes I have had the most curious feeling it was more in the nature of wishing to spare him. Listen to this: 'February second. I have drunk from the well of dreams. It is madness, but I cannot help myself. If Styles knew, he would slay the demons who feed on my soul, and that would be madness indeed.' "

"The poor woman," murmured Philippa, shaking her head. "Clearly she was out of her senses."

"Yes," Theodora agreed, "but do you see my point?"

"I'm sorry, Theodora, but it makes very little sense. In my experience, demons do not feed on souls. They are far more likely to prefer flesh and blood. I have heard of demons that will inhabit a dead body in order to attack the living or demons that kill newly born infants. There is one in Indian tradition that has the wholly disgusting habit of sucking the blood from a sleeping man's big toe. But they do not feed on souls."

"Really? A sleeping man's toe?" said Theodora, her attention arrested. "I find that very curious. It would seem far more practical to tap a vein, after all. I should think the poor man would object to having his toe sucked."

"No doubt he would," replied Philippa, "if he knew about it. Blood-sucking demons take the precaution of putting the sleeping victim and his household under a spell first. They never wake up before morning, so they never realize what has happened until it is far too late."

"But how very enterprising of them," said Theodora, much struck at the notion. "I daresay it is much the same with bankers and moneylenders. But all this is beside the point. I believe Lady Gwendolyn's demons were not demons in any real sense of the word, else why would it be madness for Styles to slay them? It would be an entirely different story if they were flesh-and-blood persons, who were using their influence to persuade her to do things she knew she shouldn't. I daresay not even the most dangerous man in England could go around indiscriminately killing people without getting into a deal of trouble. This is not the Dark Ages, Aunt Philippa. These days, the law tends to frown on such things."

"Well, needless to say, we are not going to solve anything tonight, and it is getting late." Rising, she shook out the wide legs of her *Punjab* trousers and loose-fitting over shirt and crossed to her bed. "If you insist on going to this Dr. Whatsisname's Museum in the morning, I suggest we get some sleep, though I am sure I cannot see the least point in it, when you say Styles has forbidden you to do any more investigating into his mother's journal. I daresay he will not like it in the least, Theodora."

"No," agreed Theodora, thinking it was really too bad of Styles to put her in the position of having to go behind his back, when the rational thing would have been for them to simply join forces. Unfortunately, there would seem to be little help for it now, she thought. Hugging the journal to her breast, she crossed to the door with the intention of withdrawing to her own rooms down the hall. "But then, dearest Aunt, I do not intend for him to find out. Sweet dreams. I shall expect you at breakfast at eight."

Styles, who had not the least inclination for cards that evening, made his way leisurely through the crowded gaming room. Pausing here and there to exchange greetings with friends and acquaintances, he made steadily in the direction of a gentleman, seated alone at a table at the back.

"I have often wondered, Whitfill," he announced, sinking into a chair across the table from his quarry, "why, considering your views on gambling, you choose to maintain a membership at White's. Surely it cannot be simply for the pleasure of my company."

"My views on gambling notwithstanding, my lord," replied Whitfill with what was meant to be a smile, "I find a gaming club tends to be a veritable fountain of information. I have, for example, only just heard the rumor you were attacked this evening, my lord. I comfort myself with the observation that you appear little the worse the wear for it."

"You amaze me, Whitfill, as you no doubt intended. I should be interested to know how you have come by the information in less time than it took for me to arrive here from Lady Harrington's. I should not like to think you are monitoring my movements."

"In view of recent events, it seemed the wise thing to do, my lord," replied Whitfill with an apologetic air. "In fact, their lordships insisted on it. Our man at Lady Harrington's lost sight of you in the garden, or you may be sure the attack would never have happened. As it was, he heard the sounds of a scuffle and saw a ruffian fleeing the scene as if chased by the devil. I'm sorry to say the felon eluded capture."

"Excellent, Whitfill," Styles ironically applauded. "And now I suppose I must sleep sounder knowing my safety is in such capable hands." Styles stood up. "Call your men off,

Whitfill. At once. Or inform their lordships they can find someone else to negotiate with their Serbian rebels."

Whitfill also came to his feet. "Naturally I shall tell them, my lord," he hastened to assure the earl. "Only, pray spare me a moment more. It is a matter concerning your uncle."

Styles settled back on his heels. "Umberly? What has he done to earn your attention?"

"I believe, my lord, that you should come with me. Your uncle is only a short distance from here. He has expressed a desire to see you."

The bachelor quarters near the west end of Bury Street were cramped and mean, showing unmistakable signs of decay. Styles could not but reflect that his uncle had come down a long way in the world from his former rooms in St. James's Hotel little more than a block away. But then, the unentailed property which should have come down to him on the death of his profligate father, had long since gone under the gavel. There remained little more than the manor, falling slowly into disrepair, and the grounds upon which it stood.

Beside Styles, Whitfill cleared his throat.

"The earl turned up in a raid on one of the opium dens off Limehouse," said Whitfill, opening the door for Styles. "One of the gaol guards of whom I make use from time to time brought him to my attention. I took the liberty of bringing him here. I beg your pardon, my lord, but I think perhaps you should prepare yourself."

Styles glanced at Whitfill's impassive features. The man had the look of a bloody ferret, but he was undeniably good at what he did. Nodding, Styles strode past him into the room.

The odor of sweat and sickness assailed his nostrils as he approached the still figure on the bed. Styles felt a cold knot of anger. Lord Harry had been a true Underwood, a man of weak will prey to every sort of vice, but he had not been wholly without positive attributes, not the least of which was the fact that he was Lady Gwendolyn's only sibling. At least he should be cleaned up and moved without further delay to more congenial surrounds.

"Summon my coachman," he ordered briskly over his shoulder.

Theodora, having long since given up expecting Styles to come to her room that night, sat perched in the windowseat with Percival curled, purring, in her lap.

She had been going over in her mind the events surrounding the attack on Styles, and, in spite of the fact that it stretched the imagination to think anyone could have predicted Styles would choose to make love to his wife in Lady Harrington's flower bed, she could not shake the feeling that the whole thing had been carefully orchestrated.

In retrospect, it seemed perfectly obvious that it had not been mere chance that had led Lady Damaris Gale to confront Theodora with the intent of blackening Styles's name. On the contrary, Styles had made it plain that his mama's erstwhile bosom bow had been wholly aware he would not hesitate to ruin her if ever she stepped too far over the line. Why, then, would she suddenly lose sight of that fact and commit the ultimate folly before an entire ballroom of people? The only possible answer was that it had been done deliberately.

"Indeed, nothing else would seem to make any sense, Percival," she informed her familiar, who seemed in perfect agreement with her. "The question is, what did she hope to gain by it? You are quite right to point out that it must have been something quite extraordinary to be worth incurring Styles's displeasure and forfeiting what I suspect has hitherto been a generous purse. But what?"

And then there was the matter of Phelps's lump, which she had earlier treated with a cold compress of comfrey leaves. It had not been by chance that the former pugilist had been so conveniently taken out. Someone had made sure he would not be on hand when the attacker made his move. That much seemed obvious. A deal less obvious was how anyone could possibly have anticipated Styles would be advantageously placed at the site of attack.

The answer, that it was impossible, did not in the least deter Theodora. In any hypothesis, there might be hidden variables that must be discovered before the seemingly disparate evidence formed a discernible pattern. In this case, the variables must be the motive, the desired end, and the unknown author of what would seem an insidious plot, all of which brought her back to her diminishing list of possible candidates.

At that point her ruminations were disrupted by the sound of carriage wheels on the cobblestoned drive at the back of the house. Theodora, peering out the window, was met with the sight of Styles and Hodges in the process of removing what gave every appearance of being a body from the carriage and carrying it between them to the house.

"Now, what the devil?" she queried of Percival, who was less than pleased to find himself abruptly dislodged from his cozy resting place and deposited unceremoniously on the floor. Standing stiff-legged, his tail switching, he made known his disgust. Theodora, however, thrusting her feet into slippers and shrugging into a dressing gown, was already halfway through the door.

The two men, having carried their burden through the kitchen entrance, were almost to the first-story landing, when Theodora, meeting them on the stairway, was made aware by a feeble groan that the body was not, as she had first expected, a corpse.

"Hurry, Styles," she said, instinctively taking charge. "He is in a very bad way. I shall need Thistlewaite. And hot water from the kitchens. Have Thistlewaite fetch a clean nightshirt. Oh, and have someone in the kitchens standing by. Someone with sense enough to follow my instructions. Send someone to awaken Will. I may require a go-between."

It was not until they had her unexpected patient settled on

the bed in the first floor guest room and Styles had sent Hodges to see that Theodora's orders were carried out that Theodora, helping Styles to strip the unconscious man of his coat, finally thought to ask the obvious. "Who is he, Styles? And how in heaven's name did he come to be like this?"

Styles, flinging the filthy coat aside, reached without pause for the equally unappealing shirt. "Allow me to present to you Lord Harry, or, more formally, his lordship the Earl of Umberly."

Theodora stared down at the dirty bewhiskered face over the boot she was in the process of removing. "Your uncle."

"My uncle," Styles affirmed. "My mother's only brother. Theodora, there is no need to soil your hands on him. Hodges and I between us can see to cleaning him up."

"I wish you will not be absurd. I have seen worse. Outside the opium houses on the water front." Theodora fell back to work. "How long has he been like this?"

"For nearly as long as I can remember. Not this bad, of course. He was picked up today, but from the looks of him, I should say he has been at it for weeks, the poor miserable wretch."

Theodora, after a single, assessing glance at Styles, could only be grateful when the room filled with people. With Hodges and Thistlewaite to take over the task of making Lord Harry more presentable, she did not hesitate to order Styles from the room.

She had, it was true, to remind him of her first condition, to declare in no uncertain terms that in a sickroom he would only be underfoot, and finally to assure him she was not in the least likely to succumb from practicing what was only, after all, her chosen profession; but she was, at last, able to prevail upon him to take himself off.

Her patient stripped and covered to the chin with quilts, Theodora ordered Hodges to build up the fire to a roaring blaze.

"He must be made to sweat," she said, tucking the quilts

tightly under the mattress. Instructing her assistants to keep
the fire up and her patient covered, Theodora hurried to the
kitchen. There, she occupied herself with preparing a potent
tea of herbs with cleansing and restorative properties, the chief
ingredients of which were ginseng, tumeric, and chamomille.

When the recipe had properly steeped, Theodora, issuing
orders to the chef's chief assistant to fetch chicken broth as
soon as it was ready, hurried back up the two flights of stairs.

She was met with a blast of heat as she opened the door
and slipped quickly into the room, closing the door behind
her.

"Help me, Thistlewaite, to prop his head up," she said, setting the tray on a table by the bed. "Poor man, he is very
weak."

"Weakness, I fear," observed the valet, lifting the sick man's
head, "was always one of Lord Harry's shortcomings."

Theodora glanced up from dipping a spoon in the restorative
herbal tea. "You have known him for a long time, haven't you,
Thistlewaite," she observed, gently forcing the spoon between
Lord Harry's lips.

"Since my lord Styles was a boy," Thistlewaite admitted. "I
daresay he was mostly a pleasant fellow, even likable, when
he wasn't in the influence of others. I regret to see he has
been brought so low."

"I believe it is hard on Styles," Theodora gently probed.
"Were he and his uncle very close?"

"Not, my lady, so you would notice. His Lordship did what
he could for his uncle, and that was more than his uncle deserved."

After that, Thistlewaite would say no more on the subject
of Styles and Lord Harry, and Theodora had to be content with
that rather dubious, final encomium. Which was just as well,
since soon after, the fire and the tea began to do their work.
She was kept far too busy to engage in conversation, idle or
otherwise, until little more than an hour before dawn, when
the crisis was reached.

The sun was just peeping over the rooftops when she at last judged it safe to leave her patient under the watchful supervision of Tom Dickson, who had been summoned to relieve Thistlewaite and Hodges.

Having, in the circumstances, forgotten all about her planned outing with Philippa, Theodora flung herself in bed and fell instantly into a dreamless sleep of utter exhaustion.

She did not awaken until after noon upon which she quickly dressed, made a hurried meal, and went immediately to tend her patient, whom she found resting comfortably.

The afternoon was, consequently, well advanced before Theodora was able to slip out of the house in the company of her aunt.

Fourteen

London, Theodora decided as she gazed out the carriage window in no little bemusement at the sight of Lady Winthrop, approaching from the opposite direction, was everything Styles had said it would be, and a great deal more besides.

Naturally she had arrived expecting to excite a deal of interest. After all, she was the nobody who had legshackled the most dangerous man in England. Still, she had hardly been prepared to be received with such enthusiasm that ladies of quality like Isadora Winthrop had taken to riding about town with felines of various sizes and descriptions perched on their laps. It was a phenomenon that had led in more than a few cases to minor scratches, near carriage wrecks, and not a few frayed tempers.

How very foolish it all was, Theodora reflected, an irrepressible dimple peeping forth as she settled back against the squabs. The relationship between a witch and her familiar, after all, was quite different from that of mere mistress and pet. She could expect Percival to behave with perfect decorum in her presence. They, after all, were in complete empathic accord with one another.

A pity the same could not be said of her relationship with her newly acquired abigail, she thought with a barely suppressed sigh. She had vastly preferred Millie's untutored clumsiness to Sarah Jessop's skilled competence. Indeed, Theodora deeply regretted the necessity of leaving her old friend behind in Somerset to care for the infant Annie.

Not that Jessop, as she liked to be called, had not done her best to work miracles. The abigail had, as a matter of fact, transformed a crude lump of clay into something very nearly resembling a work of art. Thanks to Jessop, Theodora thought perhaps she actually looked the part of the Countess of Styles, an achievement that she found pleasing on the rare occasions that she stopped to take notice of it.

The truth was, Theodora reflected, she was proving a sad trial to the sorely beset abigail, who obviously had never before had a mistress quite like herself. Theodora, after numerous previous failures to make herself understood to the superior servant, had at last been forced that afternoon to resort to more forceful means of persuasion. She had, in fact, declared in no uncertain terms that she liked her hair the way it was and far from change it, she would prefer to be judged the dowdiest of dowds than allow her tresses to be cut even so much as an inch. Having shocked the abigail into a stunned silence, Theodora had taken the further opportunity to let it be known she had not the least inclination to sit for hours with her fingers soaking in cucumber lotion, to submit to the torture of curling papers or irons, or to indulge herself in anything so abjectly pointless as an afternoon beauty rest. She had ended by assuring Jessop that she appreciated all that the woman was trying to do, but she simply had other, far more important matters to attend in the precious few hours that were not occupied with the endless flow of invitations that arrived daily at her door.

She supposed it was no excuse for her having antagonized her well-meaning abigail that she had been impatient to be gone on her errand and consequently had not had the time to be more diplomatic. In a few hours she would need Jessop's skills to make her presentable for another evening of social gaiety.

It was all very well to be much sought after by any number of hostesses, mused Theodora resignedly. After all, it suited her purposes to be able to circulate freely among the members of the *beau monde*. It was only that she was so greatly in demand that she was finding it exceedingly difficult to make time to do her research into the reported occurrences of vampires and the legends that surrounded them. It was why she presently found herself in the narrow thoroughfare of Holborn in the reluctant company of her Aunt Philippa.

The carriage turned off into the even narrower and dingier confines of New Street and drew up before a three-story building of soot-blackened brown brick that looked as if it had seen better days and which bore across its front a sign identifying the establishment as Dr. Galapardrasso's Museum of Abnormal and Rare Anomalous Artifacts.

"Are you quite certain, Theodora, that this is an advisable course?" queried Philippa Havelock, peering out at the less than prepossessing facade. "I cannot think Styles will be at all pleased to discover that we have slipped off without Mr. Phelps, when you know we gave our word we would do no such thing."

"*You* gave your word," Theodora reminded her aunt. "I promised only to have a care for my safety, which is not at all the same thing as agreeing not to go anywhere except in Mr. Phelps's company. Besides, you know Mr. Phelps would have gone straight to Styles when he learned of our destination. And that would not have done at all," added Theodora, alighting from the carriage. "I haven't the least doubt that Styles would not have approved of our visiting Dr. Galapardrasso's Museum, especially in view of the fact that it was specifically mentioned in Lady Gwendolyn's journal."

"Lady Gwendolyn's journal also mentioned Medvegia among other exotic locations," Aunt Philippa was quick to point out. "I trust you do not intend to seek them out as well."

"I'm afraid a trip to Serbia is out of the question, Aunt," Theodora laughed. "Fortunately, Dr. Galapardrasso is not. I am hopeful he can tell us something about the Moravian Blood Stone. Lady Gwendolyn gave every indication of being obsessed with it in the months before her untimely demise."

Lady Gwendolyn had, in fact, promised a princely sum, among other rewards of a more intimate nature, to whoever among her intimates could bring the elusive stone to her. Someone had obtained it for her if the final entries in the journal could be believed, and that someone was the Mysterious M. Unfortunately, by that time Styles, having attained his majority, had cut his mama off from his greatly depleted purse.

Theodora's eyes flashed at the mere thought of the countess's vituperative references to her son in the final pages. Clearly, her obsession with the stone had destroyed the last shreds of the woman's reason. Still, Theodora could not but be grateful that Lady Gwendolyn had seen fit to record her twisted threads of thought. It provided an intriguing insight into the events that had led up to her death.

It was clear from the final entry that Lady Gwendolyn, having the stone within her reach, but not the wherewithal with which to purchase it, had arranged a meeting with the one who had managed to find it.

A pity Styles had not pursued the matter of his mama's death with his usual keen-sighted rationality, reflected Theodora. Though she could hardly wish to subject him to the passages of bitter condemnation, he might yet have been spared a deal of grief occasioned by his own feelings of guilt.

Had Styles read the journal fifteen years before, after all, he must surely have realized that the night his mama met her death was the same night she was to have had her rendezvous with the Mysterious M of the journal.

To Theodora, it seemed obvious M had had a part in what may or may not have been Lady Gwendolyn's suicide. Furthermore, she little doubted the very same person was behind the attempt to do harm to both herself and Styles. Why else would the poisoner choose to make it appear that the Devil's Cub had, like his mama before him, succumbed to madness and then, when that failed, attempt to murder the new Countess of Styles in a manner strikingly similar to the circumstances surrounding the death of the previous countess? The two events were far too coincidental to be dismissed. Coincidences, after all, she reasoned, reaching for the door handle to Dr. Galapardrasso's Museum, were very often only incidents whose underlying relationships had yet to be determined.

Firmly opening the door, Theodora went in, followed, albeit reluctantly, by Aunt Philippa.

The jangle of a bell, hung over the door, shattered what would seem a preternatural silence. And, truly, the cramped quarters, crammed with every sort of rare anomaly, from a mummified calf with two heads to a portrait purported to be that of Duchess Margaret of Tyrol, who, noted, for her sexual escapades in the sixteenth century, had yet been notoriously ugly, was decidedly lacking in attendance. Theodora saw only a single gentleman, who, standing with his back to her and studiously bent over to examine the exhibit before him, appeared inordinately interested in what were reputed to be the skeletal remains of a mermaid on display in an obscure corner of the room, and a female of quality, who, stepping into what was presumably the curator's study, had closed the door before Theodora could get a good look at her.

"Fascinating. Dr. Galapardrasso has accumulated an impressive collection of oddities," Theodora observed, gazing with interest about her.

Aunt Philippa succumbed to a distinct shudder of revulsion.

"Good heavens, it is a dreadful place, Theodora. It is not enough that it is filthy, but it has the smell of moldering decay about it. It reminds me of an Egyptian tomb Lavinia and I visited outside of Cairo."

"But of course, dearest Aunt," Theodora smiled. "It is a museum. I daresay it would be strange if it did not smell like moldering old things, many of which were probably taken from some grave or another. Only look. Here, according to the sign, is the shrunken head of a Mr. Franklin Hobart, who had the misfortune to fall victim to headhunters in New Guinea." Theodora leaned over the glass case in order to obtain a better view of the trophy within. "How very curious. I wonder how they managed to extract the skull."

"They crushed it, dear lady, and then extracted it piece by piece," supplied a masculine voice from behind the two women, who immediately straightened and came about.

Theodora's glance flashed beyond the newcomer to note the door to the study standing slightly ajar. Curious. The lady had not emerged, and, unless there was another exit, she was behind that door listening to every word. Even more curious, the gentleman who had seemed to be communing with the mermaid was suddenly nowhere to be found.

"Dr. Galapardrasso, one must presume," declared Theodora, turning her considerable powers of empathic perception on the newcomer, who was tall and spare and had pinched features resembling the color of chalk, not to mention bespectacled eyes that put her in mind of the passionless stare of a fish.

Galapardrasso bent in a bow that was meant to be unctuous, but did not fool Theodora in the least. The doctor, she doubted not, was as slippery as an eel. "At your service—Lady Dameron, is it not. Oh, do not be surprised, my lady. Who has not heard of the charming Countess of Styles? Your name is on everyone's lips along with your reputation as a practitioner of the ancient healing arts. You honor my humble establishment with your presence."

"How very nice of you to say so," smiled Theodora, who did not believe a word of it. It was far more likely she had been recognized by the eavesdropper on the other side of the office door. "And what a fascinating place it is. I have long entertained an interest in anomalous subjects. Perhaps you would not mind showing us about."

"Naturally, I should be only too pleased, my lady," Galapardrasso replied, moving toward the displays. "Was there something in particular you wished to see? You might be interested to know that I have what is reputed to be a fragment of the thigh bone of the Witch of Endor, preserved through antiquity by the magic arts."

"I have not the least interest in anything so patently absurd, Dr. Galapardrasso," Theodora stated baldly. "I am not so gullible, sir, as to purchase holy relics. I had more in mind an oddity of historical record, a certain stone that reputedly belonged to Anna Darvulia, who, as you probably know, was the companion to the countess, Elizabeth Bathory of Beckov. I should be greatly surprised if you had not heard of her, Doctor. Elizabeth Bathory's reputation for cruelty earned her the name of Vampire."

"Vampirism, Lady Dameron?" mused the doctor, unnaturally thin eyebrows elevating above the thick-lensed spectacles. "What student of that greatest of natural anomalies has not heard of the Hungarian countess? It is said Elizabeth Bathory was responsible for the deaths of six hundred young peasant women in whose blood she bathed to maintain her beauty and youthful appearance." The fish eyes studied her speculatively. "But then, what lady of wealth and beauty would not be interested in the secret of immortality?"

"Indeed, Doctor, we women are vain creatures, are we not," replied Theodora, hard-pressed to keep either the loathing or the sarcasm from her voice. The man was a detestable creature, perfectly at home among his freakish collection of anomalies in nature. "I believe you are not unfamiliar with the Moravian Blood Stone, Doctor."

"I am, as a matter of fact, the only noted authority on the stone. An unusually fine green chalcedony with sprinkles of red, which allegedly had the power to emit rivulets of blood on command. Some legends assert the stone holds the tears of Mary Magdalen transformed into blood and that whoever commands the stone is assured of eternal youth and immortality."

"A fine story—for children and fools," muttered Aunt Philippa in obvious disgust.

"Perhaps, madam," shrugged Galapardrasso. "Whether you believe in the legends or not, the stone has had a most illustrious history. All who have possessed it have suffered violent deaths. Even Anna Darvulia, it is believed, was poisoned by her friend the countess, who coveted its powers for herself."

"Exactly my point," sniffed Philippa. "All a parcel of nonsense."

"More to the point, Doctor," Theodora interjected, "I should like to know where the stone is at present."

"Ah, there I cannot help you. I did have the good fortune to locate it for a client some years ago. Unfortunately, the stone has since disappeared from view."

"Dear, just when we were so close. What are we to do, Aunt Philippa? I so had my heart set on finding it. But then," Theodora turned to Galapardrasso as though with a sudden inspiration, "perhaps your client could help us. I am prepared to reward you both handsomely for your troubles, Doctor."

"Again I regret I cannot help you, Lady Dameron. Unfortunately, my client preferred to remain anonymous. And, now, unless I can interest you in something else, I'm afraid I must ask you to excuse me. I was on the point of closing up."

How very convenient, mused Theodora ironically. Dr. Galapardrasso was, in fact, most anxious to be rid of them, and little wonder. She doubted not that the mysterious lady eavesdropping behind his study door was growing weary of her confinement.

"Of course, Doctor," Theodora said. "You have been very kind. Perhaps you would not mind if we browsed just for a moment or two before we let ourselves out. After all, I have been looking forward since my arrival in London to visiting your museum, and, unfortunately, I haven't yet had the time to see more than poor Mr. Franklin Hobart's considerably shrunken head. I shall, of course, wish to leave a generous contribution, purely for the sake of science."

Dr. Galapardrasso's gaze noticeably wavered at sight of the roll of pound notes Theodora pulled from her purse. Clearly, she had discovered the doctor's one, real passion, Theodora reflected. "As a matter of fact, Lady Dameron, I do have a few last-minute things to do before I lock up, and naturally I should not wish to deprive you of the pleasure of satisfying your curiosity."

Theodora smiled engagingly. "You are too kind, sir."

"Kind," said Philippa with an unladylike snort as soon as Galapardrasso had turned to reenter his study. "He is a reptile, Theodora, and I should not put it past him to knock us in the head and fling our dead bodies in the river purely for the sake of stealing our purses."

"Nonsense, dearest Aunt," Theodora laughed. "I daresay he is a fish—a shark, perhaps, but a fish nonetheless. A fish that has taken the bait."

"Whatever he is, he is dangerous, Theodora, and I should sooner stroll naked in the streets than browse in this filthy excuse for a museum."

"I, on the other hand, am all eagerness to explore without the doctor present. Which is why you will take the carriage to the end of the block and wait for me."

"Wait for you!" exclaimed Philippa in unmitigated horror. "I shall do no such thing."

"You will, Aunt. Indeed, you must," Theodora insisted, urging the older woman toward the door. "It is the only way I can hope to conceal myself until the doctor leaves. Now, off with you, before you ruin everything."

Hardly had the bell ceased to ring behind Philippa's unhappy departure, than Theodora, remembering to leave her donation on the cabinet devoted to Mr. Hobart's shriveled head, concealed herself behind a sarcophagus reputed to have belonged to Cleopatra, Queen of the Nile.

The very next instant Galapardrasso thrust his head out to survey the room. "It is all right," he announced over his shoulder. "You may come out now. Happily, they have gone."

"This is all your doing, Doctor," pronounced an agitated feminine voice. Behind the sarcophagus, Theodora clamped a hand over her mouth to stifle a gasp of recognition. Good God, Lady Damaris! she thought. "If only you had listened to me," continued that lady, her skirts rustling as she came out into the room, "we should not be in the fix we're in. I warn you. Styles has been asking questions. He *knows,* I tell you. Merciful heaven, we shall all be caught and hanged."

"And I tell you he knows nothing. He was fishing, but you, my lady, may very well ruin everything. You were told never to come here."

"Where else was I to go? *You* were not at Lady Harrington's ball. You did not see the way *he* looked at me."

"You should learn to keep your mouth shut. Now, I'm afraid, you have very little choice left but to do exactly as I tell you. You will go directly home, where you will wait until I have had time to think this matter over carefully. You will go nowhere and see no one. Is that understood?"

"Yes, but—"

"Go, madam. Now, before I change my mind. You have endangered everything with your foolish tongue, and now it is up to me to decide what next we must do."

"But you have a plan? You intend to tell Morpheus that the countess . . ."

A sibilant hiss sent a chill down Theodora's spine. "Silence, woman! You would do well never to speak that name aloud. *He* would cut your heart out for you. I shall not warn you again. Leave Lady Dameron to me. If it is the stone she seeks, I might find that I am in a position to satisfy her curiosity."

"The stone? No, it's impossible. I made it all up. Or at least most of it. For poor Gwendolyn's sake. It was the game, you see. It meant everything to her. And then Mor—" Lady Damaris abruptly caught herself. *"He,"* she hastily amended, "ruined everything by claiming he had found it. But it was all a lie. It had to be. How could he find something that never existed?"

"Oh, it existed, all right. I found it for him, and I can find it again, you fool of a woman. How do you think he got his hands on it?"

Theodora tingled with excitement as she waited for an answer.

"You manufactured it for him," said Lady Damaris. "It was like everything else in this wretched museum. A fake."

"Not everything, Lady Gale. I have reason to believe the stone was real. A pity the countess did not believe it. It was one of my greatest finds, and she thanked me for it by flinging it into the sea."

Behind the sarcophagus, Theodora, struck by a startling thought, gave an involuntary jerk. Her elbow came in jarring contact with a spear, propped most inconveniently against the sarcophagus. Theodora froze, eyes clenched shut and shoulders hunched in horrified expectation of the crash that must have been inevitable, save for the fact that it did not happen.

"But enough," came Galapardrasso's pronouncement in the uncanny silence. "It is time you were gone from here, and I have an errand to run."

Slowly, Theodora turned her head and opened her eyes to stare in disbelief at a very large, very masculine hand clamped around the spear's slender shaft. Her gaze swept up and back and froze on the Devil's Cub, kneeling behind her, the side of an index finger pressed to his lips in warning.

The bell clattered twice in succession, followed by the bang of the door slammed firmly shut. A key turned in the lock.

Cautiously, Styles raised his head to peer over the top of the sarcophagus. The next moment he climbed to his feet, pulling Theodora up with him.

"I suppose there's little point in asking you what the devil you are doing here," he said, making a quick survey of the street outside before pulling the blind down over the window in the door. "I wonder if you have the faintest notion how close you came to ending up a bloody corpse in the river."

"There was not the slightest chance of that, Styles," Theodora assured him. "Aunt Philippa is outside with Tom, keeping watch. Besides," she added, slipping her hand into her reticule and then drawing it out again, "you surely cannot think I should be foolish enough to enter the lion's den without the means of protecting myself. I brought my own deterrent."

Styles froze in the process of turning from the door. "What in the deuce," he demanded, apparently much struck at finding himself staring unexpectedly down the bore of a pistol little larger than the fist that held it.

"It's a gun," Theodora quite unnecessarily informed him. "And you may be sure it is primed and loaded. Papa made sure I was thoroughly conversant in every aspect of its care and use. Otherwise, there would be little point in having it."

"Hardly any point at all," agreed Styles, taking the precaution of directing the barrel away from his chest. "Next, I suppose you will tell me you were never in any danger at all. Hell and the devil confound it, Theodora. You haven't the least idea of with whom you are dealing here."

"On the contrary, I have a very good notion of what I might expect at the hands of Dr. Galapardrasso if I were foolish enough not to take every precaution. He is utterly without scruples or principles and would think nothing of committing cold-blooded murder so long as he could be assured of doing so without risk to himself. He has only one passion. Greed. And but a single loyalty—to himself. Having been gifted with a certain degree of animal cunning, he has managed to survive by his wits for a considerable length of time. Really, Styles, I cannot understand why you should be upset. I daresay Dr. Galapardrasso is no match against a person of calm reason and practical common sense."

"Both of which you possess in abundance and neither of which will be of the least benefit to you if you are knocked alongside the head and rendered unconscious. Which is precisely what will happen if you continue to meddle in matters that do not concern you. I suggest," he added, cutting Theodora off before she could give voice to the rebuttal that was so obviously trembling for release on her lips, "that we haven't time at present for a lengthy exercise in logic. In spite of the fact that Aunt Philippa is waiting outside to rescue us should the need arise, it occurs to me we should do better to conduct a search of the study and be gone from here before the villain returns."

Unable to deny in the circumstances the sense of Styles's suggestion, Theodora clamped her mouth shut.

"Quite so, my dear," Styles applauded, odiously smiling.

"Pooh," Theodora retorted, crinkling her nose at him. "You needn't gloat. I am naturally willing to concede when I see merit in an idea. I am, after all, a creature of logic. Suppose you tell me what it is that we shall be looking for," she added, moving past him into the curator's study.

"A journal with dates, names, places—information that would be of value to a spy for the French. You appear surprised. What, exactly, did you think I should be looking for?"

"Not evidence of a traitor, I assure you. Styles, you are an intelligence agent!"

"Only in a manner of speaking," answered Styles, rifling through a drawer of the doctor's writing desk, the top of which was littered with all manner of things, including old newspapers, books, and what appeared to be the anomalous remains of a prehistoric fish.

"Why in heaven's name did you not tell me?" Theodora demanded thrillingly as she inserted an arm clear to the shoulder into the mouth of an Egyptian urn.

"Because, Enchantress, it is supposed to be a secret."

A thorough search of Dr. Galapardrasso's study revealed little of interest, save for what appeared to be a Druidical cosmic egg, which Theodora discovered while rummaging through a wooden crate, a metal coffer, containing a small fortune in gold, concealed beneath a loose board in the floor, and a scrap of paper with the name, *Saragassos,* scrawled across it.

"Is it important?" Theodora asked, peering over Styles's shoulder at the scrap.

"It's difficult to say. The *Saragassos* is a Bristol trading vessel, which has been suspected of smuggling. The name alone, unfortunately, does little to implicate Galapardrasso in anything of an illicit nature, let alone espionage activities."

Replacing the scrap on the writing table where he had found it, Styles rose to his feet. "There is nothing more to be gathered here, Enchantress. I suggest it is time we looked for an exit out of Dr. Galapardrasso's museum."

Theodora found herself moments later, perched on a window ledge, her feet dangling above a filthy, rat-infested alley.

"I am sorry, Styles," she said, pushing herself off into the Devil's Cub's waiting arms, "that we were unable to find what you were looking for. You will admit, however, that your mama's diary is connected to the events of your poisoning and my near tragic demise. It is obvious now that your mama's Mysterious M and Lady Damaris's sinister Morpheus are one and the same. Can it be that this Morpheus is also connected to your interest in French spies?"

Styles, who was gazing with wry appreciation into his wife's animated visage, could not but reflect that Theodora would seem admirably suited to investigations of a covert nature. Far from being the least out of countenance, she appeared totally oblivious to the fact that she was standing in unwholesome, not to mention, uncongenial surrounds.

"It not only can, but apparently it is connected," Styles admitted, taking Theodora's arm and ushering her through a gate into an adjoining courtyard, which, in turn, emerged on a narrow alley that must eventually take them to New Street. "I suspected from the very beginning that the purpose of the poisoning was to disrupt certain negotiations in which I have been involved on behalf of their Lordships of the Admiralty. It would have taken very little more than the suggestion that I was no longer in command either of my faculties or my several business enterprises to void the agreements. The poisoner came very near to achieving the reality. Fortunately, he could not have anticipated the interference of a white witch with acute empathic powers of perception and the analytical mind of a scientist. I'm afraid, Theodora, that you spoiled his plot. Which was why it suddenly became necessary for him to remove you from the equation."

"Yes, it would seem to explain a great deal," agreed Theodora, picking up her skirts in order to step over a pile of refuse. "I daresay Morpheus must be feeling rather desperate. Why else would he deviate from his established pattern by staging last night's attempt against your life? Had he remained true to his original plan, *I* should have been the intended victim. Especially in light of the fact that Lady Damaris had just made sure to put the notion of my untimely death in everyone's head. What I fail to understand is why he should have gone to so much trouble in the first place, when it would seem so much easier simply to have killed you outright from the very beginning."

"Because," said Styles, coming suddenly to a halt, "my death would not have suited his purposes. Good God, Theodora, you have gone straight to the heart of the matter, while I have been too occupied with political issues to see it."

"You cannot know how relieved I am to hear it, Styles," said Theodora, favoring him with a fond, if baffled, look. "I'm afraid, however, that I haven't the least idea what you are getting at."

Uttering a laugh that was totally incomprehensible to Theodora even if it did send a soft thrill coursing through her, Styles grasped her by the arms. "No, of course you haven't," he said with glittering eyes. "How could you, when you know nothing of those with whom I have been negotiating? Rebels, patriots, if you like, who are fighting for a desperate cause. Dead, I should, in their eyes, be seen as a martyr to my cause, and there is nothing so well understood as martyrdom to a rebel fighting for the freedom of his people. In the event of my sudden death, there was every chance the agreements would have stood."

"But with your very reason in doubt, you would have been discredited, your word something to be distrusted. Oh, I do see, Styles," exclaimed Theodora. Then immediately she frowned. "But then, why would Morpheus decide to chance ruining everything by sending an assassin after you?"

Styles dropped his hands. "I don't know why he should

have done it," he admitted, conducting Theodora to the end of the alley. "But I believe I know someone who could tell us. What are your plans for this evening?"

Startled at the seeming irrelevance of the question, Theodora had for a moment to think before she could answer. "I am afraid I hadn't quite decided yet. I was promised to Lady Wendover's for dinner, but I canceled in anticipation of having to adjust Lord Harry's prescribed treatment." A tinge of color flooded her cheeks as it came to her where exactly she was promised for later that evening. "As it happens, I have accepted an invitation to a masque in celebration of May Day."

That admission earned her an immediate, penetrating glance from Styles. "Dare I speculate that it is to be held at Summersgate with Andrew Moreland as your host?"

"As a matter of fact, it is," Theodora answered, her chin tilted in stubborn anticipation of Styles's probable reaction to that admission. "I have a particular wish to see Mr. Moreland's gardens, which are reputed to be not only highly unusual, but singularly impressive."

"You may be sure they are both," agreed Styles with an odd sort of grimness. "I imagine they are quite unlike anything you have ever seen before. I suppose there is not the least point in trying to persuade you to simply take my word for it."

"And not see them for myself?" Theodora demanded incredulously. "I daresay there is not."

"Somehow I knew that would be your answer. In which case, you will no doubt be pleased to have me as your escort."

Theodora was not at all certain that "pleased" accurately described what she felt at the prospect of having Styles accompany her to Summersgate, especially in view of what she hoped to accomplish by her presence there. At least she supposed she could comfort herself with the fact that he had not made things even more difficult by forbidding her to go. "But I could not be more pleased, Styles," she replied, even managing to summon a convincing smile. "Indeed, I am looking eagerly forward to it."

As by this time they had, to Aunt Philippa's abject relief, reached Theodora's carriage, no more was said on the subject of Andrew Moreland's fete. With instructions to Tom to see his mistress directly home, Styles handed Theodora up and sent them on their way.

"Swear you will never put me through such an experience as that again, Theodora," declared Philippa, collapsing against the squabs. "You cannot begin to know what terrible things I have been made to imagine while I waited for you to come out of that dreadful place. You might at least have confided that Styles would be around to protect you."

"No doubt I should have done, dearest Aunt, had I known it myself. You might say it came as something of a surprise to me. In fact, I did not even think to ask him how he came to be there. But no matter. He *was* there, and now we are safely on our way home. You will be further comforted to know that you will not be required after all to accompany me tonight to Summersgate, as Styles has decided to take that duty upon himself."

"Well, that at least is something," said Philippa on a sigh of relief. "If you must know, I am beginning to find out I am not so young as I once was. I am not even certain I wish to inquire what you were doing in that horrid museum. At least tell me if you discovered what you were looking for."

"As a matter of fact, dearest Aunt," Theodora answered, "I believe I have discovered a deal more than I could possibly have anticipated. Indeed, if I am not mistaken, I have come upon a way to make the Mysterious M give himself away. I, after all, have found the Moravian Blood Stone!"

Fifteen

Theodora, upon arriving back at the town house in Grosvenor Square, hurried to the sickroom to see to her patient, whom she had left in the charge of the butler's wife, a good-hearted woman possessed of a down-to-earth commonsensical nature. Theodora was, consequently, more than a little surprised to discover, when she entered, not the matronly Mrs. Oglesby, but Thistlewaite seated in a chair at the bedside.

Slipping inside, she raised a finger to her lips as Thistlewaite rose hastily to his feet.

"How is he?" she asked softly, coming up to the bed. "Still sleeping?"

"I daresay he has been worn out, my lady," replied the valet. "What with one thing and another. I have seen to it that he took his medicine just as you instructed."

Theodora, pressing the tips of her fingers to Lord Harry's wrist, felt for a pulsebeat, which she found, to her satisfaction, was both stronger and a deal more regular than it had been the night before. "That was good of you, Mr. Thistlewaite," she said after a moment, releasing her patient's wrist and laying a hand on his forehead. "But you don't have to sit with him, you know. I have engaged Mrs. Oglesby to look after him."

"I haven't minded staying with him, my lady, and Mrs. Oglesby was glad to take a short rest. I thought perhaps Lord Harry might take kindly to waking to a familiar face. Which he did—just for a moment or two. Though I daresay he might not have been exactly in his right mind."

Theodora glanced up from rearranging the sick man's pillows. "It would hardly be surprising if he were a trifle incoherent. Did he say something?"

"Most assuredly, my lady. Much of which would not bear repeating, I'm afraid." The gentleman's gentleman appeared to hesitate. "Lord Harry did not seem quite like himself, even taking into account the nature of his indisposition. I am not sure how to describe it, except that he seemed to be in the grip of some terrible dread. Naturally, it might only be due to the dreams that have been troubling him from time to time. I must say he spoke to me clearly and in what gave every impression of a rational manner. 'Thistlewaite,' he said. 'Thank God, it's you. I thought it was the bloody Jackal had got me. He found me, old fellow. Even in the halls of Morpheus. Tell Styles, will you, the bloody Jackal's got it in for him.' And then again, something about 'the Jackal's cursed eyes. They see everywhere.' It would seem to make little sense, I'm afraid."

"He said 'the halls of Morpheus'?" Theodora asked. "You are certain of that?"

"He spoke quite clearly, my lady."

"Odd, I wonder what he meant by it. At the very least I think we may assume Lord Harry was trying to convey a warning of some sort to Styles. I wonder who or what this Jackal could be. Does it mean anything to you, Thistlewaite?"

"I cannot say that it does, my lady," replied the valet in the manner of one who had already spent a good deal of time in contemplation of the matter. "It hasn't, to my way of thinking, the sound of a proper name, or at least any that I have ever heard. I daresay it is meant to be descriptive in nature."

"Yes, and not very flattering," agreed Theodora, gazing down at the man in the bed. "Well, we shall just have to wait, I'm afraid, until our patient is better to find out what he meant. I wonder, Thistlewaite," she added musingly. "Do you think Lord Harry would like to be rid of that brush on his face?"

The valet's impassive gaze followed Theodora's to the less than prepossessing visage against the pillows. "Now that you mention it, my lady, Lord Harry was always one to have a care for his appearance."

"Yes, I suspected as much. Tell Mrs. Oglesby for me, will you, that I shall check in on Lord Harry when I return from Summersgate," said Theodora, crossing to the door. Bidding Thistlewaite a good evening, then, she left him to resolve the matter of Lord Harry's untidy beard on his own.

She, after all, had a great deal to think about, a masque to dress for, and the less than pleasant prospect of facing an exceedingly disgruntled abigail. Deciding it would be better to deal with Jessop sooner than later, Theodora immediately sent for the maid servant.

Jessop, when she arrived in answer to her mistress's summons, bore herself into the room in the manner of one who might have walked on water had she been so disposed, observed Theodora, suppressing a sigh. Being a countess certainly presented its own difficulties, she reflected, thinking wistfully of her uncomplicated existence at Cliff House.

Theodora did not make the mistake of thinking she could treat Jessop with the familiarity she would have accorded Millie or Mrs. Tibbets. The abigail, she reasoned, would be just the sort to view such a condescension as improper in one of Theodora's exalted station. On the other hand, an abigail of Jessop's remove must naturally look to be accorded a certain respect due a servant of superior accomplishments, and that Theodora was very much afraid she had failed to do when she allowed herself to speak her mind earlier that afternoon. Somehow she must find the middle ground that would enable her to smooth ruffled feathers without sinking herself farther into ill repute in Jessop's estimation.

Wholly unaware that she had been subjecting her personal servant to what could only be described as a protracted stare

for quite some ten seconds or longer, Theodora girded herself
to take the plunge. "Jessop," she ventured carefully, "about
this afternoon."

Theodora, pausing to draw a breath, not to mention gather
her wits, ruefully beheld the abigail's humorless aspect grow
markedly more severe. It was not exactly a promising beginning, she reflected. Indeed, it suddenly occurred to her that
perhaps she should have done some research into the accepted
method of dealing with superior servants before having leapt
so precipitously into the breach. It was, however, a trifle late
for such speculations. Drawing breath, Theodora continued.

"I am very much afraid that we have gotten off on the wrong
foot, you and I. And, well, frankly, it has occurred to me that
we must have an understanding if we are to entertain any hope
in future of a congenial working relationship."

"I beg your pardon, my lady. What did you say?" queried
the abigail, deigning at last to look at her mistress, but in a
manner that Theodora could not but find vaguely disconcerting.

"I said," Theodora began again, "that we must try and reach
an understanding—"

"An understanding, m'lady. But I do understand, and I'd like
you to know my behavior this afternoon will in no manner be
repeated. You were right to set me straight, and you may be
sure that, if you were to give me another chance, I would do
my best to serve you according to your expectations."

"Well, then, that is all I ask," said Theodora, surprised that
the interview should have come so swiftly to an agreeable conclusion. "I am glad we were able to have this little talk, Jessop.
I hope you are as encouraged as I to believe that we shall in
time and with a little patience come to deal quite well together."
It came additionally to Theodora to hope the woman would
begin to show signs of unbending just a little. Indeed, she wondered if Jessop required something more to soothe her offended
sensibilities, perhaps something in the way of an apology. She
was on the point of trying to decide how one worded an apology
in terms that did not diminish one's standing in a servant's eyes,

when Jessop, as if compelled, recalled herself to Theodora's attention.

"Begging your pardon, m'lady," said the abigail, "but does this mean you intend to keep me on?"

"Keep you on?" Good heavens, the poor woman was not toplofty; she was frightened of losing her position. "You may be sure there was never any question of letting you go, Jessop," Theodora hastened to assure her "Though it had occurred to me that you might wish to be free to serve a mistress more deserving of your considerable talents. I, unfortunately, am quite hopeless when it comes to matters of fashion."

"Begging your pardon, m'lady, but that's where you're mistaken," Jessop ventured, her plain features becoming animated with conviction. "Anyone can follow the fashion. It takes someone like you to set it. The Countess of Styles is an Original, like a painting no one else has ever done before but everyone wants to copy. I was wrong to try and make you over into something you shouldn't be. If you still want me, m'lady, I'd like to stay. The truth is I can't think of anyone else I'd rather serve. I thought you must know that."

"I daresay there is a great deal I do not know, Jessop," smiled Theodora, wondering that one with her acute empathic powers of perception could have so completely misjudged the abigail. No doubt she had allowed preconceived notions in this instance to cloud her usual instincts. "Henceforth, however, I shall rely on you to teach me. And now that that is all settled, you may begin by helping me to dress. I have a masked ball to attend."

Theodora was not certain an hour and a half later whether to be relieved or piqued to receive a note from Styles expressing his regrets that he would be unable to escort her to Summersgate. Assuring her that she could rely on Phelps to give her safe conduct, he concluded by wishing her an enjoyable evening.

"Well, what do you think of that?" she demanded of Percival, who was in the windowseat occupied with grooming himself after a supper of tidbits prepared especially for him by the earl's French chef. "An enjoyable evening, indeed.

What, I wonder, has come up that is so important he is willing to send me blithely off to Summersgate by myself, when he knows perfectly well my intent is to determine if Moreland is Lady Gwendolyn's Mysterious M?"

Percival, apparently unmoved at Styles's odd behavior, extended a front foot languorously out before him, sank his claws into the cushioned seat, and stretched in a display of blissful unconcern.

"Well, I suppose one *shouldn't* look a gift horse in the mouth," Theodora conceded doubtfully, and, turning once more to the oval looking glass, surveyed herself one last time.

For the sake of disguise, she had eschewed her usual white for a tunic gown of verdant green silk, which left a daring expanse of her bosom bare and drew attention to her only ornament—a translucent green stone that, sprinkled with red spots resembling blood, hung on a silver chain around her neck.

Smiling whimsically, she wondered what Mrs. Fennelworth would say if she knew what, exactly, she had had in her possession all those years. Indeed, Theodora marveled that she herself had taken so long to make the logical connection. The truth was, however, she had all but forgotten Mrs. Fennelworth's gift to her until that afternoon, when Dr. Galapardrasso had been so obliging as to bring it forcibly to mind.

The Moravian Blood Stone. Mrs. Fennelworth had found the stone at the foot of the cliffs beneath Devil's Keep just where Lady Gwendolyn most certainly must have hurtled it in rage and disillusionment.

It would not, she speculated, require long for Morpheus, whoever he was, to come to the right conclusions, however. She would be exceedingly surprised if he did not recognize it at once. She was, in fact, depending upon it.

Theodora put on her half-mask of green satin with holes cut out for the eyes, and, tying it firmly in place, reached for her reticule and cape.

"Good night, Percival," she called over her shoulder. "Behave yourself while I am gone."

Moments later Theodora descended into the parquetry tiled entry hall to discover Phelps, looking wholly ill-at-ease and not a little ridiculous in a May Day Fool's costume of motley and bells.

Theodora fought to remain properly grave. "Good evening, Mr. Phelps," she greeted. "You are looking very colorful tonight. And how, may I ask, is your head?"

Phelps's face, beneath his loo mask, was a dusky red. "A mite tender to the touch is all, m'lady. I'm obliged to you for what you did for me. I expect it's because of you the lump was gone this morning."

"You are quite welcome, Mr. Phelps. I daresay you have already more than repaid me," observed Theodora, her eyes twinkling, as she allowed him to escort her to the waiting carriage.

Summersgate in Kensington was a turreted mansion of Jacobean construction set on a hill behind high walls and encompassed by trees. Theodora, alighting from the carriage before the house, could not but be immediately struck with the realization that masques, at least Mr. Moreland's sort, were something out of the ordinary in the way of entertainments. After all, one hardly expected to be handed down by a footman clad in little more than what amounted to a loin cloth and a slave's collar of gold clamped about the neck. Furthermore, she could hardly avoid noticing that, compared to the other arriving guests, she would seem herself to be somewhat overdressed. The prevailing feminine mode, in fact, appeared to favor something on the order of fanciful notions of the sort of gowns suited to rustic maidens and which left very little to the imagination, while that for the gentlemen who did not choose the Robin Hoods, Friar Tucks, Tom the Piper, the Fool or the hobby horse of the Morris Men dancers traditional to May Day celebrations, would seem to demonstrate a preference for whimsical costumes of various animal motifs. Certainly, there was not a coat

or waistcoat in evidence, let alone anything so obviously super-
fluous as a hat, neckcloth or gloves.

But then, the attire, or perhaps the lack of it, would seem
to suit a revelry set, not, apparently in the house, but outside
on the grounds. Certainly the distant strains of music and a
path lighted by Chinese lanterns seemed particularly designed
to lure new arrivals away from the manor and into a deepening
wood of oaks.

Theodora, drawn by curiosity, unhesitatingly started after the
others, which left Phelps, who looked anything but happy
about it, little choice but to follow.

Neither noticed a tall figure detach itself from the shadows
and enter the woods a few yards behind them.

"Beggin' your pardon, m'lady, but are you sure," queried
Phelps in accompaniment to the jingle of bells, "that you
wouldn't rather be somewhere else? It doesn't seem right, you
being here."

"I would seem to be somewhat out of place," agreed Theodora, glimpsing a figure, wearing what appeared to be the head
of a goat, in hot pursuit of a wood sprite off to her right. Indeed,
she could only be grateful for the anonymity afforded by her
mask as a feminine trill of laughter and other sounds she did
not care to identify carried to her from out of the darkness
beyond the string of lanterns. "I daresay Styles was right, and
that I shall find very little to recommend in Mr. Moreland's sort
of garden." A pity Styles was not there, she added ruefully to
herself. No doubt had he been, the gardens would have taken
on a whole new range of possibilities. She was, in fact, becoming increasingly aware that, Phelps notwithstanding, she would
have liked nothing better than to have Styles there beside her.
"I daresay we shall not stay longer than is required for me to
pay my respects to our host, Mr. Phelps."

"Mr. Phelps?" repeated Theodora in the conspicuous absence of a reply. Abruptly, she stopped, made suddenly and
uncannily aware that Phelps was no longer there. Now, what
the devil? Telling herself there was a perfectly rational expla-

nation for Phelp's seeming disappearance, she turned to glance back down the trail over her shoulder.

A wave of relief washed over her at the sight of a large figure obscured in shadows a short distance off the trail. "Mr. Phelps?" she called, wondering what had possessed the man to wander off.

At her summons, the figure straightened and obligingly started toward her.

"Thank heavens, Mr. Phelps," she exclaimed, "I was afraid something had happened to you. If you are quite ready to go on, I should prefer not to—"

Whatever it was she had preferred not to do was left unexpressed as a man, who, while undeniably impressive in size, was garbed, not in the motley guise of a fool, but in the forest green of a Robin Hood, stepped into the lantern light, and, striding forward without pause, clasped Theodora ruthlessly to his chest. It was on Theodora's lips to point out that *he* was not Phelps and to kindly unhand her, when he covered her mouth with his.

No little time later, Theodora, feeling overly warm and not a little breathless, lifted accusing eyes to her assailant. "You, Master Robin, may be glad that my husband is not here. I daresay he would take exception to the manner in which you have treated his wife."

"Unlike his wife, one must presume, who, far from showing offense, appears to have derived no little pleasure from the experience," observed Master Robin Hood, his eyes, through the holes in his mask, glittering strangely. "Do you always return a stranger's kiss with such unmaidenly fervor, Maid Marion?"

"Only in a wood when I am taken without warning, it would seem," Theodora replied with perfect candor. "Only last night in circumstances very similar to these, my husband was moved to point out that I am hopelessly depraved. Which is no doubt why he was content to allow me to come to Summersgate without him, when he knew perfectly well the sort of gardens I should find."

"Little wretch," said Robin Hood with obvious feeling. "Can you truthfully say you would not have come if he had been so obliging as to inform you Moreland's tastes ran to pleasure gardens instead of flowers and herbs?"

"You know perfectly well I cannot," Theodora retorted. "Just as you know my real reason for coming had very little to do with an interest in Mr. Moreland's gardens. I suppose it would be too much to hope you mean to tell me what you have been up to since I left you in New Street, Styles, but you might at least tell me what you have done with poor Mr. Phelps."

"Witch," declared Styles, who was far from being surprised that Theodora had so easily seen through his disguise. He had known it the moment she melted so sweetly into his arms. "Mr. Phelps, you will be glad to know—" Theodora's breath caught as demon black eyes fixed on the blood stone, then flicked, glinting, up to hers. "—was most grateful to be relieved of his duties as escort and is by now in an advantageous position to keep an eye on you from cover." A small sigh of relief breathed through Theodora's lips as without comment he slipped his arm through hers. "You will nevertheless oblige me by staying close, Theodora. A May Day revelry, especially at Summersgate, is an open invitation to take liberties with an unescorted female."

"I may be a provincial, but I am hardly blind, Styles," Theodora informed him as they started along the path. "You may be sure I knew the moment I set eyes on Moreland's footmen that this was no common entertainment. Where, by the way, *did* you go after you left me this afternoon?"

"As a matter of fact, I was employed in making inquiries into the whereabouts of the *Saragassos,* which, coincidentally enough, happens to be moored in the Pool at the present time. I set Franklidge the task of discovering what he can about her."

"After which, you no doubt hastened to Kensington for the sole purpose of surprising me. Surely you did not think I should not recognize you, Styles, as soon as I looked into your eyes?"

"If not then, then most certainly when I kissed you. My intent, however, was not to surprise you, as much as I should have enjoyed it, but to elude the men who have been following me. I prefer not to have company when we call on Lady Damaris later this evening."

"Following you. But who—" Theodora, who was still trying to digest the information that Styles was being followed, halted in startled surprise at that additional assertion. *"Are* we calling on Lady Damaris?"

"It did occur to me she could shed a deal of light on things. Of course, if you would rather not—"

"Pray don't be absurd, Styles," declared Theodora. "Of course I am going with you. You must know very well that I should only go on my own if you refused to take me."

"The thought had occurred to me," confided Styles in sardonic appreciation of his wife's sparkling eyes. It had, in fact, come to him that afternoon in New Street that, short of confining her in chains in a dungeon, any course designed to curtail Theodora's determined investigation was doomed to certain failure. It had seemed vastly less complicated, not to mention less wearing on his nerves, to simply confide in her as much as he deemed necessary and, for the rest, to join forces with his irrepressible countess. At least with Theodora under his wing, he had told himself, he would not be forced to experience another such moment as he had lived upon discovering his wife and her Aunt Philippa in Galapardrasso's unsavory den. The muscle leaped grimly along the lean line of his jaw. In that last assumption, however, it would seem he had greatly underestimated Theodora.

"I suggest, since we are here," Styles added in exceedingly dry accents, "that you first satisfy yourself that Anthony Moreland cannot possibly be Lady Gwendolyn's Mysterious M. And what better opportunity? It would appear we are just in time to witness the crowning of the May Queen."

Theodora, relieved to discover they had come at last to the end of the wood, stared in mute fascination into the wide clearing presided over by a summer house in the form of a classical ruin. In front of the ruin and surrounded by revelers stood a white hawthorn tree decorated in ribbons and flowers; and, seated on a woody throne at its base, the May Queen resided, attended by the vanquished Queen of Winter.

The fact that the latter, upon closer inspection, was clearly a man dressed in the guise of a woman was neither shocking nor in the least surprising to Theodora. The part of Winter Queen was, after all, traditionally a male role. She could not but note, however, that the bridal gown of Brussels point lace over white satin was not only exquisite, but that it seemed most peculiarly to suit its wearer. The Winter Queen's slender form moved with a provocative, willowy grace that might have done credit to the most celebrated of London's feminine beauties. Furthermore, her hair, the color of winter frost, was not only dressed in elegant curls beneath a cottage hat with ostrich plumes, but it was obviously her own, not a wig; and her face, though clearly no longer young, was masterfully painted to draw attention to the delicate bone structure, full, evocative lips, and undeniably intriguing eyes. She was, in fact, in every respect, save for the most important one, a beautiful, wholly alluring woman, who could not possibly have been Lady Gwendolyn's adoring Adonis.

"Faith, Styles," murmured Theodora, "why did you not simply tell me?"

"Because, Enchantress, you would not have believed me, and because Anthony Moreland, of all Lady Gwendolyn's intimates, was the only one who would have done all in his power to wean her from her course of self-destruction. It seemed appropriate that you discover for yourself his unique attributes."

Theodora lifted startled eyes to the Devil's Cub. "But if he was part of the game—?"

"Moreland has never been averse to enjoying pleasures of an exotic nature. He would naturally draw the line, however, at anything so indelicate as confusing blood for wine. He ceased to come to Devil's Keep when Lady Damaris introduced the game."

"How very wise of him," reflected Theodora, smiling. "I

believe I already like Mr. Moreland. Good God, Styles," she exclaimed then, as it came to her exactly what he had said, "you do not mean they actually drank blood?"

"I have it from a reliable source that they did no more than prefer their beef cooked exceedingly rare, if that is any comfort to you. No doubt it was the idea more than the actuality that persuaded Moreland to withdraw from Lady Gwendolyn's society. A decision that did not come easily to one who admired Lady Gwendolyn as Moreland did for her beauty and her wildly impetuous nature."

"I admire the way he wears a dress," confessed Theodora, watching Moreland, holding court among his guests. "I wonder if he could teach me how to wield a fan with such infinite grace."

Styles, who had not failed to note that a reveler in the guise of Will Scarlet had been paying undue attention to Theodora, took her arm and began to lead her away from the May Day celebration. "It is not a skill I should consider in the least necessary for you to master," he said, taking the path into the wood. He sent a glance back over his shoulder. Will Scarlet, he noted, had begun to work his way through the revelers in their direction, as had another in the guise of a friar. And, if he was not mistaken, there was a third with the same object. The devil, he thought, wondering where Phelps had taken himself off.

He clasped Theodora's hand in his. "You came to see Moreland's gardens," he said. "I suggest a tour would be in order."

"Styles—?" gasped Theodora, as precipitately leaving the path, he pulled Theodora after him.

"Softly," Styles said warningly. "There are three men after us, and somehow I cannot think what they have in mind is a dance around the May Pole."

Theodora, hampered by her skirts and shoes that were hardly designed with a tramp through the woods in mind, stumbled to keep up with Styles. "But who—?"

"I haven't the least notion, though you may be sure they

are not candidates for Robin Hood's merry band." Again Styles glanced over his shoulder.

Theodora, who had enough to do not to trip in the dark, was hardly prepared for Styles to come to a sudden halt. One moment she was struggling to keep her skirts from binding her legs, and the next she was colliding with an immovable object.

"Styles—!"

Strong hands reached out of the darkness and held her. "Bloody hell, Theodora," he whispered, sharp with concern, close to her ear. "Are you all right?"

"Yes, I'm fine. Who the devil are they, Styles?"

The answer came, exceedingly grim in the stillness. "That is what I intend to find out. Wait here, Theodora."

"No. Styles, wait—" Feeling him pull away, Theodora reached for him. It was on her tongue to inform him in no uncertain terms that she had not the least intention of being left behind, when she was silenced by a low hiss from Styles.

Theodora froze, her senses alert for the smallest noise. Instantly she heard it—the unmistakable sounds of a scuffle to the exceedingly odd accompaniment of bells.

"Phelps," pronounced Styles with dark satisfaction. Taking Theodora's hand, he moved toward the sounds of combat.

They had not far to go. Seconds later, they were just in time to witness Phelps, bells jingling, land Friar Tuck a facer. Neither Will Scarlet, Styles noted grimly, nor his probable companion was anywhere in evidence.

"M'lord," panted Phelps, grinning hugely. "You—and m'lady—are just in time. I was just about showing—the friar—here—a lesson in manners. When I come across him—the blighter took a swing at me."

"No, did he?" murmured Styles, narrowly eyeing the object of Phelps's instruction, who sat, sprawled, on the ground, a hand to his jaw. "Perhaps you would be so good as to help the gentleman up, Phelps, so that he can explain why he should have done anything so hasty."

"With pleasure, m'lord," grinned Phelps, reaching down to

grasp the dazed man by the neck of his robe. "Here, you, Master Tuck. On yer feet."

"If you don't mind, my lord Styles," spoke up the gentleman in rueful accents. "I believe I should prefer to get up by myself."

Styles, to Theodora's amazement, far from demonstrating the least surprise at this note of familiarity from one who was presumably only moments before in pursuit of them, appeared to have been expecting nothing less.

"By all means," he answered with insufferable calm. Styles nodded to Phelps. "It is all right, Phelps. You may unhand Mr. Whitfill. I believe he has no intention of escaping."

"Whitfill!" exclaimed Theodora, staring from one to the other of the two men.

"At your service, Lady Dameron," acknowledged Whitfill, who having climbed unsteadily to his feet, executed a bow that was somewhat less than graceful. "May I say, Mr. Phelps, that I have seldom met with a more punishing right. One must wonder what possessed you to retire from what must have been a promising career."

"Mr. Phelps was persuaded to employ his talents in my interests," Styles answered coolly. The devil, he thought. It would be remarkable indeed if Whitfill were not perfectly aware of the circumstances that had ended the aging pugilist's career. "No doubt you will pardon my curiosity, but I find myself wondering what peculiar circumstance should have made it necessary for him to use them on you, Whitfill."

"Indeed, my lord, I daresay you are," said Whitfill, baring a face, which struck Theodora was hardly more revealing of the man's inner musings than the mask that had previously concealed it. "No less am I wondering at it. It is hardly in my usual style to blunder into an ambush. Naturally, I should have realized you would have Mr. Phelps conveniently placed to guard your back. It was an oversight on my part that you may be sure I shall not make again. As it was, I could not be certain you were even aware of the danger."

"One can never be certain of anything these days, it would

seem," Styles observed in tones laced with irony. "Especially in this case. I'm afraid I haven't the least notion of what you are talking about, Whitfill. Lady Dameron and I were taking a tour of Moreland's gardens. My wife, as it happens, has a particular interest in gardens."

Theodora, who had been listening to this exchange with no little bemusement, did not fail to catch the warning light in the Devil's Cub's eye at the end of that remarkable speech.

Theodora blinked. "Why, yes. Yes, I do. As a matter of fact, Mr. Whitfill, I am seriously involved at present in making a comparative study of gardens in and about London. Naturally, I could not overlook the opportunity to explore Mr. Moreland's, which, as you are probably aware, is held up to be a model of its kind. I confess, however, that I am a little disappointed. I believe I found Lady Harrington's garden, in comparison, offered a deal more in the way of satisfaction."

She was rewarded for that piquant observation with a sardonic leap of amusement in the Devil's Cub's black, glittery orbs. "It occurs to me, Enchantress, that you are being a trifle harsh in your judgment. After all, Lady Harrington's garden had the added bonus of a full-fledged ball in progress."

"So it did, Styles. And purple and white delphiniums, you will recall," reminded Theodora. "But none of this is to the point, surely. Mr. Whitfill is under the impression we are in some sort of danger. He has even, at great risk to himself, exerted himself to come to our aid. Do you not think you should listen to what he has to say?"

"Naturally, I am all eager attention, Enchantress. Well, Whitfill?" he added to that worthy with what must have seemed to Whitfill an unnerving lack of concern. Whitfill had, in fact, begun to regard the Devil's Cub with every manifestation of unease.

"You are roasting me, my lord, are you not?" Whitfill speculated, attempting a smile that failed utterly to reach his peculiarly colorless eyes.

"When have you ever known me to roast anyone, Whitfill?"

queried Styles with deceptive mildness. "Indeed, if the matter is as desperate as you would have me believe, then you may be sure I shall be moved to treat it with the utmost seriousness. Unfortunately, the only evidence of anything untoward would seem to be your presence here."

Far from reassuring Whitfill, the Devil's Cub's observation appeared to have quite the opposite effect. Whitfill's face, Theodora could not but note, underwent a sudden, rapid change.

"My lord, you cannot think that I—" he began, only to fall abruptly silent at something he must have sensed in Styles's impassive stare. Whitfill drew himself up, his own expression guarded.

"There were two men," he said. His eyes, as he ran the back of his hand across his mouth, never left Styles's. "Surely, my lord, you must have seen them—one in the guise of Will Scarlet and the other dressed in the manner of a woodsman or some such thing. I swear, my lord, they were before me. As it happens, I had received certain information that a plot was afoot to abduct Lady Dameron. My contact, a most reliable man, had word it might be tonight. You can well imagine my concern when I heard there was a substantial sum of money promised. I thought you must have seen them coming after you, when you ducked off the path into the wood."

"It would seem the natural conclusion, Styles," Theodora pointed out, when Styles offered no immediate comment. "Phelps, you must have seen them?"

"I saw someone, m'lady," the big man admitted. "The blighter took off before I could get a good look at him."

"There, you see?" said Theodora, who, able to recall perfectly well Styles's claim that three men were after them, could only wonder what game the Devil's Cub was playing. "I daresay Phelps scared them off when he popped up out of nowhere in time to land Mr. Whitfill a facer."

"You have, with your usual acute powers of deduction, my dear, arrived at the heart of the matter," applauded Styles. "I have no doubt that is exactly what happened."

"Well, then. At least that much is settled." Theodora, sending an uncertain glance at Styles, smiled at Whitfill. "I'm afraid, sir, that you received a rather poor reward for what was meant to be a good deed. I do hope Phelps did not hurt you badly."

"Happily, my lady, I believe I shall survive." Whitfill allowed himself a wry grimace. "Though it is a pity it was apparently my ill luck to forge ahead of the two culprits. I should have preferred one of them had had the pleasure of running into your Mr. Phelps." Whitfill shifted his glance speculatively to Styles. "It's cursed odd, my lord. Have you any idea why anyone would wish to abduct your lady wife?"

"You mean, of course, other than the obvious reasons," replied Styles sardonically. "I shall leave that for you to puzzle out, Whitfill. At the moment, the countess and I have another engagement. I'm afraid I shall have to ask you to excuse us. Phelps, you will see that Mr. Whitfill finds his way back to the festivities without further incident. After which, you will return to the carriage."

"Indeed, m'lord," Phelps grinned. "I'd be only too happy to oblige the gentleman."

Sixteen

"I'm afraid Phelps does not care much for Mr. Whitfill," reflected Theodora moments later when she and Styles were alone again. "Not that I blame him. Whitfill would seem to have a penchant for secrecy, one might even go so far as to say subterfuge, which makes it difficult to form an impression, favorable or otherwise, of him. Add to that his oddly feral appearance, and I daresay the man has great difficulty in making friends. Why *do* you think those men wished to abduct me?"

Styles, who had been listening to Theodora's assessment of Whitfill with keen appreciation, smiled in swift amusement at her abrupt change of topic. "More to the point, Enchantress, is how they knew you were my wife," he observed, wrapping an arm around her shoulders as he directed their steps back through the wood toward the house. "At the very least, they would seem to have a remarkable faculty for seeing through disguises."

Theodora, who had her own theory as to how she had been recognized, one which she did not care yet to divulge to Styles, had overlooked the obvious. Ruefully, she smiled. "Now that you mention it, Styles, you would seem to have a point," she conceded. "How do you think they knew?"

"Naturally, I cannot speak for the two who got away, since I cannot be certain yet who they were. As for Whitfill, you may be sure he was already in possession of a detailed description of what Lady Dameron would be wearing before she

ever arrived. I'm afraid, Theodora, you will not like what I am
going to say, but the truth is I am reasonably certain Whitfill
has had someone watching you since you arrived in London."

Theodora's eyes flew to Styles's. "You mean I am being
spied upon?" she demanded, no little taken aback at the notion.
"Good heavens, why?"

"It is quite simple, Enchantress," drawled Styles, little
amused at the likelihood that Whitfill, far from calling off
his dogs, had taken it upon himself to extend his dubious
mantle of protection over Theodora in addition to his other
self-imposed duties. "No doubt I should explain that Whitfill
is an agent of the admiralty. He has been assigned to see to
my security until I have completed a business matter I have
undertaken for their Lordships."

"The negotiations with your rebels," Theodora acknowledged. "If Whitfill is protecting you, then why do I have the
feeling you do not precisely trust him? Indeed, what in heaven's
name was the reason for that little charade we just performed
for his benefit?"

"Perhaps, Enchantress, because I learned a long time ago it
is seldom wise to trust anyone. And in this case, Whitfill has
clearly overstepped his authority. I dislike being followed. Furthermore, I should prefer to see to my own wife's safety. It is
not the sort of thing I should entrust to a stranger."

"I certainly cannot argue with that, Styles," said Theodora,
who, on the contrary, was in complete accord with his sentiments. "On the other hand, it still does not answer my question. Why the pretense?"

"I should think it would be obvious by now to one of your
undeniable talents for logical deduction. Is there nothing that
strikes you as singular in the fact that we have been set upon
two nights in a row under exceedingly unusual circumstances?"

"As a matter of fact, I have wondered how our attacker
could possibly have guessed you would be conveniently placed
at that wall last night," Theodora admitted. "I had the uncan-
niest feeling when it was all over that the whole thing had

been carefully orchestrated. Still, it would seem implausible that anyone could possibly have known beforehand we should be conducting a biological experiment in Lady Harrington's flower bed, especially one that would necessitate our leaving in what can only be described as an unorthodox manner."

"The thing is, no one could have foreseen that particular. We were being watched. I have come to believe there must have been at least two of them—one who was waiting for his chance at the intended target—you, Enchantress. And another whose object was to draw me away from you. What they failed to take into account was your uncanny ability to arouse my primitive male passions."

"They lost us when you pulled me behind the shrubs and tumbled me on the grass," Theodora concluded with a startled burble of laughter. "The devil, Styles, what if they had stumbled on us in the flower bed?"

"I daresay it would have been most damned inconvenient," speculated the Devil's Cub with grim humor. "The thing is, however, they did find us, later, at the wall." Styles paused significantly. "Or perhaps I should say they were lying in wait for us. It occurs to me, Theodora, that things might have turned out a deal less happily if you had not called me back when the villain fled. None of which, however, is to the point."

"I beg your pardon. If it is not to the point that I very nearly escaped with my life for the second time in less than a month, I should like to know what is," declared Theodora.

"The fact that both last night and tonight someone knew or guessed a deal more about our movements than can possibly be laid to mere chance. Which brings us to Mr. Whitfill, who not only takes pride in his extensive network of contacts all over the City, but who does not hesitate to employ spies to keep an eye on those in whom he has a particular interest."

"Styles," said Theodora, apparently much struck with his line of reasoning, "you think Whitfill is behind everything that has happened."

"It did occur to me when I surmised the identity of our

mysterious Friar Tuck, that Whitfill is the one person who is in a unique position to be intimately acquainted with our movements," admitted Styles, as they emerged from the wood in the drive that led out of Summersgate. "Which is why I took the precaution of arranging for an unmarked carriage to be waiting, which, I might add, has the added advantage of being enclosed. With any luck, we may be able to make our call on Lady Damaris with no one the wiser."

Theodora, who had a great deal to think about, not the least of which was the possibility that the Moravian Blood Stone and not Whitfill's network of spies had been the means by which Will Scarlet and his accomplice had recognized her, was grateful the drive from Kensington to Berkeley Square was accomplished not only silently, but without further incident.

Fortunately, Styles, too, would seem uncommonly preoccupied, she reflected, as she slipped the chain over her head without his apparent notice and dropped the stone in her reticule. She preferred to see how the anticipated interview went before she decided whether it would serve any purpose to reveal the stone to Lady Damaris. After all, as long as Styles did not realize what it was and to what use she intended to put it, then he would hardly be likely to come up with any objections to it, she reasoned, as the carriage came to a halt.

No doubt it was a slight chill in the air that caused a small shiver to course down Theodora's back as Styles helped her down from the carriage around the corner from Lady Damaris's town house. Instructing the coachman, a stranger to Theodora, to wait, Styles guided Theodora to the back of the house.

"Are you not in the least concerned we shall be arrested for burglars?" demanded Theodora in a whisper, as Styles strode unhesitatingly up to the door.

"I consider the possibility highly improbable at best," replied Styles, drawing forth a small ring of keys and reaching for the lock. "It would, in fact, be highly irregular, since I happen to own the house."

"You own it?'' exclaimed Theodora in no little astonishment.''

"I kept it for my mother, who, on her infrequent trips to Town, preferred to have her own house," said Styles, moving to insert a key into the lock. "It was her request that Lady Damaris be allowed to continue here for as long as she wished, a request that I was willing to honor so long as it suited me. Curious," he added. Placing a hand flat against the door, he pushed it open.

"It was unlocked," Theodora whispered, the nerves tingling at the nape of her neck.

"Rather say it was ajar," Styles amended. "Stay close by me, Enchantress," he added, stepping cautiously through the service entrance into the dark interior of the kitchen quarters.

"It would seem the household has retired to bed," Theodora observed moments later, as they passed through the dining room into the withdrawing room and beyond that, into the entry hall, all of which were curiously dark.

"I believe it is more likely Lady Damaris has given the staff the evening off. You may be sure a butler of Bolton's stature would not fail to make certain all the doors were locked before retiring. In addition, the hearths are cold. There has not been a fire laid in any of the ground story rooms this evening."

Theodora, who had been aware for some time of an unnatural chill in the house, somehow did not think it could be attributed entirely to the lack of a fire in the grate. "Styles, I have the strangest feeling," she whispered, crossing the parquetry tiled floor to the foot of the stairs.

Styles opened a door off the entry hall, behind which presumably resided the butler's private quarters, and peered in.

"Just as I thought," he said, closing the door again. "Bolton is not within."

"Well, someone is." Theodora froze short of the first floor landing. From somewhere above came the muffled sounds of voices. A woman's scream, followed by the crash of a body

colliding with a piece of furniture, shattered the silence.
"Styles?"

"Yes, I hear it," whispered Styles, who had climbed the
stairs behind her. "Go below and wait."

Styles eased past Theodora up the stairs to the first floor
landing. A beam of light beneath a closed door drew him down
the hallway to the study. He reached for the door handle, then
froze as the handle turned. The door opened, and Styles stood
face to face with Galapardrasso.

What came next happened with bewildering swiftness.
Styles rammed his shoulder hard into Galapardrasso's midsec-
tion, his arm grasping about the other man's waist. As his
momentum carried them both into the study, Styles sensed
rather than saw the second figure. Too late.

A leaded weight slammed against his back between his
shoulder blades and smashed him to his knees on the floor.
Galapardrasso lunged past him to the door, and there was the
hurried sound of retreating footsteps. Cursing, Styles lurched,
swaying, to his feet.

Only then did he see her—Lady Damaris, lying in a crum-
pled heap on the floor, her sightless eyes open and staring up
at him.

Styles, tearing his eyes away from the lifeless figure on the
floor, lurched unsteadily toward the doorway—straight into
Theodora.

"The devil, Theodora," he gasped. "I told you to wait below." Clasping her in his arms, he attempted to shield her from
the sight behind him. "Theodora, those two men. Bloody hell,
if they put a hand to you."

"No, I am all right, Styles. Really I am. I ducked into a
doorway. They never saw me. But you—" Her voice caught
as she glimpsed the thing behind him. "Good God, it's Lady
Damaris. Is she—?"

Grimly Styles put Theodora from him. His hands on her

shoulders, he turned her away from the lifeless body. "I am afraid there is nothing we can do for her. It is time we were gone from here."

"But, Styles, we cannot just leave her."

"I haven't the time to argue, Enchantress. Lady Damaris is beyond our help." Taking her by the arm, Styles led Theodora, resisting, from the room. "Trust me to see to everything after I have you away from here."

"It was Galapardrasso," Theodora said distractedly, as Styles hurried her down the darkened stairway. "I couldn't be mistaken. The other man—I-I don't know. I only saw his back. He wore a cape and what curiously appeared a plumed hat, and his face was turned away. But I had the distinct impression he was not unfamiliar to me. That poor, unhappy woman!" At the bottom of the stairs, Theodora clutched her fingers in the fabric of Styles's shirt. "They must not be allowed to escape, Styles. Promise me that."

Styles felt her shudder, his enchantress who was always maddeningly collected. Grimly, he clasped strong hands over hers. "They will not escape, Theodora," he answered in a voice that sent cold shivers down Theodora's back. "You have my word. Now, however, we must get you away from here."

Theodora, steadied by the hard glitter of the Devil's Cub's eyes, nodded. "Yes, you are right, of course." Somehow she managed a wan facsimile of a smile. "I'm all right now, I promise."

"Of course you are." Or at least she would be when once he had her safely in the carriage. Styles pressed her hands, then, turning, led her through the house.

Leaving the same way they had come, they arrived in short order at the waiting carriage. Styles handed Theodora up and, giving the order for the coachman to proceed with all despatch to the house on Grosvenor Square, climbed in beside her.

"The other man was Morpheus," pronounced Theodora, as Styles sank back against the squabs. Her eyes shone huge in the pallor of her face. "It had to be. Lady Damaris was dreadfully frightened you knew something. Clearly she was on the point of losing control. Morpheus must have come to the conclusion she was become a liability he could no longer afford, especially after I showed up at the museum asking questions about things he had thought long forgotten." Theodora raised horror-stricken eyes to the Devil's Cub. "Styles, you heard him. Galapardrasso said Morpheus would cut her heart out."

"You may comfort yourself with the knowledge that she was not made to suffer mutilation," Styles offered grimly. "From the looks of it, one of them struck her. She fell and must have hit her head on something—probably the corner of the writing table. It is possible they never intended to kill her at all."

"Then what did they intend?" Theodora demanded on a rising note. "They struck her, which is far worse, you will agree, than wishing her hair to fall out. At least one might suppose her hair would have grown back again. Unfortunately, no one can bring her back to life."

Silently, Styles cursed. This was what came of disregarding his own rules. He should never have brought Theodora with him. Hell and the devil confound it! She blamed herself for what had happened—Theodora, who had never harmed anyone.

Reaching for her, Styles drew Theodora against him on the seat. "For a creature of logic, you are making very little sense, Enchantress. You did not kill Lady Damaris. Galapardrasso did, or the man with him."

Theodora shuddered in his arms. "I told her about the diary, Styles," she insisted. "And now she is dead because of it."

"Yes, she is dead, and nothing will bring her back, unless, of course, it is true that those who die violent deaths may be doomed to rise from the grave to seek vengeance on those who put them there. I am no doubt relieved, Enchantress. I was beginning to think perhaps you had become a convert to Lady Gwendolyn's belief in the existence of vampires."

Theodora, stung by his callousness, lifted indignant eyes to the Devil's Cub's. "I am a witch dedicated to the healing arts,

Styles. I have seen people die before. I have never seen one return from the other side."

Styles had long since discarded his mask, and his chiseled features shone cynically hard in the glow of the passing street lamps. "You cannot know how comforted I am to hear that, Theodora. It occurred to me that you might have allowed yourself to be carried away with your enthusiasm for anomalies. That was the Moravian Blood Stone you were wearing earlier tonight, was it not? Or a very good imitation of it."

Theodora's heart stilled, her thoughts coming sharply into focus at that unexpected observation, which, had she stopped to consider, she must have realized was his intent all along. All she could think, however, was that Styles knew. He must surely have realized what she wore about her neck the moment he set eyes on it. Indeed, she had been singularly naïve ever to have believed otherwise.

"I really do not know how to answer that, Styles," Theodora replied truthfully. "It is at the very least the stone Galapardrasso gave Morpheus to deliver to the countess. As it happens, chance or fate placed it in my keeping before I ever heard of the Moravian Blood Stone. I did not realize what I had in my possession until today in Galapardrasso's museum."

"The devil, you did." Styles suffered a bitter stab at the realization that his enchantress had so little trusted him that she could not bring herself to confide in him. Worse, he was both unnerved and appalled at the thought of the risks she had heedlessly taken. "And I suppose, realizing what it was, you deliberately wore it tonight for my benefit." By God, she might as well have published her intent in the *Gazette* as display the thing at Moreland's fete.

"You know very well I did not," Theodora retorted, nettled at what she perceived to be a wholly irrational attitude on his part. "If you recall, I had no reason to believe you would even be at Summersgate."

"You may be certain I recall every detail of the evening's adventures with perfect clarity," Styles did not hesitate to inform her with a steely edged softness. "Not the least of which is the fact that you made no attempt to tell me about your momentous discovery. I wonder if you have the least notion what went through my mind when I saw you wearing it. Perhaps you would care to humor me by telling me what the devil you thought to accomplish by showing it off at Moreland's masquerade tonight."

The devil, thought Theodora. Styles was in a rare taking indeed. Realizing she was at a distinct disadvantage in her present position, she pulled out of his arms and sat up. "I should be very surprised if you did not know exactly why I should have done it. I wore it to draw Morpheus out in the hopes that, recognizing it, he would give himself away. Unfortunately, things did not quite work out the way I had planned them. Phelps frightened him off before he could reveal himself."

Styles, who had already surmised that much the moment he saw the wretched stone around her neck, stared at her in mute fascination. "How very disobliging of Phelps. Did it never once occur to you to wonder what you were going to do when Morpheus 'revealed' himself to you?"

"I should naturally have informed you, Styles," replied Theodora, who, in spite of what Styles obviously thought, had indeed, given the matter a deal of consideration.

"But of course you would," Styles exclaimed in accents of amazement. "I wonder that I did not think of that. No doubt I am comforted by the realization that you meant, in time, to confide in me, Theodora. I wonder, however, if Morpheus would have been agreeable to the idea. Do you think perhaps there might have been the smallest possibility he might simply have preferred to do away with you in the wood?"

It was all Theodora could do not to flinch beneath the caustic bite of the Devil's Cub's final utterance. Indeed, she was very near to wishing him without remorse to the devil. "Really, Styles," she said, striving for a reasonable tone, "there is no need to be sarcastic. How was I to know Moreland would have his masque in a pleasure garden instead of a ballroom? *You* did not see fit to tell me. If you had, you may be sure I should have entertained second thoughts about implementing my plan to-night."

An incredulous laugh seemed torn from the Devil's Cub. "You are right. Clearly I am at fault. Naturally, I should have foreseen that my wife had the Moravian Blood Stone in her possession and, furthermore, intended to use it as bait to draw the traitor out. Unfortunately, my recently acquired empathic powers of perception do not yet extend to mind-reading and fortune-telling."

Theodora's chin came up, her eyes sparkling dangerously. "I wish you will not be absurd, Styles. Obviously, you could not possibly have known Mrs. Fennelworth would insist on giving me a stone she found at the foot of Devil's Keep fifteen years ago or, indeed, that it would turn out to be the Moravian Blood Stone. And as for my plan to uncover M's identity, you will agree that it was perfectly logical to suppose that Morpheus would not dare try anything in a ballroom crowded with people. I should have been perfectly safe. As it turned out, however, I confess I was relieved to discover you had decided to join me after all, Styles. Despicable as he is, I daresay I should have disliked having to shoot Morpheus."

"I could not agree with you more," said Styles, his tone heavily laced with irony. "Very likely it would have ruined your entire evening." Shoot him! Good God, he thought. She had not the least idea what it took to fire a bullet into someone. "Did you think, perhaps, you might have removed the stone when you arrived to discover your plan was already awry?"

Theodora shrugged. "Well, of course, the thought did occur to me. Unfortunately, by then I had already been seen by any number of people, so there really did not seem much point in it. Happily, in the final analysis, it would have been a shame to have wasted the opportunity. You, after all, were there to protect me."

"A pity," agreed Styles, tempted to wring the little wretch's neck for having made herself a target for a man who would stop at nothing either to achieve his nefarious ends or to protect his identity. "We may now assume that Morpheus is aware that you not only have Lady Gwendolyn's diary, but the Moravian Blood Stone in your possession. No doubt I should be pleased at the prospect that, persuaded my wife knows a deal too much about him, he no longer has any choice but to put a period to her existence."

"But that is it exactly," applauded Theodora, who could only be relieved that Styles had so quickly grasped the obvious. "I daresay we have only to wait for him to come to us, and then you will have him just where you want him."

"Oh, you may be sure of it, Theodora," Styles said with a singular lack of humor, as the carriage drew up before the house on Grosvenor Square. "Except for the fact that I," he added, opening the door and stepping out to hand Theodora down, "shall be waiting alone. You, my dear, will be on your way to Exmoor."

"Styles is not being at all reasonable, Aunt," declared Theodora some fifteen minutes later to Philippa, who had come to Lord Harry's room to find her. "He did not even afford me the opportunity to point out that I should be perfectly safe here with Phelps and Tom Dickson to look after me, not to mention a household full of servants."

Styles had, in fact, marched her straight into the house and, ordering her to proceed directly to her rooms and stay there until his return, had hurriedly changed before leaving again, presumably to go in pursuit of Dr. Galapardrasso. Recalling Styles's grimly set features, Theodora felt a dreadful hollow sensation.

"Well, I, for one, shall not be sorry to see Cliff House again," confessed Philippa, wishing Theodora would cease her endless pacing. All that nervous energy was enough to disturb the dead. "I'm afraid I am not at all cut out for a life of gaiety in London. I believe I almost miss Aunt Edna and Uncle Pervis. At least in Somerset, we do not have people going around murdering people in their beds."

"Lady Damaris was not in her bed, Aunt Philippa," Theodora pointed out. "And, in case you have forgotten, someone did try to put a period to my existence before we left for London."

"Yes, well, that was in Devil's Keep. I daresay such a thing would not have happened at Cliff House. It is all there in the emanations, you know. The Keep, I am afraid, has known far too much of strife and very little in the way of happiness."

Theodora stopped and stared at Philippa. It was true, she thought. The Keep had been an unhappy place for far too long. However, all that was going to change now. It was her pledge for the future. She, after all, was carrying Caleb Dameron's child.

Unfortunately, after tonight, she was afraid that the very fact that she was breeding might very well prove in the foreseeable future to be something of a complication. She had never known Styles to be so angry with her as he had been in the carriage, and all because of what she knew now had been a serious error in judgment. No doubt she should have told him about the troublesome stone. Indeed, in retrospect, she supposed she could hardly blame him for being a trifle upset because she had kept the discovery to herself. Very likely she would have felt the same way had their situations been reversed, she told herself. On the other hand, she was quite sure in such a case *she* would have found it in her heart to forgive him, and that was not something she could afford to take in the least for granted where Styles was concerned.

He, after all, had not lost his heart to her fifteen years before in a churchyard. Indeed, it was entirely possible that he could never find it in himself to love her as she loved him, not after the terrible muddle she had made of things. It was all so patently unfair that just when she had seemed to be making progress in breaching his formidable defenses, she should have done the one thing most certain to alienate him again.

She had failed in trust: She had not confided in him something of paramount importance to them both. How, then, was she to inform him now that she had also put off telling him something of even greater significance—the fact that she was increasing? In her present frame of mind, it seemed all too likely that he would turn from her in disgust when she finally did reveal her secret to him.

Theodora suffered a rending pang at the thought. Perhaps it was already too late to mend things between them. Styles was sending her away, back to Devil's Keep, while he stayed in London, just as his father before him had exiled Lady Gwendolyn to an existence of bitter loneliness. And why should he not, when he did not love her? Indeed, she would be very surprised if he were not having more than second thoughts about having married a witch who not only had caused him a great deal of trouble, but whom he had married in the expectation of leaving her a widow. How soon must he come to despise her for trapping him in a marriage he did not want?

What a dreadful toil she had made for herself. Indeed, she could not see her way out.

Perhaps fortunately she was interrupted in her unrewarding thoughts by her Aunt Philippa, who, calling her name, announced that Lord Harry would appear to be coming around.

"There, you see, Theodora," said Philippa, drawing her niece to the bedside. "He has opened his eyes."

"So he has, Aunt," Theodora smiled, gazing down at her patient, who, clean-shaven, thanks to Thistlewaite's ministrations, presented a far more agreeable aspect than when he had arrived the night before. "How are you feeling, my lord?"

Remarkably keen blue eyes lifted to study her face with interest. "Weak as a bloody infant, but alive, I expect, else I'd not have a pretty angel like you looking down at me. Harry Underwood is not the sort who will ever see the gates of heaven, you may be sure of it."

"Then I suspect heaven will be a far less interesting place without you, my lord," Theodora said, laughing, as she reached for his wrist, which was far too thin for his frame. "Aunt

Philippa, would you be so good as to wake Mrs. Oglesby. I believe our patient would do better with some broth inside him."

Lord Harry, who had been watching with a quizzical quirk of the eyebrows as Theodora measured his pulse, gave a comical grimace. "Broth?" he queried with unmistakable disgust. "Is that anything to offer a man who's faint for the lack of sustenance? Be a good girl and send for a beefsteak and a good Medoc if you have one. If you haven't, I'll settle for a Pommard or even a stout, but pray spare me thin broth and weak tea."

Theodora, releasing his wrist, placed a cool palm against her patient's brow. "You will settle for what I think is best for you, and for the present, you will do far better on broth, my lord. In case you are unaware of it, you came very close to expiring."

"I did, as I recall, give it a hearty go," reflected Lord Harry with an oddly twisted smile. Closing his eyes, he lay back, suddenly looking strangely old, though Theodora judged he could not have been above five and forty. Indeed, in health, he must have cut a dashing figure. Certainly, he was strikingly handsome in spite of the lines of dissipation about his mouth and eyes and a certain aura of world-weariness that his careless facade of cheer could not hide. With his dark hair and aesthetically cast features, reminiscent of an aging Lord Byron, he must have drawn more than a few feminine glances.

Theodora started, realizing he had opened his eyes again and was staring at her with speculative interest.

"Is it you whom I have to thank that I am not even now laid out in my coffin? I seem to recall in my delirium the voice and hands of a ministering angel."

"Not an angel, I fear, my lord," Theodora answered, her eyes twinkling. "But a witch."

Lord Harry's face lit with quick intelligence. "You're Theodora! By Jove, I should have guessed. I no longer wonder that Styles fell to Cupid's arrow. I'm only surprised he had the good sense to marry you when he had the chance."

"I am not sure he would agree with you, my lord," observed Theodora wryly. "I'm afraid I have proven to be a deal more trouble than he allowed when he insisted on making an honest woman of me. Be that as it may, however, I am indeed your niece by marriage, and this is Miss Philippa Havelock, my aunt."

"A pleasure, Miss Havelock," asserted Lord Harry, taking in Philippa's high-crowned cap and flowing white tunic gown without the bat of an eyelash. "It is easy to see where Lady Theodora has got her looks. I say, is that an Egyptian robe you are wearing?"

"It is an imitation of an Etruscan dress, which I designed from a description given me by an entity who visits me from time to time. But that is neither here nor there," Theodora's aunt informed him with an air of earnest concern. "More importantly, I wish you to know that, as an experienced hermeneut of metaphysical radiance, I am able to see and interpret spiritual emanations. I perceive, sir, that you are in need of spiritual counsel. It is my *dharma* to comfort the metaphysically afflicted, my lord. Should you wish to examine your past lives to discover the clue to your present *karma,* I should be pleased to serve as your guide."

"Should you?" queried Lord Harry, who was staring at Theodora's aunt with a gleam of good-natured interest that did him no harm in Theodora's eyes. "A guide, you say. That is most kind in you, ma'am. And it's true I've spent a good deal of my life wandering in a labyrinth. I cannot even say for certain where I am at this very moment."

"Yes, well, be pleased to call on me, if you decide you wish to avail yourself of my services. I should be only too happy to oblige you. And, now, I shall go and summon Mrs. Oglesby, after which I believe I shall retire to my bed. Good night to you both."

"My aunt is a student of Oriental religions," Theodora supplied kindly when her aunt had left the room. "And you, my lord, are presently in the town house on Grosvenor Square. Styles brought you here, late last night."

"So that part was not a dream. I could scarcely credit my

senses when Styles pulled me from that—er—my less-than-congenial bachelor quarters. How, may I ask, did he come to find me there?"

"You had been taken up in a raid in China Town and deposited in gaol along with a number of others. Someone who was acquainted with a man who knows Styles called that man's attention to you. It was he who removed you to your rooms in Bury Street and subsequently brought your nephew to you. Perhaps you know him. His name is Jerome Whitfill."

"Whitfill! Good God," uttered Lord Harry in fading accents. "Who does not know that bloody jackal?"

Theodora, considerably alarmed to see her patient's face go a sudden sickly grey, reached quickly for the restorative draught on the bedside table. Lifting Lord Harry's head, she held the cup to her patient's lips. "A swallow, my lord," Theodora urged when Lord Harry raised a feeble hand in protest. "I'm really afraid I must insist."

A wry gleam of amusement lit the blue orbs at the uncompromising tone in her voice. "Or you will toss it down my throat, is that it? That will not be necessary, my dear. I was never one to resist the entreaties of a beautiful woman, you see, even one who is my niece by marriage."

"I am flattered, my lord," retorted Theodora, as her patient obligingly drank a swallow or two before turning his head away with an eloquent grimace. "I daresay you are far more used to the entreaties of beauties who only pretend to be your niece."

"Good God, *tea*," was Lord Harry's response to that astute observation.

"Herbal tea, to be precise." Calmly Theodora laid his head back against the pillows and set the cup on the table. "There, that is better. Your color is already returning."

Lord Harry favored her with a baleful eye. "It was a devil of a trick to play on a man who only hours ago was at death's door. You might at least have made it a brandy."

"Brandy on an empty stomach would have ill served you, my lord. My special preparation of herbs, on the other hand, will not only cleanse your body of its poisons, but will restore your humors to a proper balance as well."

"An object no doubt to be devoutly wished for," commented Lord Harry with something less than enthusiasm. "Unfortunately, I happen to like my various poisons, and my humors be damned."

"I am, in spite of what you may think, in complete sympathy with you, my lord," Theodora assured him, as, lifting him up, she fluffed and turned his pillows before placing them once more beneath his head and shoulders. "There is nothing so annoying, after all, as having someone forcing you to do something for your own good. Indeed, you may be sure that, while, as a healer, I cannot condone your heedless behavior, I believe, after reading Lady Gwendolyn's journal, I understand why you do the things you do."

"Good God, the journal. I had forgotten about that. Are you saying you have it?"

"Yes, and I am beginning to wish I had never laid eyes on it. It has cost me a deal of trouble. And, now, if you are feeling strong enough, I really should like to know why you went so alarmingly pale a moment ago."

Lord Harry stared at Theodora, a wry gleam in his eyes. "If this is how you deal with Styles, then I cannot but wonder that he has not strangled you long ago. You, my girl, are a managing female."

"And you are an engaging rogue. And now I should be grateful if you will please answer my question."

Lord Harry settled back against his pillows with a rueful sigh. "I daresay Styles will not thank me for it, but what would you? Your Mr. Whitfill is a relentless demon of a man with eyes that see bloody well everywhere. For weeks he has been after me. Twice I was set upon by rogues and only by the luck of the devil managed to escape with my life. I have been running and hiding ever since. I thought at least in China Town I should be free of him, but alas. He managed to find me even in the halls of Morpheus."

"The god of dreams," exclaimed Theodora, who had suddenly put two and two together, or in this case, the halls of Morpheus with opium dens. The one was clearly a euphemism for the other. "Of course, I should have guessed." Suddenly a great deal would seem to make sense, not the least of which were the entries in Lady Gwendolyn's journal, Theodora realized. Morpheus had come, and Lady Gwendolyn had drunk from the fountain of dreams. It was little wonder she had hoped Styles would not hear of it. No doubt he would take a dim view of discovering his mama had turned the tower into her own private opium parlor, complete with a convenient horde of passages that provided a direct access to the sea. Morpheus could come and go as he pleased with his secret offerings and no one who was not part of the game would be any the wiser. Sickened, Theodora turned her attention back to her patient.

"How very curious," she mused, puzzled at a great deal in Lord Harry's account that would seem to make little sense. "And you think Whitfill was behind the two attacks on your life?"

Lord Harry stared at her warily. "I cannot think who else it might be. He was the one with men following me."

"Yes, of course." Theodora nodded, her eyes never leaving her patient's. "On the other hand, it would make little sense when one considers Mr. Whitfill was kind enough to give you into the care of your family. Why did *you* not come to Styles? You must have known he would protect you."

A dull tinge of color suffused the pallor of Lord Harry's cheeks. "I have been looking after myself for a good many years now," he said in sardonic amusement. "Perhaps I have not maintained myself in the style to which I was born, but, other than the loan of a few pounds here and there, I have always been my own man. Strange as it may seem, I prefer it that way. I certainly saw no reason to involve Styles, who, from all accounts, has troubles enough of his own. How is he, by the way? I had heard rumors he was suffering a mysterious affliction."

"You will be glad to know he is in perfect health, or at least he was when he dropped me off here tonight." Theodora paused, assessing her patient's mental and physical state. "Something happened tonight, my lord—"

"For God's sake, Theodora, call me Harry. Everyone does. We are, after all, relations, and I have the feeling," he added, indicating his long length beneath the bedcovers, "you have come in the past several hours to know me more intimately than most."

A fleeting smile flickered at the corners of Theodora's lips. "You may comfort yourself with the knowledge that Styles saw to your undressing," she dryly assured him. The smile faded, and she gazed down at him with a gravity that must surely have set him on his guard. "Harry, I have something to tell you which will undoubtedly prove a shock to you. I'm afraid there is no easy way to say it. It concerns Lady Damaris. She is dead, Harry. I'm terribly sorry."

Seventeen

Styles, stepping up into the carriage, ordered a disgruntled Hodges to take them to New Street. His head groom, who had not failed to make known his displeasure at being supplanted at Summersgate by a hired lackey, would be the very devil to placate, Styles humorlessly reflected. But then, nothing had gone tonight quite as one might have wished.

Lady Damaris, who might have shed light on any number of things, not the least of which was the identity of the English traitor, was dead. Lord Harry, who might or might not be able to name Lady Gwendolyn's Mysterious M, had yet to regain consciousness. And Theodora, apparently convinced that the only practical use for a husband was as a stud horse to provide her with the uniquely female biological experience of reproduction, had decided to set a trap of her own for the culprit.

"Damn her!" he uttered savagely, aware of a deep feeling of dissatisfaction with both her and himself. Having recognized from the first that she was a rare creature possessed of an uncommonly inquiring mind and an exceptional intelligence, he had treated her with a patience and tolerance he did not normally accord anyone, let alone a female of the species. And she had repaid him by going off half-cocked on her own. No doubt he could only blame himself that she was now in the unenviable position of being the quarry of a man who was not only not averse to selling out his own country, but had already